TRUST IN ME

"[This] powerful tale of redemption, friendship, trust, and forgiving shows once again that Shay knows how to pack an emotional wallop." —*Booklist*

"An unusual and compelling tale . . . I don't know when I have become more involved in a novel's characters and story."
—*The Romance Reader*

PROMISES TO KEEP

"A wonderful work of contemporary romance, with a plot ripped straight from the headlines."
—*New York Times* bestselling author Lisa Gardner

"Emotion, romance, realism, and intrigue. A love story that you'll never forget . . . a plot that will hold you on the edge of your seat, and an ending that you'll remember long after you turn the last page."
—*New York Times* bestselling author Catherine Anderson

MORE PRAISE FOR KATHRYN SHAY

"Master storyteller Kathryn Shay pens an emotionally powerful tale that leaves you breathless. Woven into this riveting plot are wonderfully written characters that grab your heart and don't let go. Bravo, Ms. Shay."
—*Romantic Times* (4½ stars)

"A fantastic treat . . . Filled with heartbreaking action, but it is the lead characters that turn this plot into an insightful read . . . Kathryn Shay pays homage to America's Bravest with another powerful novel . . . [so we might] share in their passions and adventures." —*Midwest Book Review*

"Super . . . The lead protagonists are a charming duo and the support characters add depth . . . Kathryn Shay's tale is a beautiful Christmas story." —*Painted Rock Reviews*

continued . . .

SOMEONE TO BELIEVE IN

"Kathryn Shay is an awesome talent who gets better, if possible, with each new story. *Someone to Believe In* is a wonderfully written, emotional, and extraordinary read, and truly deserves a five-star rating." —*Affaire de Coeur*

"Once again, Shay shines in this starkly realistic story . . . This powerful story will stay with readers long after they finish the book." —*Booklist* (starred review)

"Shay's writing trademark is taking seemingly impossible relationships with almost insurmountable obstacles and developing them into classic tales of true love, which is exactly what she does here . . . Another highly complex, compelling, and thought-provoking novel written by one of the best." —*Fresh Fiction*

NOTHING MORE TO LOSE

"Hidden Cove tales continue to provide superb romantic suspense thrillers . . . Terrific." —*Midwest Book Review*

"The talented Shay offers another heartwarming tale of brave men and women." —*Booklist*

AFTER THE FIRE

"Powerful, emotionally realistic . . . poignant, and compelling, this novel reinforces Shay's well-earned reputation as a first-rate storyteller." —*Booklist*

"Powerfully written . . . genuine . . . Shay pays homage to rescue workers with this exhilarating tale that demands a sequel." —*Midwest Book Review*

TAKING THE HEAT

KATHRYN SHAY

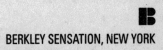

BERKLEY SENSATION, NEW YORK

THE BERKLEY PUBLISHING GROUP
Published by the Penguin Group
Penguin Group (USA) Inc.
375 Hudson Street, New York, New York 10014, USA

Penguin Group (Canada), 90 Eglinton Avenue East, Suite 700, Toronto, Ontario M4P 2Y3, Canada
(a division of Pearson Penguin Canada Inc.)
Penguin Books Ltd., 80 Strand, London WC2R 0RL, England
Penguin Group Ireland, 25 St. Stephen's Green, Dublin 2, Ireland (a division of Penguin Books Ltd.)
Penguin Group (Australia), 250 Camberwell Road, Camberwell, Victoria 3124, Australia
(a division of Pearson Australia Group Pty. Ltd.)
Penguin Books India Pvt. Ltd., 11 Community Centre, Panchsheel Park, New Delhi—110 017, India
Penguin Group (NZ), 67 Apollo Drive, Rosedale, North Shore 0632, New Zealand
(a division of Pearson New Zealand Ltd.)
Penguin Books (South Africa) (Pty.) Ltd., 24 Sturdee Avenue, Rosebank, Johannesburg 2196,
South Africa

Penguin Books Ltd., Registered Offices: 80 Strand, London WC2R 0RL, England

This is a work of fiction. Names, characters, places, and incidents either are the product of the author's imagination or are used fictitiously, and any resemblance to actual persons, living or dead, business establishments, events, or locales is entirely coincidental. The publisher does not have any control over and does not assume any responsibility for author or third-party websites or their content.

TAKING THE HEAT

A Berkley Sensation Book / published by arrangement with the author

PRINTING HISTORY
Berkley Sensation mass-market edition / May 2008

Copyright © 2008 by Mary Catherine Schaefer.
Cover art by Phil Heffernan.
Cover design by George Long.

ISBN: 978-0-425-22200-3

BERKLEY® SENSATION
Berkley Sensation Books are published by The Berkley Publishing Group,
a division of Penguin Group (USA) Inc.,
375 Hudson Street, New York, New York 10014.
BERKLEY SENSATION and the "B" design are trademarks of Penguin Group (USA) Inc.

PRINTED IN THE UNITED STATES OF AMERICA

10 9 8 7 6 5 4 3 2 1

ONE

GLANCING OVER at the firefighters who'd come into Bailey's Irish Pub for breakfast, Liam O'Neil snagged a stool at the bar and sat down. "There's a lot of them today."

Patrick smiled. He was the oldest O'Neil brother and manager of the business. "Yeah. Word of mouth, I guess. Can't believe our luck."

"Too bad about Sweeney's, though."

Dylan, the second oldest, looked up from washing glasses at a nearby sink. "Their loss is our gain."

Pat shrugged. "At least old Sweeney's retiring, not goin' out of business."

Liam yawned.

"You look whipped." Pat cocked his head at him. "This too much for you? All of them coming in here since Sweeney's closed?"

"Nah. I handled this many at the diner and got up even earlier." Liam had also had a part-time job in SoHo that he was able to quit when their other brother left the pub to pursue a career in photography. "I'm glad to be here full-time. I miss Aidan, though."

"Not me." Paddy's voice was gruff as he stared down at the list he was making. "His shit-eatin' grin since him and C.J. hooked up drives me nuts."

Liam knew the origin of that comment. He'd talked to Pat's wife, Brie, last night. She and Paddy had had another row. "Pat, I—"

"Hey, Paddy?" This from a burly firefighter across the room. His voice was gravelly, probably from inhaling smoke. "Where's the chow?"

"Where's the fire?" Pat shouted back.

They all laughed, punchy from the night shift. Mikey, Liam's son, had a thing for firefighters, and from time to time, the two of them stopped by the firehouse down the street. Liam had also researched the profession on the Internet. He didn't know how they lived with such a whacky schedule, let alone the risky job they performed. And then, of course, 9/11 had happened, changing all of them.

The door opened and the sounds of a busy MacDougal Street filtered in. Cabs hustled people to work and pedestrians were already flocking to their employment.

Another firefighter walked into the pub. Wearing jeans and an FDNY sweatshirt, she filled hers out better than the others.

Dylan murmured, "Ah, there she is."

"Who's she?" Liam asked. "I've never seen her before."

"Sophie Tyler. She works at Company 14." Pat was admiring the view, too. "Dylan thinks she's hot. I like her. She's real friendly."

From across the room, Sophie smiled at them. "Hey, Pat. Dylan." Then she nodded to Liam. "Hi."

"Come over here, darlin'," Dylan called out, "and meet another O'Neil brother."

Her smile broadened as she walked toward them. "How many of you are there?"

"Four. This one's Liam, the middle child."

Her gray eyes wide and warm, she held out her hand. "Hi, Liam. I'm Sophie."

Liam stood. Her grip was firm when they shook, and her palm callused. He noticed her other hand was bandaged.

"Nice to meet you."

"Hey, Sophie baby, get your ass over here."

She rolled her eyes. "They get worse, the more tired they are. We caught two fires last night."

"Time for bed, I'd say." Dylan's tone was flirty.

Liam envied Dylan's easy charm. It had never mattered to him before his wife, Kitty, had died three years ago, but lately Liam wished he'd inherited some.

Laughing off Dylan's innuendo, Sophie said to Liam, "Nice to meet you," and headed over to the tables where her friends had gathered.

All three men watched her walk away.

Dylan shook his head. "Man, I'll bet she's a fiery one."

Pat grunted. "Her hair's not red enough for you, boy."

"Strawberry blond," Liam murmured.

From the corner of his eye, he saw his two older brothers exchange looks.

"See something you like, bro?" Dylan asked.

In the O'Neil family, you had to give as good as you got or you were dead meat. Dropping back down on the stool, Liam picked up his mug. "What, and risk life and limb? Seems to me you've already staked your claim."

Dylan's brows raised. "You can have her if you want her."

"That's nice of you." Liam's tone was wry. "But I'd guess she'd have something to say about that."

Bracing his arms on the bar, Paddy leaned toward him. "You said you were gonna start datin' again."

"I have." He sipped his coffee, stalling for time. "I went out twice in two weeks. The women were nice, but they didn't do anything for me."

Dylan crossed his arms over his chest. "Because they were Kitty clones. You need to change it up a little."

"I *so* do not want to have this conversation." He pushed away from the bar, stood and headed to the kitchen. "I gotta get their food."

"Coward," Dylan called out.

"Back off," he heard Pat say.

"He needs a push."

"Not a kick in the pants."

"Says who . . ."

Their voices cut off as the kitchen door closed behind Liam. He took comfort in the familiar banter between his brothers and the smell of food he'd put in the oven an hour earlier. Checking the egg strata, he saw it was done, pulled out the pans and set them on the butcher block. As the food cooled a bit, he began to slice the homemade bread his ma had made before she and Pa left to visit her relatives in upstate New York.

When the firefighters in the surrounding houses were looking for a place to have breakfast after Sweeney's had closed, they'd told Pat they enjoyed a variety of foods. That's how Liam's List had begun. Every day he'd fix them a different meal from a list he'd posted. They checked it when they were in and made suggestions from the menu. Though different groups from different houses came in all week, the method was working. It was fun, and he felt a part of things.

Fun was something that had been missing from his life since Kitty had died and his son Mikey had gone into an emotional tailspin.

Don't think about that now, he told himself. He'd worry about the kid twenty-four/seven if he let his mind go there. The therapist he'd been seeing told him that was self-destructive. Instead, he thought about the firefighters. Sophie was a pretty one in a tough sort of way. Focusing on them, he managed to block Mikey from his mind.

"WHAT'S THE HOLDUP? I'm starved." John Cooper was glowering at the kitchen door. Big and brawny, with a shaved head, he scared probies with that expression alone.

"Gourmet breakfasts take a while." Company 14's captain, Jim Mackenzie, checked his pager, then sipped his coffee. His red hair, moustache and friendly blue eyes belied a good officer who could kick ass and still maintain camaraderie.

"We could just have bacon and eggs," Cooper grumbled, wrapping his beefy hand around a mug of coffee.

"Where's the fun in that?" Hannah Harper was Sophie's ex-roommate as of last month when she had married another smoke eater from Engine 46 where they both worked. "The variety of food's great." Her dark eyes danced. "And the scenery around here isn't bad."

"You checking those Irish dudes out again, Harper?" Bagatelle, one of her crew, asked. "Wait till Dominic finds out."

"Dominic knows I'm crazy about him." Hannah's expression was suggestive. "I take care of him just fine."

Bagatelle snorted.

"You're just jealous 'cuz no broad will even look at you, Bags."

"As if! The ladies flock to me, sweetheart."

Enjoying the back-and-forth, Sophie glanced over at the O'Neils. "Man, they are real eye candy."

"You get a glimpse of the other one yet? Aidan?" Hannah asked.

"No." She'd heard about him, though, because of the gentle notoriety of this place. There was an O'Neil sister, too, whom the pub took its name from. She was now the the wife of Vice President Clay Wainwright. Their story had been in the news three or four years back.

"Each one's cuter than the next," Hannah added.

Sophie thought about the brother she had just met. "Liam seems nice. But sad." And she liked his looks. Deep blue eyes, the same as the rest of them, and dark hair. But his was cut shorter and had a bit of curl.

"He's stopped by our firehouse a couple of times with his kid," Sean Murray put in. The rig's driver, he was a wiry little guy with a wry sense of humor. His demeanor was more mellow than most, unless you messed with him. "You musta missed him, Soph. The cap calls him the 'Quiet Man.'"

At Torres's questioning expression, Bilotti, the other officer on their group, snorted. "Don't you know nothin' about old movies, probie?"

"John Wayne, 1956." This from Mackenzie. "The story was better." Their captain was a reader, not a TV freak, and it wasn't uncommon to see him around the firehouse with a book.

"Story?" the probie asked.

"*The Quiet Man*. They made the film from a story in the *Saturday Evening Post*."

"Ah, finally," Cooper groused.

Sophie glanced up to see Liam coming out of the kitchen carrying a huge tray. As he got closer, the smell of freshly baked bread and eggs and cheese filled the air. Her stomach growled.

"Oh, my God." Hannah's stomach rumbled, too. "I think I'm going to have an orgasm."

"Shh," Sophie told her friend, who never seemed able to censor herself. "You'll embarrass him."

Muscles bulging with the weight, Liam set down the tray, removed the two rectangular pans and put them at either end of the table. When he put the toast down near Sophie, his aftershave filled her head. "There you go. Hope you like it."

Her coworkers dug in.

"Looks great . . ."

"Umm . . ."

"Gimme some . . ."

Liam smiled. It was a nice smile. Genuine, like he took pleasure in small things. "Need anything else? More coffee?"

"We can get it." She nodded to an urn across the way that the O'Neils had set up for them, free of charge.

"Let me. After what you all did on 9/11, we can't do enough for you."

When Liam went to fill a pitcher, there was a strained silence at the table. The anniversary of the Twin Towers bombing had just passed, and they were still feeling the effects. Their house had lost five guys—the captain's best buddy included; Cooper's cousin had died, which had sent him on a drinking binge that lasted three years. And Bilotti himself had been trapped in a stairwell but was dragged to safety by another smoke eater. All of them, including Sophie, who'd been out of the country at the time of the attacks, had worked for months at the Pile. Looking for bodies was the most gut-wrenching experience she'd ever had.

Liam returned and began to fill mugs. When he picked up Sophie's, he nodded to her hand. "What happened?"

"A few embers got inside my gloves."

"Hurts like hell," Bilotti said around a mouthful, "but she's had worse." His tone was affectionate, though gruff.

Liam grimaced and finished pouring them coffee. "If you need anything else, let me know."

The guys were appreciative. "Thanks, buddy . . ."

"This is service . . ."

"Nice of you, man."

"My kid's school is coming for a field trip at Company 14 next week."

Mackenzie nodded. "The school's getting our group. We'll look out for him."

"Thanks."

After Liam left, and they'd satisfied some of their hunger, Hannah leaned back and patted her belly. "I'm stuffed. That guy can cook."

The razzing began . . .

"Yeah, unlike you, Harper."

"Poor Dom."

"Dominic is satisfied all the time, guys, now that we're living together."

The captain tilted his chin at Sophie. "Speaking of which, any luck finding a new roommate, Soph?"

"No. I wish I didn't have to." On her third helping of the cheesy strata, she spoke between bites. "I've been thinking about getting a part-time job."

"Why don't you work here?" Hannah suggested.

"Here?"

"Yeah." She pointed to the window. A double-sided sign read WAITRESS/BARTENDER WANTED. FLEXIBLE HOURS.

"You got any kitchen experience?" Murray winked at the cap. "I mean besides what women are born with."

All the guys at the table laughed. Cooper frowned at Torres. "Who said you could laugh, probie?"

Julian rolled his eyes, but kept his mouth shut. He'd only been with them a few months and was still in the initiation stage. Yesterday, the guys had rigged a bucket full of water and flour to fall on him when he went outside for a smoke.

Sophie drew their attention from the kid. "Up yours, Murray. I cook for you morons when it's my turn and clean up after. That's plenty of experience." She stared at the sign. "Besides, I tended some bar when I got out of high school."

"No shit?"

Hannah sighed. "I'd work here just to be around them."

"Maybe. If I could earn two hundred and fifty dollars a week, I could swing the apartment alone."

She glanced across the room and saw Liam had taken a seat at the bar again. His back was broad in the green pub T-shirt he wore, but his shoulders slumped a bit. She studied him and his brothers, watched them joke around, and suddenly missed her own brother, Nate, a lot; he was a career soldier in Iraq. She was going to e-mail him tonight.

"Soph? Something wrong?" the cap asked.

"Nah, just that seeing the O'Neils make me think about Nate. I miss him."

Talk of family began. Then, as always, they got to the runs they'd had last night and the two different companies exchanged war stories. Sophie was glad to get the focus off her. She glanced at the sign again. She'd never had to take a part-time job like a lot of firefighters. She'd been one for twelve years, made enough money, and lived frugally.

But maybe she'd pick one up now. It might be fun working here. Hannah was right. The scenery was great.

DROPPING TO HER knees, Sophie crawled down the hallway behind Bilotti at a snail's pace. Pitch-black smoke blinded her and her crew, and her heart began to pound. Though she wore the regulation face mask, her throat felt gritty. On their way over to Vestry Street, they'd gotten the information on this call: seventh-floor apartment, four rooms, bedrooms in back. Occupants: mother, two kids. Her crew's job was to get the family out; Engine 33, the pumper in their house, was slapping water on the fire and her truck, Ladder 44, was conducting search and rescue.

From the radio on her shoulder Sophie heard the captain's voice. "Bilotti and Tyler, first bedroom. Cooper and Murray second. Probie stays with me."

Sweating now, and taking in too much air, she tried to slow her breathing. "Go right," Bilotti barked as they came to the doorway, of which she could only see an outline. Still on her knees, feeling her way, she bumped into a piece of furniture. A dresser. A few feet down, she banged her arm on something steel. She swore but kept going.

Finally reaching the bed, she bounced it with her hands. Heavy. Occupied. "Got somebody."

No response.

"Bilotti?"

Nothing.

Suddenly the smoke cleared. And Sophie was on the bed, dressed in a thin white nightgown. Nate was screaming from across the room. *Help us*, she wanted to yell, but no words came out. A silhouette appeared before her looking like Darth Vader and she cowered back against the wall. There were flames behind the thing. On either side of her now. Licking her bare toes.

"No . . ."

"Soph, wake up."

"No, no, no."

"Sophie baby, wake up."

Her eyes snapped open. A man sat on her bed and she whimpered. "It's me, Mackenzie. You're in the firehouse. You're not little anymore. You're not trapped."

She could feel the sweat covering her body. Smell the faint odor of the spaghetti sauce she'd made for dinner. "Yeah, yeah." She swallowed hard. Reaching over, Mackenzie picked up something from the table and handed it to her. Bottled water. She drained it. Her eyes adjusted and in the light from a streetlamp outside, she could make out the lumps of her group sleeping in the bunk room and the cap on the side of the bed.

"She okay?" Bilotti mumbled from the next cot.

"Soph?" This from Cooper.

"Yeah, I'm okay. Sorry, guys." She took in deep breaths. Shook her head and rolled her shoulders to loosen them.

Mackenzie stood. "Go back to sleep."

"What time is it?"

"Four."

"I'll just get up."

"Too early."

"I'm okay."

"Suit yourself." He squeezed her arm. "It's been a while."

"I know. Thanks." She didn't want his sympathy. Or his pity.

When he shuffled back to his bed, she slid out of hers, donned her sweat suit over the shorts and T-shirt she slept in and headed out of the second-floor bunk room. The soft sound of snoring followed her downstairs.

In the big kitchen, she crossed to the coffeemaker, flipped the switch and went to the window to watch lower Manhattan wake up. Damn it, why had she had the dream tonight? It always made her feel weak, something a female in the FDNY couldn't afford and all of them went to lengths to avoid. And why was the dream so real? She was ten again, on that bed, suffocating from smoke, while her brother screamed for help. If she concentrated hard, she could still hear Tom Carusotti say, "What's your name, honey?" Somehow she got it out. "Okay, Sophie baby, we're blowin' this pop stand. Just hold on tight to me."

The coffee stopped dripping and Sophie poured herself a cup. On edge, she leaned against the counter, sipping. She should do something. Maybe fix the guys breakfast. Better not; they'd revolt if they were deprived of their new favorite cook's morning meal.

She thought of the sadness on Liam O'Neil's face and wondered what monkey was on his back. Everyone had one, it seemed, and she didn't feel sorry for herself for hers. Except when it deprived her of sleep like now. She hoped the cook had slept better than she did tonight.

"YOU DIDN'T SLEEP last night?"

Liam shifted uncomfortably in the stuffed chair. He didn't like coming here at all. "I fell asleep but woke up at four. I forget, is that anxiety or depression?"

His therapist, Jay Yost, smiled. "The theory is that anxiety keeps you from falling asleep, and depression wakes you up prematurely."

"Based on that, I shouldn't be getting any rest."

Waiting a beat, Jay finally asked, "How's Mike?"

"I'm not sure. Some days are better than others. Last week's session went well with Dr. Lang, and he talked in school some. He's only been back a few weeks, but the teacher said he's doing okay. The kid's just so damn sad all the time."

"As is his father."

Liam's heartbeat quickened. "You think he's taking his cue from me?"

"Hell no. Don't assume responsibility for that, too."

Blowing out an exasperated breath, Liam clenched and unclenched his fist. "I'm trying to be objective. But watching your child slip deeper into himself is hard."

They discussed Mikey for ten minutes, then Jay asked about Liam's other son, Cleary. After Liam answered, Jay glanced at the clock. "Time's up for the kid discussion. Tell me about you. What's happening?"

He told Jay about the breakfasts with America's Bravest that had gone on for two weeks now. Several different companies were coming in—the same guys weren't there everyday, of course—giving the pub a steady stream every morning.

"That sounds like fun. And lucrative."

"Pat's in seventh heaven and I feel like I'm earning my full-time salary."

"You're part owner of the place, Liam."

"I know. Still, I wanna carry my own weight."

"Any women in the picture?"

"Not since the excruciating date with Eve Larkin." He scowled.

"What?"

"Dylan says I'm dating Kitty clones."

Jay chuckled. "You guys don't pull any punches with each other, do you?"

"Nah, never have. Down deep, I'm glad."

"Is what he said true?"

"Maybe. I only meet women through events with the boys. Eve's the mother of one of the kids in my Cub Scout troop."

"Should you start doing some things outside of that box?"

"Like what?"

"I don't know. A hobby. Join a gym."

He glanced at his biceps. "I wouldn't mind joining a gym. I hate the idea of picking up women, though."

"You work in a bar. Any regulars you could get to know?"

"I guess I could look around. Truth is I want to. I'm . . . lonely."

"For female companionship."

He laughed. "That, too." They'd talked about sex in the few times Liam had seen Jay. He felt comfortable enough with the guy to share the fact that celibacy really sucked.

"That's two ideas today—a gym and scoping out the pub."

Restless, Liam ran a hand through his hair. "I hate this."

"I know you do."

"I never thought I'd be here, at nearly forty-two, looking to date. I thought I'd grow old with Kitty."

"The fact that you met her in junior high and never dated anyone else also complicates things."

"I know." He thumped a fisted hand on the arm of his chair. "Shit."

"That's good."

"What is?"

"Anger. You don't show much of it."

"It builds up inside sometimes until I feel like I'm gonna bust open."

"Then let it out. Your brothers would probably go a few rounds with you."

Liam laughed. That, of course, was true.

He was feeling better when he left the session. Outside, across from Jay's office, Washington Square Park was busy with late lunchers, nannies with strollers and the ubiquitous tourists. On a whim, and because it was a beautiful September day with the sun shining, he walked to Thirteenth Street and arrived at Mikey's school as they were letting out. From near a tree, he watched his somber-faced son walk out of St. Mary's Catholic School. A little redheaded girl caught up to him. She said something, but Mike only shook his head and averted his gaze. She shrugged and walked away. He got to the curb before he saw Liam. "Dad?" His eyes widened. "Did something happen?"

"Nothing bad. I had some time so I thought I'd pick you up and we'd go get ice cream."

"'Kay."

Smiling, Liam nodded in the direction of the little girl, who was watching them. "Want to bring your friend? We could call her mother."

Mikey shook his head vehemently.

"All right, just you and me."

His son closed the distance between them and took his hand. Liam's throat got tight as he watched the other kids, whose lives hadn't been torn apart by tragedy and loss, playfully wait for rides or the bus, toss a ball to each other, hang out in groups.

Again, anger welled inside him. For his kid. And for himself. For Christ sakes, all he wanted was a normal life. Was that too much to ask?

Two

WHEN THE PUB door opened, Dylan glanced up from the stock he was inventorying. "Well, look who the cat dragged in."

His brother Aidan, an arm crooked around the love of his life, C.J. Ludzecky, came toward them. He had the O'Neil looks—black hair, blue eyes—but Aidan's disposition was more easygoing than the rest of them. It showed in his wide grin and pleasant demeanor. Patrick brooded most of the time, Liam was melancholy, and Dylan himself was usually enervated.

"Hey, Dyl." Aidan hiked himself up and hugged his brother, albeit awkwardly, over the bar. C.J. kissed Dylan on the cheek.

"You glow, girl."

"Secret Service agents do not glow." Her smile contradicted the denial. She linked her arm with Aidan's. "We're back."

"Already?"

"Yep. As of yesterday, your sister has a new personal protective agent, Kip Michaels. Good guy. Been waiting for a spot in the VPPD to open up."

Dylan studied her. Despite her denial, she did glow, with her blond hair hanging loose and her amber eyes filled with joy. She was dressed in a soft pink blouse and jeans to match. "Feeling okay about leaving the detail?"

"Okay enough. I start in the New York field office next week."

"Think this clown is worth it?"

Snatching an orange slice from behind the bar, Aidan took a bite. "Am I, babe?"

C.J. rolled her eyes. "You two." She scanned the pub. "Where are the guys?"

Just then the back door opened and in walked Liam and Mikey. "Hey," Liam said.

"C.J.!" Mikey raced to her.

She caught him on the run and hugged him tight. "How's my favorite O'Neil man?"

For a minute the kid buried his face in her neck. Dylan watched Liam watch them. They were all worried about Mike, but of course his dad was the most concerned. Having had trouble with his own son Hogan, Dylan understood only too well what Liam was going through.

Mikey drew back but kept his arms draped around C.J. "Nuh-uh, Uncle Aidan's your favorite."

C.J. whispered in his ear, "Nope, you are. And guess what? We're back in New York to stay."

Saying nothing, Mike hugged her again.

Then Aidan stepped up and reached for the boy. "Gimme him."

After more warm welcomes, they all settled at the bar. Dylan glanced at Liam, who winked at him. Aidan nodded.

"Did you hear the one about the blonde who went to see a ventriloquist show?" Dylan asked C.J.

"Not again." C.J. shook her head. "Don't you guys give up?"

"Did you hear it?"

"No."

"The ventriloquist said to the dummy, 'Got any good jokes?'

"The dummy replied, 'Yeah, there was this blonde who

went into a library . . .' He proceeded to tell three blonde jokes in a row, until finally a woman in the audience bolted up. Blond hair down to her waist, very curvy. Beautiful. 'Stop it,' she yelled. 'How can you be so politically incorrect? Color of hair does not determine IQ. When will you guys lay off?' "

"The ventriloquist turned red. 'I'm so sorry, madam. I was just joking. I—'

"The blonde interrupted him. 'I'm not talking to you,' she snapped. Then she pointed to the dummy. 'I'm talking to him.' "

Liam, Aidan and Dylan guffawed and even C.J.'s lips twitched.

Mikey's brow furrowed. Then awareness dawned on his face. "I get it. She thought . . ." He began to laugh.

C.J.'s eyes narrowed on the group and Dylan was reminded of the tough agent who'd protected his sister until she fell for Aidan. "I'm going to find the worst Irish male joke I can."

Dylan hooted. "Bring it on, baby."

While they were razzing her, the pub door opened again; a beautiful redhead walked inside.

C.J.'s face flushed. "Holy hell. I can't believe this."

"Rachel Scott, right?" This from Liam.

Mike went wide-eyed. "That's the TV lady who got Rory kidnapped."

Last summer, when Bailey, her kids and some of the O'Neils were staying at Clay's lake residence, Scott, who was a TV reporter from WNYC, had found out and publicized the Second Family's whereabouts. She'd also covered a hostage situation that Clay was involved in, with little care for her effect on their family. They'd all been furious at her sensational journalism, but Clay had been the angriest and had done his best to see that Scott's career suffered for her negligence.

Scott's face was all business as she came toward them.

"What do *you* want?" C.J. asked.

"We got word you were in town, Agent Ludzecky. I was hoping the vice president and Second Lady were with you."

C.J. stood and straightened to her full five feet eight inches. Scott was taller than she looked on TV. The woman studied C.J.'s outfit. "You're not on duty."

"I'm not on the VPPD anymore."

"What?" Dylan could practically see the newswoman's mind clicking. "Can I interview you about why?" She glanced at her watch. "I can have a crew here in ten minutes."

"What do you think?" Aidan asked, moving close to C.J.

Regally, Scott tossed back her hair. "Surely this . . . freeze has gone on long enough. I tried to apologize personally to the vice president. I sent several notes. What do I have to do?"

"Drop off the face of the earth?" Aidan suggested.

Liam stepped forward. "I apologize for my brother's manners. I'm sure you were just doing your job. But Clay's the only one who's got say here. It'd be better for you and our family if you'd just leave us alone. Please don't come back to the pub."

Green eyes flamed with frustration. They snapped to Dylan. "You're a journalist. Do you agree with them?"

Dylan wrote a weekly column for the magazine *CitySights* and loved the part-time work. "Jury's still out on that one, sweetheart."

As he knew she would, she bristled at the nickname. "I can't believe this. Well, I'm not taking it lying down." Turning on three-inch heels that made her legs look long and sexy, she strode out.

"Hmm, another fiery redhead," Dylan said. "Speaking of lying down, I'll bet she's hot in . . ."

Liam cleared his throat, reminding Dylan that Mikey was there.

"Why would she be hot, Uncle Dylan?"

"Never mind, kiddo. You'll find out soon enough."

C.J. tugged Mike off the stool. "Come on, Mike, you and I are going to stroll up to the park. We'll leave these Neanderthals to their lewd comments."

"What's a Nean . . . what does that word mean?"

"Something you, my man, will never be."

Dylan watched them leave hand in hand. "She's great."

"I am so hooked." Aidan stared after her. "And loving every minute of it. Finally, I got myself a girl." His eyes focused on Liam. "How about you? Any dates since I left?"

"Nothing I'd repeat."

"He was checking out this *strawberry-blond* firefighter who comes in here."

"Yeah? Do tell."

"I wasn't checking her out. And let's not talk about me. I've had enough of that today."

Dylan stilled. "The therapist appointment?"

Liam nodded.

"How's that going?" Aidan asked.

"Good. Glad you pushed me to do it. All of you."

"Well then, let's see what else we can push you into." Aidan motioned to the tap. "We'll have a beer and you can tell me all about the firefighter."

Dylan got drinks, wondering if Aidan could help him and Paddy come up with a plan to pull his brother out of his funk. He glanced at the door where the redheaded reporter had gone. No, she'd be too much for Liam. Damn, she'd be too much for him, and he was used to fiery hellcats.

FRUSTRATED, SOPHIE TURNED the treadmill up to seven and adjusted the incline higher. Though she was on duty, she'd snatched twenty minutes to run. Fitness was crucial to fire-fighters, but especially to women in the department. They had to develop strength to compensate for their lesser muscle mass. One reason she'd made it in the old boy's club was because she could out-lift and outdistance the majority of the guys. It didn't come easy, either, and she took every opportunity to work at it.

She also found that exercise helped her to figure things out. In the last four days, she'd interviewed eight possible roommates—roommates that she didn't even want. But she'd given it a shot by putting an ad in the FDNY newspaper, figuring if she got another smoke eater, they might not see each other much. But hell, she hadn't known there were so many weird people in the department . . .

Claire Malcolm, a paramedic, had run a hand over Sophie's dining-room table and sniffed. "Not very tidy in here. We'd need to schedule regular cleaning sessions. I won't pick up after you."

Sophie had thought, *Lady, you won't be here to pick up after anybody.*

A guy name Nick who worked on Squad 28 had seemed okay until he saw her plants. "I'm allergic to the mold in the plants."

He seemed like more trouble than he was worth.

A lieutenant Hannah knew who played in a band wanted to move in right away. Sophie was thinking seriously about it, until he told her he had to practice his sax here. She didn't think she could handle that.

Others had similar peculiarities. Looking for a roommate didn't seem to be the answer. Which left getting a part-time job.

The probie came into the workout room. He was a good-looking guy with his swarthy complexion and dark hair and eyes. Sophie had done her share of initiation—short sheeting his bed, stuffing his locker full of mothballs—but he was so enthusiastic, it was hard to be mean to him. "Cap said to tell you the kids are coming in a half hour."

"Thanks, Jules." He looked the worse for wear. "What were you doing?"

"Swabbing the floor. For the third time today."

"I remember those days. At least it'll be clean when the school gets here."

He leaned against the doorjamb. "I like little kids."

"Yeah?"

"Don't you?"

"I don't think about them much."

"You don't want any?"

"Someday, maybe. But I'm not even sure of that."

"It'll be fun having them here."

"We're out of service for two hours." She started to slow down. "I'm gonna shower first."

Jules left and by the time the second-grade class from St. Mary's Catholic School arrived, Sophie was dressed in her light blue shirt, navy pants and low black work boots. She joined her crew to meet the students, show them around and give them some instruction on fire safety.

Mackenzie led them to the common room where juice and doughnuts had been set up. "Welcome to Company 14. Why don't you get something to eat, then sit down in one of the chairs?"

The kids were cute, dressed in navy jumpers for the girls and blue pants and white shirts for the boys. She took note of the chaperones, two nuns who wore black skirts and white blouses and crucifix necklaces, a woman who was probably a mother volunteer and . . . oh, Liam O'Neil. Now she remembered. He'd told them his kid was coming today. When he caught her gaze, he smiled and waved. She nodded and glanced to the group to see which kid was his.

A little boy had turned around to face the back of the room. His dark hair was a bit curly around his ears and neck, and he had huge blue eyes. No smile, though. When he found Liam, he gave a half grin.

Mackenzie asked for quiet. "Again, welcome, all of you. We're here to tell you about the fire department and to teach you some fire safety. I'm Captain Mackenzie, and these are the five firefighters who are going to spend some time with you. After you finish your snack, we'll go look at the trucks."

"Yay!"

"The trucks."

"Super."

A boy, who'd been talking the loudest, raised his hand. Reluctantly, Mackenzie took his question. "What's that thing behind you?" the kid asked.

The cap swallowed hard. Under a banner that read, "WE WILL NEVER FORGET," a flag, a plaque with engraved names and the Maltese cross hung lovingly on one wall. "It's a tribute to the men who worked at this firehouse and were killed in 9/11."

Sophie shot a glance at Cooper and Bilotti. They were stone-faced.

Mackenzie added, "You kids were just babies when this happened, but we lost a lot of good people in the bombings by terrorists."

"Our teachers told us about it," the same kid said.

"Good." Mackenzie cleared his throat. "Now, here's how today'll work. Firefighter Tyler will explain what each rig does, Lieutenant Bilotti will take you on a tour of the firehouse, Firefighters Cooper, Torres and Murray will conduct safety drills with you."

Actually, they'd make Jules do most of the work, especially the demonstrations.

Sophie stepped forward. "You ready, guys?"

They all nodded. She led the group to the bays where two rigs were housed. She had them stand by the engine first, as it was still in service. The gleaming red truck, freshly washed every morning, could go on a run any minute now. "This beauty is Engine 33. It's called an engine or a pumper because it has an engine that pumps water onto the fire. It might get a run any minute. See those yellow layered things on top?"

Some of the kids nodded or said yes.

"Those are hoses of several widths and lengths. Most of the engines in FDNY's fleet have five-hundred-gallon water tanks. The biggest pumps go to the high-rise buildings."

They all stared at her. Was she talking over their heads? Hell, she didn't know that much about kids. She led them over to Ladder 44. "This rig is called a ladder or a truck because it carries the ladders needed in rescue work. Ladder length varies and often depends on where the unit is assigned. This one has a platform for higher places and all-different-sized ladders. Firefighters on ladder trucks are the ones who go in and find people and get them out. They also carry extrication equipment like halligans"—she pulled out the ax with a curled end—"to take down ceilings. We also have various pry tools and rams to open stuck doors."

Bilotti had dragged out some of the Hurst tools and handed her a giant scissorlike thing. "You've probably heard about this one, too. It's called the Jaws of Life and can rip open the hood of a car."

The kids' eyes widened and they murmured among themselves.

"Any questions?"

A little redheaded girl raised her hand. "How come you work here? I didn't know they had lady firemen."

"Yeah, we do." She raised a brow at the captain. "Not enough, though. There are only thirty in the entire department."

She caught Liam O'Neil's frown.

"How come there aren't very many?"

"Some people still view firefighting as a guy's job." She thought of the men who'd done despicable things when the first female firefighter, Brenda Berkman, bulldozed her way, and the way of other women, into their ranks. Even wives and kids protested. "Sometimes women are afraid to try to be a firefighter because society doesn't think they should."

"That's dumb," the girl said.

Sophie grinned. "I think so, too. Any other questions?"

"How many fires do you go to in a day?" a nun asked.

"There are eleven fires every hour in the five boroughs. We catch our share."

"Eleven?" This from the mother. "Wow!"

"I—"

A blast of static came over the PA. "Lower West Side, Box 234, Engine 33. A 10-75." Which meant a working fire.

There was rumbling from the house and six firefighters appeared in the bay. Each hustled to his pair of rubber boots and navy turnout pants that sat on the concrete floor near the engine. They kicked off their house shoes, and within seconds, they were in their goods and onto the rig, where their coats and face masks, called SCBA, were waiting in assigned seating. Not even two minutes after the call, the engine tore out of the house.

Amidst the shrill of the siren, the kids were openmouthed.

Sophie was glad they got to see a real run.

After she finished her talk, the kids headed to the common room for a safety lesson. But the little O'Neil boy hung back and sidled over to his father. Squatting, Liam spoke to his son, who shook his head and tried to take Liam's hand. Again, Liam spoke to him and when he looked up and caught Sophie's gaze, his eyes were troubled.

She walked over. "Hi. Who's this?"

Liam opened his mouth, but the boy answered before his father could. "Mike O'Neil."

"Well, Mike O'Neil, aren't you going to go in for the lesson?"

He looked down at his feet.

She squatted. "Mike, is something wrong?"

He shook his head.

"Didn't you want to come today?"

"I wanted to."

"Don't you want to do the lesson?"

He shrugged.

She stood and stretched out her arm. "How about if I take you inside?"

Finally the boy raised his head. " 'Kay." He glanced at his dad.

"Your dad will be there, too, in the back."

Dad mouthed "thank you" as she led the boy out.

Sophie sat beside Mike as the guys started with simple safety issues, like closing the doors to rooms so if a fire started, it wouldn't spread, to safety in stove use and electrical appliances. Torres demonstrated the "Stop, drop and roll" drill to teach kids what to do if they themselves caught on fire. They discussed the importance of having fire paths out of the house and gave the kids window stickers to indicate to firefighters a child's room in the home.

When the lesson was over, Sophie squeezed Mike's shoulder. "That was good, don't you think?"

"Uh-huh." Shyly he looked at her. "I didn't know they had girl firefighters, either. The ones that came for Mom were all guys."

"That came for your mom?" Liam O'Neil was married? She hadn't thought of that and was vaguely disappointed.

"When she was sick. Sometimes, we had to call the fire department to take her to the hospital."

"I'm sorry your mother's sick, Mike."

Eyes wide, the boy glanced around wildly. When he spotted his father, he bolted off the chair and darted over. Sophie followed him.

"What happened?" Liam asked, grasping onto Mike when the boy encircled his waist with his arms.

"I don't know. He was talking about the fire department coming to help your wife, and he got upset."

"I see."

"I don't know what I did."

Still holding on to his son, Liam's face shadowed with

pain. "My wife died three years ago. Mikey doesn't talk about her too much."

"I'm so sorry." Again, she hunkered down to Mike's eye level. "I didn't mean to make you sad, Mike."

His face averted, she heard him say, "It's okay."

"No, honey, it's not. I know how you feel."

He took a peek at her.

"My mom died when I was ten. I know what it's like to lose your mommy when you're little."

"Did the firefighters help her, too?" he asked.

Sophie's throat got tight. "They tried, but it was too late. My mom, me and my brother were all caught in a burning building. They did get me and my brother out safely, but not her."

Now the boy totally disengaged from his dad. "Really?"

"Yeah, really."

"I'm glad they saved you."

She smiled. "Me, too."

Liam's gaze was warm with approval. "Me, too."

THREE

MIKE THOUGHT about the firefighter lady as he lay in bed the night they had visited the firehouse. He liked her hair. Dad said all O'Neil *men* liked redheads. But Aunt Bailey had dark hair, and C.J. was blond and Mike liked them. Aunt Bailey was in Washington, but C.J. was back. That was nice. He wondered if she'd stay. Uncle Aidan said yes, but grown-ups sometimes made promises they couldn't keep.

I love you more than anything in the world, his mother used to say to him. *I'll never leave you.* Groping under his pillow, Mike took out the picture Uncle Aidan had taken of her and Mike. With his Cub Scout flashlight on, he could see her smiling, her arm around him, hugging him tight.

"Why did you have to go away, Mommy?"

She never talked back so Mike made up the answers all by himself.

"I know you were sick. But Daddy said God didn't take you. It was a just a bad thing that happened, and God would help us deal with it." He thought a minute. "If you're with God, ask Him to help Dad be happier." Bringing the photo to his lips, he kissed his mom's cheek, said, "Good night," and slipped it back under his pillow.

If his brother, Cleary, knew Mike did this every night, he'd call Mike a baby, but he didn't care. It was almost like having his mom tuck him in. Thinking about her, he closed his eyes.

FROM WHERE SHE sat at a table by the huge window with BAILEY'S IRISH PUB scripted across the storefront, Sophie smiled over at Joe Carusotti. "It's so good to see you, Joey."

Tall, fit and looking like a young Robert De Niro, he smiled back. His white captain's shirt accented his dark hair and olive complexion. "Yeah, kiddo, me, too. It's been crazy at the office."

A harried-looking Dylan O'Neil approached their table. "Hey there, Sophie." He nodded to Joe. "Sorry it took so long to get over here. We're shorthanded, again. You ready to order?"

"What's good today?" she asked

"Liam made a great turkey soup. And we got homemade corn bread."

Joe nodded. "I'm in."

"Same here."

Dylan gave Joe a sideways glance before he walked away.

"So," Joe said. "Find a roommate yet?"

"Nope. Probably because I don't want one."

"They need help at Paddock's if you're still interested in a part-time job."

"I don't wanna work at the gym. It kind of ruins the fun of going there."

Joey laughed out loud. "Only you would think sweating your ass off and depleting your muscles was fun."

"Have to stay in shape."

They were distracted from the conversation when out on MacDougal Street a cab screeched to a halt and a guy whipped out of his car and yelled at a truck that was double-parked. The truck driver mouthed several obscenities.

Joe chuckled. "Gotta love New York."

"That's what Nate always said."

"I, um, got an e-mail from him. Did you?"

"Yeah, I know he got a nasty burn in the last raid. Funny, I'm the firefighter and he's the army captain, but he gets burned."

"He sounded good, though."

"As good as any career army guy can be these days. Damn, I wish we'd get out of Iraq."

Joe laid his hand on hers. "I hate having him there, too."

Always the big brother. She grinned and squeezed his hand. "How's your dad?" His father had been on the squad that rescued Sophie and her brother twenty-some years ago. He'd recently become a battalion chief in Brooklyn.

"Good. He wants you to come to dinner."

"I'm free Sunday."

"I'll tell him you're coming."

"Will Tommy Jr. be there?" she asked.

"That's up in the air. As always, he's unpredictable."

Whereas Joe went into the fire department, his younger brother had become one of America's finest. Since they'd grown up, Sophie didn't see much of Tommy. As a kid, he'd been either hot-tempered or aloof—he still was sometimes— and she didn't know him as well as Joe, who she was almost as close to as Nate.

Talk turned to the department. "I think we got a torch in lower Manhattan."

"Yeah, I heard the guys from Squad 28 talking about it at breakfast last week. You on the case?" Joe was one of the arson investigators in the FDNY.

"Yep. With this newbie." His dark eyes twinkled. "A girl."

"Don't start. It's about time we had women in that position." Though they'd made strides in the last decade, few women chose Joe's field. It required hundreds of hours of training and police certification. Olivia Marsh was another trailblazer.

They bantered until Liam came through the kitchen door and over to their table. "Hi, Sophie. Sorry this is late. Bridget called in sick. Dylan and I are doing double duty."

Because his face was lined with fatigue, Sophie gave him a big smile. "We're in no hurry."

He set the food down and glanced at Joe. "Hi."

"This is Joe Carusotti, an arson investigator. Joe, this is the best cook in the world."

"The breakfast Boy Wonder? Glad to meet you."

"Nice to meet you, too. Enjoy."

Surreptitiously, Sophie watched Liam leave. He wore jeans and the pub T-shirt. He had a nice butt, but she was a shoulder girl. He had great shoulders, too.

"You like this place?" Joe asked.

"Um, yeah, the food's great."

"The O'Neils are quite a family."

"You'd never know their sister is Second Lady. They're so down to earth."

Only sporadic conversation interrupted their meal as they devoured lunch. When she finished, Sophie noticed people waiting at the door. Scattered around the dining room were empty tables but they were laden with dirty dishes. Poor guys.

Joe glanced back at the kitchen. "I'd like coffee but it doesn't look like we're gonna get some anytime soon."

Noticing a pot on a stand off to the side, Sophie rose, poured them both coffee and sat back down. They pushed their plates to the side. When Joe finished his coffee, he reached into his pocket.

"Don't you dare. This is my treat. And if you don't let me pay, I'm not gonna have lunch with you again."

"Well, I got a meeting in thirty minutes, and the bill isn't here." Pushing back his chair, he stood, leaned over and kissed her cheek. "You win this time. See you Sunday."

After he left, Sophie rose to go get more coffee and noticed Dylan was on the floor again; he glanced around the interior, shook his head and went back to the orders he was taking from a foursome who'd been waiting some time.

What the hell, she thought. She picked up the dishes from her table and brought them to the tub off to the side. Snagging a rag from the bar, she wiped off her table and cleared the one next to it. Immediately, six people sat down. "It's about time," a woman in a huff said to her.

"Sorry. A waitress called in sick."

Near the coffee stand were the menus. She handed them out, served water for the new people and cleared the next three tables that had sat unattended.

Again, Liam came out of the kitchen with food for customers. His eyes widened when he saw what she'd done. After he served the meals, he came over to her. "What are you doing?"

She shrugged. "I know you're shorthanded. I'm free for a few hours. I thought I'd help out."

His blue eyes sparkled like gemstones. It startled her for a minute. "*You* are an absolute doll, Sophie Tyler."

"Hmm. That's nice to hear. Shall I keep going?"

"Please. We'll owe you big time."

Sophie winked at him. "I'll try to think of appropriate . . . payment."

"You do that, lass."

She noticed he was smiling all the way back to the kitchen.

FROM THE STOVE, Liam glanced over at Dylan, who'd just come into the kitchen and dropped down onto a stool. "Damn, that was hectic."

"Where'd they all come from?"

"I don't know. We have to hire somebody ASAP." Dylan nodded the door. "Sophie was a lifesaver."

"No pun intended." Liam chuckled. "We owe her."

"Thinking of paying up, little brother?"

"Can it. She's a nice woman."

"That she is."

Thoughtfully, Liam stirred a cream sauce he was experimenting with. "She took a shine to Mikey." He explained what had happened at the firehouse last week.

"Hmm. Sweet, too."

Patrick rushed in though the back door. His eyes were flaming. "That man is gonna be the death of me."

"Who?" Dylan asked.

"Pa. I met him on the way in and he started on me about Brie. Again!"

Pa and Patrick had similar personalities and went head-to-head about a lot of things. And the fact that Pa had left the family for a while when they were all young still rankled his older brother. "Forget it. Who's sweet? I heard you say that when I came in."

Dylan glanced at Liam, who shrugged, and Dylan let any discussion of Pa go. "Sophie Tyler. She helped out today with lunch. Bridget's sick."

"Why didn't you call me?"

Silence. This time, Dylan and Liam made a point of *not* looking at each other. Finally Liam said, "This is your day with Isabella."

"I could have brought her with me."

"We didn't want to ruin your time with her."

"Translated, you didn't want to cause more trouble between me and Brie. Fuck it, I can handle my life and the pub."

"Yeah," Dylan said dryly, "we can see that."

"Don't start."

"Then don't be such a shit when we're being considerate."

"I—"

The door opened and Sophie walked in. Liam was grateful for the abrupt halt in the words that were about to erupt into a full scale fight. Paddy was short-tempered as hell these days and Dylan needed lessons in tolerance. "Hey, girl," Liam said.

Unwrapping the towel from around her hips—they were nice hips, not too slender, not wide—she smiled. "All cleaned up out there."

"I heard what you did." Pat crossed to her. "Thanks."

"You're welcome. Haven't bussed tables in years."

"Want a job?" Dylan asked, flirting again. "You're a lot prettier than any of us. I think that's why people stayed so long."

She cocked her head. The overhead lights caught the reddish strands mixed with a bit of gold. "As a matter of fact, I might."

All three brothers stared at her.

"I saw your sign and was thinking about applying."

"But you have a job." This from Pat.

"Yeah and I make good money. But my roommate just got married. I'd like the apartment to myself. I can't swing the rent alone, though. I was thinking about taking something part-time."

"When could you work?" Dylan asked.

"We're on nine- and fifteen-hour tours. I have four days off in between blocks."

"That'd be okay." Pat's mood brightened. "If we're anything, we're flexible."

"I have to be honest. I'd need two hundred and fifty dollars a week but I can work as many hours as that would take."

"Easy. Between salary and tips, you'd make that."

"I did a stint as a bartender once while I was waiting to get into the fire department."

"You're hired," all three said together.

"When can you start?" Paddy asked.

"She already did." Dylan walked over and gave her a hug. "Welcome to Bailey's Irish Pub, Sophie Tyler."

CAPTAIN YVETTE TRUDEAU wasn't nearly as pretty as her name. Oh, she was nice-enough-looking, but she was a stone-cold bitch, furthering some of the stereotypes of women in the FDNY. Everybody hated it when she subbed on their shift for the officer in charge, like today. Jim Mackenzie had furlough time, so Yvette was in charge of Company 14.

"Housekeeping duties are up," she said as she entered the kitchen. The truck squad sat drinking coffee around the scarred table that had the names of those killed on 9/11 carved into it. "Hop to it."

"There bunnies here, *Captain*?" Cooper looked innocent, but his jaw tightened. God, didn't the woman know not to mess with him?

"Funny. Get moving, Torres."

Julian jumped up. Bilotti eyed Cooper over the top of his newspaper. Sophie caught their glances. *They* could pick on the probie all they wanted—they were *supposed* to—but he was off limits to anybody else. Bilotti stood, placed his hand on Jules's shoulder and pushed him back down onto the chair. "You need more coffee, kid. I'll get it for you."

Trudeau's face reddened. "Suit yourself. Training's in an hour. You wanna do stuff last minute, it's your ass. But," she said, turning away, "letters will go in folders if housework is not done properly."

"I'm shivering in my boots," Murray mumbled.

"What was that, Murray?"

"Nothing, Captain."

She walked out and Cooper snorted. "Somebody got up on the wrong side of the bed."

Murray quipped, "She doesn't have a right side."

"Hey, you know were that term came from?" Jules asked.

Sophie smiled at the probie. "Where?"

"Left-handed people used to be considered defective. So family members tried to break the habit. They'd push the lefty's bed to the wall and made him get up on the opposite side, causing the person to be cranky."

Bilotti made a rude noise. "She's right-handed, kid."

"And I'm left," Sophie said. "Look how sweet I am."

"Yeah, sugar, you sure are." This from Murray, whose flirting and un-PC language was harmless.

They bantered a bit, finished their coffee, then headed out to check the housework detail. Sophie sighed as she read it. "Why the hell does she hate me so much?"

Cooper put his hand on her neck. "'Cause the guys like you. Even our big friend over there."

Tony Bilotti had had a lot of trouble with Sophie the first two years after she joined the group. He was one of the ones who'd believed women didn't belong in the fire department. But Sophie had proved herself over and over, and he'd finally let up.

Cooper's comment and the reference to Bilotti's acceptance of her made cleaning the toilets easier. When she finished and joined the rest of them in the bay for training, Sophie was whistling.

Standing by the rig, Trudeau shot her a frown. "You got something to smile about, Tyler?"

"I'm just happy in the morning, Captain."

The other woman's eyes narrowed. "That's not what Ray says."

"What?"

"Your ex. He says you were a zombie in the morning." She let the innuendo hang.

Bilotti came to one side of Sophie and Cooper the other. "You enjoying Sophie's castoffs, Trudeau?" Cooper asked.

The other woman's entire stance straightened. "I'll report

you for sexual harassment if you say one more word along that vein."

Cooper glared at her. Only a fool tangled with him; his bald head and bull-like appearance intimated everybody. Quickly, Trudeau looked away and picked up her clipboard. "Here's the drill. We're doing confined-space training today."

Torres stiffened. Probies had trouble with this CST. Mackenzie was waiting to broach it until Jules had been with them longer.

Stiffly, like she had a stick up her ass, Trudeau moved to the pipe, which was twenty feet long and five feet in diameter. "I'll go first to demonstrate." She dropped down to her knees at the opening. The far end of the pipe was covered so it would be pitch-black inside. "Time me."

As soon as Trudeau got inside, Bilotti said, "Bitch."

"I won't be able to do it." Jules was sweating now.

Sophie squeezed the kid's arm. "Lots of experienced firefighters panic the first few times in the pipe, Jules."

Bilotti thought a minute, then nodded to Murray, who caught Cooper's eye and signaled Sophie with a cock of his chin. They all grinned.

When Trudeau crawled out through the cloth blocking the far end, she rolled to her feet and faced them. Sweat beaded on her brow and she was breathing hard. Lay people had no idea the toll crawling through small, dark spaces took on firefighters.

"How long?"

Murray shrugged. "Oops."

Her face flaming now, Trudeau gestured to Sophie. "Your turn, Tyler."

Whipping off the FDNY sweatshirt she'd pulled on over her uniform, Sophie trudged to the pipe. She sank to her knees and took deep breaths.

"Close your eyes, Tyler," Murray called out.

She stuck her head in.

"Imagine good things," Bilotti yelled.

These were all tactics firefighters used to get through the drill. Inching her way in, she waited until she was completely inside, then stopped. Cooper's voice came from the far end. "Come on, Sophie baby. You can do it."

She waited a bit, then she slid back out the front. Coming onto her knees, she shot a dejected look up at Trudeau. "Sorry, I can't."

"Don't give me that bullshit, you're a twelve-year veteran. You've done it before."

"Sorry. Must be that it's too early in the morning for me." She arched a brow. "Regs say if we can't make it, we can try another time."

Trudeau glowered at her, then turned to the guys. "Murray, go next."

Murray knelt in front of the pipe and wiggled his body inside. He made it halfway, then crawled out backward.

"What the fuck? If you can make it halfway down, you can make it the whole way."

Running a hand through his hair, Murray couldn't conceal the mirth in his blue eyes. "Don't know what's got into me."

Bilotti finagled his shoulders through, then quit.

So when Jules positioned himself in front of the pipe, took in several deep breaths and got in a third of the way before backing out, which was typical for probies, everybody was innocence personified.

"You're all a piece of work," Trudeau spat out. "I'm reporting this to your captain."

"Guess we have to take it on the chin." Bilotti could barely control a smirk.

Trudeau stomped out of the bay.

When she was gone, Sophie raised her hand for a high five from the group.

Torres said, "Thanks, guys."

Cooper's gaze narrowed. "For what, probie?"

"Don't know what you're talking about." Bilotti's scowl was fierce.

"Don't gloat over our inadequacies," Sophie said haughtily.

God, she loved being a firefighter.

FOUR

EVEN THE QUESTIONNAIRE mocked Liam as he sat at a table in the reception area of Paddock's Gym scribbling down the required information. After the usual bio statistics, the hard questions followed.

Describe your exercise routine. Answer: Zilch.

He'd never been into working out. He'd been too busy with the kids and Kitty and the pub to devote any of his time to it.

How long and fast can you maintain aerobic exercise?

Oh, let's see, he could chase down Mikey and Cleary in no time when they were little. He still ran the bases okay when the O'Neil clan got a pickup game going.

How much can you bench-press?

Answer: A twenty-pound bag of flour? A few cases of beer.

Taking a break, he studied the reception area. Posters of men and women exercising were hung on various walls, but the space to his right caught his attention—it displayed firefighting and cop pictures along with memorabilia from each department. In the center was a framed certificate from the mayor thanking the business for its donation to the 9/11 widows fund and was accompanied by a big picture of the Twin Towers as they'd once been.

The buff blond guy with the toothpaste smile looked up from the paperwork on his desk. "Done?"

Liam blew out a heavy breath. "This isn't gonna happen." He nodded to the back rooms of the gym. He'd seen the athletic guys come and go. "I think your outfit's too advanced for me."

The trainer—Jase Smith—checked him out. "You don't seem to be in bad shape."

"Looks can be deceiving." He stood and held out the clipboard. "Thanks anyway."

"Hey, where you going?"

Turning, Liam saw the reason he was at Paddock's Gym come into the reception area. In sweatpants and a muscle shirt, with her hair in a ponytail, Sophie Tyler was frowning at him. He took a minute to admire her five foot, eight inch frame. She was solid muscle. Beautiful solid muscle. Which only fueled his feelings of inadequacy.

"This is a mistake. I don't work out, I can't run very far and I'm too old for it all."

Her eyes, when they took him in, were the color of dark gray smoke; she tweaked his biceps. "You probably aren't as bad as you think. I see you lift a lot of heavy things at work." She'd been officially employed at the pub for a week. "And I know you go hiking with the boys. Cleary told me when he came in after school one day."

Liam couldn't admit to her, here in the world of Greek God clones, that the hiking he did was with his Cub Scout troop. He was a freaking Cub Scout *leader*. It was bad enough that his brothers called him Robbie, after Baden-Powell, the founder of the scouts, and made all sorts of comments about how wholesome he was. When Kitty was alive, he used to laugh it off. Lately, it rankled him.

"Come on." Sophie tugged at his arm. "I'll work out with you."

"God no, I'd die of embarrassment."

Smith stepped forward. "I can help you, Mr. O'Neil."

Ah, so they guy knew he was the Second Lady's brother. Liam didn't often capitalize on that relationship, but what the hell—he needed help. "Appreciate that." He turned to Sophie. "Only if you go somewhere else so you don't see my pathetic attempts at getting in shape."

Her grin was mischievous. "Mmm. I think the view is pretty damn good, Liam O'Neil."

"Go."

Whistling, she wandered into another room and Jase led him into the gym proper and over to the treadmills. "We'll start you out slow. You'll be up to speed, so to speak, in no time."

Liam went at an easy pace. His brothers also teased him he had only one gear—second—so slow was good. Jase came back after ten minutes and increased the speed. The second ten had Liam breathing hard and sweating, but it felt good. He was glad he had let Sophie talk him into this . . .

She'd worked four shifts in the last week and they all liked having her around. She didn't complain about late orders or shorthandedness, was great with the customers and real easy on the eyes. She filled out the green pub T-shirt just fine, and her hair intrigued him. She wore it tied back most of the time, like now, but he'd seen it down around her shoulders on occasion. He'd been thinking about those pretty strands when they finished with the lunch crowd today, and she'd come in the kitchen; Liam and Dylan were conferring on orders for next week.

"You wanna eat?" Liam asked, hoping she'd stick around. "I made boxty stuffed with portabella mushrooms for dinner. You could have some now."

"Don't tempt me. I love your potato pancakes. But no thanks, I'm gonna go work out."

"Where?" Dylan asked.

"A place called Paddock's over on Lafayette. I've been going there for years."

Dylan nodded to Liam. "You're looking for a gym, right?"

"Yeah, sure." He still hadn't followed up on his therapist's suggestion.

Sophie's face brightened and he noticed how her complexion was just about perfect. "Paddock's is great. All the smoke eaters go there and some cops."

"Then no, thanks. I don't want to shame the family name."

"They've got great help. I could set you up with my favorite trainer."

"Go ahead," Dylan put in. "I'm free; I'll get Mikey off the school bus."

"I don't have gym stuff. Maybe I'll tag along next time."

Crossing to the back closet, Dylan dragged out old sweatpants and sneakers that were clean but nobody could remember whose they were. He tossed them at Liam. "What's your next excuse?"

"All right . . ."

"Time for weights, Mr. O'Neil." Jase had returned and glanced at the treadmill. "You did okay here for the first time. You must do some exercise."

"Just at work and playing ball with my kids. And call me Liam, please."

"Let's check your muscle mass." The trainer led him to another room with hand weights.

"No machines?" Liam asked.

"The guys prefer these."

Hesitant, Liam glanced around the weight room. "Sophie's the only woman in here."

"Yeah. A few female firefighters belong here. They're rabid about their fitness. Sophie can out-bench a lot of the dudes."

"Great."

Jase smiled. "She's something, isn't she?"

"I'm beginning to find that out."

After he did a pathetic ten reps of arm curls, bench-pressed an embarrassing poundage of weights and practically killed his thighs doing squats, the trainer told him to take a break and showed him how to stretch. From across the room, Liam watched Sophie.

Cliché though it was, she was poetry in motion. She was lifting the free weights and by the looks of the barbells, she was off the charts. No wonder she had muscles to die for. But they weren't masculine. Taking in her sturdy, supple form, he doubted anything about her was. Over the last week, he'd wondered about her life, her past and what she wanted for the future. He was thinking about asking her to go for coffee after this session when the big guy she'd been at lunch with the other day came into the room and strode over to her.

Sophie's face bloomed with smiles when she saw him. He kissed her cheek and briefly cupped his hand behind her neck. The intimacy of the gesture was loud and clear. Guess she was taken.

Turning away from the sight, Liam braced his arms on the wall. That was okay. A girl like Sophie Tyler would never be interested a staid dad—a freaking Cub Scout leader—like him.

For some stupid reason the thought made his heart bump in his chest.

"I'M THROWING IN the towel," Liam told Sophie after he finished his stretches and found her in another room; she was winding down on the treadmill, keeping an eye out for Liam and talking with Joe.

"Yeah, me, too." Flicking the switch on the machine, she climbed off. "Have a good workout, Joey."

"I will, babe. Don't forget Sunday."

She accompanied Liam to the locker rooms, but before she went into the women's side, she looked over at him. His face was flushed and his eyes were even bluer today because he wore navy sweats. She liked the way his damp hair curled at his neck. "You look good."

"Don't lie to spare my feelings. I'm whipped."

"Too whipped to go for a beer?"

He glanced behind him. "Won't your friend mind?"

"Why would he?"

"I . . . isn't he . . ." He was stuttering. It was cute. "Isn't he a beau?"

"What a nice, old-fashioned word."

Liam looked to the ceiling. "That's me. Just your nice, old-fashioned guy."

"Joe's like my brother, not my beau." She couldn't help smiling at the word. She didn't ever remember hearing anyone use it. Certainly not the rough-and-tumble guys she worked with.

"Yeah?"

"Have that beer next door with me and I'll tell you all about it."

"You're on."

After they cleaned up, Liam met Sophie in the reception area. He smelled like freshly applied aftershave—the same woody scent he usually wore, and she had to stop herself from moving in close to take a deep breath of it. He thanked Jase for his time, and they headed to the café next door.

It was a gorgeous Indian summer day in the city, so they chose an outdoor table. Late afternoon was bustling with crowds of people hurrying down of the sidewalks of Lafayette Street. Out here, the sun glistened off Liam's dark hair, showing a strand or two of gray that she found particularly endearing. When they waiter came over, he ordered a Coke.

She arched a brow. "You own a pub and don't drink?"

"Not much. I'm working tonight, too. You go ahead though."

She ordered a Corona with lime.

"So," he said, his gaze direct. "What about *Joey*?"

"Like I told Mikey that day at the station house, me and my brother, Nate, were caught in a fire when we were little. My mom worked two jobs and was out cold for the night when something went wrong with the space heater." She cleared her throat. "The FDNY got us out, but not her."

"What was her name?"

"Huh?"

"What was your mother's name?"

"Maeve Tyler."

"Maeve's an old-fashioned Irish name."

"Do you know what it means?"

"Uh-huh. Joy." He placed a hand over hers, where it lay on the table. "Tell me the rest."

"Tom Carusotti, Joe's dad, carried me out. He called me *Sophie baby*."

"The name the guys used at the pub that morning. I wondered why you tolerated it."

"Yeah, it isn't sexist, just a carryover from then and a sign of affection now." They also used it to get her out of her nightmares. "Nate and I became their *project*, I guess you could say. We went to live with my grandmother, but the fire department never lost touch with us. Tom's two sons, Joey and Tommy, were like brothers to me when we were growing up. I'm closest to Joe."

"What'd the fire department do for you as their project?"

She recounted their visits to her and Nate in the hospital, how they sent their priests to comfort the two orphaned kids, and after they were released, the guys rotated taking them places for years. "It was like I'd found hundreds of fathers. They were—are—my family."

"I can see that."

"When I was old enough, I wanted to join the FDNY."

"What year was that?"

"It was 1996. Things were tough in the department for women. The male barrier had been broken, but females were still treated like dirt. The courts forced the issue, though. I had it easy in comparison to most of the others because of the Carusottis and the rest of the guys who'd taken me under their wings. Even then, two men objected—and their wives—so they transferred out of our house."

"That's quite a story. How'd your grandmother feel about you becoming a firefighter?"

"She wasn't happy, but she died before I got in."

"Another loss."

She squeezed his hand before she drew hers away. "Which you know all about."

Leaning back, he gazed out at the street. A bus rumbled by and its exhaust puffed out smoke. "Afraid so."

"What was *her* name?"

"Mary Katherine. Kitty for short."

"The love of your life."

"How do you know?"

"It shows on your face when you just say her name."

"I met her when we were in eighth grade—we were both fourteen years old. We got married as soon as we graduated from high school. We had a great life, though it took us a while to have kids." She saw his Adam's apple work. "I guess she had problems even then. She died of ovarian cancer. A prolonged and ugly death."

"I'm sorry, Liam."

He shook his head. "Look at us. Such morbid talk on this beautiful fall day."

She raised her beer. "To fall days."

Grinning, he clinked glasses with her. *"Slainté."*

"Isn't that cute."

Sophie stilled and didn't have to look to the side to recognize the mocking voice. "Hello, Ray."

"Hey, *Sophie baby.*"

Ray was a paramedic. The absorption of EMS into the FDNY hadn't been easy, and there was still bad blood between the two divisions. But that wasn't the only reason he hated the fire department. "This another smoke eater?"

Scraping back his chair, Liam stood and held out his hand. "Liam O'Neil."

Ray was stocky, but a lot shorter than Liam. He ignored Liam's hand. "I'm Ray Cramden, Sophie's husband."

Liam's jaw dropped.

"Ex-husband," Sophie clarified.

"We took vows, sweetheart."

"What do you want, Ray?"

"Just to say a friendly hello."

It was subtle, but Liam straightened and seemed to tower over her ex. "Nice to meet you, Ray. If you'll excuse us now, Sophie and I don't have much time and she was telling me a very interesting story."

Like before when he was crossed, Ray's gaze turned chilling. "Yeah, she's full of those." He looked like he was going to say more, but Liam moved between him and Sophie's line of vision so he stalked away.

Liam cocked his head toward Ray when he sat down. "Do you want to talk about him?"

"Nah. Our history is not pretty. Let's talk about something happy. Tell me about your kids."

His face shadowed. "Not all sweetness and light there."

"Want to tell me?"

"Nah." He mimicked her tone.

"So, do you know any good jokes?"

Liam looked at her hair and chuckled. "Yeah, as a matter of fact I do. There was this ventriloquist . . ."

MIKEY STARED over the desk at Mrs. David. He liked her, except when she called on him in class and he didn't want to talk.

"Your son's done well for the first few weeks of the school year, Mr. O'Neil." She glanced from his dad to Mike. "Don't you think so?"

He shrugged.

"Mike, we discussed this. Could you answer when asked a question?"

"Yes, ma'am."

"Do you think you've done well, son?" his dad asked.

"Kinda. Not in science. I don't like it."

Mrs. David gave him a nice smile. "I think you're going to have to know science if you pursue one of the jobs you wrote about last week." She smiled at his father. "We're having a career day in November, and the children were asked to list the top five jobs they might be interested in."

"What did you put down, Mike?"

"Baseball player. Cook."

"What was at the top of your list?" his teacher asked.

"Firefighter."

His dad's smile was big and real. Mike wished he'd smile like that more. "Ah, I see."

"Many of the children chose that profession after our tribute on 9/11 to those who died in the Towers. And then, of course, our visit to the firehouse cinched it."

"A lady one works at our pub," Mike volunteered. "I like her."

His dad nodded. "She's a nice woman."

"Maybe you need to try harder at science," the teacher suggested. "Firefighters have to learn all kinds of scientific facts."

"'Kay."

"How's he doing otherwise?" His dad touched his arm.

"I wish he were more social."

Mike didn't want to hear about this so he turned his head away and made himself think about other things.

"We're working on that, Mrs. David."

"I know. And I'm glad."

The two of them talked some more, then it was time to go.

Mike stood when his dad did. He was in a hurry because Sophie was working at the pub today, and he wanted to see her before she left.

SOPHIE WAS WIPING up the bar when Cleary walked into the pub. He'd inherited the O'Neil looks, with dark hair that was a little too long, but the style these days. And there was devil in the boy's blue eyes. A lot like his uncle Dylan's.

"Hey, Cleary. How was school?" She'd been working at the pub two full weeks and had gotten to know the boy some.

"Boring." He set down his backpack on the bar and pulled his baseball glove out of it. "Where's Dad?"

"I think he's at a conference with Mike's teacher."

Cleary's dark brows drew together. Whereas Mikey kept things to himself, this one's emotions were up front and center. "Still?"

"I guess. Unless they did something afterward."

"Probably." A sulk. Now he looked like Patrick.

She rinsed out a cloth and hung it on an aluminum bar. "Something wrong?"

"Dad promised to play catch with me today."

"Then I'm sure he'll be back."

Cleary glanced at the clock. "Uncle Dylan around?"

"Just left. Some meeting at the magazine."

Patrick came into the bar area. "Hey there, kid, how you doin'?" To Sophie he said, "Thanks for holdin' down the fort."

"It's okay. I don't have to work tonight."

"You been a big help around here." He frowned. "You makin' enough money to pay your rent?"

"Yep, and then some. The pub has good tippers."

"That we do, lass." He transferred his gaze to his nephew. "What's up, Cleary?"

"Not much. Waiting for Dad."

"Want to start your homework?"

"I wanna play catch."

"Sorry, can't oblige you. I have stuff to get ready for to-night."

Cleary sulked some more.

"I can play." Sophie watched the boy assess her. His gaze narrowed just like his dad's did when he got thoughtful. "I'm pretty good."

"You don't throw like a girl, do you? I mean, you're a fire-fighter."

"Let's go see how I throw. Got an extra glove?"

Pat put in, "In the office closet."

"What do you say, Cleary?"

"Sure, why not?"

Cleary led her to the office opposite the kitchen, dug a glove and bat out of the closet and they went out the rear of the pub. From behind him, she noticed he already had wide shoulders; someday they'd be as nice as Liam's.

They stopped at the alley that backed up to the pub. The noise from the street was muted out here, and it was quiet enough to hear a few birds chirping. When Cleary jogged to only twenty feet from Sophie, she hid a smirk and held up her glove. "Sock it to me, boy."

Cleary tossed her a soft one. She caught it and returned it. Fast. And hard. Cleary stumbled back when it shot into his glove.

"Gotcha." She gave him a knowing look. "Cleary?"

"Huh?"

"That's how girls throw these days."

The boy laughed out loud and increased the distance be-tween them. He had a good sense of humor. After fifteen min-utes, he asked, "You bat, too?"

"Please, don't insult me."

He raced over and got the bat. They were into their second half hour of pop flies and run-for-them catches; Cleary's face was flushed, bringing out his freckles, and Sophie was sweat-ing in her black pants and pub T-shirt. As she leapt up to grab a ball he'd thrown over her head, she caught a glimpse of Liam and Mikey standing on the porch.

Mikey waved to her. "Hey, Sophie, you're good."

"For a girl." She gave Cleary a pointed look. "Let's take a break."

They jogged to the back porch. Up close, Liam seemed tired today, and troubled. She wondered how the conference went.

"Hi."

"Hi." She ruffled Mike's hair. "Hey, kiddo."

"Will you play with me, too, Sophie?"

She glanced at her watch. "Sure."

Liam said to Cleary, "I have some time to help with your math project if you want."

"Fix me a snack first?"

Sophie was about to tell him he could fix his own snack and to give his dad a break, when Liam said, "Uh-huh. Let's go."

Their eyes met. Liam's smile was grateful.

After she tossed the ball with Mike, they went in and found father and son pouring over a laptop computer. Off to the side were the remains of a sandwich. Still holding her hand, Mike asked, "Can I have something to eat, too?"

Liam nodded to the kitchen. "It's on the counter in the back, honey."

Saying good-bye to Sophie, Mike took off.

"I'll be going now, guys."

"I'll see you out." He stood and said to Cleary, "Be right back."

On the sidewalk in front of the pub, standing in the late afternoon shadows, Liam faced her. A few feet down the street, a FedEx truck zoomed by and stopped short behind a Lexus. Horns blared, momentarily stopping their conversation.

Liam motioned to the pub. "This is above and beyond the call of duty."

"No problem. I loved it."

"You're a good ball player."

"Don't tell Cleary, but I'm cleanup batter on the department softball team."

He laughed out loud, a deep masculine sound, one she hadn't heard before; it . . . affected her. "I'm sworn to secrecy.

Still, you must have better things to do than hang out with my kids."

"I like your kids."

"That's nice to hear. Cleary's moody these days and not always fun to be around." He ran a hand through his hair, rumpling it nicely. "I need to pay more attention to him."

"You need to pay more attention to yourself."

His expression was puzzled.

"Just an observation. Think about it. I gotta go. I'm having dinner with Hannah."

"When are you working again?"

"Not till Saturday. But our group'll be in on Thursday for breakfast."

"Oh, great. I'll fix you something special."

"Every thing you fix is special, Liam O'Neil." She had the urge to kiss him on the cheek but refrained. Instead she squeezed his arm. "See you then."

FIVE

"HAPPY BIRTHDAY to you, happy birthday to you. Happy birthday, dear Sophie, happy birthday to you."

The firefighters had strong, hardy voices, and some sang in harmony like Liam and his brothers often did when they performed in the pub. He watched them from the other side of the room where he was refilling the coffee urn. True to his word, Liam had fixed something special this Thursday morning: French toast filled with apples and cream cheese, served with a fruit cup. Now he was glad he'd fussed, though he wished Sophie had told him it was her birthday today.

As usual, the guys were joking with her. "So, Sophie baby," Jim Mackenzie said. "Getting up there, aren't you?"

"A whole thirty-two. What are you now, Cap, fifty?"

"Wiseass. Forty-five."

The young rookie who seemed to have a crush on Sophie was wide-eyed. "I can't believe you're that old."

"You just don't get it." Cooper glared at Torres. "Don't you know nothing, pork chop? Never say something like that to a woman."

"Why?"

Sean Murray—Liam was getting to know them and this one was their driver—shook his head. "He's hopeless."

Sophie squeezed the rookie's arm. "I'll tell you later, Jules. I know you meant it as a compliment."

Finished with the coffee, Liam headed back to the kitchen. "Great meal," someone from another company called out to him.

"Thanks." Feeling melancholy, he crossed to the Sub-Zero refrigerator, took out the chicken stock he'd frozen last week and left it to thaw on the counter. He was thinking about Sophie and her birthday, and then his mind went to other birthdays . . .

I got you a birthday present, Kitty had said on his last birthday before she got sick.

Yeah? He'd pulled her close. *All I want is you.*

Hmm. She handed him a box. *That's sort of what this is.*

He tore open the paper. Inside was a red negligee that had him practically swallowing his tongue. *Good Lord.*

She'd stripped then and donned the frothy confection. The lovemaking had been wild . . .

Today, alone in the kitchen, he sighed heavily. Damn it, he hated when these memories ambushed him. He was doing better and didn't wake up every day thinking about his dead wife. As a matter of fact, he was seriously considering asking Sophie for a date. Kitty would want him to see other women and finally, he wanted—really wanted—to be with a woman. He'd been seriously wondering what it would be like to make love to Sophie Tyler.

The kitchen door opened and in walked the woman he'd been thinking about a lot lately. When she'd come in this morning, she'd changed out of her uniform into some pressed jeans and a soft pink sweater. She'd left her hair down, and it curled thick and heavy at her collar. "I brought you some birthday cake." She held up three pieces covered with gooey chocolate frosting. "My favorite."

"The guys know you well," he said, oddly jealous of that fact.

"Yeah." She set the cake on the counter. "It's probably too early for you to eat this."

"Not sure I can down three pieces, Soph."

"Mikey and Cleary might like some after school."

"They will. Thanks for thinking of them." He hitched a hip against the counter, hoping she'd stay and chat. "What will you do on your birthday?"

"If I don't have to work, I usually go to the Carusottis."

"Ah."

"Then tomorrow, Hannah's taking me shopping and to lunch to celebrate." Her eyes shadowed.

"What?"

"I wish Nate were here. But he'll probably call me." She fidgeted with the watch that circled her wrist. She rarely wore jewelry, but today she'd stuck little gold hoops in her ears as well. "I guess I should be going."

"Get some sleep before you head out to your friends' house. I heard you all talking about your calls on the tour." He grinned. "Got the term right, didn't I?"

"Yeah, you did."

"Did you get *any* sleep?"

She raked a hand through her hair, messing it. "We were up all night." She smiled.

So did he. He wished he could think of more to talk about so she'd stay, but he was like a teenager with a new girl and he was afraid he'd start stuttering.

Finally, she said, "I guess I'll see you in a few days," and turned from him.

He watched her walk away. Her hips swayed gracefully; she had a nice butt, and today the soft denim clung to it. He liked the way her hair bounced when she moved. The entire package that was Sophie Tyler made him say, "Hey, wait a sec."

With her hand on the door, she looked over her shoulder, a question in her eyes. Whipping off the towel around his waist, he covered the distance between them in three long strides. She was tall, but still he had height on her. He circled her around to face him and smiled down into her eyes. This morning they were the color of warm steel. "Every girl should have a birthday kiss, don't you think?"

Those eyes widened and a slow smile spread across her face. "Yeah, I guess I do." She moved a bit closer. "You up to it?"

"I am, lass." Lowering his head, he brushed his lips across hers. For a moment, she was utterly still. Then she raised her hands to his chest and pressed one against his heart. Liam might be out of practice, but he remembered the signals: He drew her flush against him. She went willingly, tangling her legs with his. Assaulted by the flowery scent of shampoo and soap, he increased the pressure on her lips. She slid her hand up and locked it at his neck. He opened his mouth and she opened hers, then he explored her, tasting a kind of sweetness he'd forgotten existed. She made a sound of pleasure and it made *him* moan.

Steeped in the feel and taste and scent of her, he didn't know how long it was before he drew back. She stayed close and opened her eyes. They were sparking with arousal. He was hard against the fly of his jeans. She grinned; so did he.

"Happy birthday, Sophie. And sweet dreams."

She didn't say anything before she left.

But that was okay.

Turning back to the stove, Liam started whistling. His body hummed, and the painful pressure below his waist was intense. But that was all right, too. It was good to feel the sexual kick again. It was good to feel alive. Glancing at the door, he chuckled. "You pack quite a punch, Sophie baby."

"OH, MAN, BUY that skirt. It makes your legs look like a model's." Hannah watched Sophie in the mirror of a dressing room in their favorite consignment shop in SoHo. She loved coming down here to the trendy bistros and elegant cast-iron buildings with distinctive architecture. "I'll bet that'll make the O'Neil boys take notice." When Sophie didn't react, she added, "Even the quiet one."

Still waters run deep, Sophie thought, remembering the kiss in the kitchen yesterday morning. The surprisingly hot, mind-numbing kiss. Who would have thought?

Hannah laughed. "I knew it. You blushed like a Nebraska virgin. Tell all."

Smoothing down the folds of the shiny gray skirt with velvet inserts, Sophie purposefully widened her eyes. "I have no idea what you're talking about."

"Don't bullshit me. I know the signs."

Sophie grinned into the mirror. "All right. I am attracted to him. What's more, I like him. And his family."

"Me, too. As we said, they're eye candy."

"They're nice people."

Hannah perused the black tops she'd picked out to go with Sophie's skirt. "They seem to be. Nothing serious with the dude, though, is there?"

"Why do you ask that?"

"He's got a ready-made family, hon."

"Whoa. It was only a kiss."

"A kiss? *Shut up!*"

Damn, now she'd done it. She'd had no intention of telling nosy Hannah about what happened with Liam in the kitchen, even though the woman was her best friend. But that encounter had been on her mind, and she'd slipped.

"It's just a chemistry thing."

"Hmm." Hannah handed Sophie a silky top, cut low and fitted at the waist. Sophie wasn't a twig—you couldn't be in her job—and she weighed a lot more than others would think, but she was toned and this shirt would look great on her.

"So, was it slow and easy, like he is, or hot and heavy? You can't judge a book by its cover."

Slipping off her cotton T, Sophie poked her head through the neck of the top. It slithered down her body, making her shiver. Or was it thinking about Liam's mouth? Oh, hell, what fun was it to have the hots for someone and not share the buzz. "It was intense." She met Hannah's eyes in the mirror. "Smokin'."

"Think he'll ask you out?"

"Maybe I'll ask him out. Like you did with Dominic."

Hannah glanced away.

"What?"

"Nothing."

Sophie dropped down next to Hannah on the bench. "Is something wrong with Dom?"

"Maybe us both." Her tough friend's eyes filled with worry. "We haven't been using protection for a year."

"Protection?"

Sophie was thinking about firefighting gear when Hannah added, "When we have sex."

"Really? Why?"

"Because we want a kid. And we're in our freakin' thirties. Once we decided to tie the knot, we didn't care if it happened before or after the wedding."

"It didn't happen?"

Hannah shook her head. "I'm worried something's wrong."

"Have you seen a doctor?"

"This week. Dom's not happy about doing it, but we're going." She shrugged. "You know the research about smoke eaters."

Sophie did. They often had trouble conceiving a child. Exposure to extremes of heat had been linked to male infertility and there was a possibility of birth defects in the offspring of exposed mothers and fathers. Many of the chemicals in the fire environment could adversely affect reproduction. "Hannah, lots of the guys have kids. Normal kids. And the women on staff do, too. You should wait to hear what the doctor says."

"Dom will have to jerk off in a jar."

Sophie laughed. "Maybe you can help." Her comment made Hannah smile. "Do you want to talk more about this?"

"No, let's wait, like you said. It's time for lunch."

"If you're sure." Sophie stood and looked in the mirror again. "Should I get this one?"

Hannah appraised. "What do you think?"

"I look . . . good."

"There you go. We're buying the whole outfit, sister."

"Right." Sophie never had a sister, but this was what it would have been like. She hoped like hell everything was okay with Hannah.

The risks firefighters endured took all different shapes and forms.

LIAM GROANED. What had he been thinking? This was a colossal mistake.

"Come on, little brother, get with the program."

The program, as Dylan called it, was apparently to preen in front of the mirror in a men's store in the garment district over on Seventh Avenue. Right now, Dyl stood in the three-way glass and admired the way the gray pants and a matching shirt fit his trim torso. Before Liam could jab him, Aidan came out of the dressing room. He looked sharp in a navy cotton sweater and knife pressed slacks. He nudged Dylan out of the way and took center stage at the mirror.

"You two give Narcissus competition," Liam said.

"We look great, don't we, bro?" Aidan commented, still staring at himself.

"I look better," Dylan quipped.

"And you're both so modest."

They turned on him at once. Always a bad thing. Dylan went first. "You could use some confidence. The chicks dig it."

"Chicks?" Aidan choked. "Oh God, C.J. will cut your balls off if she hears you say that."

"Hey, I got another blonde joke."

Aidan glanced over at Liam. "Not yet. Let's get this guy into some decent rags."

Well, Liam had asked for this. Staring at his khaki slacks and sweatshirt, he sighed. He always ordered his clothes from L.L. Bean. Correction, Kitty had ordered them, and he kept up the practice when she died. They were nice, serviceable things that, truthfully, he never thought much about before.

Aidan stepped forward. "You said it was time for a change, Liam."

"I know. For a lot of things." He glanced away. "It's just that every time I change something, it closes another door on Kitty."

"Maybe those doors need to be shut to move on." Dylan's voice was gentle, though his words weren't.

Liam thought of Sophie. "I wanna move on."

"Then, come on, let's get you outfitted."

It took some time. But they joked through it . . .

Dylan: "Man, that sports coat is the bomb. Maybe I'll buy it instead . . ."

Liam: "I can't afford this. I got kids to support . . ."

Aidan: "Jesus, Liam, don't tuck that shirt in. Have we taught you nothing?"

Liam: "Yeah, not to be such prima donnas. You guys are something else."

They finally left the store with the sports coat, some new shirts, a great sweater and more pants than Liam needed, including jeans that cost twice what he normally paid.

They took a cab to a little Thai restaurant in the Village they'd all been wanting to try. They ordered shrimp soup and papaya salad to start with. After the soup was delivered, Liam expected the Spanish Inquisition. He got it.

"So, why the interest in new clothes?" Dylan asked.

Liam tasted the dish. "Hmm. Lime juice in this."

"Come clean," Aidan told him, though he was chowing down, too.

"Fine. Like I said, it's time for a change."

"Don't bullshit us. Remember when I started to date after Stephanie left me?"

"You bought a new wardrobe." This from Aidan.

"Spill it, Liam."

He took more time, biting into a huge juicy shrimp. Though he was a private person, he could talk to his brothers. "Okay, I want to date."

"You've *been* dating." Dylan's gaze zeroed in on him. "It's not another PTA-er, is it?"

"No. I'm gonna ask Sophie out."

"I told you you could have her."

"It's just a date."

Aidan joined in. "Did you ask her?"

"Not yet."

"How do you know she'll go with you?"

Liam fiddled with his napkin, afraid he'd flush and give himself away. "I just think she will."

Dylan's shrewd gaze assessed him. "Something already happen?"

"Like I'd tell." He sobered and put down his spoon. "It's just a date. Don't expect anything to come of it."

"You never know," Aidan announced proudly. "Look at what happened to me."

Dylan stared over his shoulder. Because he didn't join in the razzing again, Liam asked, "What?"

"I hope it is just a date."

"Why?"

"Because of what Sophie does for a living."

"The danger?" Liam asked.

"Yeah."

Aidan stared down at his empty bowl for a second, then back up at them. "It can be managed."

"For you maybe. Though we've yet to have C.J. go on protective duty." Dylan faced Liam squarely. "Nothing personal, but you're not made of the same stuff as Aidan is."

"What the hell does that mean?"

"He's tougher than you. You've always been the sensitive one in the family. And you've suffered a lot of loss."

Liam had given this some thought. He waited until the waiter cleared their dishes, then served the papaya salad. "Nobody's safe, Dyl. Kitty was a freakin' housewife and never did anything more dangerous than walk across a New York City street. And she died."

"That's one way to look at it, I guess." Dylan didn't seem convinced and just picked at the greens and fruit.

"Anyway, I can't believe Sophie would be seriously interested in somebody like me. It's just a flirtation. And it's fun."

"You're an O'Neil." Dylan's tone was insulted. Teasing again. "The weaker sex is putty in our hands."

"That reminds me," Liam said. "Who was your date with last night that had Hogan spending the night at our house?"

"A redhead."

"Now there's a surprise."

"Tell you what? You spill what happened with Sophie, and I'll tell you about my night."

"You first," Aidan said.

"Shut up, kid, you're not part of this."

Liam grinned. "Scissors, paper or rock?"

They all laughed at the old game they played as teenagers to choose who would go first. It made Liam feel good.

Almost as good as the prospect of asking Sophie Tyler for a date.

SIX

THE ALARM BELL rang. Over the PA came the static-filled message: "Report of a ten-seventy-five, Box 453, Engine 33 and Truck 44, Battalion 14." Other trucks needed would be announced in their own houses.

Sophie bounded out of the common room where she'd been watching a Yankees game with her group. She reached the bay, sent her shoes flying, stepped into the heavy turnout pants and rubber boots and adjusted the suspenders. Along with the other ten firefighters, she headed for the rigs. Murray was in the truck first, as always. Holding the computer printout of the run's details, Mackenzie rode shotgun; Sophie piled into the back with Jules between her and Bilotti.

"Ready, probie?" she asked, but gave Julian's arm a squeeze.

"Yes, ma'am." It was only his third fire, and the other two were simple ones, in a kitchen and a car.

"Stick with me, Torres," the cap told him as they pulled out of the bay onto West Third. "What did I tell you about fire?"

"Um, you can hear, see and smell it. It has a voice. I should listen for it."

"Make sure you do that. You're on the line now."

Radio communication from dispatch blared out as Murray honked the horn and darted in and out of traffic. The streets were filled with cars and cabs. "Small hotel fire on Spring Street. Heavy flames showing from the front windows on the third floor. Three alarms—Squad 28 and Engine 30 Ladder 41 already on the scene."

"I know that place." Bilotti scowled. "Remember, Murray. Me and you were on light duty a couple of months ago and did some inspections in that area."

"Right. They had a shitload of citations. We checked back a few weeks ago, some were done, others in the process."

"Let's hope more than not." Mackenzie's voice was tinged with anger. "Hell, I hate fires in a building that's not up to code. Never know what's gonna bite you in the ass."

They came to a grinding halt at the scene. Generator lights had been set up, creating beacons of eerie light, and emergency vehicles were angled at different spots in the parking lot and on the street.

Exiting the rig, Mackenzie hustled to Incident Command, from where the battalion chief would direct the fire ground. The rest waited at the rig; their assignment would determine where to park. Sophie could see the first-in engine guys raising their ladder to the second floor. On the fourth floor, smoke the color of dirt curled out the broken windows. From the truck, a gritty smell assaulted them. As they watched, more glass shattered.

Mackenzie climbed back in and told Murray to park the rig. "Heavy smoke conditions and high heat. Companies inside report second-floor flames have burned through doorways and the wainscoting is on fire. The fire room is located at a dead-end corridor." When the truck stopped, he finished, "Be prepared, they can hear screams from other rooms in the hallway."

"Is the standpipe workin'?" Bilotti asked as they shuffled out of the truck.

"Yeah."

At the southwest corner of the building, Murray hit the brakes but didn't turn off the rig. "At least they got that fixed."

"We'll raise the platform to the fourth-floor rooms on this end." Mackenzie had to shout over the noise of the truck, the water slapping inside and people at the windows calling for help. More sirens echoed in the distance.

Everyone sprang into action. While the other four operated the platform, Sophie and Bilotti dragged another ladder off the rig. Her eyes began to water as the two of them carried it to their designated location and propped it up to a second-story window where a man was yelling, "Help me. I'm stuck."

Torres came running back. "Cap said for me to heel the ladder."

"We're goin' up," Bilotti barked to Jules as he put his face mask on. "Come on, Sophie baby. It's showtime."

10:01 P.M.

"HEY, TURN DOWN the music." Patrick held up the television remote and shouted the words to Liam, who was clearing some glasses from a table. The dinner crowd had left long ago, and there was a sizable but quiet group nursing drinks at the bar. C.J. and Aidan were among them, cuddled up at one end, whispering and laughing.

Liam switched off the music and crossed to the TV. He looked up to the screen, mounted high on a wall, and saw Rachel Scott on the camera, with trucks behind her. Fire trucks. "What's she up to now?"

"Coverin' some kind of emergency." Pat turned up the sound.

"Rachel Scott reporting live from Spring Street where a fire has broken out in the Concord Hotel. It's a four-alarm blaze, which means several companies were called in."

Liam felt a few prickles of fear. "Spring Street's only a mile or so away."

Aidan took a swig his beer. "Why—oh, is Sophie working tonight?"

"Yeah. She's on the next four days."

Sinking onto the stool, blanking his mind, Liam watched the screen.

A firefighter walked by and Scott stopped him. "WNYC News. Can you give us any details, sir?"

"Step back, ma'am. You're in the way." When she opened her mouth to speak, the man, whose face was blackened with soot, barked, "Now!"

Scott retreated and the screen switched to a pan of the fire scene. Flames billowed from windows and thick black smoke hung menacingly in the air; the microphone picked up screams coming from the building.

C.J. said, "Listen to those poor people."

The camera zoomed in on firefighters laying ladders, climbing them. Scott's voice-over came on. "At this point, the FDNY is mounting exterior and interior attacks."

"Where would Sophie be?" Pat asked.

Liam had listened to the spiel about who did what only a few weeks ago when Mike's class went to the firehouse. "She could be up in the platform, on another ladder or inside looking for victims. The engine guys put out the fires. The truck crew opens the doors, does search and rescue. Outside, they'd be getting victims down with the ladders."

In a gesture meant to comfort, Aidan placed his hand on Liam's shoulder. "There's a lot of them outside. Maybe she's there. Seems like that'd be safer."

Saying nothing, Liam swallowed hard. They all knew there was nothing safe about any of what they were witnessing on live TV.

10:30 P.M.

FLAMES LAPPED at the roof of the building. The eaves were smoking and starting to light up. From below, Sophie took a sip of water in between gulps of air. She'd brought four people down the ladder, and somebody else was spelling her.

Mackenzie approached them. "Good news. Engine 30 made their way to the room over the fire. They knocked it down as well as the extension fire on the roof."

As she watched, Sophie could see Squad 28 play their hose out the window and wet the eaves. Mackenzie listened to his radio. "Smoke conditions on the sixth floor are tenable. They're cooling down the hallways and approaching the guest rooms. Get ready to go up again," he said to Sophie. "We raised another ladder for the third-floor survivors that the inside crews find."

If there were any. Sophie knew there'd be casualties. It was just a question of how many, she thought as she strode to the ladder.

"Go." Mackenzie motioned with his hand. "Victims found in the interior and are being brought to the windows."

Weary though she was, adrenaline shot through Sophie as she replaced her helmet and climbed the rungs. A firefighter from another company was at the opening where a window used to be and cocked his head at her. He was holding on to a big man with a lot of flab, who was semi-unconscious. "Shit," the firefighter spat out when he saw Sophie. It took her a minute to recognize Lance Callahan, one of the assholes who'd transferred when she came on board.

"Son of a bitch, Callahan. Just give him to me."

"Whatever you say."

It took Callahan and another guy to get the man through the window; with effort they managed to ease him out onto the ladder and into Sophie's grasp. Sophie pressed the victim's back against the rungs, jammed her hands under his armpits and grabbed the side rails; her knee slid under his groin. She grunted as she took the first step down, slowly, keeping her balance and maintaining her grip. With the man's considerable bulk, her breathing became more labored. Then he started to rouse, move. "Stay calm, sir," she told him. "Just a few more steps."

Unfortunately, the victim became agitated. "What the . . ." He looked around frantically, then bucked forward.

Sophie gripped the rails tighter. "Stop moving! We're almost at the bottom."

A boom sounded from the other side of the building and shook the ladder. "What the fuck, I'm gonna die," he gasped.

"No, we're outside, we're almost—"

The sentence broke off as the man brought arms the size of tree limbs up and broke her hold. They both fell the last ten feet to the ground.

10:45 P.M.

LIAM DIDN'T TOUCH the beer in front of him. His eyes were focused intently on Rachel Scott's face. "I'm happy to report that the blaze is now under control. We have with us Battalion Chief Dugan, in charge of public relations for the FDNY Manhattan. Chief, can you tell us the extent of the casualties?"

Somber and scowling, the chief did not look happy to be interviewed. "Not at the moment."

She edged the microphone in closer. "Were there casualties?"

"Yes."

"Patrons of the hotel? Or firefighters?"

He hesitated.

"Chief, were any of America's Bravest hurt? Or worse?"

"We had some injuries, all right? Knocking down a fully involved fire and rescuing that many people takes its toll. Some firefighters from the various companies are on their way to the hospital."

"Are there any fatalities among the crews?"

"Not that I'm aware of."

Pat looked heavenward. "Thank the good Lord. I hope Sophie's okay."

"Me, too." Liam's voice came out as a croak when he commented.

The silence in the bar was broken only by street noise and the drone of Scott on screen. Pat's cell phone shrilled out, startling Liam. His brother clicked on. "Hey. Yeah, we saw it on the news." He waited. "What? Oh, shit. Just a second, *a ghrá*." Pat handed Liam the phone. "It's Brie."

"Are the boys okay?"

"Mikey's not," she said. "He watched the newscast on a TV in the spare room where he and Cleary were supposed to be sleeping. He's . . . upset. He wants to know if Sophie's okay."

"I'll call her." He stifled his own emotion. "I'll be back in touch when . . ." If? ". . . I get her."

11:30 P.M.

IN THE EMERGENCY room of Memorial Hospital, Sophie watched the TV as she waited for her turn to see the doctor. The footage of the fire dominated the airwaves tonight.

"Soph, you okay?" Cooper asked when he came out of the treatment area. He'd had some smoke inhalation and had to have his lungs checked out after the most seriously hurt were seen.

"I'm pissed as hell."

He dropped down across from her. "How's the shoulder?"

"Hurts like a bitch. Fuck, if that guy had just held on . . ."

Cooper's brown eyes were sympathetic. "Happens to all of us."

"Yeah, well, all of you won't be accused of being too weak to hold on to the person you rescued. Goddamn it, the women in the department don't *need* this."

Cooper just grunted.

"None of us could have stopped what happened, Tyler." This from Mackenzie, who was with them but unharmed. Their truck had been taken out of service for the rest of the shift. The probie was fast asleep on a chair.

"Yeah, sure, Cap. But that's not what my fan club's gonna say."

Murray, who'd been treated for a burn and now had a bandaged wrist, sank back into this chair. "Fuck them."

"They accuse me of doing that, too. With all you jokers." She snorted. "As if."

Even Bilotti chuckled; he'd come a long way, but the women infiltrating his department—his term—wasn't his favorite topic.

Glancing at the screen, Sophie said, "Tehan's going to talk."

Rachel Scott was interviewing Mike Tehan, the structure

expert at the scene. How the hell did she still look so good? Her hair was nicely mussed by the wind, and her cheeks flushed prettily. She didn't even seem tired.

"We're waiting for news on the cause of the fire. While we do, we asked Inspector Tehan from the city's arson unit to tell us some of the problems with older buildings such as these. Inspector?"

"The issue here is threefold. First, in older hotels, the fire protection isn't always up to par. Codes were different when they were built and the city's had a problem getting all of them updated."

"You mean the city's been negligent?"

"No. I mean, we inspect, give them a grace period to get up to speed, then inspect again."

"Why don't you just close them down?"

"The law says they get a grace period."

"What needs *to get up to speed* in buildings like the Concord Hotel?"

"Some might not have sprinkler systems. Some just water in public areas. Guest rooms might not be equipped with self-closing doors."

"Can you tell our viewers what the last thing has to do with safety?"

Looking frustrated, Tehan nodded. "Fire needs oxygen to grow. If the blaze starts in a room, and the door is open, it spreads fast. That's why people even in private homes should keep their bedroom doors closed at night."

"I see."

"Yeah, sure you do, sweetheart," Cooper grumbled. "You got no clue what carelessness causes."

"What's the scuttlebutt on the origin, Cap?" Murray asked.

"Room two-seventy-eight."

"Smoking in bed?"

"Likely."

"Fuck."

"Fuck."

Murray and Cooper mouthed the obscenity simultaneously.

Sophie's phone vibrated. Frowning, she drew it from her

belt. And didn't recognize the number. She was about to answer it when an attendant called from the ER door, "Sophie Tyler?"

Sophie stood. Whoever it was would have to wait.

12:30 A.M.

"LIAM, THIS IS Sophie." She sounded exhausted. "Sorry I missed your call. When I got your message, I phoned Brie first so she could tell the boys I was fine."

Liam sighed with relief. Way too much relief. He had to clear his throat before he could say, "That's okay. Then they know you're all right?"

"Yes, your sister-in-law told them right away. I'm sorry this upset Mikey. I know he's fragile."

"He is. But you're safe? Not hurt?"

"I got a wrenched shoulder. I just had it checked out. It's sore as hell. I probably won't be able to work my next shift at the pub or the firehouse."

"No worries there. We just wanted to make sure you were safe. Otherwise I wouldn't have bothered you."

A hesitation, then she said, "I like that you bothered me."

"You do? Well, okay."

"Listen, tell the guys I'll stop in tomorrow and show you all how I am."

"Sure, good. See you then."

There was a hollow feeling in his stomach when Liam disconnected. "She's safe," he told Pat, Aidan and C.J., who'd been waiting with Liam for her call. "She was there and hurt her shoulder. She'll be out of commission for a few days."

"That doesn't sound too bad," Pat put in.

"Bad enough." He thought about Mikey's reaction, his son's fragility and Liam's own responsibility in this situation.

And hoped he'd left the tags on the new clothes he bought yesterday. In a burst of clarity, he knew he wouldn't be wearing them on a date with Firefighter Tyler.

SEVEN

LIAM BOUNCED ISABELLA on his knee, remembering when Cleary and Mike were thirteen months old; he'd loved that stage in their lives. His sister-in-law, Brie, sat across from him at a table in a front corner of the pub. The October afternoon was dreary; the rain clouds had opened up onto weary New Yorkers scurrying around outside. "She still not walking?"

"With two brothers and a sister who do everything for her, she doesn't need to walk, or talk much."

Gurgling, Isabella patted Liam's cheeks and babbled something unintelligible. She looked like her mother with her crop of reddish hair, almost violet eyes and cute bow mouth.

Liam kissed Isabella's nose. "I'd do everything for you too, princess."

Brie smiled. "Patrick calls her that."

Glancing away from the baby's face, Liam studied his sister-in-law, but before he could ask how she and Pat were doing, Dylan appeared at their table. "Here's your lunch." He set down corned beef sandwiches on rye bread. "The noon crowd's gone so we're not busy. Want me to take this gorgeous lady back to the kitchen so you two can eat in peace?" He cocked his head at Liam. "This one needs to talk to a woman anyway."

Brie gave Dylan her megawatt smile. "Sure."

Isabella raised chubby arms to Dylan; already she loved the O'Neil men and went easily to all of them.

Over sandwiches and a pint of beer, Brie nodded to him. "Tell me what's going on with you."

"You first. How are things with Pat?"

"You know, you always do this, shift the conversation away from yourself."

Liam shrugged. "Unlike Dylan and Aidan, I'd prefer not to be the center of attention."

A lock of deep auburn hair styled in a snazzy sweep fell into Brie's eyes as she leaned over. "Okay, I'll talk, then you will. Promise?"

"Scout's honor."

"We're treading water." Brie ran a polished nail over the rim of her glass. "Since Isabella was born, we've tried to avoid the knock-down-drag-outs. But one's coming up for sure."

"Why?"

"I'm expanding my business." Brie had started a company called InPlace, where she went into homes and helped people clean out their clutter. "I've hired on some new people and we're advertising in the Hamptons."

"Pretty classy."

"And very lucrative. It'll mean more of my time."

"With new people, you could cut back on your own calls, couldn't you?"

"Not really. Some clients use our services and request me, specifically. Besides, working in homes is the fun part of the business. I like straightening out other people's lives." She rolled her eyes. "Probably because I can't straighten out my own."

"You're working at it."

"You'd think after seventeen years of marriage, we'd be a bit further along." She took a bite of her sandwich. "I'm sorry, I don't mean to complain."

"Hey, this is me you're talking to. The guy whose hand you held for all those years Kitty was sick." He shook his head, thinking how much he'd missed Brie. They hadn't spent a lot of time together lately. "Work at it, Brie. He's crazy in love with you."

"I know he is. And I love him as much. It's just that . . ." She glanced away. "He's so insecure sometimes."

"You hinted at that before."

"There are things between Patrick and me that are private. Things we decided not to tell anyone."

"I can respect that."

Liam suspected Patrick's insecurity had something to do with what happened when Brie and Pat first hooked up. She'd been in college at NYU and come into the pub one night. They'd fallen head over heels for each other, but when she got pregnant with Sinead, their first child, she didn't marry Paddy right away. The details—and reason for the wait—had always been sketchy to the family. The only thing he and the guys and Bailey knew was that had been a black period in Paddy's life.

But when Sinead was a year old, something happened and they'd gotten married. They were one of those couples who'd enjoyed lots of highs and suffered lots of lows in their relationship. Funny, all Liam could remember about his life with Kitty were the highs.

"The business expansion will make waves," Brie went on. "I hope we can ride them out."

"You will."

"Now, tell me what's going on with my favorite brother-in-law. Mike got upset about Sophie the firefighter. I know she works here, but there's more to the story. Anything to do with you?"

He stared out at the street where it had begun to rain in earnest and people were darting around puddles. "I thought I'd like to get to know her better. But now, I'm leaning the other way."

"Why?"

"I could handle her job myself, Brie. I know what she does is dangerous. But as you know, Mikey flipped when she got hurt. And he's only known her a few weeks."

"Are we talking something serious here?"

"No. Just a date. I like her, and there's chemistry between us, but no, I'm not thinking June weddings."

"Then what's the problem? Go out on a date. Have some recreational sex, maybe. Enjoy each other."

Smiling, he thought of the kiss in the kitchen and how hot it had been. "I'm not wired that way."

"All men are wired that way."

"I don't know. If Mike hadn't had such a bad reaction . . ."

Gently, Brie laid her hand over his. "You can't live your life around Mikey, Liam. You've been doing that for three years."

"I know." He saw a yellow bus pull up to the curb. Mike tumbled out with the two other kids who lived in the apartments above the businesses on either side of the pub.

He watched his son's face. It was sullen today. "Look at him. He's so freakin' fragile."

Tracking his gaze, Brie nodded. "Yeah, I know."

Mike came through the door and rushed over to them. His hair had droplets in it, and his coat was wet. He took it off before he hugged Brie. "Hey, Aunt Brie, I didn't know you were coming to the pub today." He looked around. "Is Sophie here yet?"

"No, honey," Liam said after he accepted his own hug. "I told you she couldn't work for a few days."

"Yeah, but she said she'd come by to see us, didn't she?"

"I'm sure she will. Maybe not today. She's probably home sleeping."

As if they'd conjured her up out of some genie bottle, the door opened again and in walked Sophie. Her arm in a sling, she wore black jeans with a red cotton jacket and low-heeled boots. Her hair was down around her shoulders and damp as she came toward them. Liam's whole body reacted as if she *were* some supernatural creature, at his beck and call.

"Hi, Liam. Hey, kiddo." She glanced at Brie.

"This is Pat's wife, Brie. Brie, Sophie Tyler. You met on the phone, I guess."

The women exchanged pleasantries.

Mike leaned into Sophie and she circled her good arm around him. The gesture was so natural, it startled Liam. "You okay, Sophie?" Mike asked.

"Doing great today."

He touched the sling. "You got hurt."

"Just a bruise. Shoulder and arm muscles heal slow."

"I saw the fire on TV." Mike grimaced. "It looked bad."

"It was."

"Did anybody die?"

Her gray eyes zeroed in on Liam. He nodded.

"Yeah. Three guests of the hotel."

"Any firefighters?"

"Nope, none. A few were injured like me." She squatted down so she was eye level with his son. "Mike, we know how to protect ourselves. We're trained in safety on the fire ground."

"But you got hurt."

"You know why? I was carrying a man who weighed"—she nodded to Liam—"a lot more than your dad, and he got scared halfway down the ladder. He bucked and caused us both to fall off it and onto the pavement. There was nothing anybody could do about that."

As if he was waiting to be convinced, Mike nodded.

She stood and smiled brightly at Liam. Was she remembering the kiss? "How are things going here?"

"Great, Brie came in to have lunch with me."

"All done, though." Brie stood. "Hey, Michael Patrick O'Neil, want to go back and see how Isabella's doing?"

"Okay." He looked to Sophie. "You staying, Sophie?"

"For a bit."

Mikey followed Brie to the rear of the pub.

Liam had to face her. "Hungry?"

She grinned, the mischief making her eyes warm and enticing. "Is the pope Catholic?"

"Sit, I'll get you food."

"I don't want to bother you."

Fat chance, he thought as he headed back to the kitchen. She bothered him, a hell of a lot.

SOMETHING WAS WRONG with Liam, Sophie thought as he approached her table carrying a plate. Gone was the flirty man who'd kissed her senseless in the kitchen a few days ago. In his place was a polite but distant coworker. He set the food in front of her and just stood there.

"Aren't you going to keep me company?"

"For a little while." He glanced back at the kitchen. "I've got some things to do for dinner tonight."

Her heart tightened at his dismissive tone. "Go ahead, then. As I said, I don't want to bother you."

His face shadowed and he took a seat. "Are you really all right?"

"Yeah, I meant what I told Mike."

"Some big guy knocked you off the ladder?"

"Uh-huh." She chewed her food. "I'm gonna take some heat for that."

"Why?"

"Lance Callahan, the firefighter who handed the victim out to me, told his crew he knew I couldn't carry the guy down. I didn't have the muscles."

"Your muscles are better than most men I know."

"They are. They have to be, for instances just like this. Callahan's one of 'the club.' "

"The club?"

"Male firefighters who think women don't belong on the line. I'm afraid they're still in the majority. He was also one of two who transferred out of our house when I came on board. It's happened in other stations, too."

"Your group seems to accept you just fine."

"They do. Now. For one thing, I practically grew up with the department, like I told you. And I've been with these guys a long time and proved myself. I dragged Bilotti over a spongy roof when nobody else saw he was in trouble. I found Murray during a Mayday."

"Mayday?"

"Signal for a downed firefighter. And then of course, I always do my part in a run. It's just that when men haven't seen women perform well, they won't give them a break."

"I'm sorry. Will there be problems from this?"

"We'll see. Marconi, our battalion chief, said to ignore Callahan's grumbles. If it gets out of hand, he'll deal with it."

"Oh, good." He picked up the menu on the table and studied it.

"Liam, is something wrong?"

Eyes downcast, he shook his head. "No, of course not. I feel bad for you."

She cocked her head. "Were you worried?"

"A bit." Now he met her gaze. "Mike got real upset."

"I'm sorry."

"He doesn't do well with loss, or when someone he cares about is in danger. A lot went on with C.J., Aidan's fiancée, last summer and it was hard on my boy."

"I can tell he's troubled."

"That he is. Anyway, he seems okay today." He watched her. "So, how were your birthday celebrations?"

She told him about the boisterous dinner at the Carusottis' house. "I went shopping with Hannah the next day."

"Was it fun?"

"Yeah." She tossed him a flirty smile. Which he ignored. "I bought this great outfit. A black and gray skirt. A slinky top to go with it."

"Sounds pretty."

Shit, couldn't he take the hint?

"It is. Maybe you'll get to see it sometime."

"Doesn't sound like something you'd wear to the pub."

That was the last thing she expected. "Ah . . . no, I wouldn't."

"Then I'll probably never see it." His eyes were filled with something deep and lonely.

What the hell? "I was hoping we could—"

"No, Sophie, we couldn't."

Her jaw dropped. Finally she got out, "Oh, okay."

He stood abruptly, "Shall I go get the schedule?"

Her mind couldn't keep up. "Schedule?"

"For when you can work again. Or do you wanna wait until you know your arm is healed?"

"I'll be fine in a couple of days. Go get the schedule." He started away.

"Liam?" she called after him.

"I'll be right back," he said without turning around.

Sophie stared at the empty seat across from her, wondering how she could have read him so wrong.

"So, what do you think?" Pat's voice penetrated the haze Liam's mind had been in since his conversation with Sophie yesterday. He couldn't block the look of disappointment on her face and how . . . vulnerable she seemed. It wasn't a word he'd usually apply to her. "Think?"

"Jesus, get with the program," his brother growled from across the table. "Your mind's been some place else all morning while we've been trying to decide on the entertainment for November."

"Leave him alone." This from Aidan. "You've been a bear, too."

"Pot calling the kettle black. Ever since C.J. went on a protective job for the UN, you been sniveling around like a wounded puppy."

"Yeah, you're all sweetness and light," Dylan put in.

"Don't start," Pat warned his other brother, "or you'll regret it."

"Hey, just because all of you fuck up your love lives and I don't—"

"God, I missed this."

All four O'Neil men turned their cranky heads to the doorway. In it was their sister Bailey.

"Hey, B." Aidan jumped up and covered the distance between them. He took Bailey in a fierce hug. "What are you doing here?"

"I'll tell you in a minute." She smiled over his shoulder. "Come on, guys, how about a welcome for the prodigal daughter."

They took their turns embracing her. Liam went last. "It's good to see you." When he held her, he felt the baby she was carrying kick his stomach. "Hey. Little Paddy just kicked me." He drew back and placed his hand on her stomach. "Hi, guy. Getting anxious to come out?"

"Not too soon, I hope." Bailey was due to deliver her third child in four weeks. "By the way, we decided to give him a middle name to go by, since there're already two Patricks in the family. It was Pa's idea."

Liam glanced over her head. Two agents stood guard near the door. From the window, he could see others standing post outside. Mitch Calloway, the head of her division was a guy they all knew because he'd worked closely with C.J., spoke first. "Hi guys."

The men greeted Bailey's personal protective agent. Then they introduced Kip Michaels, her new bodyguard. Aidan had met him and greeted him warmly. The others introduced themselves.

"C.J. around?" Mitch asked.

Aidan explained the situation.

"Come and sit, lass." Pat nodded to the agents. "Can I get you something?"

"No, thanks."

"Mitch." Bailey's expression was stern. They'd fought this battle before. "Have some coffee."

"Maybe we will." He told Kip to stay put and got them mugs from the urn in the corner, then went back to his position.

Bailey took a seat at the table next to Liam. He picked up her hand and held it. "Why the visit, sweetie?"

"I thought I'd come up while Clay's in California meeting with the governor on a new youth crime bill." She rubbed her belly. "Besides, I probably won't be able to get back for a while after I have this little one, though I was two weeks late with both of the others."

Dylan glanced around. "Where are the kids?"

"Angel's with Ma and Pa upstairs. We dropped her off first so I could surprise you guys. Rory's home . . ." She rolled her eyes. "I mean at the residence. He's coming up after school on Friday."

"How long you staying?" Aidan asked.

"I thought maybe I'd hang around for Mike's scout ceremony on Tuesday. That way I could be here for the Halloween party at the pub this weekend. You know how much I always loved that night."

Low groans from the men in black across the room. Coverage of the Second Lady in events like a party was tough for the Secret Service. Something that included costumes was a nightmare.

Liam nodded to them. "Your guys over there don't seem happy about that."

"Then they fit right in with you four. What's going on?"

Aidan shrugged. "Guess we're all grumpy this morning." He told her about C.J.'s first stint in protection.

She said, "C.J.'s a good agent, A."

"It's hard, worrying."

"I'll bet."

"I don't know how Clay put up with what you did all those months." Bailey had worked with gang girls when she and Clay met. He was a senator at the time, and sparks flew over her safety and other things.

Patrick smiled at her. "I remember the fireworks, lass."

"*You* oughtta talk about fireworks," Dylan put in.

"Just shut up."

They always fell into old patterns when their sister was around. She'd given them nicknames. Pat was the Fighter, and Dylan, appropriately, the Taunter.

Dylan's eyes sparkled. "Let's pick on Liam."

Briefly, Liam closed his eyes. He was tagged the Manipulator because he could usually avoid conflict and still get what he wanted. Today, he didn't have the energy. "Nothing to pick on."

"No, 'cuz you turned into the cowardly lion." Dylan again.

"Man, do I regret telling you guys anything."

"As if you can keep secrets." Dylan told Bailey, "He likes the new waitress here, but chickened out asking her for a date."

"Why?"

Liam stood. "I'm not participating in this. I'll go get Bailey something to eat."

"Li—wait."

"Nope. I won't discuss it. And I'll remember next time not to tell you jerks anything."

"Hey, I understand," Aidan called out. He was the Peacemaker.

But Liam wasn't having any it. He walked away because he was no longer talking about—or thinking about—Sophie Tyler.

"TWO DEVELOPMENTS in the Concord Hotel fire, next at eleven." The male news anchor's somber expression didn't bode well.

Setting the popcorn bowl down, Sophie scrambled for the remote and upped the volume on the TV. "What now?" she asked aloud in her empty apartment.

Wasn't it enough that she'd been rejected, although subtly, by Liam O'Neil? She hadn't seen him since she went to the pub the day after the fire. She would, though, because she was bartending this weekend, then going back to the firehouse on Monday. For the life of her, she couldn't figure out what happened with him. She hadn't imagined the sexy kiss in his kitchen, or the flirtation before that. But something had changed.

Oh, who cared? It was only a fling. Hannah was right, Sophie didn't need a ready-made family.

The news program came back on.

"Rachel Scott, reporting for WNYC News. There have been two new developments in the fatal fire three nights ago at the Concord Hotel. The arson division of the FDNY has declared the fire incendiary. For you laymen out there, that means . . ."

Sophie said aloud, "It was torched."

"An inside source told WNYC several suspicious fires in lower Manhattan have had investigators spinning their wheels. We contacted the fire department but they aren't releasing any details as of yet."

"Then how do you know about it?" Shit, Joe would be really pissed about this broadcast.

"More information will follow when this news station can uncover it." Here the woman arched a subtle brow. "We believe the public has a right to know, but apparently officials of the FDNY don't agree."

Oh, great.

"Other news involving America's Bravest—one female

member of America's Bravest—is the complaint lodged by a victim of the hotel fire. Arnold Miller, the man carried down a ladder to supposed safety, notified officials just hours ago that he's filing a formal complaint against the department for his broken leg. Apparently, Miller fell several feet with Firefighter Sophie Tyler when she was unable to descend the ladder with the two-hundred-ninety-pound man. Stay tuned here for further developments."

The other news anchor faced Scott. "Are there many female firefighters in the FDNY, Rachel?"

"Thirty. There was a PBS special in 2006 about their difficult integration into the FDNY."

"Yes, remember we interviewed Brenda Berkman on her retirement? The video focused on her."

Scott frowned, as if she really cared. "It'll be interesting to see how this shakes out. I hope it doesn't give a bad name to female firefighters all over the country who are doing their job."

Sophie stared openmouthed at the screen. Holy fucking shit! Had these people really implied Miller fell because he was being carried out by a woman? That she wasn't doing her job? It was one thing for guys like Lance Callahan to accuse her of incompetence. It was another for a scandal to happen on national TV.

Her phone rang. It would be her captain. Or maybe Joey. She leapt for it. "Hello."

"Sophie? This is Dylan O'Neil. I just saw the newscast given by our friend Rachel Scott. I called to warn you."

There was an edge in Dylan's voice she'd never heard before. He was always so charming and happy.

"I saw it. Warn me about what?"

"Rachel Scott. She's given our family a lot of grief. Her coverage of Bailey and Clay has endangered them on more than one occasion."

"Really?"

"Yeah, I'll tell you all about it when you come in this weekend. But she's a shark, and she could go after you."

"About the female firefighter thing?"

"Uh-huh. Watch your back if she contacts you and I'll clue you in when I see you."

"Sure, thanks."

"Knowledge is power, babe. And you're one of ours now so you aren't alone."

She wouldn't be alone anyway. Her crew and Hannah and a lot of other smoke eaters would be at her side. But for some reason, knowing the O'Neils would have her back made Sophie feel better—for a minute. God, she couldn't believe she was going to fight *this* battle again.

EIGHT

❧

ON HALLOWEEN NIGHT, with the help of a party special-
ist, Bailey's Irish Pub had been transformed into a haunted
house extraordinaire. Ghouls and goblins hung eerily from
the ceiling, and a tape of scary sounds came over the speak-
ers up near the performing area. Cauldrons bubbled in corners and beneath an impressive array of cobwebs; lanterns
shed orange and yellow light on the patrons.

At four in the afternoon, those patrons were children. The
pub's usual meals weren't served on Halloween, but a buffet
would be provided at night. In deference to the younger set, no
liquor was available until six, when the kids would leave.

Liam had just finished setting snacks out on a table near the
window when Bailey came up behind him. He had to smile. As
always, he and his brothers were dressed as male pirates and
she was Grace O'Malley, the Irish female pirate of the 1800s.
She wore a peasant blouse with a burlap skirt, and her big
belly this year only added to the image.

"Ahoy, matey," Bailey quipped.

Liam was determined to get into the festive mood. "Shiver
me timbers, lass. You make a mighty fine wench."

Bailey snagged a carrot stick. The treats had been brought in by the Secret Service because Bailey and the kids couldn't eat uninspected food. "What does that phrase mean, anyway?"

"Shock or surprise." Years ago, Liam, the online geek, had found pirate terminology on the Internet and had shown it to his brothers and Bailey. Every Halloween when they donned their costumes, they used more and more phrases, though Dylan was into the lingo the most.

"So, are you going to enjoy yourself tonight?" his sister asked.

"Yeah, sure. I got a date."

"With Sophie?"

A pang of disappointment shot through him. "Nope. The mother of one of Cleary's friends."

"I'm sorry it didn't work out with Sophie."

Not half as sorry as he was. He couldn't believe how bad he felt at brushing her off. Nor the fact that he kept *thinking* about her. "The guys overstated the thing. I'm fine, sweetie."

"Ms. O'Neil?"

Bailey turned to Mitch Calloway. The Secret Service contingent had been increased for the night, and her personal agents were dressed as police officers. They still wore their earphones and radios, but it fit into the image. "Yes, Mitch?"

"Michaels just informed me that Rory won't stay in the designated area. We've spoken to him several times, but he's excited about today. Maybe you could have a word with him."

"Or course." She turned to Liam. "We can talk more about this, if you want. I won't get on you like the guys."

"No, thanks. It's not that important."

Once Bailey left, Liam headed to the kitchen for some drinks. As he filled the pitchers with soda, he gave in and let himself think about Sophie's return to work at the pub. She'd come in Friday night, and Dylan had cornered her about Rachel Scott. Liam was pissed, too, over the TV coverage of the fire, but Dylan seemed really concerned.

When Liam had gotten to talk to her after her shift, it hadn't gone well.

"I'm sorry about the publicity, Soph. I know it isn't your style."

Her eyes were a cold, gunmetal gray. "Do you care, Liam?"

He'd been shocked by her veiled reference to their aborted date. "Of course I do."

"Yeah, sure. I can tell." And she'd walked away.

Dylan had overheard the exchange. "You're being an asshole. At least tell her why you backed off."

"Mind your own business."

"If she leaves the pub because you can't come clean, it's all of our business."

Liam had sworn at his brother. Actually he'd told Dylan to fuck off.

Dylan had snarled. "I know why you're not telling her."

"Okay, Einstein, why?"

"Because *you* know she'd agree to do what you think is best for Mikey. The thing between you two would be over before it really got started. In that soft heart of yours, you don't really want her out of your life."

"There's nothing to be over. How many times do I have to tell you? There was some chemistry and I was *thinking* about asking her out."

"Like hell."

Their words had turned into shouts until Pat stepped in to referee. Things had been tense between him and Dylan since then, even though Liam was forced to admit to that maybe his brother had been right.

Stuffing the memory, he brought the soda out to the kids' area. Brie and Pat were watching over them. Patrick was dressed in a billowing-sleeved white shirt open halfway to his naval, black pants, and wore a bandana around his head. Brie looked stunning in a red velvet dress, cinched tight like a corset and showing a good amount of cleavage. Pat's hand rested intimately on her hip, then inched up north a bit. Liam heard his brother joke, "That's some treasure chest you got there, wench."

Brie purred, "Down, sailor. You've already had some of that treasure this morning."

Ah, so they'd made love. Liam felt envy rush through his blood. To quell it he said, "Get a room, you two."

They smiled over at him.

He glanced at the kids, who were sneaking their hands into big bowls of cooked spaghetti, which were supposed to be brains, and peeled grapes, which simulated eyeballs. Later, they'd decorate small pumpkins. "They're having fun."

"Mike especially," Brie said. "Those little Yankee uniforms are adorable." Mike and Rory had dressed as Derek Jeter and A-Rod—the outfits even had the correct numbers on them, compliments of Clay. The older boys—Pat's two, Cleary and Hogan—were here as cowboys.

"Yeah. Mike's been bouncing off the walls about the party."

"Good to see." Pat studied him. "How about his dad?"

Not wanting to ruin their glow, he bit back a nasty retort about being left alone. "Lookee, mate, if yous all don't stop askin' me about that, I'll be showin' you Davey Jones's locker."

Pat laughed out loud. "Yeah, you and whose fleet, bucko?"

Tension broken by the levity, Liam headed to the bar. It was too bad they weren't serving any alcohol yet. He could use a drink.

WHEN SOPHIE GLIDED through the doors of the pub at six, she stopped all the healthy males present dead in their tracks. Their attention was caused by her costume: a replica of the notorious white dress Marilyn Monroe had worn in *The Seven Year Itch*—the material dipped dangerously low in the front of a halter top, and the pleats accented her trim hips. She was bartending that night, and if the guys' reactions were any sign of what was to come, she was going to get a lot of tips. And show one Mr. Liam O'Neil what he was missing.

"It's working already," Hannah whispered from beside her.

"Hmm." Sophie patted her curly blond wig.

"Can't wait till Liam sees you. You look so good he'll swallow his tongue."

"Why, sugar, thanks for telling me that." She nodded to Dom, who'd moved away to talk to another firefighter. The FDNY had gotten wind of the party and a lot of them were planning to come. "You two look great as Al Capone and his moll."

"A role I've longed to play. Oh, there's Joe Carusotti, Mr. Gorgeous himself. Man, he could be right from the Old West."

Spotting her, Joe left Jules, who'd come as a football player, and made a beeline in their direction. He scanned Sophie's outfit and gave her a big-brother scowl. "Good Lord, somebody should have put you under lock and key, Marilyn."

Joe could have walked off the set of *Gunsmoke*, complete with his own Miss Kitty on his arm. "Why, Mr. Dillon, you sure do know how to flatter a girl."

They made chitchat with Joey and his date for a while, then the two of them left to get drinks.

"So, you sure you want to meet up with Dom's brother tonight?" Hannah asked.

"Yeah, why not?"

"You know very well why not. And he just came through the kitchen door."

Liam hadn't seen her, so she got a chance to gawk. His lean body was draped with a sexy pirate shirt, only half buttoned, showing great chest hair. A silver medallion peeked out from the slit. His pants were tighter fitting than usual and she longed to run her hands over his butt. She was thinking of the adage "Two can play this game" when he caught sight of her. His beautiful blue eyes narrowed on her, then his gaze raked her from head to toe with such heat she felt flushed.

"Oh, God, Dom and I are gonna have to go outside for a quickie. The sparks between you two are scorching."

Tossing back her head, Sophie grunted. "I gotta get to work."

"Good luck, girl."

Dylan met her halfway across the room. "Aye there, Marilyn. Wanna walk me plank?"

Sophie burst out laughing. "Cute." She eyed him up and down. She'd always thought he resembled Orlando Bloom and tonight he looked just like Will Turner, from the *Pirates* movie. "You're pretty sexy there, mister."

"Me? I'm singed by just lookin' at you, wench."

"Why, thank you very much." Over his shoulder she could see Liam turn away. She wouldn't let herself feel bad that he didn't come to greet her. Christ, she couldn't figure out why this bothered her so much to begin with. She rarely let guys affect her like this.

"He'll be back," Dylan whispered.

"I don't know what you're talking about."

"Yeah, and I'm Bluebeard. You two are a pair."

Sophie sashayed to the bar in three-inch red heels, slid under the opening and tied a towel around her waist. She'd just gotten the cash register ready when someone sat down. "Hi, there. I don't think we've met."

Pivoting around, Sophie found the Second Lady of the United States casually perched on a stool. Behind her were a number of cops. "Wow. Hello, Mrs. Wainwright."

"Nope, it's still O'Neil." She held out her hand and they shook. "And if you wanna know what kind of friction *that* little deed caused, you'll have to wait until we know each other better. In any case, it's Bailey. The guys told me about you."

"Oh, good stuff, I hope."

"Hmm." Bailey studied her head. "Is it strawberry blond?"

"What?"

"Your hair. Under the wig?"

"Yeah, I guess you could call it that."

"Liam did."

"He did?" She cursed the trace of delight in her voice.

"Have you met C.J. yet?" When Sophie shook her head, Bailey added, "You got a lot in common with the 'female in a man's job' thing."

"Is she coming tonight?"

"If she gets back from her assignment. She's with the king of a small country."

When Sophie looked skeptical, Bailey crossed her heart. "I swear. She's doing protective duty for the UN. It's why Aidan's so grumpy."

"I can't keep up with your family."

"So, how long have you been a firefighter?"

"Twelve years. All of them in the same house."

"Cool. America's Bravest. We all love you."

"Your husband was great during 9/11." Sophie's voice caught at the horrific memories. It was impossible to talk about, even all these years later, without it affecting her. "He visited every firehouse in the city."

"I know. He was devastated by what happened. Were you at Ground Zero?"

"Just to help clean up. I'd gone to meet my brother overseas. He's a captain in the army."

"A whole family full of heroes."

Sophie snorted. "I hear you've done your share of saving lives."

"Yeah, got a few girls out of gangs."

"You're modest."

Just then, a hook came around her neck. Sophie startled; then the person it belonged to said, "I told you, wife. If you went anywhere without my permission, a price would be paid."

Bailey giggled like a schoolgirl. "Aye, that you did, husband."

Oh, my God. The vice president of the United States was nuzzling his wife's neck right there in front of Sophie. She watched, mesmerized, as Bailey reached up and gripped his arm, which had crossed her chest. It was a tender gesture that made Sophie's heart flutter. "I didn't know you were coming, love."

"I flew in from California just for the night. I couldn't resist another O'Neil Halloween celebration."

Bailey swiveled in her seat, took the man's bearded face in her palms and kissed him thoroughly. When he drew back, he whispered, "I think we're embarrassing Marilyn."

"No, no, you're not. But stay away from me. I don't have good luck with the presidential type."

Clay Wainwright guffawed. "I don't even know your name, and I like you already."

"This is Sophie Tyler. She's the pub's new waitress and bartender." Bailey winked at Sophie. "And she's one of America's Bravest."

The vice president stepped back. He was dressed in a regal pirate's outfit complete with velvet coat, brass buttons and a plumed hat, which he removed, then bowed before her. Sophie's heart fluttered again. "I'm honored to meet you, Firefighter Tyler."

"It's my pleasure, Mr. Vice President."

He smiled. "So how do you like working at Bailey's Pub?"

"I like it a lot."

"There he is . . ."

"Hey, buddy . . ."

"Well, if it isn't our long-lost brother-in-law . . ."

"How's it hangin', Hook?"

All four O'Neil brothers had converged on Clay and clapped him on the back or punched his arm. Sophie thought of Hannah's quip that first day here. One was as gorgeous as the next. All that dark hair, those eyes in varying shades of blue. But it was the pirate outfits that accented everything tonight. They were completely and utterly yummy. Along with a very handsome Clay Wainwright, the picture the men made would make any woman's pulse skitter.

Her gaze rested on Liam. He caught hers briefly, but looked away. Someone called to her from down the bar for a drink. Sophie left hurriedly. It was too hard to see all that male beauty and have none of it for herself.

PETER PAN WALKED into the pub and caused a stir. She didn't fit the persona at all. She was statuesque and curvy with an air of authority about her. When Dylan saw her, he socked his brother's arm.

Aidan turned and tracked his gaze. "What the hell?"

Peter Pan headed their way and a smile the size of Texas bloomed on Aidan's face. When she reached them, Aidan drawled, "Now that's the finest pirate booty I've ever laid eyes on."

Peter Pan's lips twitched and she sang, "I'll never grow up, I'll never grow up." Leaning forward she kissed him hard on the mouth. "Your theme song, isn't it, O'Neil?"

"I'll sing whatever tune you want, sweetheart." He grasped her around the waist. "I'm so glad you made it." Dylan could hear the roughness in Aidan's voice. "That you're safe."

"I am, honey."

"My cue to leave."

"Oh, hi, Dylan."

"Hey, C.J." He squeezed her arm and crossed to the bar. Sophie was behind it, looking a bit flushed. And tired. "You need a break, Ms. Monroe. Wanna dance?"

"Go ahead." Pat had come inside the bar area. "You been back here all night. Take a half hour. Get some food."

"I'd rather dance."

She bent down and fiddled with something Dylan couldn't see. Patrick laughed.

"What?" Dylan asked.

Sophie held up a slipper-like shoe. "Didn't think I'd tend bar in the stilettos, did you?"

"But they do such great things for your legs."

Ducking under the opening, Sophie—wearing the heels—met Dylan and he took her hand.

He grinned. "I hope it's a slow one."

It wasn't. But Dylan liked to dance. They all did. His mom and dad, who were on the floor now, were already into the West Coast Swing. Dylan drew Sophie into one, and she kept up pretty good. That white skirt swirled around her legs . . . nicely. Liam was nearby, twirling his own redhead and executing some pretty fancy footwork. His gaze kept straying to Sophie, though. When the tune was over, a slow song started and Dylan grabbed her to him. "Now *this* I like."

"You are such a flirt."

"I know. My brother could take lessons."

"Which one?"

He snorted. "As if you didn't know."

As he held Sophie close and moved in waltz step, he caught sight of someone coming through the front door. A single woman dressed in a clown's outfit. Dylan watched her. She was scoping out the bar, looking for something.

A tap on his shoulder. "Can I cut in?"

A good-looking mobster had come up to them. The guy said to Sophie, "I'm Tony, Dom's brother. I was supposed to meet you here."

"Oh, yeah."

Dylan said, "She's all yours," and headed for the clown. When he reached her, she stepped back a few feet, confirming his suspicions. "May I help you?"

"Ah, no. I came in for the party."

He recognized her voice immediately. "Stalking the vice president of the United States is a crime."

She blew out a heavy breath. Her face was covered with greasepaint, but even that couldn't hide her good bone structure. "I'm not stalking him. I didn't even know he was here." She arched a brow. "Until now."

"Yeah, right." Though it was probably true. "You're just on a fishing exhibition."

"Dylan . . ."

Taking her arm, he ushered her out the front door. The night was cool and Dylan shivered after the heat of dancing. "You know, Ms. Scott, I was withholding my opinion on you for a while, but you're making it hard to like you after you dissed one of America's Bravest."

Her chin lifted and she whipped off her clown's wig. Skeins of auburn hair tumbled around her shoulders. And she looked surprised. "I'll have you know, I'm doing a half hour feature for our affiliate channel on females in the FDNY. I have every intention of showing the true picture. I'm even going to interview the firefighter who dropped the guy."

"She didn't drop him. He flailed and set them both falling down the ladder."

"Same thing." Pretty green, long-lashed eyes narrowed. "How do you know all this, anyway?"

"She works at the pub."

"Is she here tonight?"

"You're never gonna find out. You'll be leaving right about now."

"What *is* it with you guys?"

"We protect our own. Don't you have friends or family?"

Her brow knit. "Yes, of course I do."

"But you don't know the meaning of loyalty."

A guy dressed in a firefighter coat bumped into Dylan on his way in. "'Scuz me."

Dylan ignored him and the woman who trailed behind him.

"How did this get to be about me?" Rachel asked.

"It's been all about you from the start, sweetheart." Dylan moved in on her. "I think it would be best if you'd leave now."

Frustration flashed over her face. "All right, I'm going."

"That's what I want to hear."

She walked away, the sway of her hips visible beneath the clown suit. Dylan wondered if Sophie knew about the TV program yet. She was having fun tonight. Maybe he'd wait to bring it up. He didn't have a good feeling about this development at all and his news instincts were usually on target.

AW, AIN'T this sweet? *The place looks like a haunted house. The food's great . . . beer's cold . . . and celebrities every place you look. Along with America's Bravest. Captains. Probies. All of them. The time's not right though. I can't risk it. The vice president would have his hounds on me. They're dressed like freakin' cops. Too high profile. That's okay. I'm not in any hurry. Think I'll just scope out the place, the people. See what's what. I got a lotta time to make another move.*

LIAM WAS TALKING with his mother and father and Mona Thompson, who was in charge of the PTA, on the side of the dance floor, but he was keeping an eye on two people who'd come into the pub. He recognized the guy right away. Sophie's ex-husband, Ray Cramden. Who hated firefighters, she'd told Liam, but was dressed as one. Her ex scanned the bar, probably looking for Sophie.

Not Liam's business. Nor was the fact that she'd been sidling up to the macho Italian on her break. Liam glanced at Mona. He wasn't so innocent, either. His mother said something to him, just as Sophie gave the guy a hug and headed to the bar. When Cramden followed her, Liam stepped back. "Excuse me a minute, will you?"

Sophie detoured to the ladies' room; Cramden caught up to her right outside of it. Liam followed them and stayed behind a post, out of view, in case she needed help.

And to eavesdrop on the exchange.

"Hey, baby, if I'd known you were coming as Marilyn Monroe I woulda dressed as Joe DiMaggio."

Sophie gave an unladylike snort. "Instead you dressed as your nemesis."

"Fuck, firefighters can't hold a candle to what I do."

"Yeah, keep telling yourself that, Raymond."

He swore angrily.

"What do you want?"

"You."

"You had me. You blew it. End of story."

Grabbing her arm roughly, Cramden yanked her around. Liam was about to step in when she gave Cramden's hand on her arm a pointed look. "Part of the reason was this."

Still, the guy didn't let go.

Liam stepped forward. "Hands off the lady, Cramden."

Cramden turned but didn't release Sophie. "Who the hell are you?"

"Sophie's friend. We met at the café by Paddock's Gym."

"So?"

"I also happen to own this place. I'm thinking maybe you've had enough to drink and should head out."

Before Cramden could respond, the woman he'd come in with entered the fray. "Ray, what are you . . ." When she saw Sophie, she glowered at her. "Oh, great. Just freakin' great."

"If it isn't Captain Trudeau. How's it hanging?"

"Can't you just leave Ray alone?"

"My pleasure." Sophie shoved at Cramden and he stumbled backward. "He's all yours, Yvette."

The woman dragged Cramden away.

Sophie had shed the blond wig hours ago, and her hair fell around her face when she looked up at Liam. He saw fire in her eyes and something inside him shifted. He'd been watching her all night, how the dress swirled around her legs when she danced, how the guys were checking out those surprisingly long legs in stilettos. His gaze fell to the top of the dress; the material curved softly around her breasts, clung to them. Obviously she didn't have a bra on because her back was bare. It was probably one of the reasons she'd been center stage all night.

"I could have handled this myself, Liam."

"Yeah, you were doing a great job. A word of warning, *So-*

phie baby. You dress like that, you're gonna get hit on." He started to walk away.

"Wait just a minute." She grabbed his arm, so he had to turn to her. "What the hell is this all about?"

Emotions brewed inside him like one of the Halloween cauldrons out in the pub; finally it bubbled over. His head spun and blood thrummed through his veins.

He moved in close.

She swallowed hard, and her breath speeded up.

So did his. He moved in closer. "What's this about?" he asked silkily. Grasping her arm, he dragged her down the hall to the office.

And shoved her inside.

And slammed the door.

And plastered her against the wood. "It's about this."

SOPHIE KNEW she should protest Liam's caveman treatment. But a dark spark of excitement lit within her when he dragged her down the hall; it exploded into hot flame as he pulled her inside the office and shoved her against the closed door. The wood was hard at her back and Liam's fingers bit into her biceps.

His knee wedged between her legs. He was hard and heavy against her. As if by force of nature, she shifted to better accommodate him. He tunneled his hands in her hair; she threaded hers through his. His mouth came down on hers and he wasted no time in prying open her lips. First he tasted, explored, then devoured. Nip. Soothe. Nip. Soothe.

Sophie went wet and wanting. She clutched at his shoulders, nosed her face inside the billowy shirt and inhaled him. Licked him. Bit.

He bucked into her. The medallion he wore flattened into skin bared by the dress, and hot from his body, it branded her. His hands claimed her. They roamed, searched, teased and tempted everywhere. Still, she was shocked when he yanked at the tie of the halter top and pushed the dress to her waist

"Shit." His palms kneaded her bare breasts. "I can't . . ." His mouth replaced his hands and he suckled.

She cried out, which made him suck harder, then take her nipples between his fingers. Roll them. Scrape them with his teeth.

About to combust, she reached between them and cupped his crotch. He groaned, loud, long, beautifully.

"Sophie, ah, God, Sophie . . ."

Her skirt was yanked up.

Her panties tore.

She ripped at his belt, at his zipper and freed him. She clenched her fist around him and he swore.

"Hike your legs up around me," he said hoarsely.

She did.

"I can't . . ."

"Don't wait . . ."

"Soph, are you . . ."

"Yes. Oh, God, yes."

He plunged into her, thrusting wildly. Seconds later she came with one long, grinding shout. He was pounding into her when he erupted in the middle of her release. The sensations became more acute, almost painful; a second orgasm shot through her on the heels of the first.

Her mind blanked. Her body was no longer hers. She fell into Liam's web without thought, without resistance, without any sanity at all.

NINE

IN THE SMALL cafeteria of St. Mary's Catholic School, Liam sat alongside his Cub Scouts and listened to the Cubmaster of the pack talk to the boys and their guests. All the while, he felt like a schizophrenic. Here he was dressed in his leader's uniform of blue shirt and pants and yellow neckerchief, a representative of honor, preparedness and morality. He was about to give his official stamp of approval for the activities his scouts had done for their Wolf badge.

And two nights ago he was a wild man, having rough sex with Sophie against the wall in an office where anyone could have walked in on them.

No one had, but as soon as they were finished—oh, it took maybe ninety seconds total—Patrick came knocking on the door . . .

Liam braced one arm against the wood while holding up a half-naked Sophie with his other.

"Liam, you in there?" Pat called out.

"Um, yeah."

"Why's the door locked?"

"Give me a minute."

"Mikey's sick. I think he had too much junk food. He's with Ma but he's askin' for you."

"I'll be right out."

"What the hell—"

"Goddamn it, Patrick. I said I'd be right out."

He'd looked down at Sophie. Her eyes were still hazy with arousal, her hair tumbling around a face showing whisker burns. A few red marks marred her neck and arms. God, had he ever bruised a woman before?

Tenderly, he eased out of her; she winced, then her long legs slid down his body and she hid her face in his shirt. He brushed a hand down her hair and kissed her head. "Soph?"

She cuddled even closer. "Hug me once, close, then go. Mikey needs you."

His hand at the neck, he cradled her against his heart. "We have to talk."

"I know." The words were muffled because her face was still buried in his chest. "Go see to Mikey first. I—I need some time."

He drew back and they righted their clothes, but she wouldn't look at him. With one gentle squeeze of her arm, he left to find his son. Truthfully, he'd had no idea what to say to her right then anyway.

When he'd come back down to the pub after tending to Mike, she was gone . . .

"Troop Leader O'Neil, would you like to introduce your scouts?"

As if nothing was wrong, as if all of a sudden he wasn't Jekyll and Hyde, he stood and faced the small audience. The sight of Bailey in one of the rows calmed him. He was glad she'd stayed on an extra couple of days while Clay took Rory back to DC. Mike had been ecstatic, particularly since none of Liam's brothers could attend.

"We're happy to present to you the completion of some of the steps toward our Wolf badge. Each scout will give a short talk on what he did for his activity."

Four boys went before his son and gave accounts of their participation in activities for the areas of Feats of Skill, Your

Flag, Know Your Community and Keep Your Body Healthy. Then Mike's turn came.

Hesitant, he stood before the crowd, looking smaller in the navy Cub Scout shirt, the Wolf Cub cap with a yellow panel and a yellow neckerchief with the Wolf Cub logo. "My activity was on Making Choices. I did mine with my family. We made a list of some times when it was hard to do the right thing. When it took courage to be honest and kind. When we needed to be brave." He looked over at Liam who smiled. His son smiled shyly back, as if he needed the encouragement, and Liam felt his heart swell. "I did a drawing to show you." He held up a piece of construction paper. "This is my brother, Cleary. Sometimes it's hard to be nice to him. He says the same thing about me, but he's really a pain in the neck."

Laughter rumbled through the crowd.

"This is my dad. He's always nice to people. He'd never hurt anybody on purpose . . ."

Liam thought of how he'd ignored Sophie for days then practically attacked her in the office.

"He's gentle . . ."

Liam thought of Sophie's bruises.

"And he has integrity." Mike grinned. "I looked that up in the dictionary. It means he lives by what he believes and doesn't change his values just to do what he wants."

Liam sighed.

"And this is my mom, Kitty. She died."

There were muffled gasps around the room.

"It took the most courage in our family when she was sick from cancer. My dad helped us all through it. Aunt Bailey said he was a rock." Mike waited. "That's all."

His throat tight, Liam got up and hugged his son. He was moved by the boy's talk, but didn't think he deserved the accolades today. He hid his chagrin, though. He was used to concealing his real feelings, with the obvious exception of what had happened two nights ago when the beast he'd never known was inside him clawed its way out.

After the ceremony, Bailey waited with Mitch Calloway while the rest of the agents shepherded the crowd out. She came to the stage and embraced Mike first, then Liam. Her blue eyes were overly bright and she looked a little tired. "Congratulations, Mike. It was so cool hearing those things about your dad." She ruffled his hair. "And sad about your mom. You okay?"

"Uh-huh." Mike leaned into her. "It's why I wanted you to come."

She held him close. "I'm so glad you invited me."

"When are you leaving?"

"Tonight. I can't stay away from Angel too long." Her daughter had been taken back to the nation's capital along with Rory; both were in the safe care of their nanny.

"We got a meeting now with the Cubmaster. Can you wait till we get done?"

"Yeah, sure." She winked at him. "I can hold the plane, you know." Clay's private helicopter, DC 10, was standing by and would take her to Washington later today.

"Are you going back to the town house?" Liam asked her.

"No, to the pub. Ma and Pa are leaving for dinner out before the play and I want to say good-bye. I'll see you there in a while."

Liam hugged his sister and she left with her contingent of agents close to her.

Mikey tugged at his sleeve. "Did you like what I said, Dad?"

"Oh, honey, of course I liked it."

As he uttered the words, he couldn't help wincing inwardly. His son didn't know Liam wasn't that man anymore.

FOR THE FIRST time, Sophie was alone at the pub. Patrick had left for a meeting uptown with some distributors, Mr. and Mrs. O'Neil were going to a play, Aidan was on a photography assignment and Dylan was at a meeting at the magazine to talk to his editor about doing a piece on Rachel Scott. As she wiped up the bar, Sophie thought about Scott contacting her for a feature she was doing for the station's news program. The anchor wanted to interview Sophie about her life as a woman in the FDNY. Sophie had said no initially, but her battalion chief *strongly advised*—in other words, *told*—her to do it. Man, she wasn't looking forward to that.

The pub was empty at four in the afternoon so she tidied up the tables, swept the floor, then wandered to the back and down the corridor toward the office; she stopped at the doorway. She didn't even remember what the inside looked like. Her face heated just seeing where he'd taken her, fast and furious. She could practically hear their moans . . .

Oh, God, Liam, yes.

Soph, there?

Yeah, yeah. Ahh . . .

Who would have thought Liam O'Neil, the Quiet Man, the Cub Scout leader, would make love like that? It still gave her the shivers just thinking about it.

And scared her off. Sophie Tyler, a big, tough firefighter, was frightened by her reaction to him, by her total immersion in him, and the feelings that had left in its wake. She'd successfully avoided his calls and hadn't seen him since. But somehow, he'd been with her the whole time.

Best to get out of here. When she reached the bar area, she found Bailey coming out of the kitchen. Her agents crossed to the other side of the room and Sophie hoped nothing showed on her face as she confronted the Second Lady. "Hi, there."

"Hi, Sophie. Mind if I wait here until Liam gets back?"

"Of course not." She smiled at Bailey, but boy was it phony. "Liam's coming in? I thought Pat would be back."

"Liam and Mikey said they'd meet me here."

Sophie averted her gaze, thinking about coming face-to-face with Liam. She nodded to the kitchen. "Can I get you something?"

"No thanks," Bailey said. "I put on some water for tea in there."

Sophie sat down on a stool when Bailey took a seat.

"So, did you enjoy the Halloween party?" Bailey asked.

"Uh, yeah, it was fun."

"The guys looked great as pirates, didn't they? Even being their sister, I can tell how hot they are. Liam especially looked good."

Sophie guessed Liam's sister had no idea how good her brother really was.

"So did your husband."

Bailey laughed aloud. "That he did. I can't believe he flew in just for the night and dressed up as Captain Hook." Her eyes narrowed a bit, and her hand went to her stomach.

"Something wrong?"

"Just Braxton Hicks contractions. I had them for a month before Angel was born."

"I'm surprised your husband wanted you to stay if you're having those."

"Ha! He had no idea I was having them. Even then, he *didn't* want me to stay in New York. But I thought it was best for Mike, and that was hard for him to argue against. Besides I've got four weeks to go. This little one isn't ready to come out yet." She shook her head. "Though he has been quiet today."

"Hmm, that can mean he's ready to come."

"You know much about babies?"

"I've delivered one. A boy." Whenever she thought about the woman in a New York City cab who went into labor, Sophie could feel the joy of bringing little Juan Hector into the world. "It was great being part of the birthing process."

"I'll bet." Bailey grinned and stood. "I'm going to get my tea."

"No, sit, I'll get it."

Lowering herself to the chair, Bailey agreed without argument. Sophie returned in a few minutes, to find Bailey standing, gripping the bar, her face white.

"What's wrong?"

"Um, my water just broke. And I had a killer contraction."

Grasping Bailey's hand, Sophie called out, "Agent Calloway, get over here quick."

Three men rushed to them and Calloway drew his gun.

"You're not gonna need that." Bailey tried to joke but winced and gripped Sophie's hand so tight it hurt.

"What's wrong, Ms. O'Neil?" Mitch asked.

"I think I'm in labor."

His face paled, but he flipped open his cell and pressed a

button. "Have the ambulance standing by sent to the pub stat. Ms. O'Neil is in labor."

"An ambulance is standing by? Just for me?" Bailey asked.

"Yeah, on your husband's orders."

"He didn't tell me."

"Be glad he did it. They'll be here in just a few minutes."

"Can I do anything for you, Bailey?" Sophie asked.

"Um, maybe. Do you think you might want to be part of the birthing process again?"

"OKAY, BAILEY, BREATHE in. That's it. Now let it out slowly."

Bailey's hands went to her stomach. "It hurts."

Sophie smoothed back the Second Lady's damp hair; her own was encased in a shower cap–type thing and she was wearing blue hospital scrubs. "I know. But it'll be over soon."

"Yeah, that's what they always say."

By the time the ambulance had reached the hospital, Bailey's pains were two minutes apart, she was six centimeters dilated and almost fully effaced. It was only after she was in a birthing room that she told Sophie, once she went into labor, she'd delivered both Rory and Angel inside an of hour.

"Clay's going to kill me."

"He's on his way. His helicopter was here, but once they got hold of him—"

"Oh . . ."

"Okay, Bailey, breathe . . . that's it, girl, you're doing great."

When the contraction crested, she gritted out, "Ah, damn. Fuck."

The nurse and doctor, who hadn't left the vice president's wife since they'd gotten here and commandeered a section of the hospital, hid smiles.

Bailey shook her head. "Clay's not gonna make it."

"Doesn't look like it."

"No one will but you."

"I'm afraid so. Your parents aren't answering their cell phone. Pat's trying to get here from uptown, and Dylan from downtown. Liam's not answering, either. Traffic's a snarl from the rain and the agents couldn't get in touch with your sister-in-law sooner."

"Where *are* my agents?"

"Wearing a hole in the waiting room. Probably looks like an old movie set out there—the men pacing like useless idiots. Mitch Calloway was white on the way over in the ambulance."

"Yeah, they could never give birth. The sissies."

Sophie chuckled, Bailey laughed and then gritted out, "Oh, shit, here's another."

This time the breathing had no effect and Bailey yelled out loud.

The doctor said, "This is the last phase, Ms. O'Neil, transition. It won't last much longer."

"I hope to hell not." Bailey sighed when Sophie wiped her face with a cool cloth. "Clay was mad I wanted to stay. We had a fight."

"You can kiss and make up when he gets here."

"Don't . . ." Another contraction hit.

"Wanna ever . . ."

It peaked.

"Kiss him again."

"You will, honey. Later."

After that round was over, Bailey lay back on her pillow. Her eyes closed, she was going into herself to make it to the end. After a few moments, she whispered, "Liam's a good man, Sophie. A good father."

When one more contraction burst on her, all hell broke loose.

The doctor's voice took on an urgency that hadn't been there before. "This is it, Ms. O'Neil, sit up. It's time to push."

Helping Bailey to a sitting position, Sophie bent one of her legs while the nurse bent the other.

"We didn't do it this way for Angel," Bailey said panting now.

"No?"

"Nope. Clay got behind me on the bed, sort of like a straddle."

Sophie had seen the technique on an episode of *Grey's*

Anatomy. Funny the woman giving birth was named Bailey, too. "Do you want me to get behind you?"

There was a trace of fear in Bailey's eyes. "Would you mind?"

Kicking off her shoes, Sophie climbed onto the bed behind Bailey and encircled the Second Lady with her arms, grabbing her knees. "Okay, Doc. We're a go."

"So's the baby," the doctor said. "Push now."

Bailey pushed, grunted, moaned and waited.

Sophie glanced up. "I see his crown in the mirror, Bailey."

"Push again, Ms. O'Neil . . . okay, his head is out. Stop now while I suction out his mouth . . . Ah, there we go."

"Push again," the nurse told her.

Bailey gave it her all.

Sophie said, "He's got nice big shoulders."

"L-like my brothers."

"All right, now one more push and you'll have your little boy. That's it push . . . push . . . push . . ."

Sure enough, the baby came sliding out. "Ah, here he is."

No crying.

"Is he okay?" Bailey asked, heavy against Sophie.

"See for yourself."

The nurse placed the baby on Bailey's chest.

"Oh, God, hello, little guy. You're beautiful." She soothed down his crop of dark hair. And began to cry.

The doc held something out. "Firefighter Tyler, would you like to cut the cord?"

"I'd be honored."

Afterward, when Bailey said, "Say hi to your Aunt Sophie, little guy," Sophie herself got all misty-eyed.

BECAUSE OF HER status and to assure her safety, the hospital set Bailey up in the large birthing room instead of transferring her to the maternity ward. In Bethesda, where she was supposed to deliver, they had a private suite reserved. But Memorial Hospital did well making the Second Lady comfortable and keeping her separated from other patients.

Shimmering with a maternal glow, Bailey held her little

boy in her arms while the family cooed at him from around
the bed. Nostalgia filled Liam as he recalled his own children's births.

"You never did do anything the easy way," Pat grumbled.

"As if *you* could do this at all. Besides, I like having
everybody here to see him so soon. You weren't there when
Angel was born."

Everybody hadn't seen the child. Two hours after his son
had made his debut, Clay still hadn't made it to New York. He
couldn't connect with Rory quickly enough in DC so ended
up leaving without him, but the vice president was enroute and
expected any minute. Bailey had talked to him on the phone
three times.

"He's kinda red and skinny." Mike scrunched his nose at
the infant. "Did I look like that, Dad?"

"Yep. You were longer, though."

Patrick puffed out his chest. "My kids were bigger."

"Hogan had more hair and was more handsome, just like
me."

Bailey laughed at the brothers' competitiveness. It was
good to hear, because none of them were joking earlier when
they arrived. They'd been scared to death about the prematu-
rity of the delivery. Liam had been the calmest, even when he
discovered Sophie had coached Bailey through the whole
birth.

Sophie, who was across the room and wouldn't even look
at him. She'd changed out of the scrubs and was back in jeans
and the pub T-shirt. Now that the excitement was over, Liam
would deal with her.

"So," Pa said. "He's officially Patrick. But you'll be givin'
him a middle name to go by so we don't get more confused
than we already are."

"Uh-huh. That's what you want, isn't it, Pa?"

"Yep. Strappin' little guy that he is should have his own
name."

Patrick harrumphed. "I wish Brie were here."

"She's on a job, right?" Dylan asked.

"In the Hamptons."

"She'll be along, son."

Liam's pa looked over at Sophie and smiled. "Boy's got a guardian angel over there."

Sophie turned a big grin on Patrick Sr. and Liam felt like he'd been kicked in the stomach. "I'm glad I was here."

"You ever done this before, Sophie?" Mike asked.

"Not like this. I delivered a baby though. In a cab." She explained the circumstances.

"Awesome."

Liam still couldn't catch her eye. His chagrin at what had happened between them was diluted by the joy of Bailey's new child. In any case, Liam didn't intend to let her get away this time. He started to say something to her when the door to the room swung open.

And in rushed the very harried vice president of the United States. His face grave, he strode to the bed. Gently, he ran his knuckles over Bailey's cheek. "Hello, sweetheart."

Bailey's eyes got misty. "Hello, love. Meet your son."

Clay looked at the child cradled in his wife's arms. "Oh, Lord, he's absolutely beautiful." Leaning in, Clay tugged on a finger. "Hey there, buddy. It's me, Daddy. Couldn't wait any longer to see us?"

"Babies come in their time." This from Mary Kate. "The lad was ready."

Sitting on the edge of the bed, Clay rested his forehead against Bailey's.

"I thought you'd be mad," she said.

"I am."

Bailey laughed. "Yeah, I can tell."

Liam pushed away from the wall. "I think that's our cue to leave."

Neither Bailey nor Clay looked up as the family filed out.

But Clay called over his shoulder, "Sophie, could you make sure you wait for me out there?"

"Yes, Mr. Vice President. Of course."

Thank you, Clay, Liam thought.

In the outer area, Mike tugged on Liam's hand. "Where's Rory?"

Mitch Calloway answered. "An agent is bringing him. He came on a different plane."

"Want to go get a soft drink with me?" Sophie asked Mike.

"Actually, I'd like some time with you, Sophie," Liam said. It wasn't a question. "*I'll* go with you."

Glancing around at the others, Sophie seemed to realize she couldn't refuse without causing a scene. "All right."

They made it down the hall to a smaller waiting area that was empty. Liam drew her inside, but she crossed to the window and stood staring out at the city.

He watched her. "You gotta talk to me sometime."

"I know. I'm sorry; I needed time."

"Have you had enough?"

"I doubt anything would be enough."

Liam closed the distance between them and eased his back to the wall. "What's going on, Soph?"

She looked over. He was startled by the depth of emotion in eyes that were like thunderclouds tonight. "You want the truth?"

"Of course."

She turned to face him fully. They were close enough so he could smell her perfume, or lotion maybe. He remembered tasting it on her skin. With a small smile, she tugged at his scout neckerchief. "I'm embarrassed."

"Good Lord, I'm the one who attacked you, in the office, no less."

"I don't remember everything, but I do know I was more than a willing participant." She brushed her fingertips over his throat. "My mouth did that."

"You've got skid marks, too, sweetheart."

"Liam, what happened?"

"That night, or before?"

"Both, I guess."

He sighed heavily. "I was ready to ask you out. Hell, I even bought new clothes in case you said yes. I was so excited. But then you were in the hotel fire and got hurt."

"And you decided you couldn't take a risk on someone who walks into burning buildings?"

"No, actually, I thought I could handle that."

"After losing Kitty?"

"*Because* I lost Kitty. It may sound like convoluted reasoning, but she led a normal life, never did anything risky and she died. There are no guarantees for anybody."

"Wow. I didn't expect that."

"It's not the same for Mikey, though. He got upset when you fell down that ladder. With his therapy and all he's dealing with right now, I decided I couldn't drag him into a relationship between you and me."

"What happened on Halloween then?"

"Damned if I know." He took her hand, kissed it and brought it to his heart. "I feel like I should apologize."

She smiled a siren's smile. "Not me. It was good, Liam."

"It was the best."

They both chuckled.

"What are we gonna do?" he asked.

Sophie's features settled into resignation. "What you originally decided. Stay away from each other because of Mike."

"Dylan told me you'd say that. He ragged on me for not telling you why I changed my mind about asking you for a date. That I was afraid you'd agree with me and down deep, I didn't want you to."

"What other choice is there?"

With his free hand, he outlined an eyebrow; he hadn't noticed before how delicately arched it was. "None, I guess."

"You want me to quit the pub?"

"No. The guys would crucify me."

"I suppose we can stay away from each other outside of work. I'll try to avoid getting any closer to you and your family."

God, that was the last thing he wanted. His whole body clenched at the thought and his hand gripped hers tighter.

Just then, Clay came to the doorway with agents behind him. Liam was annoyed at the interruption but stepped back from Sophie.

"Bailey's asleep. She's exhausted. I came looking for you." Clay crossed the room to stand before them. "Sophie, thank you so much for what you did for Bailey."

"I liked pinch-hitting for you, sir."

"Call me Clay. And I'm gonna steal Bailey's thunder here,

but I since I didn't get to see the baby born, I guess I can have some fun with this."

She looked confused.

"We'd like you to be my son's godmother."

"Wow, I'm honored."

"And we're naming him Patrick, but going to call him by his middle name."

"I heard that."

"Then know you just helped bring Patrick Tyler O'Neil Wainwright into the world."

"You're going to call him Tyler?" Liam asked.

"That we are."

Sophie's face glowed. At the moment, she was so beautiful, Liam could barely catch his breath. "Oh, God, how sweet."

Clay squeezed Sophie's arm then walked out with the agents.

Liam shook his head. "So you aren't going to get any closer to my family, huh?"

"I wasn't, no."

"Gonna be a lot harder to do that now, Godmother."

TEN

THE DAY AFTER little Tyler was born Sophie arrived at the firehouse feeling like she'd been on a trip to Oz. The events of yesterday had made it impossible to sleep—she'd gone home soon after Clay's announcement about the baby's name—and today she felt drained. The early morning November air had turned unseasonably warm as she headed into the building. In the kitchen, the truck guys were seated around the table reading the paper and drinking coffee; she hoped they didn't know about the baby thing because they'd razz her unmercifully.

"How were your days off, *Tyler*?" Mackenzie asked, his nose stuck in the paper.

"Great. Uneventful. How was yours?"

"Kid's sick."

"Oh, sorry to hear that."

"Yeah, kids and babies can cramp your lifestyle." This from Bilotti, who had a five-year-old.

Sean Murray peeked over the Sports section. "So, *Tyler*, I couldn't make it to the Halloween party. Was it fun?"

"Ask Cooper and Jules. They were there. I was bartending."

His raised his eyebrows up and down. "I did. They said you looked hot as Marilyn M."

"Gee, thanks, guys."

Bilotti set down his paper. "I hear the vice president showed up."

Uh-oh.

"Uh-huh." She scanned the room. "Where's Jules?"

"Right here, *Tyler.*" He sauntered through the doorway from the common area carrying a huge basket wrapped in red cellophane. He set it on the table in front of her.

Liam sent her something? Then she caught on.

Mackenzie arched a brow. "Not every day we get a special delivery from the Secret Service."

Bilotti picked up on it. "That reads, 'Thank you for what you did for Bailey and Tyler. I'm in your debt.'"

"Oh, hell."

Cooper opened the newspaper and faced it out to her. "You're famous, Sophie baby."

The headline read, "America's Bravest Helps Deliver Second Son." Below it in smaller script, "Firefighter earns honor of namesake."

"How could the press find out about this so fast?"

"Are you shittin' me?" Bilotti grimaced at her as if she were a probie. "Any number of people on the hospital staff could've leaked it. You're a hero, Tyler."

"I was in the right place at the right time." Sophie tore at the cellophane around the basket. Inside were a variety of pastries and candies, high-end brand names like Harry and David and Godiva.

"Oh, man," Jules practically drooled. "Can we have some?"

"Knock yourselves out." She grabbed a flaky apple turnover and took a seat. She nibbled on it as the guys attacked the sweets. "I hope this doesn't follow me everywhere."

"You poor thing." Bilotti obviously wasn't going to let up. "Attention from the vice president of the US of A. The whole city knowin' what you did."

"Yeah," Murray added. "Wouldn't want to be in your sorry little boots."

"Do we have to call you something different now?" Cooper asked. "Like Fairy Godmother."

She shot them a fulminating look. "Shut up. I hate being in the public eye." Zeroing in on Mackenzie, she said, "Cap? Any news on the interview?"

"No word yet. But I'll bet my new car there will be today after all this hullabaloo." He gave Sophie a wink. "Now, if stardom hasn't gone to your head, let's divide up housekeeping duties."

The captain was right. There was news about the pending interview later that afternoon. Their battalion chief, Rocco Marconi, arrived at the firehouse about four. He found Sophie helping Murray clean off the tools in the rig and strode over to her. The gold epaulets on his white shirt gleamed in the overhead lights.

"Tyler, great job with the vice president's wife. You've done the fire department proud."

Murray snickered. "Maybe *Your Highness*?"

"Thank you, Chief. Enough to get out of that interview with Scott?"

"Nope, afraid not."

"I'm sure Trudeau would step in as a female representative of the FDNY."

"They already plan to interview her, as well as other department members. But WNYC is even more interested in you now. As a matter of fact, HR's been flooded with calls for interviews from other newspapers and TV stations."

"Oh, great."

"It is great—publicity for the department, that is."

Murray started to hum the presidential march.

"I'm sorry, Chief, I don't want to sensationalize what happened. I can't exploit Bailey and Clay."

Marconi's jaw dropped. "Fuck . . . You call them by their first names?"

Sophie groaned. This was not going well. Thankfully, the tone sounded over the PA. "Box 12. Ladder 44 go into service. School bus accident."

"Damn." Marconi turned on his heel and bounded to his truck.

Feeling a little sick to her stomach at the nature of the call, Sophie kicked off her shoes and slid into her turnout boots. She'd just hiked up the pants and was adjusting the suspenders when the guys came out.

They pulled out onto West Third and Sophie noticed the wind had picked up. On the way over, they got the details of the call. All were silently listening to the radio relate one of the most dreaded kinds of vehicle accidents. Several cars had been involved in the incident and a bus had overturned on a highway; three surrounding fire houses had been called in. They hurtled to the scene in somber silence. The rig screeched to a halt in the middle of the road.

A seven-car pileup had stopped traffic both ways and police cars were cordoning off the area. Emergency vehicle lights flashed everywhere. The yellow bus was overturned on its side, by itself in the far lane. A heavy rescue rig and Squad 28 were right behind 44, but they were first in.

Over their personal radios, Marconi barked, "Mackenzie, take the bus. Be careful, the engine could be compromised. Follow my instructions."

Adrenaline surged through Sophie as she and her crew bolted out of the rig and grabbed halligans and hooks from the side compartment. They also took some tape and a cutter in case they had to take out the windows. As they approached the bus, Sophie could hear cries of "Mommy" or "Daddy" coming from inside. Thoughts of Mike hit her out of nowhere. What if he were involved in something like this? She shook the fear off.

The wheels were facing them, big, huge tires tall enough to tower over even Cooper's height. While Mackenzie tried to pry open an emergency door in the back, Bilotti climbed up the undercarriage of the bus. Sophie followed him. Then Murray.

Mackenzie said, "Stuck. Hand me some the pry tools, Torres." He yelled out, "Murray, Tyler, you're gonna have to go in and get the kids."

On top, which was really the side of the bus, Bilotti pressed his face against the window. "The kids are right here. Leaning against the roof. Some of the seats came loose. It's disorienting as hell." He looked over his shoulder and said,

"Torres, hand us the tape and cutter. We gotta break windows."

"Then go get the K-12 saw," Sophie called out.

The cries were worse, now that the kids caught a glimpse of adults. "It's okay," she yelled inside. "Cover your heads with your coats." There shouldn't be any flying glass, but it was best to take precautions.

In less than a minute, they crosshatched two windows, cut around the edges and when they struck it with the end of the ax, the glass fell outward in a sheet.

From the ground, Mackenzie yelled, "Tyler and Murray, go, go, go."

Sophie whipped off her helmet and coat as did Murray. He was smaller and wiry and could squeeze through the opening as easily as she could. Feet first, she wiggled inside.

"It's okay, guys, we're gonna lift you out." She picked up a little girl. "Shh, sweetheart. You can go first."

Outside, Bilotti and Cooper began lifting the kids through the windows. Sophie could hear them grunt from the exertion. Other members of her crew would take the children down the ladder they'd raised.

Murray had a little boy in his arms. The child screamed, "Get Tommy."

"Tommy?"

"He's back there. Under the seat."

"I'm on it," Sophie called out.

She made her way down the narrow space of the bus. From below one of the seats, she heard someone crying. Sophie found a small boy wedged between the bench and the hump-like, metal things found in buses. His head was bleeding.

Huddling close to the child, she said, "Hi, Tommy, I'm Sophie. We're gonna get you out of here."

The boy roused. Huge tears in his blue eyes reminded her of Mikey again. "'Kay."

From above, Jules cracked another window and poked his head in; wordlessly, he handed her a saw. She said, "Close your eyes, Tommy. And try not to be scared. This is gonna be loud."

The earsplitting sound of the K-12 rent the confines of the small space. As carefully as she could, Sophie cut through the metal leg. Finally it snapped off. The seat hit Sophie's chest and knocked her flat on her ass. Scrambling to her feet, she handed out the saw and slid her arms around Tommy, who moaned. Sophie whispered, "Just a little while longer, honey." She lifted him up to Jules. Glancing down the bus aisle, she saw it was empty.

"Tyler, get out of there," the cap yelled into her radio. "I'm worried about the tank."

She hoisted herself up and was halfway out the window when she saw a WNYC news reporter and a cameraman. They were being pushed back by a group of cops. Sophie climbed out onto the bus, hustled down the ladder, and raced from the vehicle. In seconds there was an explosion behind her. She wasn't far enough away and she felt the heat, stumbled, but righted herself. When she was a safe distance away, she turned and saw the inferno behind her. Flames ballooned out of the front of the bus. When she pivoted back around, the camera was on her. Fuck. In no time, that footage would be all over the TV. She wondered if Mikey would see it.

DR. LANG was real pretty with brown hair and eyes. She was nice and friendly, too. Dad told him Uncle Dylan and Hogan went to see her last year, and Hogan was cool, so she had to be okay. Except sometimes she asked him questions he didn't like to answer.

Today, she smiled at him from the chair. He sat on the couch. Next to her were pink flowers. She always had a vase of them and they smelled good. His dad used to bring his mom flowers all the time.

Dr. Lang said, "There's been a lot of excitement at your house, hasn't there, Mike?"

He brought his baseball mitt in with him and stared down at it. "Aunt Bailey had a baby. His name is Patrick but they call him Tyler. After Sophie."

"I read today's paper about it." She smiled at him. "Sophie's the firefighter you were so upset about a while back. The one who fell off the ladder."

His heart started to beat fast. "She didn't get hurt bad."

"But it scared you."

"Uh-huh." He bit his lip.

"What, Mike?"

"I heard Dad talking to Aunt Brie about it. He thinks I shouldn't be around Sophie anymore."

Dr. Lang waited. She did that a lot when she wanted him to talk more.

"Because I got scared for her."

"Does that make sense to you?"

Sliding on the glove, Mike punched it. "Not really. I like her. I just didn't want anything to happen to her."

"Why do you think your dad doesn't want you to see her?"

"Cleary says Dad's overprotective. That means he worries too much about us."

"Partly. It also means that he makes decisions based on what he thinks is best for you guys."

Mike wondered how his dad could always know what was best.

"Do *you* think it's best for you not to see Sophie?"

"I dunno."

"Mike?"

He looked at the doctor. "I wanna see her. I want her to help me with my Wolf badge stuff."

"Did you tell your father? Maybe he can explain why he feels as he does."

"Dad's been sad again since the Halloween party."

"Why?"

He shrugged.

"Again, maybe you should talk to him. Getting things out in the open makes them less scary."

"I know sometimes adults don't tell me stuff."

"To protect you."

"It makes me more scared."

"When you get scared, is that why you don't want to talk or participate in anything?"

Mike dropped the mitt and came to the edge of his seat. "Sometimes. Can I ask you something else?"

"Of course you can."

"There's this girl at school. She's in Brownies and she

wants to be a firefighter. She's going to work on a safety badge for her troop."

"And?"

"Maybe if Sophie works with me, Cara could come, too."

Leaning her head back against the seat, the doctor grinned. "I think that's a great idea."

Mike frowned. "I wonder if Dad will."

"Ask him."

He wrinkled his nose. He'd have to think about that.

Later that night, when he was in bed, Mike pulled out the picture of his mom. She smiled up at him and made him feel better.

"I wanna ask Dad something but I'm not sure."

She had always told him he could ask his dad or her anything.

"I like Sophie, but Dad doesn't think I should spend time with her."

She'd say his dad wanted what was best for him.

"I miss you, Mom." He put his nose to the picture. Sometimes he could still remember the smell of that bath stuff she used to use. But not lately. It made him kinda sad.

He wondered if she missed him in heaven. She told him before she died she'd miss him until he came to heaven, too, but that she'd be happy there. And he should be happy here.

Kissing the picture, he tucked it beneath the pillow, turned off the flashlight and pulled up the covers. His mom was smart. Probably she still knew what was best for him.

AS SHE STARED over at Rachel Scott, Sophie wondered if she wore the makeup, had her hair styled and bought killer clothes if she'd be as pretty as the news anchor. Probably not. The woman had panache, something you were born with.

"We're going to be taping the interview, if that's all right."

Hmm. From her pocket she pulled out the device Dylan had given her. *Use this so you'll have a record of exactly what you said.* Placing it on the table, Sophie smiled innocently. "Of course not. Just as you won't mind if *I* tape it."

Scott glanced at the recorder. "Fine." She checked her

notes. "I'll probably be calling you Firefighter Tyler most of
the time, though I might slip into the more familiar if it feels
right."

"You plan all that out?"

"Yes."

Sophie raised her chin. "Why did the vice president
blackball you?"

The other woman's mascara-laden eyes widened. "He feels
I covered a difficult time in his life irresponsibly."

"Did you?"

"I don't think so. In any case, it's what he thinks that
counts."

"Then you'd better be nice to me on camera. I'm in his
good graces now."

"I'll remember that." Scott smiled, and it made her face
softer.

"What's the final program going to look like?"

"I plan to do a quick history of women in the department.
Then we've got some live footage of women fighting fires,
like yesterday at the bus, of them teaching classes, hanging
around the firehouse. I'm hoping to get some shots of you at
your station. Then there will be interviews with other females
in the department and with guys—some who embraced
women in the department, some who didn't."

"That oughtta be a show."

"We have to be fair. For the record, Sophie, I think what
women have accomplished in the field of firefighting is re-
markable and very admirable."

"You do?" Maybe this wouldn't be so bad.

Scott chuckled. "Yes, I'm not the cast-iron bitch the
O'Neils think I am."

"I saw some of your tape from when the vice president was
taken hostage."

"Broadcasts get edited." Her lips thinned. "Sometimes, the
emphasis isn't what you thought it was going to be."

"Oh, terrific. That makes me *really* excited about this interview."

When Scott threw her shoulders back and lifted her head,
Sophie saw a glimpse of the formidable woman inside the

glossy exterior. "I've been assured I have full approval over this show. Give me a chance, Sophie."

The woman could be on the level. In firefighting, people had been biased against Sophie without knowing what she could do. And she'd gotten a raw deal more than once. She decided to give Rachel Scott the benefit of the doubt. "Why the hell not."

They began the interview when the camera rolled. So did Sophie's tape. Scott said she'd just ask a lot of questions and Sophie should answer without worrying about making a mistake. They'd edit around them.

"I'm here with Firefighter Sophie Tyler, who's gotten a lot of press lately. Let's get that out of the way, first. How did you come to help deliver the vice president's child?"

Sophie had resigned herself to that question. She gave a shortened version of the events with Bailey; Scott asked a few discreet questions, then turned to another topic.

"You also work at Bailey's Irish Pub, which is owned by her brothers, right?"

"Yeah. I'm a waitress and bartender."

"Do most of America's Bravest have second jobs?"

"Many do."

"Why?"

"To make ends meet."

Scott checked her notes. "It says here, the average pay is in the FDNY is about sixty thousand a year. With benefits, it goes up to around ninety. Officers' pay is even higher and there's all that overtime." She raised an eyebrow, her silent question loud and clear.

"That's a nice chunk of change but to live in New York you need more."

"Before 9/11 people believed firefighting *was* a part-time job. Stereotypes of hanging out at the station house . . . cooking and eating dinner . . . watching ballgames on TV. What do you say to that?"

Sophie faced the camera directly. "Just this. New York City has about eleven fires every hour. We go to work knowing we might walk into buildings that could fall down on top of us, or choke the air from our lungs. And we may not walk out. You do the math on the salary."

"Touché, Firefighter Tyler. Now let's talk about being a woman in the department. Do the guys harass you?"

"Look, you know the stories. You probably saw the documentaries. We had a tough time getting in, staying in. But things are changing. Some guys are still in the dark ages about it, and some are more liberated. I can tell you that my crew are the latter."

"Though when you got to your current station house two firefighters transferred out."

"Their prerogative if they want to be Neanderthals."

They talked about the men some more, and Sophie tried to be honest but not make any sweeping negative statements. Actually, she managed to say several good things about her group.

"You grew up in the fire department, didn't you?"

"Yes."

"Would you tell us about that?"

After Sophie finished, the woman's eyes glistened. "What a nice story, Sophie."

"Yeah, Rachel, there are those kinds in the FDNY."

"Tell me about the Concord incident."

Man, the woman switched gears as fast as a truck ripping through the streets.

"Nothing to tell. I fell off a ladder with a man who weighed . . ." She inspected Rachel. ". . . maybe twice what you do. He got scared, flailed and we tumbled down."

"Men say women don't have the physical ability to be firefighters."

Sophie explained her workout routine, how much she could bench-press, her strength and stamina. "Women have to work hard, but we can do the job."

"The man who fell doesn't see it that way."

"Nothing I can do about that."

"Are you taking heat for it?"

"Probably. But not to my face."

"And it's a very pretty face, Sophie. Does that impact you? Being an *attractive* woman in the FDNY?"

"Does it impact you?"

"Excuse me?"

"Well, you're really asking if I have it easier in the department because of my looks. Or maybe if I sleep around. I'll bet you get the same questions about being in the male-dominated world of TV news."

Scott looked startled. Then she smiled. This time it was bright and genuine. "Again, Firefighter Tyler. Touché."

Though Sophie knew her question wouldn't make it into the broadcast, she smiled anyway.

LEANING AGAINST the wall of the kitchen in Bailey and Clay's town house in New York, Liam said to Dylan, "It's not too crowded in here."

"No. As long as the kids stay in the basement"—which had been finished off—"and some of the secret agents are outside."

Liam chuckled at the joke. When Pa was at the lake with Bailey and the kids last summer, he'd called the Secret Service that and it stuck.

He nodded in the direction of the family room. "Our sister's holding court."

"I'd say little Tyler was." Dylan smirked. "Everybody loves babies."

"You want any more, Dyl?"

"I don't know. You?"

"I don't know, either."

That question had been uppermost in his mind since it dawned on him that he and Sophie hadn't used birth control Halloween night. If she was pregnant, would she know by now? And if she was, how would she feel about it? He couldn't believe he'd been so irresponsible, but then again, his behavior was anything but normal that night.

"Liam? Where'd you go?" Dylan asked.

"I was thinking about how Rory asked if they named the baby after Ty Cobb, whose real name was Tyrus, by the way."

"Instead they named him after your girl."

"Don't start. We've had enough excitement for a while," Liam said.

"The bus thing was rough. She looked like the hero from *Die Hard* coming out of the smoke with the explosion in the background."

Liam had practically had a heart attack when the footage came on TV as a trailer to the news and he'd seen her back-dropped by all that fire.

"She coming today?"

"Clay invited her personally to thank her and say good-bye."

Bailey and Clay had stayed in New York for a few days after little Tyler was born. They could have traveled back on the VP plane, with a doctor in attendance, but Bailey wanted to spend the first week of November in the city with her family.

"She said she'd be here." Liam scowled at his brother. "Listen, Dylan, we talked. I told her the truth about changing my mind because of Mike and she agreed. You were right, she said it's not a good idea to get involved."

"What happened on Halloween?"

He felt his face heat. Turning to the cooler, he grabbed a Corona. "What do you mean?"

"Ha! I knew it. You were locked in the office with her. Pat said something funny was going on."

It had hardly been funny. Uncapping the beer bottle, he took a long swig before he turned back around. "I'm going to ask you nicely to let this go. What you're doing isn't helping me. Please, Dyl."

"Okay. Sorry. I just think you're wrong in letting Mikey determine the course of this." He wiggled his brows. "And I wanted some prurient details."

"I'm gonna go hold Tyler."

"So there are some . . ."

Liam walked away while his brother was still talking. In the family room, he found Bailey holding the baby, his ma, Brie and C.J. gathered around her. The men, and Angel and Isabella, were in Clay's den solving the problems of the country. "Can I hang out with you ladies?" he asked, squeezing Bailey on the shoulder.

Bailey grasped his hand. "You just want to hold Tyler."

"That I do, lass." He lifted the child from her arms.

A surprising sense of longing shot through him. The baby smelled like powder; his weight was slight and his little arms flailed as Liam cuddled him to his chest. He closed his eyes, remembering when Mike and Cleary were infants.

Bailey said, "Bring back memories?"

"Hmm. Good ones."

"You were a fine father," his mother commented. "Those little ones were as attached to you as they were to Kitty."

Lowering himself and the baby into the rocker beside his mother, he hugged Tyler to his chest. "I loved every minute of it. Especially since we had to wait so long before and in between the guys."

"Speaking of the guys, how's Cleary doing?" Brie asked.

"Okay, why?"

"I think he and Hogan got into it Halloween night."

"Anything serious?"

"Some shoving. Sinead broke it up." Sinead was Pat's oldest son, who'd started at Fordham this past September.

"Nobody told me."

"Huh." C.J. sipped from a beer bottle. "I wonder where they learned to push around their relatives?"

"From my wonderful big brothers."

"Did I hear my name?" Aidan asked as he walked into the room. Liam watched as his gaze rested on C.J. He had to look away from the poignancy of Aidan's expression.

"Hey, A. How's the male contingent doing?"

"They're talking about Rachel Scott. Since I don't like to blast anybody, I thought I'd join the distaff side." He crossed to Liam. "Give him to me."

"No. Why don't you just go have your own?"

"Aye, I agree with that," Mary Kate put in. "You're forty, Aidan."

"Tell her," he nodded to C.J.

"Don't gang up on me. I just got *Matka* and my sisters off my back thanks to my brother's impending fatherhood." She rolled her eyes. "Besides, we're not even married yet."

"I tried to get her to set a date."

Bailey shot a fake grimace at C.J. "Let's get to that, girl."

The doorbell rang.

C.J. sighed with relief. "Saved by the proverbial bell."

"I'll answer it." Aidan started out. "Don't think you're home free, woman."

Aidan ushered Sophie inside a few minutes later. With a guy! What the fuck?

Bailey beamed at Sophie. "Hey, there's my birth partner."

"Hi, Bailey. Mrs. O'Neil." Sophie greeted the other women, and nodded to Liam. "This is Tony Caruso. A friend."

Tony—he was the Italian guy falling all over her at the bar on Halloween—greeted Liam's family. Liam forced a nod and a greeting, then caught Sophie's gaze. She shrugged as if to say, *We agreed.* He smiled back when in reality he wanted to smash his fist through the wall.

A fuss was made when Clay came out and found Sophie had arrived. Between Clay's attention and *her date*, Liam didn't have a chance to talk to Sophie privately before they ate.

But all afternoon long he watched her like a hawk. He appreciated the way her purple corduroy skirt swirled around her calves and how the lilac top she wore with it outlined her breasts. They were full and heavy. He knew because he had held them in his hands only a week ago.

He also watched Caruso. They hadn't slept together. Yet, at least. The guy touched her frequently—a hand on her back, a brush of fingers down her hair, a lean into her. But Liam could tell there was no intimacy between them by the way Sophie inched back each time. He wasn't surprised. She wasn't the type to fuck one guy one week and another the next. And he guessed that's all they'd done, just fuck. The thought made him sad. So after they'd cleaned up dinner, he snuck upstairs to the spare room, which was fully furnished with a TV, and stretched out on the sleigh bed. He switched on the baseball game, feeling shitty. Huh! What else was new?

SOPHIE GLANCED UP the stairs for, oh, about the tenth time. Bailey came up beside her. "He's okay."

"Excuse me?"

"Liam, he's okay up there. He always sneaks away at gatherings like this. Sometimes it makes him sad to see all these happy families."

"He loved Kitty a lot, didn't he?"

"Yeah. They were good together." She gave Sophie's shoulder a squeeze. "But he needs to move on."

"I know he does."

When Tyler let out a lusty cry, Bailey turned away.

And before she could stop herself, Sophie climbed the steps. She checked two bedrooms and found Liam in the third. The Yankees game droned from the TV and she watched him from the doorway. He was all masculine grace, asleep on a blue windowpaned quilt amidst a mound of pillows. His navy slacks outlined his long legs and the matching silk T-shirt hugged all his muscles. She wondered if these were the new clothes he'd bought for the date with her that they'd never had. More than anything, she wanted to climb on that bed and wake him with kisses and intimate caresses. The feeling was so strong, she grasped the edge of the doorjamb to keep herself where she was.

He awakened. It was wonderful to watch—first he stretched his arms overhead with his eyes still closed. Then he opened them, blinked, and saw her.

And for a moment, there was nothing between them but their feelings for each other. He smiled, and so did she. "Hi."

"Hi." He glanced at the clock. "I must have fallen asleep."

"I came to see if you were okay."

"Did you?"

"No. I wanted a few minutes alone with you."

He studied her for a minute. "Why'd you bring him?"

"You know why. If we're going to do this, we have to do it right."

The *this* didn't need explanation. "If?"

"We are."

His gaze was intense. "Sophie, there's something we haven't talked about. There wasn't time at the hospital. But I've been thinking about it."

"What?"

"At least come and sit." He patted the side of the mattress and moved over.

She sat close enough to him on the bed that she could see his clear blue eyes and the little nick he must have gotten shaving.

He picked up her hand. "On Halloween night, we didn't use any protection."

"I know." She'd realized the slip, too, the next day. "It was irresponsible."

"Where were you in your cycle?"

"At the end."

"Still." He touched her stomach. "We could have . . ."

"No, Liam, I'm on the pill."

His eyes widened. "Oh."

"Not because I'm sleeping with anybody. It's just easier to be a firefighter if my periods are regular and short. This pill does that."

"I see."

"And I don't have any kind of STD. We get regular HIV tests because of the blood we come in contact with." She hesitated a moment. "Are you clear?"

"Um, yeah. I am."

"Do you get tested?"

He looked away.

A thought struck her. Oh, God, it couldn't be. "Liam, have you slept with anybody else since Kitty died?"

Blowing out a very heavy breath, he faced her. "Nope. I'm just a clean-cut Cub Scout leader."

Sophie laughed out loud. "You are so *not*. I was there, I know what's inside you."

"I know what's inside you, too, lass."

Again she chuckled. He reached up and cupped her face. "Soph, I—"

Brie appeared in the doorway. "Liam—" She stopped short. "Oh, sorry."

"What's wrong?"

"Dylan wants you downstairs. Cleary and Hogan are at it again."

ELEVEN

❧

THEY TOOK *the rigs out of service this morning, so the fire house is quiet. Traffic's whizzing by, but I can tell from over here there ain't any action going on. Wonder if they're talking yet about the fire yesterday. That was a real beauty. The damage I did! Perfecto, if I do say so myself. Scared a shitload of people. And it's me that's responsible for all the fuss today. I like that they're upset, worried, even if they're more on guard now. But hell, if you can't scare them, why do it? Gotta have some fun. And I don't want it to be over too soon. It'll have to end—don't have a clue how—but right now, I'm just enjoying myself.*

TRAINING IN THE fire department was a double-edged sword. Sometimes it was a boring and tedious, but most firefighters knew it was necessary and could save their lives. Today, Sophie didn't mind the classroom shtick because Joe Carusotti was running it.

He was just about to speak when Torres rushed in. "Sorry I'm late."

The guys grumbled but Joe cut them off. "Get some coffee and a doughnut, kid. Now, if everybody else has had their fill, I'd like to start this little show."

"Your food wasn't as good as the pastries the vice president sent Tyler," Bilotti quipped.

"Yeah, well, we're not all stars." He rolled his eyes. "She a pain in the ass to live with these days?"

"No more than usual," Murray put in.

"Bite me," Sophie said. Then she narrowed her gaze on Joe. "You'd better watch your tongue, Carusotti. I can tell tales on you. Like the time you were fifteen and I found you in the backseat of your father's—"

"Whoa! Mea culpa." The others laughed; Joe sobered when Jules took a seat next to Sophie. "On to the task at hand. Squad 28 caught another fire last night that was incendiary. The administration batted around doing these training sessions anyway, and that cinched it. You're my virgin run-through with this information."

"Anybody get hurt last night?" Mackenzie asked.

"Uh-huh. The probie." He nodded to Jules. "Listen up, Torres."

"Yes, sir."

Joe described the incident. The captain had gone first into a two-story apartment building with a forcible-entry team. Upstairs, in the public corridor, they encountered black smoke. After crawling down the hall, the captain tested the door, tried to open it, but it was stuck. The irons man wedged in the end of the halligan between the door and the frame. The probie drove in the tool with a long-handled ax. Two other smoke eaters pulled back the halligan and the door popped, but would only open a few inches. They tried to shoulder their way through, but couldn't. They managed to widen the entrance enough for the captain to get his hand inside, where he found a wire holding it closed.

"Shit," Mackenzie said. "The torch didn't even try to cover this one up?"

"Nope."

"How'd the probie get hurt?" Jules asked.

"He went in after they cut the wire and tripped over other wires that had been rigged."

"The guy was trying to *get* the firefighters?" Jules asked, wide-eyed. Sometimes his naïveté about the nature of people shocked Sophie.

"You gotta expect the unexpected, probie, especially since we know there's a lunatic out there."

Mumbling among the crew.

"Torres, tell me about the kinds of lunatics out there."

Jules flushed. He'd made it through the academy, but Sophie knew he had trouble with book learning. She'd helped him at the firehouse review things he needed to know.

"Revenge. Profit. Vanity fires. For kicks."

"Right so far. What else?"

He thought hard.

Come on, Jules.

"To cover up crimes."

"That all?" Carusotti asked.

A frown. But no answer.

"It's the number one cause."

Jules shook his head.

"Mackenzie?"

"Kids. Juveniles start the most incendiary fires."

"Fuck," Jules said under his breath.

"He didn't remember because he *is* a kid," Murray joked.

"This morning we need to cover what to look for when you're on the scene. I know, I know, even with your flashlights, you can't see your hand in front of your face most times. You gotta find the fire or look for victims. But you can still help us by being aware of a few things." He clicked into his PowerPoint presentation, which was displayed on the wall behind him. "Sophie, read them."

She read the list out loud.

1. *Are the doors and windows opened or closed?*
2. *What is the color of the smoke?*
3. *Trace the burn pattern.*
4. *What is the point of origin?*

5. *Note any obvious starting devices or flammable accelerants around that indicate arson.*

"Now," Joe said, "let's talk about what these are exactly, and why they're important. I know you've had all this training, but we're dealing with a dangerous criminal right now, and everybody in the department has to be up to speed."

Jules choked on his coffee when Joe used the term *dangerous criminal*. But they took Joe's instruction seriously. Because purposely set fires were the leading cause of all fires, and they claimed the lives of too many firefighters. Because purposely set fires were unpredictable and firefighters had a greater chance of getting hurt in them. And sometimes, because purposely set fires were ignited by another firefighter.

When the training ended, Joe thanked them for their patience. He spoke briefly to Jules, then approached Sophie. "Hey, kiddo, you doing okay?"

"Yeah. You did a good job here."

"Necessary. Your guys were better than the rest are gonna be."

A little loudly, she said, "Well, they're not *always* morons."

Joe squeezed her arm. "Taking the heat about the vice president?"

"Yeah, but who cares? It was great helping with the delivery."

"You like the O'Neils, don't you?"

One in particular. She could still see Liam lying on the bed, rumpled from sleep. The need to climb right in with him, kiss him, make love to him had been so strong, her body tightened just thinking about it.

"What?" Joe asked.

"Nothing."

"Your face flushed."

"Did it?"

He studied her. "Yep. But I gotta go, so I can't drag it out of you. Call me if you wanna talk."

"Sure, I will."

As she watched him walk away, Sophie was grateful for his concern, but she knew she wouldn't talk to Joe about Liam. It wouldn't help. Nothing would. Like other things in her life, she'd just have to get over it.

MAN, LIAM THOUGHT, he couldn't catch a break here. Circumstances kept conspiring against him and Sophie being able to keep their distance. Right now she was at the front of the pub, working with Mikey and a little girl named Cara. It had shocked the hell out of Liam when Mike had asked if Sophie could help him with safety activities for his Wolf badge, and if Cara Cahill could join them; she was a Brownie and had to do similar activities for a badge. Liam didn't even think about objecting because Mike rarely asked friends to come over these days. He saw their heads bent together and had to chuckle. Even his kid liked redheads.

Making his way to the table by the window where they sat, he glanced outside. A light drizzle had begun, and the sky was gray. "How's it going?"

Mike glanced up with a sparkle in his eyes. "Great, Dad. We're drawing our houses and making a plan for . . ." He frowned.

"Hazards," Sophie said. "And an escape route."

"Sounds productive." He asked the little girl, "Cara, can I get you something?"

"I don't wanna be a bother," she said quietly. She was intent on her own drawing.

"No bother. Do your mom and dad let you have soft drinks?"

"Sometimes."

"Me, too, Dad."

"I'll get you Cokes. Sophie?"

"Yeah, sure. Thanks." She kept her gaze on the papers they were working on.

When he returned to the table and set down drinks, Mike pointed to his paper. "Look at what we should do, Dad."

He dropped down onto a chair next to his son. "Tell me about it."

In the next ten minutes, Mikey talked more than he had at one time since . . . Liam didn't remember how long it had been. His son told him about the fire hazards where they lived and escape routes. "Sophie said she could do better if she saw the house."

Quickly, Sophie added, "But this is enough, Mike."

Liam sat back and steepled his hands. "Yeah, it's enough toward your badge, honey."

"I want her to come to our house. She could see my room. Make sure it's safe." He glanced at Cara, then to Sophie. "Could you go to hers, too?"

"If her mother says it's okay."

Feeling helpless, Liam tried to cut this off. "Mike, I . . ."

"My mother will say it's okay. I'll call her."

They both bolted up. Mike grabbed her hand. "I'll show you where."

"You can use my cell—"

But the words trailed off as the kids rushed away.

Backdropped by the window and the clouds, Sophie's eyes were steel gray and troubled. "Everything's working against us staying apart."

"Not everything."

"What do you mean?"

"Tony Caruso."

She stiffened.

"Did you have fun after you left Bailey and Clay's town house?" He wasn't happy with the edge in his voice.

Again, her gaze focused on the plans. "Yeah, sure, I guess."

"Look at me, Sophie." When she did, he asked, "What did you do?"

"Liam, this isn't helping."

"I wanna know."

Her sigh was heavy. "We went back to my place."

"And?"

"Watched some TV."

"And?"

Her glass hit the surface of the table hard. "What do you want to know, Liam? If he kissed me? Yes, he did. Did he touch me, like you did? No. Okay?"

Now that he knew, the fist around his heart loosened, but he also felt embarrassed. "I'm sorry. It's just your being around so much makes me crazy."

"Can you talk Mike out of wanting me to go to your house?"

"I could forbid it. But even though he's quiet, when he digs his heels in, he's a lot like me."

"How?"

"In the end, he gets what he wants."

Her brows raised.

"I guess there's always a first time." He stood. "I'll check on them, then we'll set up a time."

SOPHIE DIDN'T KNOW what she expected, but it wasn't what she found at Liam's house in Brooklyn. The gray-sided building was nestled in an old neighborhood, with other old houses like the one he'd lived in with Kitty.

"I didn't realize you were a landlord," she said when he answered the door on one side of the duplex.

"It was the only way we could afford a place, even though Kitty's parents gave us the down payment. And, of course, prices were unbelievably lower twenty years ago."

"It must be worth a fortune now."

He smiled sadly. "In more ways than one." He stepped aside. "Come on in."

"Who lives on the other side?"

"A businessman did, but he's moved uptown. Dylan's thinking about taking it."

"Would you want that?"

He closed the door and leaned against it. Wearing dark brown jeans and a gauzy, tan rolled-up-at-the-sleeves shirt, he looked terrific. "I'd love to have Dyl and Hogan there. Wouldn't you wanna live near Nate?"

"More than I can say." She glanced around the foyer. "Mike didn't tell me the structure was a duplex. It poses more fire hazards."

"I hadn't thought of that." From behind her, he placed his hands on her shoulders and left them there for a few seconds, then helped her remove her leather jacket. Carefully, he hung it up in the closet. "Come on, let me show you around."

A living room opened up off to the right. Spacious and bright, it had a beautiful stone fireplace and comfortable sofas and chairs. On the walls were family photos. And not a thing out of place. "It's beautiful yet homey. And neat."

His brow furrowed. "It wasn't always. Kitty didn't fuss about those things. Only after she got sick did we become so . . . tidy." He ran a hand through his dark hair. "In retrospect, I guess it was something we could control."

She squeezed his arm. He stared at her, then covered her hand with his. The contact was warm, supportive, but set off sparks nonetheless. Sophie noted how his body stiffened; her stomach clenched.

A room that might have been a dining room, but was now set up for the kids, was straight ahead. It housed two computers, a big table and chairs. "You must have renovated."

"We did. The place was shabby inside and out when we bought it. Patrick was a huge help—he's the handiest of us all. Dylan pitched in because he can do anything he puts his mind to. Which I think is another reason he should move in the other side. Aidan was useless, though."

She smiled at the thought of his charming brother trying to wield a hammer. "We helped Bilotti remodel his basement and that was a chore."

"We?"

"Our company. And some others from the department."

Liam led her down a hallway, off of which was a half bath. "This is the pièce de résistance."

The kitchen was a chef's paradise. It was huge, with a bank of tall windows, oak cupboards, granite countertops and tile on the floor, all in shades of brown and tan and splashes of terra-cotta. Gleaming pots and pans stood guard over a center island. Now it was filled with the scent of baking pastry, but she could detect herbs growing in pots near the window. There was a glassed-in eating area beyond the kitchen. "Liam, this is wonderful."

"The backyard was big so we could go out several feet and

could expand the space on both sides." He hesitated. "We redid it all just before Kitty got sick."

"Did . . . did she cook?"

"Nope, couldn't boil water. It's how I got into cooking. She was a nurse before we had the kids, so she worked crazy hours." He gave a sad smile. "She wanted me to have this as my domain."

Sophie was instantaneously jealous of the smile that claimed Liam's face. Fuck, she was envying a dead woman.

Liam cleared his throat. "Mikey should be home soon."

"Yeah, it's almost four."

"Want something?"

"Coffee would be good."

He tipped her chin. "You look tired."

"I subbed for another firefighter yesterday. We had a slew of calls. No arsons, though."

His beautiful blue eyes widened and he dropped his hand. "Arson?"

"Uh-huh. There's a torch loose in lower Manhattan. It's been in the papers."

He moved to the other side of the room and took coffee beans from the cupboard. "I see."

"I'm sorry. I shouldn't have said anything."

He didn't look at her while he ground the beans. "I, um, don't read about fires."

"Why?"

"Call me crazy, but I hate to think about you inside burning buildings."

"I'm sorry," she repeated. There was nothing else to say.

"None of the guys read about it anymore or watch the news when it's on, except Dylan. He didn't mention an arsonist."

The front door opened; a few seconds later, Mikey and Cara, dressed in their cute uniforms and carrying backpacks, rushed into the kitchen. Sophie was glad for the end of her conversation with Liam. Talk of arson had upset him.

Mike put his things away in a closet, then crossed to Sophie. "Hey, Sophie."

Liam's back was to her as he assembled the coffee so he didn't see Mike hug her. Cara said a polite hello, and Liam told them to sit. He'd put out juice, fruit and dip, and some kind of tarts that looked delicious.

Cara seemed wary of the dip, but tasted it. "This is good, Mr. O'Neil."

"Thanks."

"Can I show Sophie my room, now?" Mikey asked.

"After your snack." Liam joined them with mugs of coffee. "And don't rush it."

Sophie took a tart. It was flaky with raspberry inside. They made small talk about what happened in school today, and when the kids were finished eating, Mikey looked at Liam.

"Go ahead," he told them.

"I want you to come, too, Dad."

Cleary's room was first down the hallway; it was small and not quite as neat as downstairs.

Mike said, "Mine and Cleary's rooms used to be one big one, but when we came along, Dad and my uncles divided it in two."

"Cool." She noticed a patchwork quilt on the bed, but didn't get close enough to see what it was made of. On the walls were baseball posters. No computer, but a boom box. Lots of books. "Does Cleary like to read?" Sophie asked.

Mikey took her hand. "Mom used to read to me all the time, and even to Cleary."

"Ah."

Liam smiled. "Those are nice memories."

"Come see mine." Mike tugged her out the door.

When she reached his bedroom, she chuckled. The décor was a hodgepodge. Cara said, "This is way cool."

It was. Dinosaurs roamed one wall. Stars twinkled from the ceiling. Sports figures dominated another area. "It sure is, Mike." She took note of the layout. "But you need to keep that window more accessible. The desk's too high to be in front of it. It'd be hard to get out in case of a fire."

" 'Kay."

Pulling the pad she'd brought from her pocket, Sophie began writing notes. As she walked around the room, she had a few other suggestions, like moving some items and getting rid of a stack of papers.

She stopped short when she got a good look at the bed. "What's this?"

Mike came up next to her. "It's a quilt my mom made." He coughed. "It's of all the stuff from me when I was a baby."

Her throat got tight. "It is?"

"Yeah, I'll show you." He pointed to a square. "This is from my baby blanket. It's still soft." He drew her hand to it. "Here, feel."

Moved beyond words, she touched the yellow fleece.

"And this is from my first pair of jeans." He went on to describe the Yankees jersey, the crocheted booty sewn into a patch, part of his baptismal gown, which he wrinkled his nose at.

When he finished, she whispered, "I've never seen anything more beautiful in my life."

The room was quiet. Then Mike said, "She made one for Cleary, and Dad, too, only his had her stuff on it, too. 'Cuz they were married."

Kitty had united them in a quilt for eternity. Slowly Sophie turned away from the almost tangible presence of Kitty O'Neil. She caught sight of Liam in the doorway. The expression on his face wasn't sad, but more nostalgic. Full of good memories, like he'd said.

They left Mike's room and she stopped to check out the smoke alarm in the hallway—and to regain her emotional equilibrium.

At the end of the corridor was another room. Liam and Kitty's. She didn't want to see it. Didn't want to witness their quilt, the place where they'd made love. But what could she do? She braced herself when Liam opened the door.

But once again she didn't find what she expected. Inside was a perfectly nice, masculine setting. Sand-colored walls. A hardwood floor that was covered with a dark blue rug shot with a circular brown pattern. And on the huge bed was a modern coverlet with geometric shapes tying in the brown of the wall and accented with shades of blue. A bathroom off of it boasted the same color scheme. "Liam, this is wonderful."

"Brie did it."

"What?"

He glanced down the hall where Mike was still in his room showing something to Cara. "She helped me clear out Kitty's things, then planned this out. We went ahead with it about a year ago." He nodded to the closet. "Our quilt is stored in there."

"Did that make you feel bad?"

"In some ways. But it helped me along emotionally." He searched her face. "I *have* made progress, Soph. I'm ready to go on with my life."

"I know." And standing here, in his bedroom—and it *was* just his—she wanted desperately to be part of it.

TWELVE

THE NIGHT was rainy and cold, befitting Liam's mood. He'd been feeling like shit since Sophie visited his house. He needed to get out of this funk, and when being home alone had gotten to him, he headed to . . . where else? The pub. When he entered through the front door, the familiar scent of the lamb stew he'd prepared that afternoon enveloped him. Comforted him. Pat looked up from where he was wiping the bar. "What are you doin' here? It's your night off."

"I'm restless. No kids. Ma and Pa have Mikey and Cleary's at a lock-in with Hogan and Sean at church."

"We're all kidless," Brie said from the end of the bar. She wore a beautiful tapestry jacket over a sage green top. "My parents came down. The girls are with them. When they fell asleep, I headed over here."

Liam glanced around the pub. The only other people in the place were tucked away in the corner, sharing some popcorn and gazing goofy-like into each other's eyes. A feminine giggle or masculine chuckle intermittently drifted over. "Why are the lovebirds here?"

"Not sure. They came in around midnight."

"Where's Dylan? He's on, right?"

"Here I am." From the corridor where the office was located, Dylan appeared carrying a box. "Game time, kiddies," he announced.

"Count us out," Aidan yelled back. "We're making wedding plans. I'm pushing for Valentine's Day."

Standing, C.J. tugged at his hand. "No way am I gonna miss one of the infamous O'Neil trivia marathons."

Sophie exited the kitchen; with a jacket on her arm, she was obviously headed out. Her hair was curlier and the T-shirt she wore tonight seemed to fit her snugly. Maybe it had shrunk. Fuck!

She bumped into Dylan in the middle of the pub. "What's that?"

His brother slid his arm around her shoulders and they walked toward the others. "We have these little trivia contests regularly. To see who's the smartest. It's me of course, but I continually have to prove it to these jokers."

"And pigs fly," Liam said, suddenly cheered. "I'm in."

"Of course you are." Brie clucked her tongue. "Mr. Study-Everything-on-the-Internet."

He glanced at Sophie. His latest *study* had been arson. "Not so much anymore."

"I was just leaving," Sophie told them.

"Stay, darlin'," Pat suggested. "You can be on my team."

Brie crossed to two tables that were already pushed together. "No way, guys against the girls, as usual."

"You're outnumbered, lass." Pat smiled fondly at his wife and she returned it.

Sophie shook her head. "If I don't play, you'd have even teams."

"Be a sport, Sophie." C.J. had joined Brie and Aidan hung back with his brothers. "Let's show these men our stuff."

"Already seen it," Pat and Aidan said together.

"Watch it, guys," Liam pointed out. "We have a guest in here."

Sophie laughed out loud. "I work at a firehouse. Those guys would make all of you blush."

Before she could object again, the seven of them were

seated, genders on opposite side of the tables, with a pitcher of beer between them.

Dylan began taking cards, pencils and pads out of the box. "Explain the rules to her, Liam."

Liam liked the way Sophie's eyes had lit with mirth. Smiling at her, he said, "Each side gets to pick cards according to their dollar amount. The more money a card is worth, the harder the question. If you get the answer right, you keep the cash. Wrong, and you subtract it. First thing to decide is whether you'll go low or high."

A delicate snort from Brie. "The guys always go low. They're chickenshits at heart. We women take chances."

"And who usually wins, *a chroi*?"

"So you're ahead two games." She smiled at Sophie. "Maybe Sophie will be our good-luck charm."

"Don't bet on it. I'm not very good at games."

Done with setting up the board, Dylan gave one box of cards to the girls and held another. "All right, huddle up."

The guys picked questions of values $1,000, $2,000, $10,000 and $14,000 for the first round.

C.J. was giggling when they announced theirs. "Six thousand, sixteen thousand, twenty-four thousand and a whopping sixty-four thousand dollars."

"Oh, *leanbh*, you're goin' down." Dylan smirked. "Pat's gonna have his way tonight."

Brie's pout was sexy. "Like he doesn't always."

"What are you talking about?" Sophie asked.

"Couples compete for . . . personal prizes," Dylan explained. "We won't go into the details of who pays who what."

Sophie glanced at Liam. Was she wondering what the stakes were for him and Kitty when they played this game in the past? Maybe she was imagining what she'd offer him. That's what *he* was thinking about.

"Here's the first one, scaredy-cats." Brie read the card. "What's the name of the game where you have to break your opponent's hidden code of colored pegs?"

Pat looked at Dylan, and then Liam, who answered, "Mastermind."

C.J. snickered. "Measly one thou." She wrote down the score.

"The eight-thousand-dollar question for the girls." Pat read the card. "Shit. She's gonna know this."

"Shut up, Paddy." Dylan always took this seriously. "You'll clue her in."

"It won't matter." With scorn, he said, "Who starred in the movie *Spartacus*?"

"Kirk Douglas," Brie shouted. "I *love* him. He was gorgeous when he was young."

"You wound me, lass."

She grabbed his hand and kissed it saucily. "Maybe later."

When Brie handed her the cards, Sophie read the next question for the guys. "What type of vehicles were zeppelins?"

"Airplanes." Liam again.

"Liam should be forbidden to answer them all," Brie whined.

"Hey, you wanted guys against girls." Dylan frowned. "Though he is making the rest of us look bad."

"Not hard," C.J. said.

"Not yet," Aidan quipped.

"You're pathetic," Dylan put in. "Here's yours, ladies. What kind of roses did Marie Osmond sing about?"

"Paper." Sophie blurted the answer and seemed to surprise herself. "When the song came out, the guys at the firehouse hated it. I used to play it just to rag on them."

Brie straightened. "Okay, we're up, twenty-four thousand to three thousand."

"It ain't over till it's over." Pat was having fun, which was good to see.

"Here's yours, sore loser." C.J. was reading. "Which dam is in the state of Nevada?"

No one answered. Finally Pat turned to Liam. "You can't keep quiet just because they picked on you."

He shrugged and lied. "I don't know."

"Bullshit."

"You guys figure it out."

"I think it's the Hoover Dam . . ."

"No, the Washington Dam . . ."

Aidan said, "Maybe the Jefferson Dam . . ."

"*Is* there a Jefferson Dam?" Sophie asked.

Finally they decided on Dylan's guess. "Hoover Dam."

High fives all around when they were right.

Enjoying himself, Liam reached for the cards. "My turn to read." He looked at the question and chuckled menacingly. "Oh, *a chuisle mo chroi*, you're never gonna get this."

"Where did all this Irish come from tonight?" Sophie asked, interrupting the game.

"We always fall into it when our guard is down. When we're relaxed." Pat grasped his wife's hand over the table. "With those of our heart."

For a change, Liam's guard *was* down and when Sophie caught his glance, he winked at her. She was of his heart, and it was fun to be in the spirit of things. After a meaningful stare, he picked up a card. "Who was originally named Emanuel Goldberg? I know this."

C.J. rolled her eyes. "Of course you do."

"I'll give you a clue. His first name is Edward."

"What the fuck, what are you doin', Liam?" Pat's tone was outraged.

"Shut up. It's a hard one."

They guessed Eddie Murphy. It was Edward R. Murrow.

When they called it quits at 3 a.m., everyone was mellow from the beer and the good company and a whole lot of fun. Liam was definitely feeling better.

Sophie checked her watch. "I'm out of here."

"You're not goin' home alone." This from Pat, who stood and linked Brie's hand with his. "We've got our car. We'll take you."

"I always go home alone."

"Not this late."

"I'll get a cab."

Dylan glanced at Liam. When he said nothing, Dyl made a disgusted sound. "I'll ride with you, Sophie."

His heart beating faster, Liam watched them. Brie watched him. Pat scowled at him, and C.J. asked, "What's going on here?"

Sophie's face flushed.

"Forget it." Liam grabbed his coat. "I'll see her home."

"You don't—"

"Hush, girl," Pat said. "He does."

THEY DIDN'T TALK in the cab. Liam sat as far away from her as he could get, but he could smell her lotion, as he had all night; he knew now what it would taste like on her skin, how soft that skin would be, and how she would get goose bumps when he touched her. Fuck! When they arrived at her apartment, he said to the cabbie, "Wait here."

"Gonna cost you, buddy."

"You have no idea."

Frustrated from watching C.J. and Aidan, Pat and Brie trade sexual innuendos all night, he climbed out of the backseat and tugged Sophie with him. At the stoop of her building, he stopped. The wee hours of the morning in early November had turned cold, and Liam tucked together the flaps of Sophie's leather jacket so she wouldn't get chilled.

Hesitantly, she looked up at him. In the moonlight, her eyes were liquid with emotion. "I'm sorry. This is awkward." When he didn't say anything, she added, "Again! Damn it."

"It's not that." He put his hands on her arms, rubbed up and down from shoulder to elbow. "I'm tired of this, is all."

"Of me?"

"Well, of wanting you, yeah. But of dancing around life in general. I know we decided we'd do what's best for Mike, and maybe me, too, but Christ, Sophie, it isn't working. I think about you *more* every day." Moving closer, he felt the warmth of her body seep into his. "And dream about you. Sometimes I feel like I'm gonna jump out of my skin if I can't touch you again."

Leaning in, she rested her head on his chest. "Me, too."

His hand cupped the back of her neck, felt the silkiness of her hair. He kissed her crown and felt her shiver. From the cold, or his touch? "Think once more would hurt?"

Muffled laugher. "We're kidding ourselves."

"I know." With his arms tight around her, he put his mouth on her ear. "Tonight, I don't care."

She waited a moment, and he thought he'd lost until she said, "Pay the cab off."

SOPHIE LAY PRONE on her bed, her face buried in a pillow. "Liam, please. *Please.*"

Naked at the other end, he held her foot in his hands. "Please what, *muimin.*" The Irish lilt had come from nowhere. "That means 'darling.' " He increased the pressure on her instep.

"How can the foot be an erogenous zone?"

He kneaded harder. "Is it?"

"You know damn well it is." She sighed and snuggled into the bed. The mattress had been cold when they got in, but now heat blazed from every inch of it. They'd been at this awhile. "I want more."

"You'll get it. Not yet, though." He picked up her other foot and kissed her arch before he began to rub. "Remember, I told you my brothers said I had only one gear . . . second? This is it."

"You were in high gear on Halloween."

"I lost my head."

When he finished with her feet, he kissed the back of her legs all the way up to her knees, where he spent an excruciatingly long time with his tongue. Continuing the path, he had her moaning as he caressed her butt, gave it a pat, and caressed it again. "A little slap and tickle?" he joked.

Where did he learn all this?

He spent time massaging her neck and shoulders. "Knots here, sweetheart. You tense?"

"I am now!"

"All right, if you insist." Instead of turning her to face him, he sidled onto the bed behind her and drew her backside flush against him. She could feel his rock-hard arousal as he pressed against her.

"What—"

"Shh, just enjoy." His hands flirted with her breasts, her abs, and one slipped between her legs where he explored her thoroughly. Her moans turned into deep, tortured groans by the time he got down to serious business; first, he rolled her nipples between his fingers until she was squirming. Then he made her come with his hands. It happened lightning fast. She was still gasping for breath when he whispered in her ear, "There now, that'll take the edge off until . . . later."

"Later?"

"Hmm." He nuzzled her neck.

When she was sane again, she rolled over and faced him. "Your turn, Liam."

With a smug masculine smile, he lazed back into the pillows. "Oh, yeah."

"No mercy for you, either." She took his lead and did the same to him as he'd done to her. It was a hell of a ride.

LIAM SLID INSIDE Sophie as if they'd done this all their lives, not just once in a frantic encounter. His body was taut and humming; hers was practically steaming.

"Oh, God, you're going to kill me."

"Wouldn't think of it, sweetheart." He kissed her nose and began to move. Gently at first.

She smiled up at him with such feeling, his heart clenched in his chest. Tunneling his hands through her hair, he stared at her and increased the pressure, the pace. He took great pleasure in seeing her eyes glaze. He felt his own body flush, tighten, but he made himself wait until her spasms began.

"Oh, Liam . . . oh, oh, my God . . ."

She was beautiful as she came on one long moan, accompanied by *yes*es, and *hmmm*, and *there, oh, there* . . .

When she was done, really done this time, he let himself go. His world lit up behind his closed eyes, and the light, the warmth, the fullness was mind-numbing. One last thrust and he burst inside her to a cacophony of sounds and light and sweetness.

They lay together in the darkened bedroom, illuminated by the moon coming in through the slats of her blinds. The air felt cold again, and Sophie cuddled into him, his scent filling her head, the feel of his muscles engulfing her. He pulled the covers up around them.

When she could breathe normally, she said, "Wow. That was something for a Cub Scout."

"Our motto is to 'do your best.' "

"*That* had to be your best."

"Well, it ranks right up there." He drew her closer. "You had a few tricks up your sleeve, too, lady. Where did you learn to do that thing with your tongue?"

"I'll never tell."

He waited a beat. "I will. So you don't have to ask. I always took secret pleasure in the fact that my brothers assumed I'd be having a boring, stuffy love life."

"Goes to show how much they know."

"Kitty and I were adventurous right from the start, Soph. I don't want to talk about her now, but just know that we learned together, experimented, watched X-rated movies, visited certain websites."

"Good for you." She was surprised that his confession didn't bother her. Of course, she'd been the beneficiary of that experimentation—more than once. And besides, she'd known when she visited his house, saw the quilts, that she'd have to accept his life with Kitty. She did—and she was glad he'd had it. Mostly, she was sorry he'd been hurt so badly.

"What are we gonna do about this?" he asked after a while.

She didn't insult him by pretending innocence. "I don't know. We said twice this wasn't going to happen again, and look at us. But it's not just the sex, Liam. I can't stop thinking about you, wanting to be with you."

He held her so tightly, he seemed to meld into her. "Same for me. I get so angry that I've found someone I could care about . . ."—He kissed her head—". . . do care about, but could even more, and circumstances are such that I can't have you."

"We haven't done a good job of staying apart."

"I know. I don't want to even try anymore."

"Me, either." She kissed his breastbone, ran her hand through his chest hair. "What about Mikey?"

"I've been thinking. Would you go to my therapist with me?"

"Your therapist?"

"Yeah, I see this great guy. We've been working on some depression issues and he's helping me see where my life is going, how I should handle Mikey, that kind of thing. Maybe he could give us some advice."

"Of course I'd go." Though she'd never seen a counselor in her life, at that moment, she knew she'd do just about anything to be with Liam.

They were silent, both lost in this new plan and what effect it would have on their lives.

Finally he said, "In the meantime, we could see each other and just keep it to ourselves. Not hide it, Soph. I'm not asking you to sneak around . . ."

"I know what you mean. And I'm not insulted. I agree, let's be sane about this."

Suddenly, he flipped her to her back and covered her body with his. His weight pressed into her; it felt wonderful. "Okay, but not right now. Let's not be sane now."

Again she laughed out loud. "Well, you did win the trivia game. I guess I'll have to do whatever you say."

"Good to hear, *a ghrá*."

"What does that mean?"

"My love."

Thirteen

Liam stared over at Sophie and his heart swelled in his chest. She wore ordinary jeans, a peach blouse and a vest, but she looked like a supermodel to him. Besotted. That was the word to describe how he felt after just four days of their new arrangement. He'd made a therapy appointment for next week, but in the interim, they'd thrown caution to the wind, played hooky and had actually gone out together today.

Crossing the room and coming up behind her and, as if he had the right—which today, he did—he placed his hands on her shoulders. "What are you looking at?"

They were at the New York City Fire Museum on Spring Street, which wasn't far from the pub. The building itself was a renovated firehouse and had character.

"This is so cool. These old-time fire engines are set up like they're on parade. Can't you just picture them coming down the streets of a nineteenth-century New York City?"

Mostly, in his mind, he could just picture her. Had been able to picture *only* her for days. "Yeah, sure."

He took her hand as they moved from apparatus to apparatus in the fire engine collection. They'd already seen the 9/11 memorial and stood before it silently. He'd sensed a rightful sadness in her, and wondered what it was really like to be a firefighter and lose all those brothers in the Twin Towers.

Off in another room were hand-painted parade hats, speaking trumpets and leather fire buckets. Liam found these most interesting and read the descriptions earnestly.

All the while, they chatted like a normal couple, and that felt good, too. Really good. When they came upon the collection of modern firefighting equipment, he was fascinated by the tools of her trade, especially the Jaws of Life. The brutal-looking spreader with jagged edges on the blade was daunting.

"Have you used these, Soph?"

"A time or two. It depends on what else has to be done. The last call we needed them on was a few weeks ago. Bilotti ripped open the roof of the minivan because I was . . ." Her voice trailed off. She often stopped herself in the middle of a sentence.

Squeezing her neck, he said, "You can tell me, sweetheart."

"You said you don't read or watch the news about our runs."

"Things are different now. You can talk to me about your work. I won't go ballistic."

On the Internet, Liam had discovered that a perennial problem with firefighters and their significant others was how to include the people they loved in their work and not scare the hell out of them. He was determined to handle her stories. If they were to make it together, she had to be able to tell them to him.

"I was in the vehicle trying to get a kid out."

She was inside a car that had to be torn apart. He imagined the engine was compromised, like in the bus accident last week, but didn't ask her about it. "Did you get her out?"

"Yeah. A three-year-old girl."

"Good."

They meandered around the museum, commenting on the various displays until they came upon a section where a tour was just about to start. The guide with a tag that said "Retired FDNY" smiled at them. "Want to come in? We've got room for one more."

"No," Sophie said vehemently.

Startled, Liam looked at her.

"It's a fire simulation. I don't want you to see it."

"I can handle it."

"Liam, I . . ."

He kissed her cheek. "Wait here."

After listening to the introduction, Liam ducked inside with the others. The room was a mock apartment, equipped with lasers, black lights, safe smoke and other devices that illustrated common fire hazards and promoted safe living environments. Though it all fascinated him, the most striking thing was when they started the smoke—it was a white mist, really—Liam couldn't see anything. *Nothing.* Sophie went into buildings like this? Blind? As he made his way through the apartment by holding on to a rope along with the others, his heart began to beat fast, he started sweating and he felt disoriented. Jesus!

She was waiting for him when he stumbled out. He strode over to her and drew her off to the side. Almost reverently, he took her face in his hands. "You have to be one of the most courageous people I've ever met."

"Why?"

"Because you routinely go into those kinds of environments."

"Anybody could do it with enough training."

"I couldn't." He brushed his knuckles down her cheek. "I admire you so much."

"I don't know what to say."

Again, he took her hand. "Let's go look at the gift shop. I want to buy you something."

That something turned out to be an FDNY baby-doll T-shirt. It was pink and lettered with "Real Women Drive Fire Trucks" across the front. She said, "Oh, God, if the guys knew I had this, they'd rag on me bad."

"Don't worry. You're certainly not wearing this skimpy little thing to the station house."

She giggled like a schoolgirl. Down the aisle she found something for him—a pair of boxers. On the butt was scripted, "Find 'em hot, leave 'em wet."

He laughed and took them to pay. At the counter they found a collection of chili. Liam leaned over and whispered, "Let's get a package of this, go back to your place, cook it and eat it in our new undies. Just these and nothing else."

"Sounds good to me."

"The chili?"

"That, too."

"LIAM O'NEIL, if I wasn't married, I'd go after you with all I got." Hannah grinned at Sophie. "Any sane girl would."

"Why, darlin', you made my day." This morning he'd forgone the pub shirt and wore a black long-sleeved thermal top with gray jeans. He looked sleek and sexy. He'd continued to work out and it showed.

The guys chimed in. Cooper asked, "How often do you serve a real Irish breakfast?" The meal consisted of bacon and other pork products, as well as eggs, potatoes and Irish tea Liam had made today.

"Not often." Next to Sophie's chair, he bent over to clear plates. His arm brushed hers and she could feel his heat. "It's bad for your arteries." He winked at Hannah. "I don't eat it much because I have to keep my girlish figure."

"How's the gym working for you?" Murray wanted to know. Sophie's coworker had mentioned he'd seen Liam at Paddock's the other day.

"Lately I'm only getting there twice a week. I need to go more." He threw Sophie a pointed look. "I've been . . . tied up."

The guys talked while Liam finished up and cashed them out. His movements were swift and economical, but Sophie knew he could be slow and smooth. When she handed him a ten, his brows knitted. "You work here, Sophie."

"Not today. I pay my way."

Reluctantly, he took her cash.

As he stacked dishes, the guys talked as if he were one of them. "Another arson last night," a firefighter from another truck company said. "Don Lucas from Squad 28 got hurt."

Almost imperceptibly, Liam stilled. Sophie saw his eyes narrow.

"Any leads on the torch?"

"Tyler?" Murray asked. "You talked to Carusotti?"

"Joe said it's looking more like the guy knows what he's doing."

"Can't believe it would be another firefighter," Jules commented again. He seemed to be having a lot of trouble with that possibility.

"It'll be a shame if it is." The captain blew out a heavy breath. "I hate what that does to morale."

They lapsed into talk about other arson cases, then slowly began to leave. When Mackenzie reached the door, he glanced back at Sophie. "You coming?"

"No, I'm gonna stick around and help Liam finish up."

When he came out of the kitchen with a cloth to mop up the table, Sophie was alone in the pub and staring down at the jukebox. "They all gone?" he asked.

"Uh-huh."

From her peripheral view, she could see him cross to the door and lock it. Bailey's didn't open for lunch until 11:30. He came to the machine and braced his arms on either side of her, effectively imprisoning her from behind. The sensation was more than pleasant as his body, his scent surrounded her. She leaned back into him. "What are you doing?"

"Stealing some time with you." He kissed her neck. "Good morning."

"Good morning."

"Aren't the guys coming in?"

"Nope, Pat has the day off and Dyl called last night and said Hogan had something at school today he'd forgotten about. And Ma and Pa are out shopping."

"So it's just you and me."

"I like the sound of that, Sophie baby."

Moving to the side, his hand slid into his pocket and changed jingled. "Wanna dance?"

"No thanks, I watched you Halloween night. And Dylan told me your mother taught you guys ballroom dancing."

He arched a brow. "You mean I can do something physical better than you?"

"Forget it."

He dropped change into the slot. They still had an old-fashioned jukebox, not a digital one. Some sexy Latin music blasted out. "Liam, I—"

"Hush, I'll teach you the salsa." On the dance floor he set them up facing each other. "Now, here's the routine. You go back in a one-two-three step. Quick, quick, slow." He demonstrated the move. "And I go forward. The man always leads."

"Of course he does."

"Let's try it."

His hands settled at her waist, his touch firm, possessive. "Added benefit." His eyes crinkled at the corners. "I get to hold you in public."

They did the simple step. "Pick your feet up, don't bounce."

She caught on quickly; he went further, showing her another step where they turned to the side. Intent, and completely focused, it took her only about a half hour to get them down.

"This is fun."

"Nah. This is the fun part." Placing his hands on her hips, he ran them up and down. "Hmm. Now move your hips. Swish them. Yeah, that's it." He pulled her close and pressed his lower body into her. She could feel his muscles tighten like they always did when he was around her.

"I do like this."

"A dance for lovers," he whispered in her ear.

"I think I could dance with you all day."

"Maybe some of the day. Then we'd get to the lover part."

AT THE END of the week, Sophie worked the last of her night shift and Liam went over to her place after he'd cooked breakfast at the pub. He brought with him some DVDs. She took one look at them and shook her head. "Let's not watch these."

"I wanna know more about your job."

This wasn't good. She felt it in her gut. When she was married to Ray, they used to watch all the firefighter shows like *Third Watch* and *Rescue Me* and the movies that came out, but he was a paramedic in the business and knew what the job was like. She didn't want to subject Liam to the nitty-gritty.

"*Backdraft* isn't very realistic. They show guys going into burning buildings without face masks, and there're flames in the scenes, but hardly any smoke, which is just plain stupid. A fire doesn't happen that way."

He put in one of the discs, led her to the couch and pulled her down beside him. "Yeah, but there's that scene on the fire truck where William Baldwin makes love to his girl. I wanna see that."

"You're a sex maniac."

"Hey, I'm making up for lost time."

"Fine by me." She reached for the remote.

He stayed her hand. "What happened?"

She looked down at her wrist where there were crisscross burn marks. They'd puckered up and looked like hell. Shit, she'd forgotten. "I took my glove off to test a door. A beam fell nearby and shot burning pieces of wood every place. One caught my wrist."

"Does it hurt?"

"Nah."

His face was pained. "I'm sorry." But he shook whatever he was feeling off and turned to the TV.

They watched all of *Backdraft* and had started *Ladder 49* when Sophie felt her eyes close. The next thing she knew, Liam was picking her up. She nosed into him, felt herself being carried then laid down and covered. He started to draw back.

She grabbed his hand. "Get in with me."

"If I get in, you won't sleep."

"I will. After."

Chuckling, he stripped and slid into the bed with her.

She felt like she was floating in a half-dreamlike state. Everything he did was hazy, all his tender ministrations and even her orgasm was soft and fluid.

She awoke about four, fully refreshed. She had to be to work at the pub by five. Intuitively, she sensed Liam was gone. Rolling over, she found a note on the nightstand. "See you later, Sleeping Beauty."

Grinning, she leapt out of bed, showered, dressed in nice black slacks and the pub T-shirt, took a few minutes to fuss with her hair, and yeah, put on a little makeup. She arrived at the pub forty-five minutes later.

"There she is," Patrick said from behind the bar. As she got closer, his gaze narrowed on her. "You look fantastic. Good day?"

"Hmm, the best."

"You work last night?"

"Yeah, but I got enough rest." She removed her leather coat. "I'll just hang this in the back. Is, um, Liam there?"

"Yep. Mike and Kathleen, my girl, are with him."

Sophie headed for the kitchen and found Liam at the stove. He'd changed his clothes and put on soft jeans and a pub T-shirt over a long-sleeved navy top. The two kids were on either side of him, each standing on chairs, each watching a pot.

"How long does it take to boil, Uncle Liam?" Kathleen asked.

"Not too long. Just remember to stay back so steam doesn't burn your face. It can be as dangerous as hot water."

In a minute, he handed them noodles. "All right, put these in. Be careful you don't splash the water . . . there, that's right . . . good girl, Kathleen. You too, Mike."

When they finished, he carefully helped each kid down from their perches. He was whistling as he turned and looked up.

"Hi, Liam."

"Sophie." His voice was husky.

"Sophie!" Mike raced to her and hugged her around the waist.

"Hey, Mikey."

He drew back and his hand slid down her arm. She jerked when he grasped her wrist. Mike frowned, looking really like an O'Neil. "What happened?"

"I got a little burn."

He stilled.

"Does it hurt?" Kathleen asked.

"Not now."

Mike's brows were knitted when he looked up at her. "Dad just told us how bad burns can be. How they hurt."

"I was talking about boiling water, Mike."

"A fire's gotta hurt, too, Dad."

Sophie squeezed his shoulder. "Uh, yeah, it does."

"I saw the picture of you climbing out of that school bus." He hadn't mentioned that before. "It blew up."

"I was far away when the engine gave."

The back door opened and Aidan came in. Even Sophie could feel the strain in the room. He said, "What's going on?"

"Nothing." Liam shrugged.

"Sophie got hurt, Uncle Aidan."

She held up her arm. "Just a burn."

Nonchalantly, Aidan crossed to Sophie and inspected her wrist. "Ah, that's nothing. Remember when C.J. got hurt saving Rory?"

"Uh-huh."

"That was worse than this and she was okay." He ruffled Mike's hair. "People get hurt. They mend."

"I guess."

"Come on, you two, let's go have a Coke." With a quick glance at his brother, Aidan shuffled the kids out.

Sophie hated the look on Liam's face. "This is what we're dealing with," he said. "Sometimes I forget."

"I know." Thinking about the dreamlike state she was in when she and Liam had made love only hours ago, she added, "Reality sucks!"

JAY YOST SAT on a stuffed chair across from Liam and Sophie, who were next to each other on the couch. "Nice to meet you, Sophie."

"You, too. Liam speaks highly of you."

He nodded.

"Jay won't tell you I talked about you in these sessions, Soph. But I want you to know I have."

She smiled shyly and gave a nervous shrug of her shoulder. He noticed she'd dressed up, too, in a long maroon skirt and white sweater. "Good stuff?"

"Yep."

"So, what can I do for you today?" Jay asked.

"We need some help. It's about Mikey. I know you don't

normally let me talk about him for the whole session, but this is different."

"Shoot."

"Sophie and I are seeing each other. We tried not to, but it didn't work out."

"Is that a bad thing?" the psychologist asked.

"No, it's good. But we haven't gone public with our relationship because of Mike."

Jay gave him a pointed look.

"I know you don't think I should build my life around him, but if we tell him about us, and he gets even closer to Sophie than he is, we're worried about his mental state."

Sophie added, "He got upset when I fell off a ladder in a fire and had a bad reaction to a burn I got the other day." She sighed. "He also saw a school bus blow up behind me—just after I climbed out of it."

"A lot for anybody to take in."

"We need ways to help him cope with the danger of Sophie's job," Liam said. "If we're to keep seeing each other."

"Are you?"

"Are we what?"

"The first question I have to ask would be is this a fling or are you serious about pursuing a relationship? Because if it's a fling, I recommend you leave Mike out of the whole thing."

No response from either of them.

Finally, Liam picked up her hand. He was feeling a little anxiety himself right now. But fuck it, as he'd told her, he was done dancing around life. "It's not a fling for me."

"It isn't for me, either," she answered quickly.

Liam's heart lightened. His grin, when it came, matched hers.

Jay smiled, too. "Well, then, let's get down to business."

Keeping her hand in his, Liam addressed the therapist. "I've been reading about childhood anxiety disorders on the Internet."

"Mike might have that to a degree, but since there's no irrational fear here—Sophie *is* in danger every time she goes to work—he doesn't fit the parameter that a lot of the kids' fears are manufactured. Not real."

Liam frowned.

"But we can apply some of the tenants of dealing with child-hood anxiety to your predicament. The first thing I'd recommend is that you don't put the burden of your relationship on him."

"What do you mean?"

"If he thinks you'll stop seeing each other if he reacts badly, it'll cause him even more anxiety."

Sophie asked, "But how do we work with him if he doesn't know we're worried about him."

"Just tell him you're seeing each other without implying he has a say in it. That it's a fait accompli. Then talk openly with him. Tell him Sophie's in danger—don't hide that. He knows it already and if you cover it up, he'll be confused. Instead, help him express what he's feeling."

Liam nodded. "We can do that."

"Let him express his fears, encourage him to. He can cry. Say he's worried when he is." He took a bead on Liam. "That's something you should think about."

"What do you mean?"

"I imagine you worry about Sophie, too."

"If I do, I can control it."

"Maybe." Jay didn't look convinced. "But don't deny your fears, either."

Sophie squeezed his hand. "You do that sometimes."

"I'll think about it."

"Also, Mike's going to need coping skills to handle his anxiety."

"Like what?"

"Karen Lang can help there, but you can, too. It might be something as simple as having someone else he can talk to about this, besides you two. A place to vent where he doesn't have to worry about you."

"Dr. Lang?"

"Yes, and maybe one of your brothers or your sister-in-law."

"He's close to Brie and C.J."

"Another thing you can do, Sophie, is take him to the fire-house, explain precisely what you do. Tell him what's reasonable fear and what isn't."

"The guys on my group have families. I can ask them how their kids deal. Maybe he could talk to kids of other firefighters."

"Good idea."

"Cara Cahill's father is a policeman," Liam said thoughtfully. "I just found that out."

"That's his little friend?" When Liam nodded, Jay agreed. "He might talk to her. Check with her mother, first." He thought for a minute. "We could also get him into a more formal support group."

"Aidan was in one." Liam explained how the Secret Service had set up a group for spouses of agents after an agent was killed protecting Clay. "And there was an online group he belonged to."

"Maybe *you* should visit that. Like I said, I'm worried about you dismissing your fears."

He wished they wouldn't keep bringing up his feelings. "Let's concentrate on Mike for now."

"All right, today we will. But next session it's all you, buddy."

"Where do we go from here?"

"Let me talk to Karen. I'll tell her what we brainstormed, and see what she has to say. Meanwhile, take the first step. Let Mike know you two are dating. Be casual about it. Will he be glad?"

Liam smiled over at Sophie. "How can he not be? He cares about her, too."

When they left the office and walked outside, the wind blew and the air was cold, so Liam drew Sophie off the street under an overhang. He cupped her face with his hands. "Some big admissions in there, woman."

The expression in her eyes was warm and loving. She smiled broadly. "I meant everything I said, Liam."

"I did, too."

"So, onto the next phase I guess. Telling people."

"My brothers are gonna have a field day."

"Will they be happy?"

"Yep."

"Are you?"

"You betcha, baby." He grabbed her hand. "Let's take the next step."

FOURTEEN

BILOTTI AND SOPHIE were checking the ladders on the rig when he stopped and stared at her. His dark eyes narrowed. "What's with the smiles, Tyler? We're on fifteen hours. It's cold as a bitch tonight. Don't seem like much to be happy about."

"Not all of us are sourpusses like you."

He grunted. "You must be getting some."

She laughed. "Which means *you* aren't?"

"That'll be the day." Though Bilotti was divorced, he was big and very male and had plenty of female company. "The TV thing's on tonight." He tested a rung on the ladder. "I hate shows about the department. They always manage to make us look bad."

"Rachel Scott seemed okay, but you can't trust the media." She watched him. "Tony, we're square, right? I mean you had a tough time when I came to the group and now all this shit with Scott going on . . ."

"We're square. Don't let that broad go plantin' ideas in your head."

Jules appeared in the bay. "Chow's on."

"What'd he cook, probie?" Bilotti asked, putting away the last of the ladders.

"Some kind of fish."

"I hate fish."

Sophie sniffed. "It smells good."

"It's still fish."

At dinner, the subject of the TV broadcast came up again. Eleven of them gathered around the table because they ate with the engine's crew and often Chief Marconi joined them.

"So, Tyler, what'd you say about us?" Murray asked.

"That you're Neanderthals, but I love you anyway."

After some talk of the show, the chief leaned back in his seat and his eyes sparkled. Sophie groaned, knowing what was coming. Good thing she was prepared.

Marconi said, "Good dinner. Which reminds me . . . how do you know that the female firefighter cooked dinner?"

"Don't know, Chief." Murray loved when people picked on her. "How?"

"The smoke alarm goes off."

"Hmm." Sophie pretended to think. "How many chiefs does it take to change a lightbulb?"

None of the guys responded.

"Chickenshits," she said under her breath. "It takes one. He holds the bulb up to the socket and the world revolves around him."

That set them off on all kinds of firefighter humor, much of it black, until they finished dinner. Then they got a call for a kitchen fire. When they arrived, it was a false alarm, and they were back in the firehouse by nine in time for the beginning of *Timeline, USA*.

Rachel Scott appeared on the screen wearing a dark suit and a peach silk blouse. Her hair was full and styled, and her makeup perfect. She arched delicate brows. "Women in the fire department? Today, it's a fact of life. Laws and social pressure have forced fire departments across the nation to join the twenty-first century. The numbers are low—there are only three hundred fifty female firefighters, or firefems as they were once called, in the country. The typical fire department is a culture that prides itself on machismo and an old-boy's-club atmosphere. This, however, is about New York City and the FDNY. The last bastion of *firemen* who went kicking and screaming into integration of many sorts."

A shot of a firehouse came on. Engine 46. It was a standard, two-story building, brick front. The camera went inside to find the crew in the kitchen, eating dinner. The lens focused on Hannah Harper. She looked tough and savvy in her fire department blues and was joking with the guys.

The voice over continued, "Though this is a common occurrence today in an FDNY house, when the first woman, Brenda Berkman, forced her way into the department you wouldn't have seen this kind of camaraderie because the male firefighters wouldn't buy her food"—the camera panned to a full meal set on a table—"fix her dinner or let her eat with them."

The next shot was of Sophie, entering Company 14. She was wearing a blue shiny jacket with FDNY on the back and was carrying a backpack. She smiled at the camera, but it was forced.

"You look good, Tyler," Cooper said. "A little heavy maybe . . ."

"Back at ya. You're getting that paunch again."

The camera followed Sophie into the kitchen, where the guys greeted her without fuss.

"This is another scene that wouldn't have been the same back in the day. When Berkman walked into a firehouse for the first time, she was met by a group of wives of firefighters who were protesting the entrance of women into the department." A newspaper clipping of the event came on screen. A slew of women were gathered outside of a firehouse with placards that read, "Not with our husbands."

Then there was a clip of Rochelle "Rocki" Jones, who was now a very good battalion chief, explaining that on her first day, she was met at the door by a male firefighter who told her he didn't want her there.

The next cut showed Yvette Trudeau climbing a rope at the academy. Scott's voice-over continued. "One of the biggest fears of the men in the department was whether woman had the physical ability to do the job."

Then live footage of the Concord Hotel fire appeared on-screen, showing Sophie descending the ladder with the giant of a guy.

The camera was still on her when they fell.

"Do they really have the physical capability to be firefighters?" Rachel Scott asked.

"Fuck," Sophie said.

"Goddamn it." This from Jules. "She shouldn't get away with that."

Other more colorful expletives from the guys followed.

When Scott appeared again, she was the picture of innocence. "Let's take a look at the history of women coming into the department."

On screen came a shot of the FDNY's training academy.

"Women candidates who passed the written exam were given a physical test here at the academy, called the Rock. All ninety failed."

"Damn it, that test was rigged," Sophie said. "I told her that people testified it was the hardest test ever given. When men were offered the chance to take it, to prove it wasn't too hard, they wouldn't risk it."

"Calm down, Sophie," Mackenzie said. "Maybe it gets better."

But the litany continued. A picture of Brenda Berkman came on. "In 1979 Brenda Berkman, a law student, brought a class action suit against the city of New York, forcing the city to reevaluate its test. Many said the resulting test given in 1982 was 'soft,' which in department vernacular means easy."

Lance Callahan's ugly mug came on. "I think women are a liability in the department. They can't keep up physically. I always said I wouldn't want one at my back. It's why me and another guy transferred out of the house when a woman came on board."

More rounds of swearing. Sophie got up and stood behind the group, too angry to sit anymore.

Then Mackenzie appeared on screen. "Of course women can do the job. In some ways better. They use up their air slower. They can get in tighter spaces. And their endurance and stamina can beat out ours."

Bilotti growled, "I don't know about that."

The cap shrugged. "My opinion."

Scott looked out at the camera, her expression puzzled. "But they don't have the upper body strength of men, do they? For instance, could Firefighter Tyler carry you out of a building?"

A cut to the ladder scene again and of them toppling to the ground.

"Nobody gets carried out of a building if we can help it, Ms. Scott. Victims are dragged. It's dangerous to the firefighter and the victim to carry them."

"But victims do get carried down ladders."

Cut away from Mackenzie.

He slapped his hand on the table. "Fuck it, I answered her damn question, then I told her that Sophie had dragged out some of our own men. That the incident at the Concord could happen to any of us."

Scott's face came on screen again, but she was alone. "Despite the protests, in October of 1982, women graduated from the academy. But their entrance, as already indicated, wasn't a cakewalk. Women reported the following: slammed doors in their faces, firecrackers under their beds, colleagues who wouldn't trade shifts with them, car tires were slashed, pornographic material displayed everywhere." She peered out the camera, her expression hard. "However, the worst occurrences were getting beat up at a company picnic, having their air bled out of their tanks only to go undiscovered until right before a fire, and rape and sexual assault."

Another newspaper clipping came on screen and showed the legal ramifications of the latter. Berkman had been assaulted by a doctor. After pressure from the ranks, the then-mayor had to fire the doctor. "No other legal action was taken, which this reporter finds unconscionable."

"At least she got that right," Sophie grumbled.

"In any case, the pressure continued. Much like the nineteenth-century fights for civil rights, when abolitionists and suffragettes banded together, so did the Vulcan Society and the females."

A black firefighter came on screen. "It's abominable. Out

of nearly twelve thousand firefighters, there are only three hundred and thirty African Americans."

Scott asked, "Why are there so few?"

"It's called a hostile atmosphere. Some people—African Americans and women—don't apply because they're not wanted."

Scott alone again. "Still, women persevered and even rose in the ranks of the FDNY. Now, there are women battalion chiefs, captains, lieutenants.

"But it isn't all warm and fuzzy. Like Berkman took flak from her female coworkers, so it goes today."

Another flash to Trudeau. "In my opinion, Tyler should have been able to carry the guy down."

Utter silence in the firehouse.

Then the alarm bell rang.

THE O'NEIL FAMILY gathered around the pub's TV but there was none of the usual joking among them.

"I can't believe Scott's pulling something like this again." C.J. sipped a beer. "It's amazing how she can slant things."

Dylan's scowl was fierce. "Clay's gonna be pissed when he hears she criticized little Tyler's namesake."

Liam said, "She's on again."

This part of the program started off all right. The camera focused on Sophie, who looked great in her firefighter uniform with a sparkle in those gray eyes. Scott briefly questioned her on her experience with Bailey. Then cut to a shot of the pub. In an voice-over, she said, "This is where Firefighter Tyler works part time. She says many firefighters have second jobs because they can't make ends meet. When asked about the average salary being $90,000, she admitted . . .

Cut to Sophie. "That's a nice chunk of change." Then she said, "You do the math."

Dylan swore. "That was taken out of context. You can tell from the hesitation. Goddamn it, I wished I'd listened to the tape she made."

His mother touched Dylan's arm. "Son, don't take the name of God in vain."

"Sorry, Mama, but geez . . ."

"So how are you treated today, Sophie, in comparison to the early eighties?"

"We had a tough time getting in. Some of the guys are still in the dark ages. Nothing you can do about backward men."

"What about your group?"

"My group . . . well . . . some guys are Neanderthals." The camera cut her off.

"Oh, God, she can't have said just that, left that implication," Liam put in.

"It was spliced," Dylan told them.

Scott asked about the guy she dropped.

"Look, I fell carrying a man who weighed twice what you do. Nobody, male or female could have prevented that."

"Are you taking heat for it?"

"Not to my face."

Scott turned back to the camera. "And such a pretty face it is. This is Rachel Scott from WNYC News."

"That's it?" Pat asked.

"Shit." Liam was furious. "I know she told the whole story about her connection with the fire department. Where's that?"

"You should call her, Liam." This from Brie. "She must be pissed."

Fishing out his cell, Liam punched in her number.

"This is Sophie Tyler. Leave a message."

He hung up. "She's not there. She's working tonight and they probably got a run."

"Then she didn't see this." Dylan got up, crossed to the TV and took out the DVD he'd taped the show on. "Here, Liam. Take it over."

Liam was already shrugging into his jacket. "I'm on my way."

He got to Company 14 just as the trucks were pulling in from a run. It was eleven at night and cold. He waited until the rigs were inside the bay and the crew tumbled out.

Every single one of them had drooping shoulders, blackened faces, and heavy steps. They'd had a fire, a bad one, he guessed. Liam hated to lay this on them, but they needed to know what had happened: while they were out risking their lives and saving people, Rachel Scott was slandering their ranks.

Despite the gravity of the situation, he took pleasure watching Sophie take off her suspenders and bulky pants and boots. She yanked the tie out of her hair and shook it back. There was grumbling, until one of the guys—Murray—looked out of the bay.

Liam strode up to the building.

"Hey, there's our favorite chef. Come to cook for us?"

"I will if you want. Meanwhile, I got something to show you." He held up the DVD. "It's Rachel Scott's show. I imagine you didn't see it."

Sophie came forward. "We got a call right in the middle of the history part." Up close, he could see her eyes were bloodshot and she was squinting. She had a headache from the carbon monoxide. He knew it happened to firefighters in most fires. "Is the rest of it bad?"

"Yeah, Soph, it's bad."

DYLAN APPROACHED the TV station at 12:30 a.m. The wind whipped around him and he turned up the collar of his bomber jacket. Rachel Scott had been the live anchor tonight, so he knew she'd be here. He was breathing fire and ready to spit it at her. He waited by the building, and when she came out the door approached a nearby town car, he stopped her with his words. "So, you found new blood."

Startled, she slapped a hand over her chest. Slowly she turned and saw him in the shadows. "You scared me half to death."

Her driver had gotten out of the car and come up to her. "Is everything all right, Ms. Scott?"

"Call off your dog. I want to talk to you."

"It's very late. And I'm tired."

"I'm Clay Wainwright's brother-in-law." He knew the trump card would work.

She said to the driver, "Give us a minute, Sam. Go inside

and get some coffee." Nodding regally to Dylan, she crossed to the car, opened the door before he could get it for her and slid inside. He followed.

The interior was plush and full of leather. As a connoisseur of good clothes, he noted that her coat was a camel-colored cashmere. "Nice, if you can manage it."

"I can." She lifted her chin. "I imagine this is about the *Timeline* broadcast."

"You got it, lady."

"I thought it was all right." He noticed her fiddling with the strap of her purse.

"You gotta be joking. It was the most biased, inaccurate, glaringly edited show I've ever seen."

"Well, the edits did give it a different slant."

His newsman's sixth sense kicked in. "What does that mean?"

"Oh, come on Mr. O'Neil. You know that in broadcasts— and movies and songs I might add—edits can make or break a show."

"I'd say it broke yours."

Her shoulders stiffened. "It most certainly did not."

"Loyalty is good, Ms. Scott, but it's going to bury you this time."

"What do you mean?"

"I mean, my family's had it with you."

"Your family?"

"You don't get it, do you? Then listen up. Sophie works at the pub."

"She's an employee, I know."

"She's more than that. She's one of ours now, especially since she helped deliver Bailey's son. You just crossed another line and you aren't going to like what you find on the other side."

"I have a meeting with the vice president when he's in town next. We're going to clear up the thing about last summer."

"Don't bet on it. Once Clay sees your little show, he'll be angrier than ever."

She reached out. "Please, Dylan, don't let that happen. This . . . wasn't my fault."

"Same old, same old. Not only won't I help you, I'm going after you myself."

"In your little column?"

Again he laughed. This woman was a piece of work. "My little column, as you call it, has a lot of clout. So watch out, babe." He moved to the door, opened it and climbed out.

She didn't say anything more and neither did he. Yet!

SOPHIE TURNED off the recorder. Thank God Dylan had recommended she tape the interview with Scott. After they'd seen the rest of the show, she'd sworn it was edited to make her look bad and played the original interview for her group.

"Can she be sued?" Mackenzie nodded to the TV. "The taped interview and the TV show told a totally different story."

Jules's face was red with anger. "She should be more than sued."

"I don't think I can go after her." Sophie ran a hand through her hair. "I *did* say those things."

"Out of context," Liam put in. "Dylan'll know if you have recourse."

"It doesn't matter. I'm so buried. The guys in the department will crucify me."

Liam gave her hand a quick squeeze and let go. "Maybe not."

"We gotta be able to do something." Bilotti pointed to the tape recorder. "Can we make this public?"

"We might be able to do that," Mackenzie said. "HR will get in on it, but we need legal advice."

Cooper, who'd once been president of the FDNY's union, said, "We'll call the UFA in the morning, get advice from them."

"Meanwhile," Murray said, "we gotta do some salvage and overhaul." The aftermath and cleaning up after a fire. "If it's possible."

"I can't believe this. Damn it, I told Marconi I didn't want to do the fucking thing."

Liam glanced at the clock. "How about some breakfast? I can make it quick."

All agreed. Sophie suspected he was giving her some alone time with the guys. When he went to the kitchen, she faced her crew. "I don't know what to say."

Murray stood, joined Sophie and slid an arm around her shoulders. "We'll figure it out."

"Yeah, sure."

They batted around some ideas until the food was ready. Then when Liam called them, they went into the kitchen, sat down and began to eat.

Just as dispatch came over the PA. "Report of a ten-seventy-five, Box number 98. Engine 33 and Ladder 44 go into service."

"What's a 10-75?" Liam asked as they bounded up from the table.

"A working fire." Sophie waited until the guys were out. Then she bent over and kissed his cheek. "I'm sorry about breakfast, Liam."

He said, "Go. Call me later."

Instead, for some reason, she reached in her pocket and took out her house key. "Go there? After the kids get off to school?"

"You're on."

In minutes they were in the rig. Her mind was reeling from the events of the night. When she forced herself to stop thinking about Scott's broadcast, she wondered about Liam. How had he taken to seeing the reality of her life?

FROM THE BATHROOM, Liam heard Sophie enter her apartment. Then she called out his name.

"In here."

She appeared in the doorway. Fatigue etched itself on every feature in her face. Veins showed in her fair skin and she was squinting again. "What are you doing?"

He held up a bottle. "I found this. Temptress?" he teased about the name of the lotion and bath salts she used.

"Oops."

"It smells great. Like you do." He pointed to a pillow on the side of the tub. "I guessed you like baths?"

"My weakness." She closed her eyes and leaned against the doorjamb. The scent filled the air, blocking the smell of smoke still in her hair. "Every muscle in my body aches."

"Bad fire?"

"Yeah, pieces of a ceiling fell on me."

A slight hesitation. "Then, you need to soak."

"I do." She crossed to him and gave him a quick kiss on the mouth. The smell of smoke still lingered on her. "It means a lot, your being here. What about breakfast at the pub?"

"I cooked it before I came over. Dylan can serve it."

"You've been up all night?"

"I caught a few hours of sleep." He went for the buttons on her blue uniform shirt. "Let's get you out of these."

"I like the sound of that."

"No funny stuff, lady. You need a bath, food and sleep." He whispered in her ear, "Besides, I like my women conscious during sex." He removed the shirt, exposing a serviceable black sports bra. "It'll all work out, sweetheart."

"I know." She turned to the mirror.

"Good Lord."

She frowned at him in the glass. "What?"

"Your back."

Pivoting, she pulled out the medicine cabinet mirror. Her upper torso was a series of black and blue marks. "Oh, damn. I knew it hurt."

"Should you see a doctor?"

"No, this has happened before."

"How often?"

"Um, I don't know. A time or two." She angled around so he couldn't see the bruises.

Too late, Liam knew. He'd never forget the sight of her battle scars.

Her face was pained, and so he kept his feelings to himself. "Go ahead, finish undressing and get in." He dipped his hand in the water, feeling the silkiness of the water. "It's ready."

"Thanks."

He knew she didn't mean for the bath. "I'm okay, Soph."

"Sure, me, too."

He left the bathroom and found his way to the kitchen.

Opening her fridge, he stared blindly at the contents. Last week she'd said reality sucked; tonight the *reality* of her job was all over her back.

He said a quick prayer that he could handle the battered and bruised woman he'd left to take a bath. For a few seconds in the bathroom just now, he hadn't been sure he was man enough to do it.

FIFTEEN

THE FOLLOWING WEEK, Sophie took the subway to Liam's house to have dinner with him and the boys; they were planning to tell Cleary and Mike they were dating. As she listened to the chug-chug-chug of the train, she felt the effects of the rough week she'd had. The TV broadcast fallout had been exhausting to deal with.

First, Sophie had taken it on the chin from a lot of the guys in the department, the ones who hadn't heard the original tape of the show.

"So we're Neanderthals," Lance Callahan had snarled on a fire her truck had caught with his engine. "I should have said more nasty stuff."

"You did just fine in that regard, Callahan."

"So did you, *Sophie baby*."

Other guys gave her dirty looks, and some made outright comments, too. Her own group tried to stifle the outbreak of bad feelings, but then they started getting razzed and called pussy-whipped, so Sophie told them to stop defending her. She'd meant it to protect them, but her words came out wrong and Bilotti, under pressure, had told her to fuck off.

After hearing the original tape, the brass took the interview in stride, saying the whole thing would blow over. Of course, she'd reminded them she didn't want to do the interview in the first place, so there wasn't much they could blame on her. Many of the female officers had contacted her to give support. And to be fair, a lot of guys, like Dom Caruso and his group, which included Hannah, offered support, too. The union was still looking into legal recourse for her.

As she got off the train and headed to Liam's in the crisp November night, she buttoned up her jacket against the cold and thought of the calls she'd received from the O'Neil women.

From Bailey: "Honestly, that woman! Clay's furious, and I'm thinking of having a talk with Rachel Scott myself. Now that I'm not feeling so vulnerable with pregnancy, I'm up for a fight. Tyler sends his love, by the way."

From C.J.: "Screw her, Sophie. She's made it on her looks and we did it on guts and brains. She's just jealous. Do you play racquetball? I need a worthy opponent."

From Brie: "I'm so sorry, Sophie. I hope this doesn't affect you and Liam. He told me you two were dating. Want to have lunch sometime?"

But the biggest shock came from Mary Kate O'Neil: "I remember those days here in the city. For the life of me, I couldn't figure out why women wanted to work at a firehouse. But fair's fair and I thought they should have a shot if they wanted one. That Scott person did you wrong, just like Bailey, and we O'Neils hold grudges."

With all that support, Sophie thought as she reached her stop and walked the short distance to Liam's house, she did feel better. On the front stoop, before she could ring the bell, the door to the other side of the duplex opened. And out walked Dylan.

"Hey, Sophie, just the girl I want to see." He nodded to Liam's side of the duplex. "Did he tell you I was moving in?"

"He mentioned you might."

"I did." He grinned and held up the cell phone he carried. "I just got good news. This is the kind *you'll* want."

"I could use some."

"I'll tell you and my brother together."

Without knocking, Dylan opened the door to Liam's house. For a minute, Sophie longed for her own brother to live nearby, and for her to be able to walk in his house unannounced. She missed having that kind of closeness with Nate.

They found Liam in the kitchen, wearing a cute apron that said, "Irish men rock!" He looked up. "Hey, Dyl." Then he saw Sophie and his face lit up like fireworks. Sophie's whole world shifted at his uncensored delight in seeing her. "Hi, there."

"I found her on the porch."

Liam scowled at his brother. "You're not staying for dinner."

Dylan laughed. "Wouldn't dream of it. I wanted to share my news."

Crossing the room, Liam kissed Sophie on the cheek.

Dylan watched them. "Am I missing something here?"

"Yep, but we'll tell you tomorrow. What's your news?"

"I want to print the entire transcript of Sophie's interview with Rachel Scott as my column next week."

Sophie was shocked.

Liam said, "Why didn't I think of that?"

"Because you're not as smart as me. My editor's all for it."

"Don't you usually take a point of view?" Sophie asked. "Or will you write something about Scott's journalism, too?"

"I will. Later. But I think the transcript will stand better on its own. I've got Hank Sellers on board to publicize it in the *Voice*, and some other colleagues are gonna give it a nod." He snatched a carrot out of the salad Liam had fixed. "And I think we should send it to every firehouse in the city."

Sophie felt her eyes tear. "Oh, Dylan." She threw herself at him and hugged him tight.

He held on to her. "Well, now, darlin', I like your kind of payback."

From behind her, when Liam spoke, his voice was raw. "Thanks, Dyl."

"You're welcome."

Sophie drew away and Liam grabbed her around the waist. "I'm glad for you, Soph."

"My cue to leave." He studied Sophie. "You don't happen to have any sisters, do you?"

"Nope, sorry."

"And you can't have her." Liam drew Sophie even closer. "She's mine."

"So I see." He winked at them. *"Go mbeannai Dia duit."*

"What does that mean?" Sophie asked Liam as his brother left.

"He gave us his blessing."

MIKE ENTERED the house and got a whiff of his dad's pizza. He liked all the food his father cooked, but pizza was his favorite, especially when his dad put a lot of cheese and sausage on it. He knew Sophie was coming to dinner and bet she'd like it, too. He wished Cleary had a ballgame or something tonight. He'd been a jerk lately and Mike tried to stay out of his way.

His dad and Sophie were in the kitchen. She looked pretty in a pink sweater. Her hair was all fluffy. And she was smiling. So was his dad. They made Mike smile. "Hi," he said.

"Hey there, buddy." His dad crossed to him and hugged him. He took Mike's backpack and jacket and put them away while Mike hugged Sophie.

His dad got him a glass of juice. They were drinking beer. "Did you have a good time at Cara's?"

"Uh-huh. Her dad works funny hours like you and he was home. He played video games with us, and showed us how to draw with a new computer program."

"Sounds like fun."

"Do you like her dad?" Sophie asked.

"Yeah. He's a cop." He smiled at Sophie. "I like firefighters better, but he's cool."

She ruffled his hair. His mom used to do that, too. "Thanks." Mike climbed up on a stool at the center bar.

"School good?" his dad asked.

"It was okay. Will you read to me later?" he asked Sophie.

"I'd love to."

The front door slammed again. Oh, heck, Cleary was home already.

His brother came into the kitchen in his gym clothes. His hair was sweaty and his face red so you could see some of his freckles.

"Hey, son."

"Hi, Dad." He eyed Sophie. "Hi."

"Hello, Cleary."

"Didn't have time to change after basketball practice?" their dad asked.

"Nope." He dropped his coat on a chair and tossed his gym bag there, went to the fridge and got a can of soda. His dad didn't say anything, even though they weren't supposed to drink pop before dinner and Cleary had been reminded a thousand times to put his stuff away.

"When we eatin'?" Cleary asked.

"It's almost ready. You can join us after you put your things away and clean up."

"I'll take a shower later."

"Sorry. We have a guest, and in any case, I'd rather you didn't smell like a locker room at the table."

Cleary mumbled under his breath. His dad was cool about it, like he always was with Cleary, but Sophie got a funny look on her face. She didn't say anything, though.

When Cleary left, his dad shook his head. "Thirteen going on thirty. My favorite age."

Sophie looked at him. All soft-like. And goofy.

They ate fifteen minutes later. Cleary didn't say much at dinner—he was probably still mad at Dad—but Sophie talked to him and Mike and his father smiled the whole time.

Like he used to smile when their mom was alive and they all ate together.

When dinner was over, Cleary pushed back his chair so it made a loud scrape on the floor. "I got homework."

His dad frowned. "When did we stop excusing ourselves?"

Cleary clucked his tongue. "May I be excused?"

"No. Sophie and I want to talk to you guys."

"About what?" Cleary's tone wasn't nice.

His father leaned back but he didn't look relaxed. "We wanted to tell you that we're going to be dating from now on."

Mike liked the sound of that.

Cleary shrugged. "You dated before, Dad."

"I know. This is a bit more serious."

"No shit?"

Uh-oh.

"Cleary!"

His brother blushed. "Sorry."

"And yes, it is more serious." He turned to Mike. "We wanted to tell you both to expect her to be around, but also to say that if you get worried about her working at the firehouse, you can talk to us about your fears."

"I'm down with it," Cleary said. Down meant okay, Mikey knew.

Mike said, "Me, too, Dad."

Sophie zeroed in on him. "Did you hear what your father said about worrying, Mike?"

He didn't want to think about that. "Uh-huh."

"You can talk to us about anything, guys, you know," his dad put in.

"Anything?" Cleary asked.

"Yes."

"She gonna stay overnight here with you?"

"I think that's inappropriate to ask, son."

"You said I could ask anything."

"That's all right, Liam, I'll answer his question. I won't be spending the night, Cleary. But I hope to be around a lot."

His dad stood. "Come on, Cleary, you and I are going upstairs for a talk." He looked at Sophie. "Could you and Mike clean up?"

"Sure."

Cleary didn't look happy. Mike was glad he wasn't in his brother's shoes right now. His dad was cool, but when he got mad, Mike got scared.

And right now, he looked plenty mad.

LIAM HADN'T EXPECTED this. He must have been too worried about Mikey to consider Cleary's reaction to the news that he and Sophie would be dating. Jesus, sometimes he just couldn't keep up with two kids and his own life. He turned the chair at Cleary's desk around and lowered himself into it while his son flopped on the bed. "What's going on?"

"Nothin'."

"Why are you acting so surly?"

"Hey, Pop, I'm a teenager."

"Don't be a wise guy."

"What do you want me to say?"

Liam thought a minute. "Tell me what you're feeling these days."

Picking up a baseball from his nightstand, Cleary threw it up in the air and caught it when it came down. "I'm dope. Things are mag at school."

"That's not what I mean."

"Look, I got homework."

Liam stood and on Cleary's second toss, grabbed the ball midair. Then he sat down on the side of the bed. "Cleary, this is me you're talking to. I used to be your best friend."

For a minute his son's face got so sad it startled Liam. "Not since Mom died."

"Excuse me?"

"It's not like it used to be, Dad. You're always worried about Mike, and now you got a girlfriend."

"And I don't pay enough attention to you?"

"That's stupid, I'm not a baby."

"What are you saying?"

Cleary looked away, then began to pick at the quilt Kitty had made for him. "I dunno. I just feel funny sometimes. And it makes me wanna do bad stuff."

"Why?"

"Things are jumbled up inside me."

"Cleary, if you wanna talk about anything to me, I'm here."

"You already told me about the birds and the bees."

Ah, so that was it. He should have caught on sooner. When he and his brothers were teenagers, sex was always on their minds, but they'd had each other to talk to. "Yeah, well, there's got to be some confusing things going on inside you now."

"Maybe. I dunno."

"Is that why you asked if Sophie would be staying overnight here?"

"Sort of." He took a long look at Liam. "Will you be staying at her house?"

Gently, he put a hand on Cleary's shoulder. "If you're asking me if I'm going to have sex with Sophie, that's a private matter right now. I'm not comfortable sharing that with you."

"You want me to share stuff like that with you."

"I know. I'm your dad. I can guide you. But my relationship with Sophie is too new to talk about." He studied his son. "If this was about your mother and me, I'd share more, son."

Cleary gulped, a kid again, a nice kid who must miss his mom, miss seeing his parents together and knowing that the whole world of sex was going to work out somehow.

"Let's do some things by ourselves again. You're right, I don't spend enough alone time with you."

"Whatever."

He stood. "And take it easy on Sophie." He kissed Cleary on the head.

"Okay." Liam reached the doorway and heard Cleary called out, "Dad?"

"Hmm?"

"Soon. Let's do something together soon."

Liam smiled all the way downstairs.

"AND THEN TOMMY saw the water tower."

"I like the water tower parts."

Sophie held the Hardy Boys book in one hand and cuddled Mike close to her side with the other arm. "Me, too." She read the rest of the chapter with a new and beautiful feeling inside her. "That's it, buddy. Your dad said nine, and it's past that."

"'Kay." He laid his head on her shoulder and yawned. His eyes had been drooping for the last five minutes. "I'm glad you're gonna be here more, Sophie."

She kissed his head. "Me, too." Easing away, she knocked

a pillow on the floor. Along with it went a flashlight, which she picked up. "What's this?" she asked, her tone teasing. "Do you read after the lights are off?"

His eyes widened.

"Mike, what's wrong?"

He glanced down at the bed. She tracked his gaze and saw there was a photo on top of the sheet—one of him and his mother. Sophie cleared her throat. "Honey, do you look at this picture when the lights are off?"

"Sort of."

"What do you mean?"

"I . . . talk to Mom." He whispered, "Don't tell anybody."

"Oh, Mike, it's okay that you do that."

"Cleary would dump on me. And Dad would feel bad."

"You know, I talked to my mom for years after she died. Every night when I prayed." She looked down. "May I?"

He nodded.

With reverence, she picked up the picture and smiled at it. "Hello, Kitty."

Mike scooted closer. "She says hello back." He added, "Wanna ask her something?"

"Do you want me to?"

"Maybe."

"I'd like to." There was a lump in her throat. "I know all about you, Kitty. How much your boys and Liam loved you. I'm glad." She peeked at Mike then focused back on the picture. "I . . . I was wondering if you'd think it's okay that Liam and I date."

Quiet. Then Mike whispered, "She says it's okay. She says you make Dad smile again."

"Whew! I was worried about that."

Mike yawned and slid down on the bed and closed his eyes. " 'Night, Sophie."

"Good night, Mike."

She stayed where she was until his breathing evened out. Before she left the bed, she looked down again at the picture she still held in her hand. Kitty O'Neil was delicate and ethereal and very much the perfect wife for Liam. She traced the woman's face. "Oh, Kitty, how can I compare to you? Do you really think I'm good enough for him?"

Kitty didn't answer this time. Sophie wished like hell she would.

IN THE HALL just outside of Mikey's room, Liam felt his eyes moisten. He swallowed hard and backed away. He didn't know about Mike and the picture of Kitty. He didn't know his son talked to his dead wife every night. And in his heart, he didn't know how he felt about that.

But seeing Sophie talk to Kitty's picture, seeing Sophie ask her permission and voice her fears to his wife clarified one thing for Liam. He was pretty sure he was falling in love with Sophie Tyler.

The glow of that realization lasted until midnight when Liam woke to a scream. He rushed into Mikey's room to find his son sitting up in the bed shouting, "No, Mommy, no, don't go into the fire."

SIXTEEN

CARRYING FORTY POUNDS of gear and axes each, all of Sophie's group was breathing hard when they reached the roof of the eight-story building on Sixth Avenue. A loft on the seventh floor had caught fire, and the blaze had spread faster than normal. Four alarms were called in. The engine groups were slapping water on the Red Devil, and thick black smoke billowed from the seventh- and eight-floor windows. Despite the fact that they were sweating, the wind swirled around them on the roof, making the November air up here even colder.

Ladder 45's men had followed Sophie's group up, and Bilotti, who was the lieutenant in charge on the roof, yelled to them, "Give me some ventilation, guys." Then he spoke into the radio to Mackenzie who was helping to coordinate efforts on the fire ground. "We're here, Cap."

"There's a woman on the fifth floor in the southwest exposure. Your side of building. She's at the window, waving her hands, shouting. She's ours." A pause. "Christ, she just crawled out on the ledge. Talk to me, Ladder 44."

"We're on it, Cap." Bilotti faced his group. "Cooper, get the rope. Start tying up. Tyler, take off your air pack."

"Yes, sir." Sophie disposed of her SCBA and came to the ledge. The wind blew harder out here, tugging a few stray hairs loose, despite the helmet she wore.

"You're goin' over."

She knew the drill: she'd rappel down the side of the building past the burning floors, get the victim hooked up to the rope and bring her into a lower floor where other firefighters would be waiting to pull them both inside. Briefly, Sophie remembered the first time she'd taken the lead on rappelling. Bilotti himself had been a regular firefighter and had grumbled to the officer in charge that a *girl* shouldn't go over. But the cap had bitched him out and sent Sophie, who was more trained, if not more experienced, down the side of the building. She'd executed the maneuver flawlessly. Must be Bilotti remembered, because he didn't even blink this time when he called for her.

The guys held the harness and Sophie stepped into it; Torres secured the clip. "Make your side tighter, probie."

"Anchor that flap lower on her hips," Bilotti put in.

When she was strapped up tight, he pulled at the contraption. "Good?" She nodded. He checked her radio then grasped her shoulders. "Take it slow, even though it's cold. Account for the wind. You'll get there." He glanced at the sky. "Snow's holding off, so at least it won't be slippery. Try to keep the victim calm and don't let her jump out at you."

"Copy, Lieutenant."

Bilotti checked out the guys. The rope had been tied around the waists of Cooper and Murray, who were sitting down on the roof's surface, feet braced on a concrete abutment. They would also grip the line. Torres stood by for backup if needed. "We're ready, Sophie baby," Cooper shouted.

"Got your back, kid," Murray added.

Torres yelled, "Good luck."

Sophie climbed over the rim of the roof, stopped and made a smacking sound with her lips. "See you soon."

Below her on the ground, people were yelling and she caught a glimpse of the crowd. Shit, it was late afternoon and pedestrians had gathered around to watch the show. Blocking them out, she motioned with her hand for more rope as she shimmied spread-eagled down the brick surface of the building. Her boots got purchase on it as she descended. Inside her turnout coat she felt the sweat drip, but her face was cold. As she got closer to the window, the woman's screams became more frantic. "Help me, I'm gonna die."

"Nice, nice, Tyler." She heard Bilotti's gruff voice in her radio. "Good job. She's there," he shouted to the guys.

When Sophie came even with the window, she braced her feet on the sill. "Calm down, ma'am. You're not gonna die. I'm gonna get you out of here."

The victim's soot-smudged face contorted. "You're gonna knock me off. Watch out, you're gonna knock me off."

"I won't knock you off. I'm gonna get you tied up to this line; when that's done you can hold on to me, too." From the corner of her eye, she glimpsed flames blowing out of the window next to them, like an angry fire-breathing dragon.

When the woman saw the flames, she screamed, "It's gonna get us," and catapulted herself at Sophie.

Sophie grabbed for her, got hold of her under the armpits, thank God, but they began to plummet. With the added weight, and abrupt movement, the rope unraveled at lightning speed. Sophie's muscles strained as they fell. Her knees and the victim's back knocked into the side of the building.

As they spiraled downward, a picture of Liam flashed into Sophie's mind. Then one of Mikey. And Sophie panicked at the thought of something happening to her. The rope stopped abruptly right in front of the fourth-story window; Sophie froze and hung suspended.

Someone shouted, "Tyler, here. The window."

After a split second, she recognized the guys from Engine 46 and went into action. Swinging to the opening, she braced her feet on the ledge and handed the woman in. Two smoke eaters grabbed for the victim, then the guys dragged her inside.

"You okay, Tyler?" Bilotti's voice from the radio sounded worried now.

"Yeah, I'm inside. I'm fine."

One of Engine 46's crew, Hanson, was staring at her.

"What?" she asked.

He said nothing.

Dom Caruso came up to them. He was a captain on Engine 46, which had helped knock down the fire. "You okay?"

"Yeah. Banged my knee is all."

Hanson said, "Not so sure about that. You looked dazed when you got to the window. Just for a second."

Sophie frowned. "Shit, you'd look fuckin' dazed, too, if the rope slid out on you."

"Maybe." He walked away.

"What's eating him?" she asked.

Dom shrugged. "Guys are still stinging over the interview thing."

"Oh, great. Now they're looking for me to screw up." She pulled off her gloves and bent over and massaged her knee.

"Go to EMS and check that out."

"I'm okay."

"That's an order." He put a hand on her arm and nodded to the others. "Go, Soph. And don't worry about all this. It'll blow over."

A loud round of clapping burst out as she exited the building; it embarrassed her. Several smoke eaters patted her on the back, but some turned away in disgust.

When she reached the EMS truck, she saw that Ray was working on the other side of it. Great, just what she needed. He was giving a little girl oxygen. When he saw Sophie, he scowled.

"Get me away from him," Sophie said to the female paramedic who approached her. The nametag read "Celia Shortino."

"Gotcha." Shortino led Sophie off to the side of the bus. "Ditch the bunker pants and roll up your trousers."

When Sophie undressed, Shortino inspected her knee. "Not that bad. Scraped. Swollen some." She looked Sophie in the eye. "I watched. You're a better broad than me, Tyler. I woulda shit my pants when the woman jumped out."

"You get used to it."

But when Shortino went to get ice, Sophie felt like a hypocrite. Something had happened up there. She was scared, of course. There was a saying in the FDNY that if you weren't scared, you were crazy.

But Hanson had been right, too. She'd thought about Mikey and Liam when she was suspended a hundred feet above the ground and, for the first time in her twelve years as a firefighter, Sophie had frozen. Split second or not, she'd fucking frozen.

So she's a hero. She just keeps racking up the points. Makes me so mad, I wanna freakin' puke. I did a good job on that fire, so it'd look like a crack junkie was freebasing in the cellar. Mr. Hero himself, Captain Joe Carusotti, will discover it just fine. Fuck them, I want them to know what I can do. I want fame, even if I can't take credit.

They'll never catch me. Never even suspect somebody like me.

Maybe I should have some fun with her. *Take her down a peg or two. I don't like her getting credit and me getting none. Have to think about that one. Better get back. Don't want anybody to wonder what I'm doing here. But hell, what's the fun of it all if you can't watch.*

WHILE MA, PA, Aidan and Dylan covered the early dinner crowd at the pub, Liam waited for Patrick at a place in TriBeCa to try out a vendor who'd been hired by the restaurant to provide meals once a week. The guy cooked steaks out back in a trailer, and the owner served his food to the customers. This kind of thing was becoming popular upstate.

Pat looked harried when he rushed in and joined Liam, who sat in a booth nursing a beer. "Sorry I'm late."

"Weather hold you up?" Liam had been watching big, fat snowflakes hit the window and was thinking about the holidays and how he needed to talk to Sophie about plans for them.

"No." Pat looked older tonight, with lines deeply etched around his mouth; the gray at his temples seemed more prominent.

"Something happen?"

"No. Yeah. I guess so." He motioned for a beer and while the waitress was there, they put in their orders for rare sirloins and steak fries. "I was tryin' to get a cab over on Sixth Avenue when I saw a crowd gathering in front of this building." He shook his head. "It was on fire, Liam."

Gripping his glass, Liam forced himself to stay calm. "Sophie's crew there?"

"Yeah. Sophie wasn't hurt or anything."

"I've never seen her in action."

"Believe me, you don't want to. I'm only tellin' you this because you might see it on the news, or Mike could catch a glimpse of it on his computer."

"She wasn't hurt, right?" Pat shook his head. "What was she doing?"

"Dangling from an eight-story building."

Jesus. "Tell me all of it, Pat."

"I came by just as she was being lowered down the outside of the building in some kind of harness to rescue a victim two floors below. But the whole thing went south when the woman jumped out the window at her."

"Tell me she hung on to the victim."

"That she did. On one hand, it was the most incredible thing I've ever seen. On the other, it was freakin' crazy. With the added weight, the rope unraveled down the building two stories until it came to a stop abrupt enough to get whiplash. The firefighters at the window where she landed dragged them both inside."

Liam took a deep breath. This was why he tried not to watch TV or read the papers about rescues in the lower West Side.

"You all right, buddy?"

Liam stared over his brother's shoulder. "I guess. I know she does these kinds of things . . ."

"I did, too, Liam. But hell, seein' it. I'm . . ." Pat looked away.

"What?"

"I'm wonderin' if she's good for you. And for Mikey and Cleary."

"I told you my feelings on that. Kitty died and never did anything dangerous."

"Three hundred forty-three firefighters bought it in the Towers."

"I know, Paddy."

"I'm just sayin' I'm worried about it."

Liam frowned. "You encouraged Aidan and C.J. to get together."

"Yeah, and she ended up quitting the detail where she was riskin' her life every day."

"I suppose."

"Would Sophie ever quit the line?"

"Can't see that happening. It's in her blood. Any compromise has to come from my side."

"And your kids." He sipped his beer. "And the rest of us." When Liam didn't respond, Pat added, "Anyway, I had to tell you."

"Yeah, you did. But for your own sake, Paddy, you also gotta let go of all of us a little. You take on too much responsibility. I can handle this. You look like shit."

"I know. Bad time with Brie last night. To top it off, Pa guessed something was wrong and he got on me about it. As if he's so innocent."

"Ma and Pa worked out their problems, Pat. Just like you and Brie will."

"He said that, too."

"Wanna talk about Brie?"

"I guess. But first, I need to know something. Is it too late to cut this thing off with Sophie?"

"Uh-huh." He'd filled his brothers in on the therapy and the tack they were taking with Mike. "I'm in love with her, Pat."

"Then I hope it works out for you. Love isn't always enough."

"THIS IS DECADENT."

"Hey, girlfriend, anybody who dangles off the side of a building hanging on to one hundred sixty pounds of flesh deserves some freakin' pampering." Hannah sat next to Sophie in a chair at a little salon in the Village. Her feet were propped up and being painted a candy-apple red by a little Vietnamese lady who didn't speak English but made it clear she loved America's Bravest. Her assistant worked on Sophie.

Sophie herself was having her toenails and fingernails done in a pretty peach. "This seems so silly," she said, glancing at her hand. "Next tour will just ruin the manicure."

"You're off till Sunday. Plenty of time to enjoy it. Your man will like it, too, when you scrape those claws down his back."

The thought of Liam and what his reaction would be to the girly things she was doing before she went to work at the pub tonight made her grin. She was already wearing her pub uniform of black pants and the green top with a matching green sweater over it so she and Hannah could play all day. "Hmm. He will. How about Dom?"

"Are you kidding?" Hannah's brown eyes were filled with affection. "He goes nuts over makeup and polish. Just like when I dress up. I think it's the contrast to being a big, tough firefighter on the line."

Sophie chuckled.

"He said you did great yesterday."

Remembering the fear that had frozen her, Sophie shrugged. "I did okay. Hanson got on me."

"Yeah, Dom said. He's an asshole."

"I hate having to prove myself over and over, Hannah."

"The pricks. Women are here to stay but they're never gonna make it easy for us. And they're picking on you because of the interview. Maybe they'll back off when they see the transcript in Dylan's column."

"Maybe, but it sucks just the same. The column should help, though."

"We're getting it run off and sent to all the firehouses, as well as putting it on e-mail."

"Through official channels?"

"What do you think?"

"Thanks, Hannah."

"You're welcome."

For a while, they sat in silence and enjoyed being spoiled. Then Sophie asked, "How's it going with the baby thing?"

Hannah scrunched her nose, making her look young. "We're giving it our best shot. Tests came back. Dom's little soldiers are moving slow."

"That's happened to other smoke eaters. Because of the heat."

"I know. Dom heard that around the firehouse. We're thinking about helping them along."

"How?"

"Artificially. Putting my egg and his sperm in the same vicinity so they might hook up."

"That sounds like a plan."

"Shit, I hate this."

"I'm sorry. But if you get a baby that way, who cares?"

"The docs tell you to make love right after so you never know how the little one was conceived." Hannah studied her. "You're not thinking about babies these days yourself, are you, Soph?"

"Me? No."

"It's serious though, with Liam, isn't it?"

She transferred her gaze from her feet to her friend. "It is. I know you didn't think a ready-made family was a good idea, and it hasn't gone that far, but I really care about him, Hannah."

"Oh, hell."

"Please, be happy for me. It's so good, in so many ways."

"All right. How'd he take what happened yesterday?"

Liam had been working at the pub last night, but called her. "He seemed fine. He's a strong person and knows himself well. I like that about him."

"Sounds like you like everything about him."

"I've never felt this way about a guy."

"Ah, I remember those infatuation days. Hard to even think about anything else."

"Yeah." Sophie waited then decided she could trust Hannah. "Did it ever affect your work? Falling for Dom?"

"Sure. The guys ragged on both of us because we were in the same house. I took more grief than he did, of course."

Sophie was quiet.

"Soph?"

"Did you ever"—God, this was hard to say—"get scared or anything because you loved somebody now and were worried about your safety?"

Hannah waited a beat. "No." Then, "Did that happen to you yesterday?"

"I don't know. I did think about him while I was dangling off the roof."

"Life flashing in front of your eyes kind of thing?"

"Maybe."

"I hope that's all it was."

"Better be." Sophie held up her hands. "I'm done here, I think."

Hannah wiggled her toes. "Me, too." As they stood, she said, "Don't mention what you just told me to any of the guys, Soph."

"Do you think I'm nuts? It wasn't really anything anyway."

"Sure. You're just second-guessing yourself because those jerkoffs are ragging on you. But until it passes, keep what you told me quiet."

Hannah's warning bothered Sophie as they cashed out and left the salon. If Hannah wanted her to be quiet about it, then had something actually happened?

IN DEFERENCE to the November wind that was rattling the kitchen windows, Liam had made a hardy Irish stew. The main dish would be served with a special salad his mother was concocting at the butcher-block counter. She and his father usually went to Florida for October and November, but they weren't heading south until January this year because of his dad's heart attack last summer. Right now, she'd put on some Irish music and was singing along with "Danny Boy."

Wiping his hands on his apron, Liam crossed to her and spun her around.

"What are you doing? This salad won't make itself, boy."

"There's always time to dance, Mama. Remember how you used to tell us that?"

"So I did." She went easily into his arms and they fell into a slow rumba. A head shorter, she felt slimmer these days, but despite her gray hair and the wrinkles that claimed her face, she was as beautiful to him as she'd been when she taught him to dance. He told her so.

"You're full of the blarney, that you are." Her eyes misted, though.

"What is it, Mama?"

She sniffled. "It's nice to see you so . . . lighthearted. I've said novenas to St. Theresa for you."

"They must have helped. It's been a rough three years— five since Kitty got cancer. But I'm finally moving on."

Like the young woman she used to be, Mary Kate O'Neil did a series of turns that made Liam smile. "And would it be that girl who's comin' in tonight that's got you happy?"

"That it would."

"You and Aidan." His ma shook her head. "Couldn't find a safe one."

He waited. "I had a safe one, Mama."

"I know, *a stor*." She patted his back.

From the doorway, Pa said, "What's goin' on back here?"

Liam winked at his mother. "Just dancing with my best girl."

"Harrumph. Thought she was *my* best girl."

"That I am, Patrick O'Neil."

"When Irish Eyes Are Smiling" drifted from the CD player. Liam led his mother over to his pa. "Go ahead, Pa. You love this song."

His father took his mother's hand, said, *"Mo chroi,"* and held her close.

Leaning against the wall Liam watched his parents dance around the kitchen. It reminded him of his childhood and warmed his heart. He remembered what he'd told Patrick yesterday—that the two of them had had issues in the early days. Liam always thought his pa was too controlling, a lot like Patrick Jr., and his ma was strong-headed. But they worked it all out. *See,* he told himself, *all couples have issues. You and Kitty didn't.*

He pushed the thought away. The door next to him, which led to the bar, creaked open and he smelled Sophie before he saw her. His whole body responded to the sensual awareness. She didn't say anything, just crept inside and sidled in close. Her coat was over her arm, but he could feel her heat.

Still silent, he slid his arm around her shoulders; she moved even closer and they both watched his parents execute some pretty fancy maneuvers.

When the song ended, Liam clapped. Sophie joined in. Liam said, "You two still got it."

"Aye, we do, boy." Pa was staring at Ma, then kissed her. She kissed him back.

Without a trace of self-consciousness, his pa looked over at them. "Hello there, Sophie."

"Mr. O'Neil. Mrs. O'Neil."

"It's time you called us by our names, don't you think, lass? You're Tyler's godmother, after all." Pa took a bead on Liam. "And more, from the looks of things."

Sophie nodded. "That would be nice."

Dylan burst through the door. "A group of ten just came in, guys. Sophie, you're needed at the bar."

"I'm there."

Liam reached out. "I'll take your coat."

She gave it to him and he grabbed her hand. She'd had a manicure. He looked at her face. And makeup done. He cleared his throat. "You tryin' to kill me, darlin'?" he whispered so his parents wouldn't hear.

She raised up on tiptoes. "Nope. Just trying to keep you interested."

"If I was any more *interested*, I'd never make it through the night. As it is, these pants are fittin' mighty tight."

"Hold the thought." She kissed his cheek and left.

After the party of ten was served drinks and food, Liam took a break and went out to the pub. Aidan must have come in and was sitting on the other side of the bar flirting with Sophie. When Liam reached them, he heard Dylan telling them a joke.

"This brunette, redhead and blonde worked in the same office. Every day, their female boss would leave at noon and return at two. The brunette caught on first. 'You know, we can leave, too. Do errands, take a longer lunch.' The others agreed. The brunette went to have her nails done. The blonde ate at a fancy restaurant." Here he winked at Aidan. "But the redhead went home. When she got there, she found her husband's car in the driveway next to another one she didn't recognize. She crept inside. Up to the bedroom. Through the crack in the door she saw her husband with another woman on the bed, doing the nasty. The woman was her boss. The redhead flew out of the house and back to the office. When the brunette and blonde arrived, they told how much fun they had in the two hours. They were going to do it again tomorrow. The redhead frowned and said, 'Not me. I almost got caught.' "

Even Liam joined in the laughter. Sophie gave them a sham look of disapproval. "Let me guess. If you told that to C.J., it would be the blonde who went home."

Dylan kissed her on the cheek. "Of course, lass. We're equal opportunity chauvinists."

Sophie got Liam a Coke and he sat down next to his brother. "Where is she tonight, Aidan?"

His brother's face lost all its mirth. "Working again. An ambassador from Italy is here and needed an armed guard. My girl got it because she speaks fluent Italian."

Dylan said, "You're not gonna be a crybaby about it every time she has protective duty, are you?"

"Shut your mouth," Aidan said. "I don't need your shit."

"Grow up," Dylan told him and went to the end of the bar.

Liam stood. "Come on, Sophie, I don't want to get in the middle."

"Yeah, you're good at fence-sitting."

Clapping Aidan on the shoulder, he leaned over. "I'll let that go because you're upset, kid, but learn to deal."

From the jukebox, Liam selected Cole Porter's "I've Got You Under My Skin" and swirled Sophie onto the dance floor. He pulled her close and buried his face in her neck. "I love this lotion."

"Hmm."

"I like the sweater, too." He whispered, "I'll like it better when it's lying on the floor of your bedroom with your other clothes tonight."

"Think you're going to get lucky, Mr. O'Neil?"

"I know it."

She nosed into his chest. "Fine by me."

"You okay?" he asked. "I forgot about your knee."

"No problem. I had my feet up most of the day between the manicure, pedicure and facial."

"Fuck, you got a pedicure, too? They drive me nuts."

"Hannah's husband, too."

"Witch."

"Liam, are you all right about yesterday?"

He knew it needed to be addressed, but he hadn't wanted to spoil the good mood. "I think so. Pat saw you, you know?"

She drew back. *"What?"*

"He was on his way to meet me and he saw you dangling."

"Oh, wow. That's too bad."

"I know it was on the news but I didn't watch it."

"Did Mike?"

"No, but I told him about it. He was scared for a bit, but did okay."

"I need to bring him to the station house soon. So he can see the equipment, like the harness and other safety things."

"I agree. You were gonna talk to the other guys about their kids, too."

"I'll do it as soon as we get back on tour."

"Good." He pulled her close. "Now, let's forget about danger lurking in every corner."

"It's a deal."

The deal was off, however, when at eleven o'clock that night a man dressed in a suit entered the pub. Liam was on a stool, Sophie was wiping off the bar and Dylan was cleaning a table. The man looked around, saw Aidan stacking glasses and crossed to him.

Alarm bells went off inside Liam's head. When Aidan looked up, they got louder. "Hi, Jim. Did you . . ." Aidan's face paled. "Something happened to C.J."

Jim said, "Yeah. She's all right, Aidan, but she got shot tonight. She's at Memorial Hospital and I came over as soon as I heard. I got a car to take you there."

Aidan froze. Dylan came down the bar and Liam had gotten close enough to see his brother's face was totally devoid of color. "I'm going with you," Dylan said.

"Me, too. I'll get our coats." Liam looked at Sophie. "Close up here and meet us there?"

"Of course." Sophie squeezed his arm and Aidan's.

They were out the door and into a black Suburban in minutes. No one spoke. Liam wondered if they were all remembering their earlier exchange and how they'd ragged on their little brother about worrying too much.

SEVENTEEN

GRIM-FACED, Liam and Dylan sat in the emergency waiting room at Memorial Hospital. Even in here, the smells were acrid and antiseptic, reminding Liam of all the times he'd been in a place like this with Kitty. When they arrived at the hospital, Aidan had rushed inside the treatment area with the agent who'd driven them over and the two brothers had kept vigil ever since.

Liam glanced at Dylan. "We always do it, you know. Nothing to feel guilty about."

"I wish I'd kept my mouth shut. Jesus, I never expected her to get hurt."

"Danger lurks around every corner." Why the hell was life so hard?

Dylan ran a hand through his hair. "I guess when you put yourself in harm's way it does."

Liam frowned at his tone. "You encouraged me and Aidan both to go ahead with these relationships."

"What the hell do I know? Sometimes I think I'm full of shit."

"You're just feeling guilty. Let's wait and see what's going on with C.J."

The agent, Jim Bradley, came into the waiting area, cutting off further discussion. "You can come back." Liam nodded to the sign on the wall that indicated one visitor at a time was allowed inside. Bradley tracked his gaze. "The service has pull."

They followed the agent through the winding corridors of the emergency room. A few patients were out in the halls, looking frail and sick. C.J. was in a curtained-off cubicle, sitting up in bed, her left arm bandaged. She was pale, but alert. His brother slouched in the only chair, scowling.

"Hi, guys." C.J. smiled weakly. "Nice of you to stop by."

"Don't fucking joke with them," Aidan said.

"He's wigging out."

"A bullet passes through the arm of the woman I love and I should be happy about it?"

"Grazed, honey. Passing through is worse."

Liam stepped forward and kissed C.J. on the cheek. "You okay?"

"It hurts like a bitch, but they gave me a pain reliever. God bless modern medicine."

"You going to be out of commission long?" he asked.

"Not nearly long enough," Aidan mumbled.

"A few days at least."

Dylan approached the bed and squeezed C.J.'s arm. "More time to plan the wedding."

Aidan's glare was brutal. "If there is a wedding."

They all stilled. Then C.J. laid her head back and closed her eyes. "Can somebody talk some sense into him?"

Abruptly Aidan stood and stalked out of the cubicle. Dylan started after him, but Liam stayed his arm. "Let me go, Dyl." To C.J. he said, "Don't worry about this," and left.

After searching the waiting areas, he found Aidan in the main lobby of the hospital staring out one of the windows into the New York night. He put a hand on his brother's shoulder. "Aidan?"

"Leave me alone."

"I won't talk if you don't want to, but I'm staying with you."

Liam leaned back against the wall so he was in his brother's line of vision. Finally, Aidan looked at him. His eyes were dark and turbulent. And something else Liam recognized. Fear. "I'm not sure I can do this."

O-kay. They'd been here before. But now, it was different, for Liam at least. "You're scared and angry is all."

"Yeah. Both. Doesn't change what I said." He pounded his fist on the window frame. "I thought I could handle it. I knew she'd be doing protective duty. Still, I thought I could handle it."

"You can. If you love her enough."

He shook his head.

"What's the alternative, A.?"

"Call off the wedding."

Crossing his arms over his chest, Liam thought about the right advice to give Aidan. "Don't make any rash decisions tonight. You're in a bad place."

"I guess." He locked gazes with Liam. "She could die in her line of work."

So could Sophie. "Anybody can die, Aidan. We all know that."

"Like Kitty. I thought you were right when you said that before. About her dying when she led a safe life. Tonight, it doesn't make as much sense."

Not to me, either.

"I don't recommend this, Liam."

"What?"

"Falling for a woman who risks her safety when she goes to work. It's too late for me, but—"

"Too late for me, too."

"Fuck."

"Don't say anything more to C.J. about calling off the wedding."

"I meant it."

"No, you didn't. Give yourself a breather. And right now, she needs you. She's brave, but she's in pain. And she shouldn't have to worry about you."

"I'm being selfish."

"Human, really, but you gotta rise to the occasion."

"You're right." He turned and they headed back to the emergency room. "I hope you do better than me, Liam, with Sophie."

"Tell you what," he said with a lightness he didn't feel. "We'll work on this together."

The small smile from his brother made Liam's lie more palatable. He was able to keep the fear at bay as he followed his brother in to see C.J.

MIKE BOLTED UPRIGHT, panting hard. Where was he? His eyes adjusted to the darkness. He saw the dinosaur on the wall and the stars overhead. His hand grasped the quilt. It was the one his mother had made him.

He just sat there a minute, trying to get his breath. Then he rummaged around for the flashlight and turned it on. The clock on the table said 3:00. His dad would be home. Climbing out of bed, he crept downstairs. On nights like this where his dad would be out, Mrs. Carpenter stayed with them and went to sleep in his dad's bed. His father slept on the pullout couch in the living room. But when Mike got down there and shined the light into the room, his dad wasn't there. He *never* stayed out this late. Something must be wrong.

Feeling like a baby because he wanted to cry, Mikey trudged upstairs and stopped in front of Cleary's room. His brother was sprawled out on his stomach, his face in a pillow and his leg sticking out of the covers. Mike went over to the bed.

"Cleary?" He shined the light down on the floor. He'd be even madder if Mikey woke him with the light in his face.

Cleary just moved on the bed.

Mike shook his shoulder. "Cleary, wake up."

"What the . . ." He turned to Mike. "Go away."

"Dad's not home."

"Go *away*."

"It's three o'clock in the morning."

"Jesus."

"I'm scared."

He thought his brother went back to sleep but finally he turned on his back. Mike lifted the flashlight a bit.

"You have a bad dream?"

"Uh-huh. About Mom."

Cleary just stared at him and Mike knew he was gonna yell at him, or at least call him a dweeb. Instead, he moved over in the bed and pulled out the covers. Mike climbed in, not too close, because Cleary didn't like that.

"Where do you think Dad is?"

"Screw—" He stopped. "Maybe he's on a date with Sophie."

"He never stays out this late."

"I know."

"Something bad happened."

"You just think that because you had a dream about Mom."

"I miss her."

"Me, too."

"I like Sophie."

No answer.

"Do you?"

"She seems cool. Sometimes it bothers me that Dad's dating."

"Mom woulda wanted him to."

Cleary was looking up at the ceiling.

"C-can I stay here?"

"I guess." He added, "But you gotta turn off the flashlight."

"Okay."

Downstairs, Mike heard the front door open and close.

"There's Dad," Cleary said, but he didn't sound mad. "See, everything's all right."

Mike had to know for sure. He called out, "Da-ad."

Footsteps on the stairs. His father came to the doorway. "Mike? Cleary?"

Cleary said, "Mikey had a bad dream and got scared."

"I'm sorry, honey."

"Where were you?" Mike asked.

"Let's talk about all this in the morning."

Sitting up fast, Cleary grabbed the flashlight and turned it on. It made a scary glow against the wall. "No, tell us now."

His dad came inside and sat on the edge of the bed on the other side of Cleary. "I was at the hospital."

Mike gulped. "Sophie got hurt again, didn't she?"

"No, not Sophie. C.J. She's fine, though."

"C.J.?" Mike never thought about that. "What happened to her?"

"She was on protective duty like she used to do with Aunt Bailey, and . . . somebody shot her in the arm."

"Holy shit, Dad," Cleary said, "She got *shot*?"

"Just grazed, really. The bullet didn't lodge or anything."

Cleary's eyes widened. Mike stilled.

His dad said, "Mike, did you hear me? C.J.'s okay."

"Uh-huh."

"You can see her tomorrow."

He nodded.

"Come on, Mikey." His father stood up. "Let your brother get some sleep. I'll take you to your room."

"Dad, can he . . . uh, stay here?" Cleary's voice sounded funny, like he was scared, too.

His dad stared down at them. "Yeah, sure." He waited a while, then went to Cleary's closet and came back with a sleeping bag. "I'll bunk on the floor."

Mike didn't say not to do it. Neither did Cleary. After his dad got pillows from the linen closet and was settled in, Cleary turned off the flashlight.

" 'Night, Dad," Mike whispered.

Cleary reiterated it.

"Good night, guys. Don't worry, everything's gonna be all right."

With Cleary next to him and the sound of his father's breathing coming from the floor, Mike almost believed that maybe things would be okay.

TWO DAYS AFTER C.J. was shot, Sophie met Mike at his school. She'd arranged to take him and Cara to the firehouse on her day off, show them around and subtly get into some safety issues with him. She arrived just as St. Mary's let out. Mike was waiting in the school behind the front door with Cara because it was freezing out. Sophie was glad she'd worn her long leather coat.

"Sophie!" Mike yelled as he came rushing toward her, his heavy jacket unzipped and flapping open. His welcome filled her with a rush of feeling. Maternal, she guessed. Geez, who would have thought? She gave him a warm hug, then bent down to zip up his coat. Cara joined them.

"Hi, Cara."

"Hi, Sophie. Thanks for letting me come."

"I hope you can use the visit for your Brownie badge."

She and Liam had decided the explanation for taking the kids to the firehouse was to get more information for their Brownie and Wolf badges. They hadn't wanted to hit Mikey over the head with their tactics and risk making him more insecure. Because of that, they also agreed that Liam shouldn't accompany them.

She hadn't seen much of Liam since C.J. had been shot. That night, after she'd closed up the pub, she'd gone to the hospital, sat with the family, then headed home alone. Liam needed to be with his kids, and there was no fulfillment of the teasing promises they'd made each other at the bar. She felt guilty even thinking about missing that with him when C.J. lay shot in the hospital and Aidan was a wreck.

"So, you guys excited about this?" she asked as they got on the subway to go to the firehouse. Both their faces were red by the time the reached the entrance.

"I am." Mike grinned at her. "I like learning about equipment."

"You gonna let us go down the pole?" Cara asked.

"Maybe. If the captain says it's okay. We don't use it anymore, you know."

Cara nodded vigorously. "It causes injuries. My dad told me."

"Cara's dad is a cop."

"I heard that."

The subway exit was right across from the firehouse. Each kid took one of her hands when they got off the train and walked into the bay. Another group was working, of course, so she was surprised to see Bilotti by a rig. "Hey, Soph," he said when he spotted them. His gaze narrowed on her hands.

"You subbing?" she asked.

"Hmm. Officer in charge." His expression was tender when he knelt down in front of the kids. In one of his more sensitive moments, he'd confessed that he missed living with his daughter since his divorce. "Hi. I'm Lieutenant Bilotti."

Mike said, "We met you when we came with our school."

"Uh-huh. What are your names again?"

"I'm Mike, this is Cara."

"Welcome to Company 14."

"We're gonna look at some of the safety equipment," she told Bilotti.

His expression was puzzled. "Go ahead."

First Sophie took them to her turnout gear. "This is what we wear in fires. It's specially designed to keep us insulated from the heat. It's nonflammable, which means it can't catch on fire."

Mike's eager face was fun to watch.

Cara said, "That's a lot like my dad's protective vest."

"Uh-huh." These things"—she picked up her gloves—"are made of special material called Nomex. They keep our hands and head covered and safe." She smiled. "Wanna try them on?"

Mikey laughed as he donned the hood, and Cara put on the gloves, both of which were way too big, of course.

"This smells like smoke." Mike wrinkled his nose. "The whole place does."

"Yeah." She often had a hard time getting it out of her hair and her pores—a perennial firefighter problem.

"What's that?" Cara asked, pointing to a huge accordion-like pipe that ran from the truck to wall.

"That's for the rigs. It vents the exhaust."

Then she explained the SCBA pack, with special emphasis on the PASS alarm. "If your air is low, this signal goes off indicating that it's time to leave the building." She pressed it briefly and the noise was loud and obnoxious.

"Cool."

She didn't tell them that one of the scariest things about being a firefighter, other than working blind, was when the alarm went off and you knew you were out of air. Many a probie had panicked and gotten disoriented and had to be rescued. Jules had been one of them.

When she finished explaining the gear that would keep them protected, she moved to the truck that held the rappelling equipment. Mike scowled at it. "You wore this when you rescued that lady."

Liam had told Mike about the incident, but Sophie also suspected he'd seen some of the footage on TV or in the news. "Uh-huh. It keeps us safe in those situations."

"My dad's afraid of high places," Mike told her.

Sophie chuckled. "I didn't know that."

"Yeah, he won't even go on a ride at the park." A scowl. "Like last summer at the lake. He wouldn't take me on the Ferris wheel. C.J. did." He watched Sophie for a minute. "She got hurt then, too. And two nights ago somebody shot her."

"My dad's been shot." Cara said the words matter-of-factly.

Mikey turned to Cara. "No kidding?"

"Yep."

"Were you scared?"

"Uh-huh. Mommy cried."

"He's okay though, isn't he?" Sophie asked.

"Yeah. He got better, fast."

"Well, so will C.J."

From the special compartment in the rig, she pulled out the safety harness. "This is what kept me up." She stepped into it. "It goes on like this."

Bilotti joined them. "Let me help." They secured the ropes and clips, explaining what they were doing. The kids were wide-eyed. "See, I was pretty safe."

Both kids nodded. She undid the contraption and stowed it away.

"We put out cookies a woman we rescued brought us today," Bilotti told them. "Want some?"

They all headed for the kitchen.

As the kids settled in with chocolate chips and milk, Bilotti drew Sophie aside. "This just came in."

She stared down at the paper he handed her. "What is it?"

"The transcript of your interview with Scott. The e-mail said it was in *CitySights* today. That's your boyfriend's brother's doing, right?"

Sophie faced him squarely. She hated that they'd taken

some steps backward after she'd struggled hard to win his respect. "Yes, Tony. He published it so everybody would know that my words were taken out of context."

Though he had heard the tope, Bilotti grunted. "I can't believe you really said all those good things about our company."

"Well, I had to lie about it."

His expression turned serious. "I'm one of the ones you alluded to who had trouble at first."

"You were, Tony."

"Scott's a bitch. She butchered what you said."

"Yeah, she did."

"I . . ." He scowled. ". . . I shouldn't have said what I did when the guys started on us. About taking care of yourself."

"It got bad, Tony. They don't let up."

"This'll help." Nodding to the kids he said, "One of those is an O'Neil. You playing Mommy these days?"

"Not exactly."

He gave her a quick squeeze on the arm. "See you in a couple of days."

"Okay." He started to walk away. "Tony?"

"Hmm."

"I'm glad we had this talk."

"Jesus, don't go soft on me, Tyler."

She smiled. "Wouldn't dare, sir."

As she led the kids to the Hurst equipment, she was grinning. Dylan had come through for her. She'd have to find a way to thank him.

DYLAN'S OFFICE at *CitySights* was small and stuffy. He only wrote the one weekly column, so he didn't need more space. Sometimes, he dreamed of having a bigger job at the magazine, but never pursued it. Just like he never pursued his dream of turning his columns into a book. He was forty-three years old, with a ruined marriage, a troubled son and a job at a pub. Huh!

"Somebody's here to see you, O'Neil." His coworker John came to announce his visitor.

Odd, he wasn't at the office often enough to have people

looking for him here. Anybody who wanted to find him would go to the pub. "Who is it?"

"Some chick in a pink suit, killer boots and mounds of red hair. You are one lucky bastard, O'Neil."

"Don't bet on it." The description of the visitor fit Ms. Rachel Scott. And if he gauged correctly, he thought, glancing at his column that came out today, more than her hair was going to be flaming.

He sauntered into the reception area, which wasn't very big, either. "Hello there, sweetheart."

Her eyes sparked green fire. "Cut the chauvinistic remarks. I'm on to you. You just do that to make me mad."

"You're already mad."

She glanced around, sending her full, lush hair swirling. "Is there somewhere private we can talk?"

An anteroom jutted off the reception area. He led her to it and closed the door. Immediately perfume filled the air. He'd bet it was French and expensive. Before he sat, he pulled out a chair for her. Her brows rose.

"My mama taught me well," he said, amused at her surprise.

"So I see."

He dropped down across from her and lazed back into the seat, propping his foot up on his knee. "What can I do for you?"

She held up a copy of the magazine. "This is your doing."

"You mean my *little column*?"

Her glare was blistering. "It made me look like a fool."

"No, darlin', you did that all by yourself when you took Sophie Tyler's words out of context."

"Editing happens. You know that."

"I'd say this was a lot more than editing. Slanting. Skewing. Slandering, maybe."

She averted her gaze. Hmm.

"I told you we'd fight back."

"Why? What's in it for you?"

"Sophie. She took a lot of grief from other firefighters when you made her seem like she was putting them all down."

Nervously, she placed her cashmere coat on the chair next to her. "Those things blow over."

"Sensitive, aren't you?"

"More than you know." She bit her lip, which was covered with a pretty raisin-colored lipstick. "I'm sorry she was hurt by the interview."

"Something's going on with all this, isn't there?"

"What do you mean?"

"You said before that broadcasts get edited. Without your consent?"

"No, of course not."

"I don't believe you."

"I don't really care, Mr. O'Neil."

"Then why are you here?"

Her chin lifted. "I got a call from the vice president's secretary. He was supposed to meet with me when he came to town for Thanksgiving."

"Let me guess, he's called it off."

"Did you engineer that?"

"Clay's his own man. I didn't have to. I do know my sister was pissed as hell when she saw the broadcast."

"His freeze is affecting my career."

"And I should care why?"

"Because I'm asking you to."

God, did she really think she could sway him? Sure, she was pretty as hell, like his ex-wife, Stephanie, was, with all that red hair no man could resist. But he wasn't getting sucked in again by pure female beauty. He'd found that beneath it often lay fluff. "Not enough. You've got so many black marks against you I don't wanna touch you with a ten-foot pole."

"I read your back columns. You're usually more fair than this."

"I'm flattered."

"When you went to the school about the bullying, you showed both sides. When you took on DSS for that homeless man, you gave credit to the good things and demanded reforms in inadequacies you saw."

"That's because there were two sides in those cases. You, on the other hand, are a prime example of self-advancement in our field."

"What do you mean?"

"You'll step on anybody to get to the top."

"I've had to be tough, yes, to get ahead. And all right, I want more. But—"

"What?"

"Excuse me?"

"What more do you want?"

Her jewellike green eyes narrowed on him. "Fine, I'll tell you. I'm shooting for a position as foreign correspondent with the station. But I have to prove myself with tough assignments first. A lot of people covet the spot."

"Ah, the plot thickens. If you can't even get Clay to let you in on domestic things, going overseas is a moot point."

She drew in a heavy breath.

"Your loss, I guess." He stood. "I'm not helping you."

"Dylan, please."

For a second, he imagined her saying that to him in other circumstances. But he'd let his cock lead him in this direction once with a pretty face and killer body and it had practically ruined his life.

"No." He opened the door.

"I'm not leaving yet."

"Well, I am, sweetheart. Have a nice life." He left her there, staring openmouthed at him.

And the rest of the day, he metaphorically kicked himself in the butt for remembering—and wondering about—that mouth.

EIGHTEEN

"YOU'RE SMOKIN', BABE."

"*You're* crazy."

Liam kissed Sophie's fingertips. "For you, hot stuff."

"Cut it out," she said when he began to suck on her pinky.

"Hey, I spent a lot of time on the Internet planning this."

"Lovemaking is supposed to be spontaneous. You're not supposed to plan out what you say."

"There's another one. Spontaneous combustion. That's what we got going for us." He bit her lightly. "Now help me out here."

"Okay." She sighed with pleasure when he turned her hand over to kiss her wrist. "I'm a fire waiting to roll. Make me go up in flames, big guy."

He stopped and faked an offended glare. "Are you mocking me?"

Giggling, she got out, "Of course I am."

"Tsk. Tsk. Guess I'll just have to keep you smoldering for a while."

He did and also kept up the banter. He spent another ten

minutes kissing her, licking her everywhere. She tasted so sweet and he was having a great time.

"This make your blood boil, Soph?"

"Mmm."

"Are you fully involved yet?"

"Oh, yeah."

Brushing his lips over the swell of her breasts then her breast bone, he whispered, "You're like wildfire, sweetheart."

As was his intent, he had her simultaneously laughing out loud and hot as hell by the time he made his way down her body. His mouth closed over her. "Explode for me, babe. Let's see some of that flashover."

The sounds from her as she came made his heart full and his cock harder than granite. When she was finished, she sucked in a few breaths, then bolted up and pushed him to his back.

"Hey, what . . ."

"Okay, wiseass, I'm gonna make some of my own fireworks here."

He laughed out loud. "That's my little firefighter."

An hour later they were still in bed, watching mid-November turn dark outside the window at only 4 p.m. He sighed, not wanting to move. "I gotta go. I'm serving supper at the pub tonight."

"Where's Mikey now?"

"Dylan got him off the bus. He tried like hell to find out what I was doing."

"You don't, like, talk about this with them, do you?"

He raised dark brows. "Talk about what?"

"Sex. I watch those shows, you know. Like *Rescue Me*. The guys share intimate details of their love lives."

"Oh, that. Sure, I do." *Not*. "All men do."

She started to sputter. "Y . . . you . . ."

"Gotcha." Leaning over, he kissed her hard. "You're as easy to get going as matches to tinder."

"Oh, God, stop with the firefighter lingo."

Grasping her arms lightly, he stared into her deep gray

eyes. "No, of course I don't tell my brothers intimate details. Hell, it's hard enough talking about the emotional stuff."

"But you do that, right?"

"Yeah. Always have. It's the O'Neil curse. Just with each other, though." He slid out of bed. "I'm gonna shower, okay?"

"Get a little sweaty?"

"Yeah, you, too, lady. What time do you have to be at work?"

"Tour starts at six."

Liam cleaned up in her tiny bathroom, wishing he didn't have to come and go like this. Wishing Sophie lived under his roof. It was too soon for all that, he knew, but it didn't make him want it any less. When he came out in the pub attire he'd brought along, he saw she was still in bed.

"What are you smiling at?" she asked.

He leaned against the jamb. "I love you, is all."

Her jaw dropped. It took him a minute to realize why. Crossing to the bed, he stood over her. "Oops. Forgot I hadn't said that out loud to you. I've just felt it for a long time."

"Y . . . you have?"

"Yeah. You don't have to say it back. I know you care about me." He kissed her head, then started for the door. "Gotta go."

She grasped his arm. "Hold on a minute."

At his questioning look, she tugged him around fully. "I've felt it for a while, too."

The sun shone in his heart, which had been full of thunder clouds for a long time. "You have?"

"Yes."

Lowering himself to the bed, he drew her up into an embrace. "Then tell me right, woman."

"I love you, Liam."

His heart beat a steady rhythm as he held her next to it. There was no passion this time, just a deep sense of connection, of gratitude and of hope—something Liam hadn't experienced for a long time. He said only, "Good."

He'd reached the bedroom door before he remembered something. "Oh, shit, I keep forgetting to tell you this. Next week, on Thanksgiving, we close the pub and have a family dinner there. Everybody comes. Are you working?"

"Um, yeah."

"That's okay. It goes on all day and night. You can come before or after your tour." Though he didn't like that, he'd have to reconcile her schedule with his life and was proud of himself for being able to do it.

"Liam, I'm sorry. I can't come at all. I'm working twenty-four hours."

"What? Your house is on nine- and fifteen-hour tours."

"We are. But a while ago, I said I'd work overtime for one of the guys on another group so he could be with his family."

"Why the hell did you do that?"

"Because, at the time, I didn't have anywhere else to go."

"What about the Carusottis? Wouldn't you go there?"

"They have a big shindig for firefighters. It's not really like eating with your family. So I gave this young guy with kids a break."

"Tell him you can't do it."

She looked confused. "I wouldn't do that to him. His family is counting on it."

"I was counting on you."

"I'm sorry."

Instead of hurt, anger started to well inside him. Jay Yost said getting mad was better than taking everything on the chin. "That doesn't help, Sophie."

"I—"

"What about Christmas?"

"Excuse me?"

"Have you already made arrangements for Christmas?"

"No, I was hoping Nate might get some furlough. I've got time off."

"Don't make any plans to work."

"Yes, sir."

"I'm pissed."

"I can tell."

"I'll deal with it." He crossed to her again and this time kissed her hard. "You got family now. Remember that."

She was wide-eyed at his tone. He was a little surprised

himself. When he left, he was still mad. But it felt good. He was gonna fight back, fight for her, and no fire department, no previous commitments were going to change that.

"WHAT'S GOT YOUR panties in a twist?" Cooper sat across from Sophie at the kitchen table where they were all feasting on the lemon meringue pie Mackenzie's wife had baked for them.

"Nothing."

"Boyfriend giving you trouble?" Bilotti asked between bites.

"He's pissed at me."

"You sound shocked."

"I am. We've never had a real fight. This wasn't a real one, either, but Liam never gets mad."

"It's always the quiet ones." Murray joined in. "My ex is the same way."

Throwing back her chair, Sophie set down her fork. "I gotta go think about this."

"Can I have your pie?" Bilotti asked.

"Knock yourself out."

She headed upstairs to the bunk room for some privacy. In one sense it felt good to know she would be missed at the O'Neil Thanksgiving. In another, she felt apprehension: the guys talked all the time about schedules being a problem with their family lives. In her brief marriage to Ray, he'd been on the medical bus and they both had to juggle time together and no one was the guilty party.

She was sitting on her bed, leafing through *Firehouse* magazine, when Jim Mackenzie came in. "You okay?"

"Yeah. Wasn't in the mood for razzing."

"Want to talk without it?"

"I have been meaning to ask you a few things."

His smile was warm. Dropping down on the bed beside hers, he sat facing her. "Yes, Shirley and I fight over work. No, it's not the end of the world. And yes, I get pissed off about her not understanding my job."

"I'm that obvious?"

"Uh-huh. Unfortunately, this is a common problem." He cocked his head. "It's tough, Sophie. Just when you think things are going great, shit happens. What was it this time?"

"I'm doing twenty-four on Thanksgiving. I didn't know when I said I'd work for Cameron that I'd have a freakin' boyfriend. Truthfully, I didn't want to be alone."

"Ah, the holidays. Tough. Even tougher with kids. He has two, doesn't he?"

"Yeah. How do your kids deal, Cap?"

"With the schedule?"

"For one thing."

"They take their cue from Shirley. If she's pissed, so are they. I've missed a birthday or two. It's never okay; we just pretend it is." He waited a beat. "You should know what you're getting into."

"It's even more complicated." She told him about Kitty and Mikey's problems with abandonment.

His wince didn't comfort her. "Damn, that's too bad."

"Can your boys deal with the danger of firefighting?"

"I think so. After 9/11, everybody's kids and wives were really freaked. Eventually things evened out but it was tough for a while. Remember, though, that's all most of our families have ever known. I was a smoke eater when my boys were born."

"You're not helping, Cap."

"Sorry. We could arrange for my kids and Liam's to get together. Hang out. Maybe something would click."

"That would probably be good for Mikey. Cleary's another story."

"How old is he?"

"Thirteen."

"Then he's probably my son Terry's soul mate." The tone sounded and the cap stood up. "Think about it. Now let's go battle the Red Devil."

A flurry of activity followed, but in minutes they were on the rig and speeding toward Box 66, a 10-75. It was slippery out from the snow that had fallen earlier, but Murray was in control and glided the rig though the streets with expertise.

When the radio blared out that the run was a church fire, Bilotti swore. "I hate these."

Agreement all around. There had been a spate of church fires in Atlanta a few years ago that got national coverage. They were incendiary. That people would intentionally burn down houses of God was often harder to handle than other arson cases.

And of course, arson posed more of a threat to firefighters. Damn, Sophie wondered, why had she thought of that statistic?

The rig came to a screeching halt beside Engine 9 and they all piled out of the truck. Immediately Sophie was assaulted by the smell of burning wood, gas and the putrid scent of thick charcoal-gray smoke that was puffing out of the roof. Usually, she never noticed the smell, but today she did. Despite the heat from the blaze, she shivered inside her turnout coat.

The cap strode over to Incident Command while Sophie's group yanked pry tools out of the truck. She was handing a halligan to Spike Lawrence, Jules's sub, when the cap returned. "They laid a three-incher and a couple of hand lines. The roof's been ventilated."

"Anybody inside?" Cooper asked, strapping on his air pack.

Mac nodded off to the right. A group of people were huddled together: several women, gray-haired, slight, draped in blankets.

"Shit, they're all old."

"Rosary Society meeting tonight." Mackenzie's frown said he was bothered, too. "We're going in. A woman's missing."

Donning their SCBA and helmets, Sophie and her group followed their captain into the church. The smoke wasn't too thick and, with all their flashlights on, they managed to find their way through the huge narthex to the sanctuary, where the meeting had been held. The smoke was gray in here. The fire was out but Sophie knew it could spring up and devour them if it got hungry again. There were a few pops and snaps and something fell behind Sophie as she started down the aisle.

Into their radios, Mackenzie said, "Murray and me will go left. Bilotti, go right with Lawrence. Cooper and Tyler, take the altar. Search under those pews where the choir sits."

The heat increased as Sophie neared the altar. The crucifix overhead was dangling at an odd angle, badly charred. She and Cooper turned right and the others went left. She shined the light on the first pew in the choir area, the second, then the third. An arm was visible beneath the fourth.

"Shit," she shouted into the radio. "Got a body."

Reaching under the pew, she tried to drag the woman out. "She's stuck," Sophie reported into the radio. "Cap. We need help."

Mackenzie, Lawrence and Bilotti were there in a flash. Laying herself out flat, Sophie slid as far under the pews as she could get. "She's still breathing." Whipping off her mask, Sophie gave the woman air and coughed herself with the sudden influx of smoke into her lungs. Finally the older woman roused.

"Get back, Tyler. We gotta pry the pew loose."

Sophie rolled to her feet.

There was a loud boom on the opposite side of the building. "Holy shit." This from Lawrence, who'd staggered backward.

Over her radio, Sophie heard the command. "Evacuate the building. Firefighters are to evacuate the building. Flames are visible from the fellowship hall and origin of the explosion unknown." Outside the bullhorn signaling an immediate exit sounded almost simultaneously.

Sophie looked down at the stuck woman.

And froze.

"Pry the pew," Mackenzie hollered.

Bilotti went into action but Sophie just gripped the ax she held.

"Tyler, what are you waiting for? Get the right leg of the pew."

I love you. I've just felt it for a long time.

"Tyler!"

Startled, Sophie angled the ax at the claw of the pew and swung it hard while the guys finished with the other legs. Wood cracked from several different places. Bilotti and Lawrence lifted the heavy bench off the woman. She moaned and seemed disoriented. Bending down, Mackenzie removed his face mask and gave her some air. "Let's get her out of here."

Grabbing the victim under the arms, Lawrence nodded. "There's a side exit."

Cooper took her feet.

In seconds they were out the door.

Turning, Sophie saw the fellowship hall was fully involved. And the church had reignited.

FUCKING A. That was close. Almost didn't make it. I like the looks of that smoke. Real pretty curling up out of the flat roof of the hall. Smells like freakin' dog shit, though. Not like the rag in my hand. Sweet, sweet gasoline.

Noise on the other side. Ah, lookee here. Five of them stumbling out with an old lady. I'd better get back in the bushes. Hide. They can't see me in the evergreen shrubs. But I can see them. Hear them.

Coughing. Bending over. Giving the victim air.

The paramedics hustle around the corner, carrying a stretcher. "We've got her," one of them says.

Another asks, "Everybody out?"

"Yeah."

They scoot the woman away.

The new guy sits on the ground. Next to the girl. Ah, the girl. Timed this one right.

The big one, Bilotti, stands over her. "What the hell happened in there, Tyler?"

Her hair falls around her shoulders as she looks up at him. Always was pretty. "Nothing."

"Like hell. The tool didn't freeze up in midair by itself."

"I got something in my eye. I couldn't see. I was trying to blink it out."

"Back off, Bilotti," the captain barks. "Come on, let's go find out what we need to do next."

Conflict. Music to my ears, guys. An added bonus. In a few minutes, I can go out front, too, watch it all wind down. Meanwhile, look at that beautiful, beautiful fire.

SOPHIE DID HAVE something in her eye. After the medic washed it out, he gave her a gauze cloth to blot it with. But in her heart, she knew her eye wasn't why the halligan had frozen midair. The realization, and the cold out here on the street, made her shaky.

I love you.

She'd thought about Liam saying those words when the explosion hit. She'd thought about maybe dying in a burning church, and fear had paralyzed her for a minute.

"Hey, kiddo, you okay?"

The familiar voice soothed her. Until she realized what it meant. "Yeah, Joe. Something in my eye, is all." She frowned. "Another torch?"

"Looks that way. Initially in the church. Burn patterns indicated arson, so they called me."

She shook her head.

"See anything?"

Visualizing the scene, she watched herself going down the aisle. "Stained-glass windows were open on the right side. A couple of them."

He wrote that on a notepad. "Anything else?"

"I don't think so."

"The lady okay?"

"I heard she was. What was the boom in the fellowship hall?"

"More than likely the oven. Bet my ass there's evidence of gasoline rags there. That's the easiest way. Not sure our guy is the brightest lightbulb in the pack."

Over his shoulder Sophie saw someone approach. "Hey, there. Nice to see you."

Tommy Carusotti was taller than his brother, but slimmer. His dark hair didn't have the gray Joe's did, but his brown eyes were more world-weary. Maybe because he was a cop in a busy district now.

"Aren't you a sight for sore eyes." The men hugged, then Tommy kissed Sophie's cheek. "Long time no see, girl."

"Been busy. You, too?"

"Yeah." He winked at her. "Got a new lady in my life."

"Shut up!"

"How come I don't know about this?" Joe asked. He was good at playing big brother.

"Remember when you stole Susie Summers away from me in high school?"

"Hell, we were kids then."

The cap came over. "Hey there, Tommy."

"Mackenzie. How's it hangin'?"

"What are you doing in our neck of the woods?"

"I had business up this way. I saw the trucks, so I stopped to see the show."

Odd terminology, Sophie thought, but then Tommy was always a little off. One minute he was friendly and fun, the next sullen and sulking. Apparently tonight, he was the former. He slung an arm around her shoulder. "I miss you. Wanna have dinner sometime?"

Joe smiled. "I'll come, too."

"Freakin' hell you will. I wanna talk to her and you monopolize her when there's three of us."

The captain said, "Sorry to interfere with your social planning, but I need Tyler at the rig."

She kissed both men's cheeks. "See you later, guys. Call me, Tommy."

As they headed across the road, Mackenzie asked casually, "How's the eye?"

"Got it washed out." She held up the gauze.

"How'd stuff get through the face mask?"

"I took my SCBA off when I gave the woman under the pew air."

"Ah." They reached the rig and found Jules there, dressed in civilian clothes. The cap asked, "What are you doing here, Torres?"

"I heard it on the scanner. Wanted to see. I'm pissed I missed a fire."

"How'd the class go?"

"Good. The book is hard, though."

"Bring it to work," Sophie told him. "I'll help you."

Mackenzie stared at the fire, which was smoldering now. There was still smoke coming out of it. "Hell of a thing, isn't it? Torching a church."

Jules made the sign of the cross.

"Never did understand what kind of asshole would do

something like this." Murray sounded disgusted. She knew he went to church with his kid. "The guy must be twisted."

"Couldn't this be a woman?" Jules asked.

"Most of the fires set by women are revenge fires," Sophie answered. "This could be one if she had a grudge against the church."

They all climbed on the rig. For some reason, the thought of a female torch bothered Sophie all the way back to house. It covered the worry over what had happened to her in the fire. And the shame over why she'd thought of Liam's declaration at the moment she froze.

That night, they all fell asleep early.

Suddenly, Sophie was under a church pew; Liam stood over it. "I love you, Soph. Don't get hurt, please."

She struggled and struggled but couldn't get free. Then, she was in a stairway of the Twin Towers above the ninetieth floor. She heard the second plane hit and knew she was going to die.

Bolting up, she realized she was in bed, in the dark, breathing hard. They guys were all zonked, so she must not have screamed. Tiptoeing out of the bunk room so she wouldn't wake anybody, Sophie made her way downstairs. In the dim light from over the sink, she fixed coffee, then took a seat at the table with a mug of it—and tried not to panic over what she'd done in their run.

"Sophie?" She looked up to find Mackenzie in the doorway.

"Did I wake you?"

"No, the smell did. I don't sleep more than four hours at a time anymore."

"Another joy of being a firefighter."

After pouring himself coffee, he crossed to the table and took a seat. "Yep. Like I said before, there are a lot of them that people never know about. What woke you?"

"A dream. About 9/11."

"Jesus, nobody's had one of those in a long time." For months after the attack, firefighters nationwide had experienced nightmares about being trapped in the Towers.

Sophie swallowed hard just thinking about it.

For a few minutes, the cap didn't say more. Then he started to talk. "When Terry was born, I thought about quitting the department."

"What? Why?"

"I kept seeing his face when I walked into a burning building. I was a father. I had responsibility. It was a hell of a time for me."

Oh, God. Did he know? "W-what'd you do?"

"I took a leave. Got my head on straight. When I came back, I was okay."

"Glad it worked out."

His gaze was direct. "Sophie, we depend on you to do your job."

"Aren't I?"

"Eye or no eye, you froze in the church. If I see it again, I'll have to deal with it."

She started to speak.

"No, don't say anything. I don't wanna know details. I just want you to know my position."

They watched out the window as a few taxis sped by.

And suddenly, Sophie was flooded with doubt, and the fear that emotion often brought along with it. Firefighting was her life, the only stable part of her life, the only thing she could depend on. My God, she couldn't afford to lose it.

NINETEEN

THANKSGIVING DAY dawned bleak and gray in the Big Apple. Liam saw the dawn because he set the clock early to go to the pub and put in the turkeys. Luckily they had two good-size ovens. With the entire O'Neil clan coming for dinner, they'd need all the space they could get. The Secret Service had provided the food and drink, but the O'Neils were cooking it.

He dressed in clothes to cook in—jeans and a long-sleeved thermal shirt—wondering if Sophie was still asleep. He hoped so. She was on twenty-four-hour duty today and had told him the holiday would be hectic with kitchen fires and electrical short outs. Uptown, the FDNY would be busy because of the Macy's parade. Hell, he hated thinking about Sophie in the midst of all that action. She should be relaxing with family on Thanksgiving.

As he walked to the subway in the cold, windy morning, he thought about how distant she'd seemed this week. Since he'd told her he loved her. And she'd said it back. Maybe it was too soon to declare their feelings, but Liam didn't regret the words. He knew the tenuousness of life.

Especially hers.

He kept thinking about their troubled relationship as the train approached, and he got on and rode to the pub. When he was at the back door, he was still stewing about her. "Fuck! This is *not* easy." He raised his eyes to the sky. "Come on, give me a break!"

Once in the kitchen, he prepared the birds and shoved them into the ovens. The whole time, he talked to God. "I try to be a good person . . . I put the needs of my kids first, most of the time my family's . . . I lost the woman I'd loved since I was a kid. Can I *please* have something go right again?"

The back door opened, startling him. His brothers were coming in to help prepare food, but it was too early for that.

"Hey there, handsome." Sophie. Already in her uniform, wearing her shiny blue outer jacket, her cheeks were rosy from the cold morning. Her hair was down and fluffy, and the lights caught the reddish strands and played with them.

"Aren't you the answer to my prayers."

She sashayed toward him, slid her arms around his neck and kissed him thoroughly. Thoughts—and prayers—fled from his mind. He drew her closer, deepened the kiss and she gave him tongue action. After a long time, they pulled back. "Well, Happy Thanksgiving to you, too."

"I can stay for a while."

"Great. Did you eat?"

"No, but that's okay."

"Let me make us something. I'm hungry." He gave her a quick nuzzle. "Very hungry, after that kiss, darlin'."

"I'll help." She removed her coat, draped it over a chair and crossed to the counter.

She worked on toast and he fried bacon and eggs; they did the chores in relative silence, sipping the strong coffee she favored and he'd brewed earlier. Once they were seated on stools at the butcher block with full plates in front of them, she motioned to the kitchen. "You fixing the meal by yourself?"

"No. The guys are coming in a couple of hours. I told them to sleep in some. No sense in all of us getting up at the crack of dawn."

"You're a nice guy, Liam O'Neil."

"I was just telling somebody that."

"Who?"

"Never mind." He arched a brow. "But I was kind of hoping *you* were seeing a different side to me."

"Oh, I am. A very sexy side. But you're still a nice guy."

He watched her on the sly as she attacked the breakfast. He loved how she ate with passion. "The whole family's coming?" she asked between mouthfuls.

"Then some. Brie's parents are in town, so they'll be here. And Cara's dad's working today, so Mikey invited her and her mother. I think Dylan has a date."

"With who?"

"Some redhead, of course." He rolled his eyes. "Then the Secret Service will descend. I cooked an extra turkey just for them."

"No kidding?" She shook her head. "It's amazing how your sister lives."

"It'll be worse if Clay runs for president."

"Who knows? You might be having Thanksgiving dinner in the White House someday."

He waited. "Just me?"

"And the kids, of course. Your family."

"That's not what I meant." At her questioning look, he said, "Maybe you, too, sweetheart."

She just stared at him.

Her reaction pissed him off again. "Soph, people who love each other make plans."

"Don't you think it's too soon for that?"

"No." He stood and cleared his plate. "But obviously, you do."

"I didn't say that."

"You didn't have to. All week, by the way."

"What does that mean?"

He put the dishes in the sink, then turned toward her. "That since that night we confessed to loving each other, you've been acting strangely."

"We had some rough fires. I've been distracted."

"So you admit the behavior change."

"Don't put words in my mouth."

Liam shook his head. Just a few minutes ago, they were practically jumping each other's bones. Nothing like this had ever happened with Kitty, this change of mood so fast it left him floundering. "Is something wrong? Because if it is, we can talk about it."

He could tell he hit a nerve by how her mouth tightened.

"What is it?"

"I didn't want to talk about this with you yet."

Coming back to the counter, he braced his hands on its edge. "You can't leave me hanging, now."

She sipped her coffee, then looked up at him. "Liam, after you told me you loved me, I had a hard time in the fire."

"Define hard time."

"I sort of froze when the fellowship hall of the church exploded."

"As any sane person might."

"No, it's deadly for a firefighter to freeze, even for a split second."

"Are you saying this is my fault?"

"In a way. I was thinking about you. And it happened when I was rappelling, too. I thought about you and Mikey and froze for a minute suspended in midair."

"Jesus Christ, buildings exploding and dangling hundreds of feet up in the air are things to freeze about."

"Not for firefighters. My captain caught on. He gave me a warning."

"For what?"

"That if I can't do my job and be in love, then I gotta choose."

"This is crazy. Other firefighters are married. Have kids."

"Maybe they've been through this before. Mackenzie said it was hard for him after his son was born, knowing he risked his life every day."

"There you go."

"He took some leave, got his head on straight."

Now *that* would be an answer to his prayers, at least temporarily. "You could take some time off."

"No! People would see me as a weak female who can't handle the job. I can't afford to show any vulnerability. I'd be a sitting duck for their criticism the rest of my career."

"Sweetheart . . ."

"No! End of discussion. I have to deal with this alone."

"Not alone, Soph. You've got me."

"You're the *problem*."

"Is that what I am now?"

Shoving back the stool, she stood. "I shouldn't have told you."

"No, you should have. It just makes me mad to think you feel bad about loving me. Loving the boys."

"If it destroys my career, I do."

"That's a pretty big leap." She just watched him. "What are you going to do?"

"Nothing. Now. I'm hoping I don't panic on runs today."

"So, I should be waiting with bated breath to see how you react in fires and if it's bad, we're done? Great Thanksgiving day."

She crossed to him and surprised him by sidling between him and the counter and resting her head on his chest. It was an incredibly tender gesture and had his arms coming around her. "No, we wouldn't be *done* if that happened. It would just tell me if this is an aberration or the norm. Then I'll deal with it."

"Oh, that makes me feel better. I'll have no say."

Abruptly, she pulled away. "Give me a break, Liam."

"I'm sorry, this is . . . unexpected."

"For me, too." She glanced at the clock. "I gotta go. I'm sorry if I ruined your Thanksgiving."

"I'll be okay. Don't worry about m—" He shook his head. "I guess that's the issue."

"Can I call you today? Just to hear your voice."

Now he felt like shit. "Of course you can. Try to enjoy your turkey dinner."

"It won't be as good as yours." She kissed his cheek. "I do love you."

"I love you, too."

Which, he thought as she walked out, was not as joyful as it should be on Thanksgiving day.

DYLAN HAD ALWAYS thought he came from a normal family. But as he scanned the pub, he had to chuckle at how wrong he'd been. Like always, the kids had their own tables, and Cleary, Hogan and Pat's sons Sean and Sinead were jabbing each other. The younger ones, Kathleen, Rory, Mike and the little girl he'd invited, were tucked in a corner and quieter.

But it was the big table—really several smaller ones pushed together—that was *not* Norman Rockwell. The vice president of the United States and the Second Lady were at one end. Angel was in a high chair next to Bailey, Tyler closer to Clay asleep in a carrier. Standing post ten feet away at the front of the pub, and at the back door, were black-suited Secret Service agents.

Bailey lifted her glass. "To my brother, for this wonderful meal. Thanks, Liam. *Slainté.*"

After they all raised their glasses and toasted Liam, Dylan pretended offense. "You know, we helped. I made the onions and applesauce."

Pat waved his hand. "I fixed the sweet potatoes and vegetables."

Aidan, who was having a hard time enjoying himself—that kid could be impossible—tried a smile. "Mama and I made the desserts, right, beautiful?"

"You watched," C.J. said. Before they'd gone to her mother's house for a few days of Ludzecky-style celebration, Aidan had *helped* Mama bake.

Ma patted her youngest son's arm. "He was good company."

The joking began again. But Liam got up and crossed to the buffet table. Dylan sensed something was wrong again, and he'd bet it was spelled S-o-p-h-i-e. Excusing himself from his date, Colleen Lucas, a dancer with a small ballet company, he followed Liam. "Need more food out?"

"Yeah, the service is going to eat in shifts."

"Bring on the second turkey."

"This will be the fourth, buddy."

"I'll help." He followed Liam to the kitchen; Liam lifted another turkey from the oven where it was warming, and Dylan handed him the knife. They talked as his brother sliced the bird in quick, efficient movements.

"Your date's a looker."

"Gotta love those dancers."

"Hmm."

"Why don't you call her?"

Liam stopped slicing. "Honestly?"

"Uh-huh."

"I'm afraid to. It bothers me that she's out on the streets today. I don't want to know the details."

"Just tell her you love her."

At Liam's surprised look, Dylan chuckled. "It's obvious. But I could always read you like a book anyway."

"Time for a change of subject. How's Hogan?"

"Glad to be here."

"Where's Stephanie?"

"In Paris. She never lets up, even on holidays."

"What is it with our women? Brie's not around enough to suit Pat. Stephanie chose her career. Aidan's still pissed off about C.J.'s protective duty, and Sophie's schedule is impossible."

"I was just thinking how we always used to be a normal family." His dark brows narrowed. "I never expected life to turn out this way."

Liam transferred meat to the platter. "We don't sound very grateful for all we have today."

"No, I guess not."

Handing Dylan the first tray of meat, Liam gave him a fake smile. "Here, take this out."

When Dylan brought the turkey to the buffet table, his sister stood and crossed to Mitch Calloway. "All right, this was the deal. Organize the shifts now so you can take turns eating."

Mitch's lips thinned. "It's not protocol, Ms. O'Neil."

"I'll sic Clay on you."

"All right."

Dylan slid his arm around his sister. "Rules with a velvet fist, this one."

"Not so velvet," Mitch grumbled.

But he got the guys—and one woman who'd been added to Clay's detail—to get ready to eat. C.J. stood, talked to a couple of the agents, then came over to Dylan.

"How's the shoulder?" he asked.

"I'm back at work." She smiled but looked tired. "You'd think I was at death's door."

"He gets scared."

C.J. nodded. "I know. I hate that my job worries him, but I gotta be who I am, Dyl."

He'd heard that from Stephanie. The good thing in his brother's situation was that C.J. loved Aidan wholeheartedly. Whereas Stephanie—who knew where her head was at. "He'll be okay."

"I know." She wrinkled her nose. "I just hate fighting about this again."

Dylan glanced to the kitchen. Suddenly he felt really sorry for Liam. His brother was right—his life with a New York City firefighter was never going to be easy.

"Is THE GRAVY hot?" Al Daniels asked.

Sophie tested it with her finger. "Yep."

"Think we'll get to eat this meal?"

"I've worked several Thanksgivings. I'm running about fifty-fifty."

Al smiled over at her. "Nice of you to sub for Cameron. His wife rags on him about holidays."

Join the club.

"How about you, Al? Any family to miss you?"

"Divorced." He moved the turkey from the stove top to the counter. "I couldn't make it work with the wife." He nodded to the living area. "Notice how few family members came?"

"Yeah, I did. Too bad."

"I dig this job, but it's got its drawbacks." He nodded to the table. "Put the gravy on the hot plate and get the salads out of the fridge."

As she worked, Sophie thought about the four runs they'd had this morning.

A kitchen fire that Daniels said he could have pissed on and put out.

A Christmas tree lit for the first time that burned out part of a living room.

A car accident over in the Village. Sophie had had to climb inside the cab again.

And a bar near Bailey's Irish Pub whose stove had caught on fire.

Minor runs. No panic.

His back to her, Daniels said, "Call the troops."

Sophie went into the living area. There were about twenty-five people in here. Two dozen smoke eaters. Two battalion chiefs. Two wives. Six kids. The mother and sister of one of the guys. Sophie tried to imagine Liam here for dinner and missing the holiday with his boisterous family. She tried to picture Mary Kate O'Neil, or Patrick, spending mealtime at a firehouse. No way. And that didn't even touch the vice president and his family. As she studied the group assembled, she wondered if she was kidding herself. Was she ever going to fit into his life or him into hers?

When everybody sat down and the battalion chief had given a blessing, the tone sounded.

"Box 66. 10-75. Two alarm. Engine 33 and Truck 44 go into service."

The swearing was kept to a minimum in deference to the kids, but the faces in the room told a story loud and clear . . . pouts from the children . . . rage on one wife's face . . . a mother's sadness.

With a heavy heart, Sophie strode out of the kitchen to the bay.

SOMETHING WAS WRONG with his dad. Mike could tell. He was smiling, but not with his eyes. His mom used to say that was how you knew when Dad was pretending. So Mike left his cousins and went to the kitchen. "Dad?"

His father was over by the window staring at the snowflakes

that fell outside. He turned around. "Hey, buddy, need something?"

"Nope." He glanced at the phone on the table. "Sophie call?"

"Uh, no."

"I feel bad she isn't here."

"Me, too."

"Why don't you call her?"

"She said she'd call us. She might have runs and not be there. Aren't you having fun out there?"

"Uh-huh."

His dad squatted down. "Come here, Mike." When Mike crossed the room, his father grasped him by the shoulders and looked him in the eye. "You miss Mom? You said last year that you missed her most on holidays."

Mike had talked to her picture last night. Asked her if it was okay that Sophie was in their lives this Thanksgiving and Christmas. She said yes.

"Not as much as before."

His dad seemed surprised.

"I like having Sophie around."

A big, fat frown from his father.

Mike didn't understand. "You don't feel better with her being with us?"

"Yeah, I guess I do. I just didn't associate it with missing Mom or not."

"Is that bad, Dad?"

"No, of course not. Your mom would want you to be happy."

"You, too."

He just nodded.

"You sure I can't call her?"

"I guess it'd be okay."

His dad gave him the phone and he punched in Sophie's cell phone.

"You know her number by heart, son?"

"Yeah, sure. Don't you?"

Mikey heard, "This is Sophie. Leave a message."

He clicked off. "She's not there. Think she's fighting a fire?"

"Could be."

"I'm going back out to see Cara."

"All right."

He hugged his father. "I wish you weren't sad today."

"I'm not, honey."

Mike shook his head. His dad was lying. That made Mike even sadder.

AS MIKE LEFT, Cara's mother, Julia, a nice-looking blonde with a cute smile, walked into the kitchen. She ruffled his son's hair as they passed each other.

"Hey, Julia. Need something?" Liam asked.

"I was hoping I could help you. I feel useless."

"You're our guest."

"Please, let me do something."

Liam smiled over at her. "The wine you brought was enough."

She held up the glass she'd carried into the kitchen. "I know your sister and her husband can't drink this, but would you like some?"

"Sure, I'll have a glass."

She poured him some, handed it to him, then said, "Put me to work."

He sipped the wine. "Hmm, good. You can slice more bread. Some of the agents might want sandwiches."

Near to her now at the counter, Liam noticed several things about Julia Cahill. She was very pretty, but her eyes were weary. Though she was dressed in a nice peach skirt and sweater, she seemed a bit pale.

"Sorry your husband couldn't make it."

Lines formed around her mouth when she looked up. "Hazard of the job."

"Tell me about it." He glanced at his cell phone, which he'd put on the table for when Sophie called.

Julia tracked his gaze. "I noticed Sophie isn't here. I like her and appreciated the interest she took in Cara."

"I wish she could have had dinner with us."

"Work?"

"Yep." He cocked his head and impulsively asked, "How do you do it, Julia? Make it work when your husband has a dangerous job with a crazy schedule?"

A pause. "I don't do it very well."

Liam stilled. "I'm sorry. I didn't mean to pry."

"No, that's okay. It's been tough for me for a long time. We're at a low point now. Johnny wants another baby, and I can't handle any more responsibility as pretty much the sole caregiver."

"I know all about that, too. Single parenting is hard."

"Cara doesn't suspect anything's wrong, but Johnny and I talk about divorce . . . oh, maybe every six months."

"Have you tried counseling?"

"He won't go. He says it's the nature of his job and he can't change that." She shook her head. "Listen to my mouth running. I must have had too much of my own wine."

"I'm sorry. If it's any help, I truly do understand."

"And I'm sorry for rambling." She nodded to the turkey. "I guess you couldn't go to the firehouse for dinner."

"Excuse me?"

"Families of firefighters can go to the firehouse on holidays. I always envied that about them, as opposed to cops."

"Uh, she didn't invite me."

"Well, you couldn't have gone anyway."

"Yeah, right."

She nodded to the second platter of turkey. "Go, take that out. I'll follow with the bread as soon as it's sliced."

Liam served the food thinking about Cara and her mother, discouraged by Julia's admissions. And about the noninvitation to the firehouse. God, was no one happy?

When he returned to the kitchen, Julia had her back to him and was holding his cell phone in her hand, speaking into it. "Um, yes this is Liam's number . . . I'll get him." She turned. "I saw you looking at the phone. It rang so I answered it. I think it's Sophie."

"Oh, thanks."

Liam took the phone, and Julia said, "I'll be leaving."

When he was alone, he spoke into his cell. "Hello?"

"Who the hell was answering your phone, Liam?"

SOPHIE WAS UP in the bunk room and had given a lot of thought to calling Liam. Now, she wished she hadn't. "I asked who that was."

"I heard you. How could I not? You were yelling." His voice sounded strained.

"I'm sorry. I didn't mean to snap. I just didn't expect another woman to answer your phone." No response. "Who was it?"

"Julia Cahill."

"Cara's mother?" Tall. Willowy. Blond.

"Uh-huh. Mike invited them because her husband had to work today." He added, "New York's Finest don't get a break, either, I guess."

O-kay. She had a choice. Ruin the call, or forget about Liam keeping company with a beautiful woman he had a lot in common with. "How was dinner?"

"Great. It's a zoo, though. The Secret Service has to eat in shifts. We just got their food out."

We. "Crazy life Bailey leads. How's my namesake?"

"Holding court. Between him and Angel and Isabella, people are getting their fill of babies."

"Sweet."

"You want a baby, Sophie?"

A long pause on her end. "Where did that come from?"

"I don't know. I just thought of it. Do you?"

"I guess. I don't know how I'd balance that, too."

"I agree it'd be a problem."

Of course you do.

"Do other female firefighters have kids?"

"Yes. You know that."

"Any working today?"

"Liam, where is this going?"

"Sorry. I'm melancholy, I guess." He waited and so did she. "How was your dinner?"

"Cold. We got a run as soon as it was served."

"Oh, sweetheart, I'm sorry."

"We ate when we got back, but it wasn't the same."

"Been busy?"

"Uh-huh. Routine stuff mostly."

"Catch any fires?"

"Minor ones."

In the background, she heard, "Hey, Dad, come on, the Secret Service just brought in Sean's birthday cake."

"Be right there."

"I'll let you go."

"What time will you go to sleep, if you don't have a run?"

"Around midnight."

"I'll call you before then, when everyone's gone."

"Okay. I love you," she whispered.

"I love you, too, *a ghrá*."

Sophie clicked off her phone and stared at it. Stretched out on the cot, she closed her eyes. It had been a very unsatisfactory phone call. Added to what happened earlier . . .

A rolling fire. A roof that needed to be ventilated. And when it was, flames shooting up through it. Al Daniels had been burned.

And once again, for a few seconds, Sophie had frozen.

TWENTY

BEFORE SOPHIE went to work at the pub on the Tuesday after Thanksgiving, she headed to the Secret Service Field Office. C.J. had told her how to get to the undisclosed location when Sophie had called and asked to see her. At the entrance to the nondescript building she stopped at the reception desk. "I'm Sophie Tyler. I'm here for Agent Ludzecky."

The uniformed guard, who was a member of the second branch of the Secret Service—C.J. was a special agent—checked the list. "I'll show you to her office."

He led her through several corridors; off of them were some cubicles and one larger room with desks where agents were looking at numerous wall screens and a maze of other equipment.

C.J.'s office was at the end of one of the hallways. She was sitting at her desk with earphones on, taking notes on a pad. It was odd to see her in the traditional government outfit of a black suit and white blouse and the American flag lapel pin. When she looked up, she motioned Sophie in.

Wandering around, Sophie studied the wall plaques behind C.J., the large window looking out at New York City and the computer setup that looked like it came from an episode of the *Outer Limits*. The desk was organized, and there was a picture of C.J.'s family, and one of Aidan, perched on it.

After a minute or so, C.J. took off the device. "Sorry about that. We've got a threat and the accent of the caller is tough for even me to crack. Take off your coat. Have a seat."

Removing the wool peacoat she wore over jeans and a sweater, Sophie sat in a chair. "Your job must be exciting."

"Yeah, it is. Not quite the merry-go-round the vice presidential detail was, but it keeps me busy and happy." She cocked her head at Sophie. "Wish I could say the same for my fiancé. Which is why you're here, right?"

"No, I didn't come about Aidan."

C.J.'s hazel eyes flickered with understanding. "Ah. Then it's about Liam having trouble with your job."

"Did he tell you that?"

"No, Aidan used it as ammunition when we had our last fight about my getting shot."

Sophie frowned. "Liam seems to be dealing. Aidan's not?"

"He's being a baby." She shook her head and a few blond tendrils escaped the knot at her neck. "We already rang this bell, and now he's reneging on his promise to handle my job. I'm furious at him."

"You got shot, C.J."

She rubbed her arm. "I guess I'm overreacting, too, but hell, he's talking about calling off the wedding."

"I'm sorry."

"He won't. He's just mad. Amazing how you forget you just wanted to be together and would work *anything* out to accomplish that." She watched Sophie. "But let's talk about you and Liam. Can I ask you something first?" Sophie nodded. "Is it serious between you two?"

"I'm in love with him."

C.J. smiled broadly. "And he feels the same?"

"Yes. But there are issues." She recounted their concerns about Mikey and the schedule Liam was already having trouble with. Hell, he'd even brought up having babies.

"Those O'Neil men. They're all alike."

"I was hoping you could assure me that things will work out for me and Liam."

"I think they will." She leaned back; her expression conflicted. "I'm not giving up on Aidan, if that's what you're asking."

No response.

"Sophie, you were supposed to say you weren't giving up on Liam, either."

"There's something I need to ask you. I'd appreciate it if you'd keep it confidential."

"Whatever you want."

"As an agent, you must have learned to control your own fear along the way. I know I had to as a firefighter."

"Yes, of course."

"After you fell in love, did it change? Did you ever get scared in a way you hadn't before?"

C.J. stared hard at her. "My answer needs to be confidential, too. If Aidan ever found out . . ."

"So you did."

"I do. Fleetingly. I think about him and it makes me scared for a just a second."

"Does it affect your ability to perform your job?"

"No. I've learned to cope with it. And it doesn't happen much anymore. When I got shot, it wasn't Aidan I was thinking about." She waited a beat. "You having a problem with this?"

"Just a couple of times. It's thrown me, though. And my captain caught on."

"Not good. But for what it's worth, I do think it's manageable."

"If it isn't?"

"I don't know, Sophie, maybe you'd have to choose."

"You made a choice. You chose Aidan."

"I could live without the VPPD but not without him." She motioned to the office. "Luckily, I can still do work I love."

"I don't know anything else but line firefighting. It's been my dream since I was ten. It's who I am."

"Don't panic. Maybe the fear thing will even out like it did with me."

"Maybe. I hope so."

Sophie left C.J.'s office unnerved. She hadn't gotten the assurance she'd wanted. It hit her when she boarded the subway that maybe what she wanted was impossible to get.

WITH THE WIND kicking up snow and reddening their faces, Liam held Sophie's hand as they walked down Fifth Avenue. Silver garlands and red bows decorated posts and storefronts. The odd Christmas carol drifted out of cars and businesses and bell ringers were on every corner. Despite the weather, December in New York was one of his favorite times of year. Hers, too, she said.

"Wait." She stopped at a Salvation Army red bucket. Digging under her wool peacoat into her pants—she never carried a purse—she pulled out some bills. He took a minute to admire how the black jeans hugged her hips, and the boots she wore accented them.

When she was done, he pulled up the coat's hood and took her gloved hand again. "Let's go in FAO Schwarz. I want to get some things for Tyler and Angel and Isabella."

She chuckled. "Three babies. Fun to buy for at Christmas."

He bit his tongue. They could have a baby of their own by next December twenty-fifth. He'd been thinking about that since Thanksgiving. But he was determined not to spoil today. They had a whole day together, for a change, and he was sick of the bickering.

As they entered the world-famous store, they were greeted by a three-story clock tower singing "Welcome to Our World of Toys." Little kids ran from display to display screeching with excitement. Liam grinned at them, broadly. "Man, I love this place."

She'd taken off her hood and unbuttoned her coat. "I can see. Were your Christmases fun when you were young?"

"Let's head left. Yeah, they were fun except for the year Dad was gone. We were all a bunch of sad sacks on Christmas morning, even though he came over."

"That's right. You said your parents split for a while."

"Yeah, they were both bullheaded then. Problem was Pa

hooked up with another woman for a few months and ended up with a daughter that he never knew about."

"Wow, you never mentioned that."

"It's tough to talk about. Pat has trouble with Pa on occasion because of the whole thing."

"What happened to her?"

"She was in a gang and died." He looked down at her. "People have issues—huge ones—and resolve them, Soph. Anyway, to answer your question, we didn't have much money, but they managed some great gifts and there was always good food. My brothers and I doted on Bailey so she got more than usual."

"Sounds wonderful, with or without a lot of material things."

"How about you?"

"We had almost nothing until I was ten and my mother died. She didn't really do Christmas. Then, everything changed."

"The fire department."

"Gifts flooded in every year after we went to live with my grandmother. It was almost embarrassing. The Carusottis helped us give some away to children's shelters. Tommy never liked doing that though. He said we should keep them."

"I haven't met any of them."

She stood on tiptoes and kissed his cheek. "Soon." They arrived at Spanky, the Gund Where Bear, where they could get directions. "Doll department," Liam said.

After Spanky told them where to go, Sophie socked Liam in the arm. "Seriously, we're getting them dolls?"

"Uh, yeah."

"Tyler, too?"

"Uh-huh."

"You're lying. You weren't planning on that until I said something."

"Of course I was." He raised his chin. "Then we're heading to the baseball section and getting them all mitts. That was the plan, scout's honor."

"Yeah, sure."

They did purchase the dolls—baby ones with big brown eyes and cute outfits. And pint-size mitts like he'd bought his boys when they were little. When he and Sophie were finished at the store, they walked outside to blasts of cold air. They both buttoned up. "Hungry?" he asked.

"Are you kidding?"

"There's a sushi bar down the street. Let's eat there." He pulled her as close as the gifts would allow. "Then maybe head to your place."

"Now I believe you planned *that*."

The restaurant was crowded at three in the afternoon with businessmen and women dressed in suits and shoppers with bags from the toy store, Bloomingdales and Macy's. Halfway through the meal, Sophie's cell phone rang.

He grasped her hand across the table. "Don't answer it."

"I have to see who it is. I won't take it unless it's Nate."

"Fair enough." He popped a spring roll into his mouth as she checked the caller ID. Her eyes were apologetic when she looked up. "It's him."

Faintly irritated, he said, "Go ahead."

"Hi, buddy."

He felt guilty as he watched her eyes moisten when she heard her brother's voice. He knew she really missed him. For a minute he wondered what it would be like to be separated from Pat, Dylan and Aidan. It was bad enough having Bailey in DC.

Sophie glanced over at Liam and saw him staring at her with a scowl on his face. He was irritated about this call. Jesus.

"So, how's my favorite sister doing?" Nate asked. Static made him hard to hear.

"Great. Did you get my last e-mail?"

"Yeah. But your tone doesn't match what you said in it."

"You're breaking up, Nate," she said, hoping like hell they didn't lose the connection.

"Just a sec. That better?"

"Yeah"

"You sound upset, Soph."

"No, no. I'm out for lunch with someone."

"Liam?"

"Uh-huh."

"How's it going?"

"So-so."

"Well, I got great news."

"I could use some."

"I got a week at Christmas just to spend with you. We have to meet over here, though, or it'd be just a few days."

Uh-oh.

"Soph? Did you hear me?"

"Yeah, I heard you. It's great news. What and when did you have in mind?"

"Greece. There's this little island called Santorini. You'll love the sunshine. We can veg, catch up. And this is the best part—I've got the actual day of Christmas off. You're not working that week, right?"

"No, I took it off like we discussed last year. What about flights?"

"Pulled some strings. My colonel's daughter is a bigwig at one of the airlines. She already got you a ticket."

Again a silence.

"Honey, I need to see you." His voice was gravelly—how it got when he was upset. "It's been tough here and I have some things I have to talk to you about."

"Of course. Anything you want. I can't wait to see you."

"Sweet. I'll work out the details and be in touch." After a moment he added, "Are you sure you're okay?"

Until I get off the phone. "Yep. I love you, Nate."

"Love you, too. See you soon."

When she clicked off, Liam angled his head. "You're frowning. Bad news?"

"No. At least I don't think so. Nate has furlough at Christmas."

"Hey, great. I can't wait to meet him."

"You won't. He only has a week. I have to fly over to Europe to be with him."

His face blanked. "You're joking, right?"

She shook her head.

"Sophie, you can't do that. We're invited to DC for Christmas at the vice presidential residence. It's all planned."

"Without consulting me?" she asked.

"I knew you had the time off. I was saving the good news as a surprise today."

"Well, I am surprised."

"Yeah, me, too." His voice was cut glass cold.

"I'm really tired of this seesaw."

"We agree on that, at least."

Music filtered around them. The song currently playing was "I'll Be Home for Christmas."

Liam glared at her. She matched it.

Suddenly, the day had gone south, like too many of their times together lately.

"It's not working." Liam faced Jay Yost over his desk and said the words out loud for the first time. They made him cringe.

"With Sophie?" Liam nodded. "I'm shocked. The last time you were here together, things were great. What happened?"

"The *latest* is the holidays. But that's not all of it."

"Tell me about the holidays first."

As he told the story, he got angry all over again. "I suppose I could handle it this year, but fuck, Jay, I don't want to live this way. And I'm concerned about Mikey and Cleary."

He told Jay how his youngest had come to him soon after Sophie had dropped the bomb about her brother . . .

Mikey held a little Christmas tree ornament in his hand. It was crudely shaped like a helmet and decorated with a number. "Do you think Sophie will like this? We made it in school. For our mothers in the shape of whatever they did for a living." Mikey's face wasn't sad, though. "It's okay if I made it for Sophie, isn't it?"

"It's fine. She'll love it."

"I'm gonna give it to her at Aunt Bailey's house."

"Maybe you should do it before, buddy."

"Why?"

"I don't think she's going to make it to DC."

Mike's face had flushed. "You mean she won't be with us on Christmas, either?"

"No, she's flying over to Europe to see her brother, Nate. Remember, he's in the army."

"You said she'd be with us." His voice rose. "That she couldn't spend Thanksgiving here, but she would Christmas. Dad, she's got to spend Christmas with us."

"I'm sorry, son. She hasn't seen her brother in a long time."

Mikey had stomped off, and been sullen the rest of the night. It had broken Liam's heart when he found Sophie's gift in the trash that night . . .

"Did you take it out of the trash?" Jay asked.

"No. I thought about it, but then he had a bad dream that night. About his mother."

"Tough situation, Liam. You said Cleary was upset, too?"

"Uh-huh. Mike told him about Sophie's Christmas plans, and he came stomping downstairs . . ."

Dad, you need a new girlfriend. This is bullshit.

Cleary, you like Sophie. I know you do.

Yeah, but what good is it if she doesn't want to be with us? I vote for finding somebody else.

"What about you, Liam?" Jay asked after he told the therapist that story. "Do you vote for finding another woman?"

He was seriously considering it. Especially after what happened when they made love after the fiasco at lunch. Almost wordlessly, they'd gone back to her place. And had nearly brutal sex. It had only made things worse.

"What are you thinking?"

"That maybe Cleary's right. Maybe I need to consider my options."

"Want some advice?"

"Of course."

"Don't burn any bridges. What you do now will affect the course of the rest of your life. And your kids."

"Either way. If I marry her, we're in for a lifetime of these ups and downs."

"You were lucky with Kitty. Most relationships are up and down."

"Yeah, but you can hedge your bets. Falling for a New York City firefighter wasn't one of my best moves."

"But you did fall."

"I did. I'm in love with her."

"Be sure to consider that in what you do now."

"I get the point. I won't be rash."

"Wow, Brie, this is lovely." Sophie followed C.J. in to Patrick and Brie's house in Rockaway Beach. It was a redbrick, two-story structure, with a beautiful foyer and rooms spread out from each side.

"Thanks. We like it. Come onto the porch." They followed Brie down a ceramic-tiled corridor that flowed into a kitchen that was a chef's paradise.

"Won't the porch be a little cold?" Sophie asked. Her hands were freezing because she'd forgotten gloves.

"It's heated." C.J. was already whipping off her outerwear. "It's sweet being out there when the snow falls."

C.J. was right. It was fun to sit on the flowered rattan furniture and watch the snowflakes kiss the six glass sliding doors. As the tiny crystals fell to the ground they melted. "How long have you lived here?"

"My grandparents left me the house. I'm an only child and they were from the city. Pat and I moved in when the kids were little."

"Brie's rich. Don't hold it against her."

It was obvious the two of them were close enough to joke.

Brie shrugged. "My family's well off. What can I say?"

"You are, too," C.J. added. "You're raking it in with your business."

Again, a very genuine smile. "I'm doing all right. We've been able to renovate to make it like we want."

Sophie watched Brie as she crossed to a side table to fix drinks. She had to be the most stylish woman Sophie ever met. For today's *girl's lunch*, she wore an emerald-green lounging outfit that made her eyes look like jade. On her feet were little gold slippers that Sophie would never have thought of buying. Hair, nails, makeup—everything was perfect.

She didn't seem like Pat's type at all.

"Eggnog or wine?"

Both women chose wine, so Brie opened a bottle of

Chardonnay. When it was poured, she joined them and they all lifted their glasses. "Shall we toast to the O'Neil men?" Brie asked.

"Who drive us crazy," C.J. added.

Sophie's eyes misted and the other two women lowered the glasses.

"What is it, Sophie?" Brie asked.

She shook her head. "You two *have* O'Neil men. You're married or engaged. This is all new with me and Liam and I'm not sure we're going to make it."

Brie blew out a heavy breath. "Join the club. I've never been sure Patrick and I will last."

"You're kidding, right?"

"Trouble from day one. We separated for a while."

"I didn't know that."

"Isabella was conceived in the middle of it. Separation sex."

C.J. chuckled. "Aidan and I had it, too, when we broke up."

"Would you have reconciled anyway?" Sophie asked Brie. "Or is that too personal to ask?"

"Who knows? We have a shaky history. I got pregnant when I was in college. We had Sinead but didn't get married until he was a year old. A long story I don't talk about much."

"Wow."

"My point is there are no guarantees in a relationship. In making one or staying in one." She shook her head. "But I love him so much. I just hate how he acts sometimes and how strained our relationship gets."

"I'm sorry, Brie. I was whining about my own problems with Liam."

"I'm telling you this because I love Liam like he was my own brother. And I know he loves you. Please, tread carefully with his heart. It's been broken once, and we all thought that was irreparable."

C.J. squeezed Sophie's arm. "We're not ganging up on you, girl. Just . . . trying to make you part of the family, I guess."

"I don't feel ganged up on. I appreciate your honesty. As I

said, I love him. I want our relationship to work." She swallowed hard. "Your stories help."

Brie's cell rang. She leaned over the table. "Speak of the devil. It's Liam." She put her finger to her mouth. "Don't talk. Hey, Liam . . . *What?* Oh, my God. No, no, he's not here. Um, no, he's not with them, either. Because C.J. and Sophie are sitting right across from me. What can I do?" Another pause. "Yes, of course. I'll tell them, too."

"What is it?" Sophie asked, panicking at the part of the conversation she'd heard and the way Brie had gone totally pale.

"Liam can't find Mikey. The schools had a half day today, and he didn't come home on the bus."

"What?" Sophie whipped out her cell to check her messages. "Nothing from him on my voice mail." She stood. "I'll head back to the city and call Liam on my way." Forcefully she suppressed the thought that Liam hadn't called *her* nor had he asked to talk to her. This wasn't about their relationship.

C.J. stood, too. "I'll come."

Brie wrapped her arms around her waist. "Liam asked me to stay home in case Mike makes his way out here by himself."

Now, Sophie felt a different kind of fear. One that she'd never, ever experienced before. "Stay in touch. Here's my number."

After Brie punched it into her cell, C.J. and Sophie left.

All the way back to the city, Sophie felt the worry in her heart increase with each mile. It was a mother's worry for her child.

"HEY, MISTER, can you help me?" Mike shivered; he was wearing his winter jacket, but he'd forgotten his gloves and hat this morning.

The cab driver who was hanging out on Thirteenth Street rolled down the rest of his window. He'd been smoking and blowing white puffs out the opening. "What'd you say?"

"I need a cab."

"What are you, eight or nine? I got a kid that age."

"Eight. I need a cab." He handed the guy a piece of the phone book he'd torn out of the yellow pages. "To here."

"Sorry, I can't . . ." The driver looked down and frowned. "Somebody you know there?"

Mike nodded. "I got cash." He took his stash out of his backpack. "I know how much it is. My dad took me there. I got enough to come back, too. Cleary says cabs wait for people."

"The meter runs while I wait. You got enough money to cover it?"

Mike didn't know that. He just stared at the driver, his heart beating fast, his lips beginning to tremble.

"What the hell? Get in. I'd just worry about you getting picked up by somebody else who'd do God knows what."

Mike climbed in the cab. It smelled like smoke, but he didn't care. It reminded him of the firehouse where Sophie worked. He watched the scenery pass as the car went through the city, then out a ways. "It's the second entrance with the arches. By the big stone thing with the huge angels." He knew where to go because his dad had taught him how to find it.

When the cab pulled up to his destination, Mike had trouble with the door because his hands were shaking, but he finally got out. It was even colder here. And nobody was around. "Y-you're gonna wait, right?"

"Yeah." The cab driver looked at him. "Ain't you got no gloves or hat?"

He shook his head and felt the shivers travel though his body.

"Then hurry up, kid."

Mike trudged over the bumpy gravel; the wind howled, scaring him. But he kept going. Finally, he was there. He knelt down, feeling the ground beneath his knees. "Hi, Mommy. I came out here because I was hoping you could hear me better." He touched the cold headstone, which read *Loving Wife and Mother*. "I feel bad. I thought you said it was okay to have Sophie with us. But she didn't come to Thanksgiving, and she can't come to Christmas, and she's in danger all the time. You gotta tell me. Are you sure this is okay?"

LIAM HAD CHECKED everywhere. Called everybody he could think of. And nothing. He'd come back to the pub, hoping Mike was here or had called. The only way he was getting through this was by blocking everything but the ways he could find his son. When he entered the front door of the pub, Dylan and Aidan looked up.

"Nothing," Dylan said. "You?"

"Cara thought he got on the bus. He didn't tell her or anybody else where he was going." His heart thrummed in his chest. "So that must mean he didn't go anywhere of his own free will."

"No, it doesn't." Aidan circled around the bar and came over to him. "Don't go there. It's only been a couple of hours."

"If a child isn't found in the first twenty-four hours, chances are he won't be."

"Right now, I wish you never went on the Internet."

"I saw it on TV."

The front door burst open and in hurried C.J. and Sophie. For some reason, they'd been together at Brie's.

"Liam?" Sophie asked. "No word?"

He shook his head. "I even went to the firehouse. He isn't anywhere. Nowhere." It was inconceivable that this could happen to their lives.

And in a staggering moment of clarity, Liam knew he'd never be able to deal with something happening to Mike. It would, quite simply, destroy him.

C.J. crossed to Aidan and Sophie came to him. She put her hand on his arm. "What can I do?"

He stared at her. "Nothing. Nobody can do anything."

"I can." C.J. fished out her cell phone out. "I'm calling the police. I have a lot of contacts there. The service works closely with them."

"Isn't it too soon?" Liam asked.

"Not this time. Not for the nephew of the vice president."

"Oh, my God, I hadn't thought of that."

"I'm sorry." C.J. spoke into the phone. "I didn't mean to scare you more."

Liam dropped onto a stool and buried his head in his hands. "Somebody went after Rory. They could go for Mike. I never thought of that."

"Rory's a whole different story." Sophie was rubbing his back. "Hang on, Liam. Don't buy trouble yet."

He didn't have to buy trouble. He had enough of his own.

A half hour passed. He was dimly aware of his mother making coffee. Of C.J. talking on the phone. Of Cleary in the corner, playing a video game. Liam needed to go talk to his other son, so he forced himself up. As he passed by the front door, a yellow taxi swerved into the curb and stopped.

"Oh, God. Oh, God. Oh, God."

Outside in the late afternoon shadows, Mikey said something to the driver, then calmly walked toward the pub.

And Liam fell to his knees sobbing.

His boy opened the door. "Dad?"

He heard commotion behind him. Bursts of crying. He felt a hand soothing on his back again.

"Mike, where were you?" Dylan asked.

"I went to see Mom."

That made Liam drop his hands. "Mom? At the cemetery?"

"Uh-huh. I'm sorry I worried you. But I had to go."

"Any one of us would have taken you, honey." This from C.J.

"I wanted to talk to her alone." Mike crossed to him. "I'm sorry, Dad."

Still on his knees, Liam grabbed his son and clutched him to his chest. He was real, and solid and here unharmed; nobody had taken him. Right now, that was all that mattered.

TWENTY-ONE

LOOK AT THEM scurry around. If I didn't know better, I'd think they didn't have a clue what to do. Okay, okay, now that the fire's out, the truck guys will go in again. Truck guys and girl . . . she's here. Just like I planned. This time, it's gonna be even better.

Jesus, it's cold. My fingers are frozen. Almost can't hold the device. Almost, but not quite. Just one little push on the button inside my pocket. The timer'll do the rest.

Ah, this is what I'm waiting for. The arson investigator extraordinaire. He says, "Hey, Mackenzie. Another one?"

"Yeah, only I don't get it," the captain answers. "It's so obvious. We found the accelerants out in the open. It's like he wants us to know."

"Not good. We're dealing with a lunatic, I think."

Watch out, Joey boy. You don't want me to get any madder.

"Who's inside?" Carusotti asks.

"Engine 33 and Truck 44. Salvage and Overhaul."

"I'm heading in."

You do that. It's just what I want. That's it. Go inside. Look

at the burn pattern on the first floor. Go upstairs. I'll wait.
That's it. Go check out the girl.

Twenty. Nineteen. Eighteen . . . Ten. Nine. Eight. Seven. Six.
Five. Four. Three. Two. One.

Boom.

RAY CRAMDEN watched from the medic bus as another explosion sounded from inside.

Yvette Trudeau, subbing on Engine 7, swallowed hard when the building reignited.

Julian Torres turned toward the sound from the rig where he was getting some water.

Tommy Carusotti pushed off from the tree and moved closer to the building to get a better look.

Between cupped hands, Hannah Harper yelled something.

Inside, Sophie Tyler and the rest of her crew were buried under a collapsed ceiling.

THE PHONE AT his bedside blared into the night. Dylan rolled over to check the clock. Three a.m. Hogan? No he was here, asleep. At least Dylan thought his son was in the next room, but you never knew with that kid. His heart pounding, he pushed off the covers and fumbled for the receiver. "Hello."

"Dylan O'Neil?"

"You got him. Better be important."

"This is Rachel Scott."

He blinked at the clock. Yep, 3 a.m. "Christ, lady, do you know what time it is?"

"There's been an accident at a fire on Bleeker Street. Sophie Tyler's trapped in a building. Word has it the ceiling fell on her and her crew."

"Oh, my God."

"I'm calling out of courtesy. I didn't think you'd want to hear this on the morning news."

"No, we wouldn't. Give me the address."

She told him exactly where the fire was.

"Rachel, it's not good, is it?"

"No, it's not good. It's arson, and looks rigged."

"Rigged?"

"Like somebody intentionally trapped the crew. I'm sorry, Dylan."

"Thanks. And thanks for letting me know."

Dylan set down the phone and for a minute, didn't know what to do. But long ago he and his brothers made a pact never to keep things from each other. As far as Dylan knew, with the exception of intimate details about their relationships with women, they'd kept the promise.

First, he called Aidan and Patrick and told them to meet him at the fire site. Then, he threw on clothes, grabbed a heavy parka, left his house and went next door to Liam's side of the duplex. The frigid air hit him like a hard slap in the face. Taking a deep breath of it, he let himself into Liam's side. It was quiet and he assumed everyone was asleep. He switched on a small foyer light. Upstairs, he heard somebody moving around.

Crossing to the bottom of the steps he called out, "Liam, it's me, Dylan."

His brother appeared at the top of the staircase dressed in pajama bottoms. "What's going on?"

"It's Sophie." Dylan saw Liam grip the banister. "She's trapped in a building over on Bleeker Street. Rachel Scott's on the scene and called me."

"Sophie's not all right, is she?"

His poor brother. How could he handle this, too?

"I don't know. Get dressed and we'll go there now."

"Dressed?"

Dylan climbed a few steps. "Yeah. We'll head over to the site," he repeated. "We'll leave the boys a note and lock up the house. One of us will come back by seven if it isn't all over by then."

"All over?" Rooted to the floor, Liam was obviously shell-shocked.

"Come on, Liam. Just get dressed."

Liam turned left. Dylan jogged up the rest of the stairs and went down the corridor. He had a bad feeling about this, and his brother was going to need all their support.

SOPHIE CAME AWAKE. Something heavy crushed in her chest. Something sharp dug into her back. She could hardly breathe.

Muffled voices. Shouts. Whooshing noises.

Weight lifted. More of it. And more, until she could take in air. Her eyes still closed, she heard, "Sophie, come on, wake up." The voice was familiar.

She tried to move her lips and couldn't.

But she could hear. "Get some more men. Beams are pinning Carusotti."

Scuffling. Joey was here, too?

More weight was lifted off her until her chest felt light. Somebody brushed stuff away from her head. She opened her mouth and tasted grit. After two tries, she raised her lids. Her eyes stung so she closed them. Blinked.

"Sophie. Can you hear me?"

She nodded, which made her head split in two. The guy yelled, "Tyler's awake. Where's the board?" Then the voice clicked. It was her ex-husband, Ray.

"W . . ." She coughed and piercing pain arrowed through her chest. "What happened?"

"Ceiling caved. Just lie still. We're gonna get you out."

She became aware a grinding pain in her hand. The room was semi-filled with smoke. "The fire was out, Ray."

"Yeah, but the bastard had a timing device. Waited until crews went back inside." He squeezed her arm.

Sophie felt herself lifted. Slid onto a backboard. She managed to keep her eyes open and turned her head to the side. Fallen timbers, dry wall, and shards of jagged wood and steel everywhere. Backboards were scattered around the room. "Wh . . . who's hurt?"

"Your group. Minor injuries. Basically, they're okay."

"Joey?"

Somebody leaned over. "Sorry, Sophie."

Sorry? For what? Pain at the movement. She moaned and her mind got cloudy. "Joey?"

No response. Then darkness

She came awake again outside. The air was freezing, and somebody yelled, "Get a blanket."

Another person came up close. Ray said to him, "Excuse me, mister. Please move."

"Listen, buddy, I know you got a job to do, but we're looking for Sophie Tyler."

Someone else in her line of vision. Did she recognize him? She squinted. Dylan. "Is Liam here?"

"I'm right here." He was on her left. He came in close, took her hand. His touch hurt and she moaned. "Sweetheart, are you all right?"

"I'm sorry," she said.

Another person on the other side. "Hey, sweetie." Hannah?

"Joey? Is Joey okay?"

"Oh, honey."

"Tell me."

"He's hurt, bad. He's on his way to the hospital. He got crushed by a beam."

A beam? A beam? No, no . . . She remembered. "He pushed me away. The beams . . . were gonna hit me. He pushed me out of the way."

"Shh. You can talk later." Liam again. His hand let go. "I'll see you at the hospital."

SITTING BY SOPHIE's bed, Liam watched the sun come up through the window of her hospital room. Over the course of four hours, she'd been in the ER, X-ray and the casting room; finally they'd brought her to ICU. She was breathing better with the oxygen hooked into her nose. The heart and blood pressure monitor blinked at him, their occasional beeps sounding in the room. From what he was told, she was lucky she only had a concussion, broken wrist and some bruised ribs. Hundreds of pounds of plaster and timber had fallen on her. It was a miracle she was still alive.

And Liam knew he was running out of miracles.

She stirred.

"Hello, *a ghrá*."

"Hey." The glazed look in her eyes was from the pain medicine. "W . . . what time is it?"

"Almost seven."

"Can I have some water?"

Retrieving the glass with a straw, he held it to her mouth so she could sip. As the haze cleared a bit, her eyes widened. "Joey?" At his blank look, she added, "Carusotti. How is he?"

"I don't know."

"Did anybody die in the fire?"

"Not that I know of." Liam touched her arm. "A lot of people were hurt."

"Where's my group?"

"Some are still out in the waiting area."

"Go get one of them."

"Sophie, you need to rest."

"Please, I have to know about Joey."

Fine, he could handle this. She wasn't herself, and Joe Carusotti was like a brother. Liam found Jim Mackenzie in the waiting room. Other firefighters were there, faces blackened, some bandaged.

His eye swollen and his arm wrapped in gauze, her captain crossed to Liam. "She okay?"

Not on your life. "She's resting, or was. She's worried about her friend, Joe Carusotti."

The look on Mackenzie's face was not encouraging. "He's bad."

"But not dead, right?"

"No, a beam hit him hard."

"Sophie said he pushed her out of the way when he saw the beam heading for her."

"No shit? Nobody knew that."

Her friend Hannah did. She'd been there when Sophie told them.

"How bad is he?"

"Still unconscious."

Liam shook his head. "I don't think she's strong enough to hear this."

Mackenzie waited a beat. "I know you mean well, Liam. But in our line of work . . . we don't lie to each other."

"Just don't tell her."

"Same thing. We don't do that. We can't afford to. We depend on each other to tell the truth, no matter how bad it is."

Liam cocked his head, realizing he had no say in how to handle this. Briefly, he wondered if Sophie were his wife, if he could make the call.

"I'll tell her," Mackenzie said. "You don't have to."

"Only one person can go back at a time. You probably should, since I don't know the details."

Mackenzie squeezed his arm. "I won't stay long."

"Take as long as you like. I have to go home and break this news to my kids. Tell her I'll be back later."

"Liam, don't take offense."

"None taken. Give her my love."

Outside, the early morning was biting cold. He wondered what it was like to fight a fire in this kind of weather. Did water seep through the gloves? Did it freeze in your hair or on the guys' moustaches? He made his way home, thinking about all kinds of minute details of her job. And hating every single one of them, especially now.

Dylan had left the hospital and gone back to their house in case the boys woke up early. They hadn't and he found his brother in the kitchen, drinking coffee. Its rich scent filled the kitchen. "How is she?"

"Groggy. In pain. Worried more about her friend than about herself, though."

"Common, I'd guess, in her profession."

Liam shed his coat and threw it on a chair. Dropping down at the table, he let Dylan pour him coffee and shook his head as he sipped.

"Coffee's not that bad."

He didn't laugh. "I can't do it."

Dylan stared at him. "Don't make any decisions in the heat

of the moment." Almost his exact words to Aidan a short time ago in the very hospital where Sophie now lay.

"It's not good for any of us. God knows what'll happen with Mikey when he hears. We're still not over his visit to the cemetery last week."

Where he asked his mother if Sophie should be in their lives, for Christ's sake.

"What do you think Kitty would say about all this?" Dylan asked.

"To do whatever makes me happy. Makes the boys happy." The sober truth was becoming clearer every day. "This isn't cutting it."

"Then maybe you're right."

Dylan's acquiescence drove the reality home. The pain of it sliced through Liam.

"Dad?" Cleary stood in the doorway, dressed in pajama bottoms and a thermal shirt. "What's goin' on?"

"Come sit."

When Cleary reached the table, Liam struggled to keep his voice neutral. "There was a bad fire last night. Sophie got a broken wrist and bruised ribs when a ceiling fell on her."

His boy's eyes widened. "She all right?"

"She will be."

"Jesus, Dad, her job sucks."

"I know, Cleary. A lot of firefighters were hurt last night."

"Is she dead?" This time, Mike had come to the doorway; apparently at the tail end of his revelation to Cleary. Mike's face was white. "Is Sophie dead?"

"No, no, buddy, she just got hurt."

Mikey started to cry, rushed across the room and hurtled himself onto Liam's lap. Cleary rose and crossed to them. He knelt down and laid his head on Liam's shoulder, shocking the hell out of him.

As he hugged his boys, he wondered how he could condemn them to mornings like this? How could he sign them up for a lifetime of bleak dawns and nighttime terrors? "Shh," he whispered, his mouth close to Mike's head and gripping Cleary's shoulder. "It's all right, guys. I promise it'll be all right."

Over them, Liam's gaze locked with Dylan's. His brother nodded to him, and Liam nodded back.

TWO DAYS AFTER the fire, Hannah and Dom drove Sophie home from the hospital. Hannah accompanied her inside, while Dom tried to find a place to park. He'd spotted a police officer down the way and was going to try to get the cop to let him sit and wait in the tow-away zone.

"Here you go, girl." Her friend set Sophie's bag on the chair. She'd been the one to bring Sophie clothes and other necessities she needed in the hospital. "Wanna go to bed, or sit in here?"

"I *wanted* to stay at the hospital."

"Sweetie, you almost fainted in Joe's room."

"I'm so weak, I can't believe it."

"The guys promised they'd call if there was any change." A lot of firefighters were keeping vigil at Joe's beside.

Gingerly lowering herself to the couch, Sophie groaned as she propped her arm on a pillow and her legs up on the table. She took in a deep breath, but that made her ribs hurt like a bitch. "What if he doesn't make it, Hannah?"

"Don't think like that."

"He got crushed by a beam and twice as much plaster as I did. How can anybody survive all that?"

"It's the head injury that's causing the coma."

"Coma?" Her heart began to beat fast. "They're calling it a coma?"

"You can handle this, Sophie. We've been through it before. In 9/11, when Jake Simmons . . ."

"Died, Jakey died. And so did all those guys in the Towers."

"And you lived through it."

"Not Joey." She ran a hand through her hair, which was limp. "If he dies because of me . . ."

"Joe got hurt by a fuckin' asswipe who set not one, but two fires that night. They think the last one was to trap your group."

"I know. The cap told me."

Hannah's face was pale, too. She seemed peaked today. "How's Tommy? And his dad?"

"Big Tom's taking it better than Tommy." Sophie shook her head. They'd both been visibly upset when they visited her. Tommy had prowled around like a caged tiger and cursed a blue streak, whereas his father was stoic and said little. "Big Tom's a smoke eater," Sophie told Hannah. "We do so well, closing ourselves off."

"Speaking of that, where's Liam?"

Purposefully, Sophie suppressed her feelings. "He never came back to the hospital after he went home the morning of the fire. I think I offended him by telling him to go get Mackenzie and being so concerned about Joey."

"That doesn't sound like our Liam."

"My guess is that *our* Liam's had about as much as he can take."

"What do you mean?"

She explained about Mikey's foray to the cemetery.

"How is that your fault?"

"Mike went to see his mother to ask her if it was okay that I was a part their lives."

"His mother's dead."

"I know. But he talks to her. I did, too."

She remembered the picture under his pillow and asking Kitty the same thing. Sophie had been so hopeful then, so sure she and Liam could make it. But now . . . Mikey, the fear she experienced in tight situations, Liam's feelings of exclusion and his all-consuming worry . . .

Must be Kitty had been wrong when she said Sophie was good for them.

"This isn't working out with me and Liam."

Hannah didn't contradict her.

"Firefighters should just be with other firefighters, like you and Dom."

"You get no argument from me. But I don't think you should make any big decisions while you're flat out in pain, emotionally drained, and worrying about a man who's been like your brother your whole life."

Sophie laid her head back on the cushions. "Oh, I don't

know. Maybe this is the best time. When things are good, I don't see the downside clearly."

"Want me to stay?" Hannah asked.

"No, I'm going to sleep." With effort, she stood and couldn't help groaning. "In the bedroom."

"You hurt, don't you?"

"Yeah. My ribs." She held up her arm. "And this cast itches like a son of a bitch."

Settled in her bed, with water, her pain pills, the phone and TV remote on the table where Hannah had put them, Sophie smiled at her friend. "Nobody understands like you. Thanks for telling me everything. For not shittin' me about stuff. You're a true firefighter, Hannah, in every sense of the word. Thank God."

Hannah just stared at her. Oddly.

"What?"

"Nothing. I'm heading out. Go to sleep." In an uncharacteristic move, Hannah kissed her on the head. "It'll be okay, girlfriend."

"So long as Joey makes it."

"We'll call." She switched off the light. "Go to sleep."

The pill she'd taken worked. In minutes Sophie's eyes closed. She welcomed oblivion. There wasn't much she wanted to think about right now.

LIAM DIDN'T GO to see Sophie until three days after the fire. Staying away was a rotten thing to do, but he had to have his head on straight before he talked to her again. He'd finally figured things out.

As it was midday, he rang the doorbell, thinking she'd be awake. He had a key, but didn't feel comfortable using it. When she opened the door, he saw she was dressed in a peach sweat suit and her hair was damp around her shoulders. She looked small and vulnerable. "This is a surprise."

"I'm sorry I haven't come before."

"Dylan came. Aidan called and Patrick stopped over with Brie. They said you needed some time."

"I did. Can I come in?"

Stepping aside, she watched him walk in, then led him to the living room. She raised her chin when he faced her. "Did you get enough time?"

"Yes." He lowered himself to the couch, but didn't take his coat off. "Sit, sweetheart."

She sat with difficulty. Once, Liam cracked a rib sliding into a base, and it hurt like hell. She must be sore.

"How's the arm?"

"Better. Pain meds help."

"How long for the cast?"

"Five more weeks."

"What will you do? Some kind of desk duty?"

"Maybe. Listen, are we gonna talk about the weather, too?"

"No." Her gray eyes were muddy with fatigue and pain and he knew he shouldn't lay this on her now, but he had to. "I can't do this, Sophie."

"I'm not surprised."

"Even if it weren't for Mike, and Cleary by the way, I can't keep living with three a.m. wake-ups and seeing you battered like this."

"As I said, I'm not surprised. Hurt and angry, but no, not surprised."

He swallowed hard. He was taking a risk, but there didn't seem to be any other option. "I want you to quit the fire department."

Her shoulders stiffened. *"What?"*

"I want you to quit being a firefighter. I'd concede to a desk job, or you being an instructor at the academy, but I don't think that'd make you happy." When she didn't respond, he continued. "I know this is a lot to ask, but that's why I haven't come for three days. I can't find any other way around our situation."

She eased back, away from him. "Maybe there isn't a way around it."

"Jesus, you could be lying in that hospital bed dying like your friend."

Her eyes widened. "How can you say that to me? Do you have any idea what I'm going through, worrying if Joey's gonna make it or not?"

He shook his head at how ludicrous her statement was. "Listen to what you just said, Sophie. Of course I know *exactly* how it feels."

She stared at him; he saw the answer in her eyes before she spoke. "I'm not quitting the fire department."

"Then I can't see you anymore."

"It's your decision."

"No, it's yours really."

"Does it matter? I still haven't dealt with the fear I experience because of you and the kids. It's obvious everything's conspired against us being together. So whoever's decision this is, I guess it's made."

Liam felt like somebody had cut out his heart and stomped it on the ground. It took him a minute to regain his voice. "You obviously can't work with that arm, anyway, but I don't want you to come back to the pub, either."

"Huh. Losing my guy and my job all in one day."

"You don't have to lose me. You can make this all right."

"Back at you."

He sighed heavily. "Let's not fight, Soph. I'm not sure I can bear leaving you like that. I love you so much."

Shoulders sagging, her face filled with emotion, she whispered, "I love you, too. But you're asking too much."

"Maybe. I had to try, though." Moving closer, he drew her to him. Clumsily her casted arm went around his waist and she buried her nose in his chest, the way she liked to do. The way he loved her to do. That little gesture threatened to level him.

His hand went to her hair. He inhaled its lemony scent. Stroked the silky strands for the last time. "I'm so sorry I'm not a better man and could not handle all this."

"You're the best man I've ever known. I'm sorry I can't be the kind of woman Kitty was."

He couldn't speak around the lump in his throat.

"I'll never forget you, Liam."

It was then that he realized she was crying.

But so was he.

TWENTY-TWO

SANTORINI GLEAMED like a jewel in the Mediterranean Sea as Greece's noonday sun beamed down on Sophie and Nate. They were staying in a nice hotel built into the side of a mountain. Beautiful foliage and the traditional whitewashed exterior and peacock-blue roofs of the island backdropped them as they stretched out on lounge chairs at the pool. Sophie stared out at the sea and blanked her mind.

"You okay, Soph? You haven't said much since we got here."

"I'm fine." She glanced over at Nate. He'd shaved his head and it was a good fit for him. It made his blue eyes stand out more. He'd also built world-class muscles since he joined the army years ago. "You're lookin' good, bro."

"You, too. What's with the one-piece suit?"

"Um, black-and-blue marks."

He winced. "Ribs still hurt?"

She touched them gingerly. "Not much. Sore, mostly."

He nodded to her cast. "That really cramps your style."

"I'm managing. At least I have some strength back."

"The sun, good food and great company."

With her uncasted arm, she reached over the chairs and squeezed her brother's hand. "How true." Trying to get the focus off her, she nodded out to the volcano that sat in the middle of the sea. "So are we gonna climb the caldera tomorrow?" On Christmas day.

"Whatever you want, babe."

"I wanna do that. The history of this place still boggles me."

Santorini had been a normal, circular island until the volcano in its middle had erupted, making the land mass crescent shaped, with the active volcano out hundreds of yards in the middle of water. It was rumored to be the lost city of Atlantis.

Nate motioned to a waiter who was serving patrons at the pool. "I'll have another beer."

"Me, too."

When the ice-cold Mythos was served, Sophie sipped it and forced herself to stay in the present. Forced herself not to think about Liam and Mike and Cleary today on Christmas Eve or tomorrow morning, opening presents, spending their holiday with the O'Neil clan.

Which she would never be a part of. That was a done deal. Over. *Fini*.

"Where are they?" Nate asked.

"Excuse me?"

"I know you said you didn't want to talk about Liam, that it was over between you two, but you're thinking about them, so we might as well hash it out."

"I don't want to hash it out. I want to forget them."

He stared at her in the way he always did until she caved.

"They're in DC at the vice presidential residence. Shit, they're having Christmas day dessert at the White House."

Nate laughed. "And yet he's an ordinary guy."

"They all are."

"Sorry I never got to meet him."

"Me, too. There isn't a person alive who doesn't adore him."

He waited a beat before he said, "Including my big sister."

"Nate . . ."

"Okay, change of subject. What's the latest on Joey?"

"When I left, he was out of the coma. Thank God." The

relief she'd felt when she'd gotten the news had briefly eclipsed the gnawing pain inside her at losing Liam and the boys. "Joe's pissed as hell that he's got to turn the arson case over to his new female partner. Especially after we were all hurt by the guy."

"Joey's all bluster. He's a feminist if I ever saw one. He was your biggest supporter when you wanted to join the FDNY."

"Yeah, he was." She laid her head back and let the hot sun beat down on it. "Be grateful for the people you *do* you have in your life, I guess."

They spent the rest of the afternoon at the pool, talking about the Carusottis, their jobs; finally both dozed in the chairs.

At seven, they decided to go into Fira, one of the towns nearest the hotel, for dinner. Sophie donned a peach sundress, which looked good with the tan she'd gotten today. She added strappy flat sandals for the walk down the sloping narrow pathways to the shopping area.

A variety of stores lined the cobblestone walkways, winding around the curves and jutting out after them. Sophie smiled at the colorful clothing and admired the expensive jewelry.

She noticed Nate checking out the jewelry shops. "What interests you there, kid?"

"Nothing. Just admiring the craftsmanship."

He linked their arms and the made their way through the throngs of people to Nicolas's, a restaurant rumored to be the most authentic Greek eatery in the area. As they waited for a table in the small entrance, they laughed as they watched the waiters bring out lamb, beef stew and fish, all the while being grumpy with the patrons.

"Eat up . . ."

"What do you mean you're not going to dunk the bread in the artichoke sauce?"

"Aye, Americans!"

It reminded her of places in Little Italy.

Once they sat and ordered, she said to her brother, "Is something going on, Nate?"

"Like what?"

"I don't know. You're hiding something, aren't you?"

His phone rang.

"Who's calling you in Greece?"

"I don't know. I'll check later."

"Nathaniel!"

"Okay, okay, let me get this then I'll come clean."

He ducked outside, and Sophie tried to take interest in the wall décor—mountainous scenes of Greece, a faded vineyard mural, some bronze shields and crests. When she'd exhausted that distraction, she tried to think about the pretty church they'd seen yesterday, and how they watched the sunset on Io with five thousand other people.

But it was no use. Her mind went back to New York City— walking the streets decorated for Christmas, with Liam holding her hand. At the pub, watching him cook at the stove and seeing him smile over at her intimately. In bed. Damn it! Damn it! Damn it! He'd be in DC now, with the kids in front of a fire maybe, with a huge tree in the background.

When Nate returned, she said, "Spill it."

"Okay, okay." He plunked down. "I got a girl."

"A girl?"

"Uh-huh." He shrugged. "I was going to tell you about it this holiday, but when I found out what happened with you and Liam, I changed my mind."

"You jerk. I can be happy for you under any circumstances. Tell me about her."

"She's a soldier, too. A captain, like me. Married and divorced. She's on her last tour of Iraq." He smiled like a man in love. "We have so much in common. We're both career military."

"Will you always be stationed together?"

"If we get married."

"Married?" she said with a gulp. Then, she added, "I get it, that's why you were scoping out the jewelry stores."

"Uh-huh. Wanna help me pick out a ring? Her eyes are blue and I thought diamonds and sapphires."

"How sweet. Where is she now?"

"At her parents' house, telling them, too. She's from Kansas."

"What's her name?"

"Anna."

Sophie picked up her napkin and wiped her mouth. "I can't wait to meet Anna." She took out money from her pocket. "My treat. You save your cash for some bling."

This time they thoroughly investigated each jewelry store and finally settled on one. Nate was like a little kid. Sophie joined in the fun and refused to let her own aborted relationship interfere with this monumental occasion in her brother's life.

But it was hard when the jeweler asked her to try on the rings so Nate could see them on a woman's hand. As she slipped a beautiful marquis-cut sapphire surrounded by diamonds onto her finger, she felt a sense of loss so great it stole her breath.

No matter what she said to anyone else, or told herself, down deep, she'd been hoping Liam would be the one to slip a ring on her finger this Christmas.

THE VICE PRESIDENTIAL residence on Observatory Circle was big enough to sleep all the O'Neils. The kids took over the basement opposite the Secret Service office down there, and the adults shared the bedrooms. Liam was in the great room, staring out the window at the snow that drifted to the ground just in time for Santa, when his mother came up to him.

"Wasn't Mass nice?"

He smiled at her, all dressed in red and green, looking like a present herself. "Can't believe the monsignor came here to say it."

"Even your father was impressed."

Over her shoulder, Liam caught a glimpse of the Christmas tree, high enough to touch the ceiling. "We're going to open a few presents before bed, right?"

"That we are. Aidan and C.J. have to leave early tomorrow morning to get to her parents in Queens for their Christmas." She thought for a minute. "I'm praying the youngsters will go to sleep, being together and all."

"Clay told the big kids they'd better play along about Santa." He slid his arm around his mother. "Remember when the guys told me and Aidan there was no Santa? You had a fit."

"You didn't believe them. Aidan did. He punched Dylan. But you refused to believe Santa Claus didn't exist."

"That's me, the eternal optimist."

"Nothing wrong with that." She petted his arm. "Even if it gets your heart broken."

What was there to say? His mother was right . . . his heart was broken, and he missed Sophie so much he could hardly function. He knew from experience that the pain would recede and eventually he'd feel better. But damn it, how many times would he have to go through this recovery process?

"Where is she, son? I haven't wanted to ask since you're seeming so upset about it."

He told his mother about Greece and the plans Sophie had made with her brother. He didn't tell her how they'd fought about it. How they'd fought about pretty much everything in the last month.

"I always wanted to see Santorini. I hear it's lovely."

"Pa should take you." Still thinking about Sophie, he added, "At least she's got Nate. I'd hate to think she was alone on Christmas."

"Did you get her a present?"

He thought about the ring he'd been eying at Tiffany's. "No."

"We all love you, *a stor*. I'm wishing something fierce I could help you."

"I know, Mama, thanks."

An hour later the family gathered around the tree to open some gifts. After the kids finished theirs and went to play or listen to music, his mother was first to go among the adults. With "White Christmas" in the background, the mood was cheerful. "Oh, what's this now?"

"Pearls for you, Mama," Aidan said of Dylan's idea. "From us guys."

"Why is it you would spend so much on me?"

"Because we love you."

Dylan, Aidan and Pat had gotten Liam a slick leather sports coat. The three of them had gone in on an expensive headset Dylan wanted, then on a watch for Patrick. The whole family had bought a soft-looking cashmere sweater for Bailey that matched her eyes and one in red for Clay.

They gave Brie a glittering gold choker, and for C.J. a Coach purse that was supposed to be a big deal but looked like any other bag to Liam. Seeing the girls open their gifts made Liam wonder if there were any presents for Sophie that had to be returned to the store.

Finally, they finished and Liam needed space. He took a glass of eggnog into the library for some peace and quiet. After a while, his sister came in.

"Babies down?" he asked her.

"Yeah, finally."

Before she sat, she went to a closet and took out a big brown bag.

"What's that?"

"I hope this is okay. It's from Sophie. There're gifts for the boys and for you."

Liam shook his head. "They shouldn't have them. It'll just be harder to deal with her absence."

"The note said it was your call."

"No."

"Okay. I'll just leave it here for you, in case you want yours. If not, I'll send them all back to her."

He nodded.

"Liam . . ."

"Don't, honey. There's nothing to say. It's over."

When he was alone again, he stared at the bag for a long time. Then, when the clock struck twelve, and it was Christmas day, he got up and walked out of the room, leaving the presents and Sophie behind.

FEELING LIKE A cooked noodle after the ten-hour flight back from Greece and a slippery cab ride into the city, Sophie dragged herself into her apartment. Nate had flown back to Iraq in time to meet Anna for New Year's Eve, when he was planning to propose. Sophie was truly happy for her brother.

Setting her suitcase down in the foyer, she noticed a package by the door. Without opening the cardboard box, Sophie knew what it was that her neighbor Mrs. Conklin had brought in for her. Bailey had returned her gifts for Liam and his kids.

Just perfect.

God, she wished she could go to work. On January second, she was meeting with Chief Marconi to find out what light duty she could do. She couldn't stand this idleness. Any kind of work would take her mind off losing Liam. She looked at the package again. Fuck! Heading straight to the bedroom, she stripped and fell into bed.

The shrill ringing of the phone woke her.

She blinked at the bright sunlight coming in through the window. The clock on the nightstand said it was noon. The next day? She rummaged for the phone. "Hello?"

"Sophie Tyler?"

"Yes." She didn't recognize the female voice.

"This is Anna Lund."

"Who?"

"Nate's . . . friend."

"Oh, Anna, hello." Maybe she was calling about the ring. No, wait . . . he wouldn't have given it to her until tonight, New Year's Eve. "How are you?"

"I'm hoping you can make me better. Did Nate leave Athens when he was supposed to?"

"Yes. I watched him get on the plane . . . must be two days ago . . ." She sat up in bed and her heart catapulted in her chest. "Two days, Anna. He should have been back long before this."

"I was afraid of that. He never made it to the base."

"What?"

"There was some action on the route he would have taken here. I was praying he never got on the plane."

"What are you saying, Anna? That he's *missing*?"

"That's exactly what I'm saying. The brass is checking it out, but they don't know anything yet. And it's been forty-eight hours, Sophie. Forty-eight hours."

No, no, this couldn't be happening. Not this. "Oh, God."

"I'm sorry to call with bad news. I waited a day, thinking

maybe he was just delayed and couldn't phone us for some reason."

Sophie swallowed hard. "Can I do anything from here?"

"No." The woman's voice broke but the soldier pulled it together. "I don't think we can do anything but wait."

Wide awake now, Sophie pushed back the fear lodging in her throat. "Don't bet on it. Give me a number where I can reach you. I'll call you back."

After taking Anna's information, Sophie climbed out of bed and, still holding the phone, she stumbled over to her desk. Her hands were clumsy as she searched for the number she'd been given months ago. She found it in the middle drawer and managed to punch it in.

He answered after three rings. "Clay Wainwright."

"Clay." She had to swallow hard. "I-It's Sophie Tyler. You said to call your private number if I ever needed anything."

"I remember, Sophie. What happened?"

"I need some help."

"Then I'm your man."

ON NEW YEAR'S Eve afternoon Liam was at the pub getting the food ready for the big evening ahead. At least he'd have something to do tonight—celebrate with mobs of people. When his phone rang, he left the Irish lasagna he was making and picked up the cell from the kitchen's butcher block. "Hello."

"Liam, it's Bailey."

"Hey, Sis. Happy New Year."

"Something's happened."

"Happened?" Please, please, God, not to them. "To you? Your family?"

"No, to Sophie."

She wasn't fighting fires yet. How could she be hurt? "Tell me."

"It's her brother, Nate."

Liam was stunned when he got off the phone. Poor Sophie. He knew how close she and Nate were, and more so, he knew what it was like when your family was in jeopardy. Hurrying out to the front of the pub, he found Dylan loading beer into the coolers. "Dyl, I gotta go."

"Go? You can't go. We got a big night ahead of us." He finally looked over. "What's wrong?"

He explained about Nate as he whipped off his apron and donned his L.L. Bean jacket. "I'm going over to her apartment."

"Give her our love and stay in touch."

A half hour after he got the call from Bailey, Liam arrived at Sophie's doorstep. This time he used his key, which he'd never returned. It was dark inside the apartment. For a minute, he wondered if she was home. Switching on the light, he could see a figure shift on the couch. "Sophie? It's me, Liam."

No response.

He crossed the room. Still, no movement. Kneeling down in front of her, he took her hands in his. They were ice-cold. "Soph, I know."

Her eyes were bruised when she looked up. "I asked Bailey not to call you."

"We don't keep secrets in this family."

"It doesn't matter."

"Do you want to talk about it?"

"No." She drew in a heavy, shaky breath. "You should go, Liam. I'm bad company."

He stood and shed his jacket, sat on the couch and slid an arm around her. "I'm not going anywhere." When he tried to tug her close, she resisted, just for a minute. Then she curled into him and buried her face in the sweater he wore over his pub shirt.

Later, the doorbell rang. Sophie startled. She'd dozed off and Liam had, too. He checked his watch and saw it was seven. Once she roused, Sophie flew to the door. On the other side was his mother. "Mrs. O'Neil?"

She held up bags. "I brought you supper."

Liam joined them at the entryway and took the food. "Thanks, Mama."

"It's hot now."

"We'll eat. Want to stay?"

"No, I'll be needed at the pub." She grasped Sophie's shoulders. "Have faith, girl. We're all praying for you."

"T-thank you."

After his mother left, Liam led Sophie back to the couch. He took the food to the kitchen, portioned out the lasagna, cut the bread and brought it and two beers into the living room. He set the tray down in front of her.

"I can't eat."

Her stomach growled loudly.

"You body says otherwise. When was the last meal you had?"

"I don't remember."

"Eat. We don't have to talk. But you gotta keep up your strength. Want me to turn on the TV?"

She stiffened. "Do you think anything will be on there about Iraq?"

"Someone would have called you, love."

"No, then."

They ate in silence. She managed to down most of the lasagna and a chunk of bread. When she finished, she laid her head on a pillow and stared up at the ceiling. She was dressed in navy sweats, socks and her hair was pulled up into a ponytail, and once again he was reminded of her vulnerability.

"I do feel better. Not so weak."

"I'm glad for that at least." He picked up his beer, sat back, too, and linked their hands.

She held on tight. "He's the only thing I have, Liam. I don't know what I'll do if he isn't found alive. I just don't know what I'll do."

"Let's not jump the gun." Bringing their linked hands to his mouth, he kissed her knuckles. "And he's not the only thing you have."

"Not you. Not anymore."

"No, not like we planned. But I'll always be here for you. So will my family. And you have the Carusottis, your crew."

"All related to the fire department."

"You told me they were second families to you."

She shrugged.

"So hang on to that. And we're in no way giving up on Nate."

At eleven, Bailey called. Liam answered this time. "There's no news. Clay's been working on this all day long."

"No news," He said to Sophie. Then into the phone, "I appreciate this, Bay."

"We're doing everything we can here, Liam. And if Clay has to fly to Iraq to get to the bottom of this, he will."

"Here, talk to Sophie." He handed her the phone and Bailey must have reiterated everything.

"I hope he doesn't have to go over there." Sophie's voice broke on the last word and she gave the phone back to Liam.

An hour later, they'd switched on the TV and watched the ball drop from Times Square. Sophie was leaning against him, absently stroking his chest. Neither commented on the arrival of a new year.

Finally Sophie said, "You can go. Catch the end of the celebration at the pub."

"Forget it." Easing her to her side, he stretched out on the couch with her, covered them with a throw, and clicked off the TV. "Maybe things will be better tomorrow."

She nestled into him. She didn't share his sentiment, he knew, but he was trying to have faith.

AGAIN, SOPHIE AWOKE to the doorbell. Liam stirred, but stayed asleep. She slipped off the couch and hurried to the door. This time Patrick and Brie stood at the entrance.

"What are you doing here so early?" she asked.

"It's ten, honey." Brie held up a basket and Patrick carried coffee. "Breakfast."

Sophie smiled weakly. "More food."

Pat hugged her. "Sometimes there's nothing else you can do."

They came inside and she nodded to the couch. "Liam's still asleep." She led them back to the kitchen where Brie hugged her, too. "I'm so sorry. Clay's doing everything he can."

"I know."

"So's C.J." Patrick said. "She went to the office today to see if she could find out any intel. She's got connections."

Brie set coffee in front of her at the table.

"Are Mike and Cleary okay?" Sophie asked.

"They're at our house. They wanted to come to see you but Pat thought it best they didn't."

"Probably. I'm a mess." And she felt like a zombie. But now that she was conscious, the terror was seeping back in.

"You're entitled, lass."

Brie made herself comfortable in a chair. "We're staying for a while."

"You don't have to do that."

"Yes, we do. For you and Liam."

"You're his family."

"We care about you, too, Sophie." Pat touched her arm. "No matter what's happened between you and my brother."

Her eyes moistened and a few tears slipped down her cheeks.

A couple of minutes later, Liam came into the kitchen. He acted like it was nothing out of the ordinary to see his oldest brother and sister-in-law at the table.

The four of them made it through the day watching football, though much of the time was passed in somber silence. Pat and Brie left at six, and Aidan and C.J. showed up at seven. She'd put some things in the works and had her cell phone to be contacted when any news came in.

"Guys," Sophie said. "Really, this isn't necessary."

Aidan scowled at her statement, C.J. hugged her and they joined the vigil.

A half hour later, Liam stood. "I'm gonna go check in with the boys. See if I can do anything for them." He squeezed Sophie's shoulder. "I'll only be gone an hour or so."

"Liam, you don't have to come back."

"Hush." He kissed her nose. "See you in a little while."

Cleary and Mike were reassured by Liam's visit, he told Sophie when he returned ninety minutes later. Aidan and C.J. left shortly after.

Liam nodded to her wrist. "Can you shower with that?"

"Yeah, but baths are easier."

"I'll run you one."

"Do I need it?"

His smile was soft and warm. "Well, I cleaned up at home." She hadn't noticed he'd changed into a Syracuse football sweatshirt and jeans.

"Okay, I'll take a bath."

He left her alone after he drew the water, and she wished he hadn't because the demons came then. Images of the war she'd seen on TV. Nate's smiling face in his uniform. The broken and bloody possibilities that threatened to level her. She hurried through the rest of the bath, put on pretty blue pajamas Nate had given her for Christmas and found Liam in her bedroom, stretched out watching the news.

"Anything on there?"

"Yes. But Clay just called to tell us in person. There's a report of a landmine going off near Karbala. Four soldiers were killed. Four are missing."

Sophie gripped the edge of a nearby dresser. "Did they release the names of those killed?"

"No, pending notification of relatives."

She felt her knees go weak. Liam leapt up, caught her and led her to the bed.

The phone rang again. "It's me," Bailey said. "He isn't dead. He's missing."

Sophie began to cry. Once again she had to hand the phone to Liam. At least there was still a chance.

When he clicked off, he squeezed her hand. "It's good news, love."

"I know." She swiped at her face. "We should call Anna."

Anna burst into tears when she heard the news that Nate wasn't among the dead. They promised to stay in touch.

Drained, Sophie lay down on the bed with Liam and cuddled in close. He covered them with a light blanket and just held her, with the low drone of the TV in the background. She could hear the thump of his heart and it calmed her some.

She was still there, four hours later, when the phone rang again.

"Sophie, it's Clay. Nate's all right. He wasn't captured. He and three other guys who were on their way back to base hid out in the city. He managed to contact their colonel. The group was picked up just a bit ago."

"H-he's not hurt?"

"Some scrapes. One of the other guys lost a leg, though. Nate saved his life."

Relief flooded her and tears flowed again. "Clay," she said between hiccups. "I don't know how to thank you."

"You already did, girl. By the way, the offer still holds, if you need anything else. Now go celebrate. We've notified Anna Lund. She's on her way to the hospital in Karbala."

When Sophie ended the call, she looked over the bed at Liam. Stretched out with his arm crooked, his head resting on his palm, he smiled at her. "I take it he's all right?"

She broke into sobs, between which she explained what had happened.

"As I said once, heroism runs in your family."

Finally composed, Sophie stood and went to the bathroom to put water on her face. "I feel like a whipped puppy, now." She picked up her brush and ran it through her hair. "Thanks for staying with me," she called out to him.

"You're welcome."

He hadn't moved from the bed when she came back into the bedroom. He was all masculine grace and beauty, just waiting for her. "What do you need now, Soph? I won't be offended if you want me to leave."

Watching him, she thought of how he'd been there with her the whole, awful time, took care of her and asked nothing in return. All of this after they'd officially broken off their relationship.

So her answer to his question was to release the first button of her pajamas. Then the second, the others.

She slipped the top off and crossed to bed. There, she let the bottoms slide to the floor.

TWENTY-THREE

Looking out at the new recruit class that started mid-January at the New York City Fire Academy, commonly known as the Rock, Sophie studied the young hopefuls, wondering how their lives as firefighters were going to shake out.

"So, Tyler, like your light duty?" Manny Campoli, the battalion chief in charge of the academy, spoke from beside her. A big guy with broad shoulders, a bald head and sporting a moustache, he looked pretty much the same as he had twelve years ago when he'd helped train her.

"It's better than doing nothing," she said.

"I hear ya. I got hurt when I was a line smoke eater, too." He nodded to her arm. "How's it with the cast off?"

"At least I can shower and take a bath without it taking forever."

The mention of baths called to mind the one Liam had drawn for her when Nate was still missing. Once again, her heart began to hurt. She still thought about Liam all the time; the pain seemed to be worse, not better.

Manny motioned to the recruits who were assembling for the day in the gym. They'd done roll call already, where the recruits dressed like her and Manny in uniforms, but now they'd put on FDNY sweats. "So, you ready to beat on the guys?"

"And two women, don't forget."

"How could I with you around?"

"All right if I lead the run this morning?" Every day the recruits went five miles to keep in shape. "I need to build stamina."

"Knock yourself out, kiddo."

Sophie led recruits on laps around the gym. Usually they ran outside, but it was particularly snowy today and slippery. She savored the exercise; she'd been running the streets of New York and doing some arm curls for three weeks now and felt good to be getting back in shape. She wondered if Liam was keeping up with his workouts. She hadn't gone to Paddock's because she didn't want to bump into him. Had he increased his aerobic capacity? His muscle mass. Not that he needed the latter. He had great . . .

Fuck! Don't do this, girl. She had to remind herself every time he popped into her head not to think about him, wonder about him, wish she could touch and kiss and hold him again.

At the end of the run, she was spent and sweaty. She sent the recruits to the weight room and was sipping from a water bottle when Hannah came into the gym.

"Hey, Soph. How's it hanging?"

Every time Sophie saw her friend these days, Hannah was smiling. "Good." She nodded to Hannah's middle. "How's the little one?"

"Like he's not even there." She patted her flat stomach. "Geez, you think I'm ever gonna show?"

"I'll remind you of that in seven months when you can't see your toes."

Hannah, big, tough Hannah, giggled. "Lunch today?"

"Yeah, sure. Meet you in the mess hall at noon."

As Hannah strutted away, Sophie thought about how she'd shown up at the academy for the first time two weeks ago and found Hannah working here . . .

What are you doing at the Rock?

Um, light duty.

Did you get hurt and not tell me?

No, I got knocked up and didn't tell you. I've known since December. But things were so bad for you . . .

Truth be told, it had been hard at first, seeing Hannah as a mother-to-be. And so cautious. Women no longer had to go off the line if they were pregnant, but Hannah said she wasn't taking any chances after trying so hard to conceive. This change in her friend's life, and her impending motherhood, had made Sophie wonder if her own life was passing her by. Would she ever have kids? If she couldn't make it with a man as great as Liam O'Neil, what hope was there for her?

And what would it be like to have his baby? A sister maybe for Mikey and Cleary. She could just see all three guys vying to hold a tiny little bundle of pink.

Sick of her thoughts, she joined the recruits in the huge weight room and did some light curls to strengthen her arm. Soon, she could go back to the line.

But as when she slowed down, images swamped her again. Of that last time with Liam . . .

I love you, Sophie. I'll always love you. He'd slid inside her and the sensations were so familiar she'd wept.

It doesn't matter where you are, or who you're with, know that.

She'd protested. *No, you have to go on with your life.*

I will. But you'll always be in my heart, a ghrá. *Always.*

She hadn't seen him since.

But she had gotten a visit at the firehouse from C.J. . . .

We're getting married on Valentine's Day.

So, you worked it out?

No, not exactly. Aidan's going back to a support group he attended for a while. She shrugged. *And we're thinking about having a baby, so I'd be off protective during the pregnancy. Nothing's a hundred percent, I guess. But I know one thing. I'm not letting him go.*

You're a better woman than I am, then.

Am I, Sophie?

"Firefighter Tyler?"

She looked up into the face of a female recruit. The girl was sturdy looking and raring to get on the line. Like Sophie had been once. "Yeah, Carson?"

"We're done with the weights."

"Super." She yelled to the recruits, "Get your turnout gear on and report to ladder training in the gym. Then we go to the smoke house." Where they'd practice their skills on a building that they'd purposely set on fire. Precautions were taken to insure the safety of the recruits, but it was damn near the real thing.

As the others filed out, Sophie followed them, wondering how long this open wound in her heart would last. On that unhappy note, she went to prepare to teach her class on venting a roof. Then she'd have lunch with Hannah.

And hear more about babies, babies, babies.

"DAD'S GONNA kill us, Cleary."

"I don't care. If he's too chickenshit to do this, I'm not."

From the backseat, Mike's gasped at Cleary's language when he was talking about their dad.

Sinead, who was driving the Honda Civic his grandpa had given him, looked in the rearview mirror at Mike. "Mom'll kill me, too. For driving you way out here."

A few days ago, Cleary had looked up on the Internet where the academy was. It was located up near a bridge connecting three of the boroughs in New York. A long way from them.

"Thanks for doing this, Sinead," Mike said.

He grinned, which made him look just like his dad, Uncle Patrick. "I'm down with it. I like her, too."

Ten minutes later, they pulled up to the Rock.

"Holy shit," Sinead said. "This is humongous."

"Twenty-seven acres," Cleary told them. "Eleven buildings."

"How do you know which one she's at?"

"There's a reception area. We'll ask there. I got the number of the building from the website."

Cleary directed Sinead where to go. When they pulled up to the front, and Mike and his brother got out of the car, Sinead went to park it in a lot and wait for them.

There was a big door up ahead, and they went through it. A

guy was sitting at a desk in a uniform like Sophie's. "Hey, kids, can I help you?"

"We're looking for Sophie Tyler." Cleary sounded strong and confident and even looked older today.

"Tyler?"

"Yeah, she's working here since she broke her wrist."

"Oh, yeah." The guy cocked his head. "You her kids?"

"N—"

"Yep," Cleary interrupted. "We're her kids. Just tell her Mike and Cleary are here. She's expecting us."

"Don't know about that, but I'll call Campoli and he might be able to locate her." The guy picked up the phone and Mike and Cleary moved off to the side.

"You lied," Mike whispered.

"So add it to my sins."

Mike giggled and Cleary laughed. Their plot about Sophie and his dad had made them be better friends.

The firefighter hung up the phone. "She's at lunch." He looked across the room. "Ruocco, show these kids to the mess. They're Sophie Tyler's."

"Tyler isn't married."

"Just do it."

Luckily the lunchroom was in the same building. Mike spotted Sophie sitting at a table with another girl. Hannah, her friend, who came to the pub a lot. But Mike couldn't take his eyes off Sophie. He hadn't seen her in weeks and his heart hurt looking at her. She didn't seem sick anymore. Man, he hoped she didn't get mad at them for coming here.

She looked up when they reached her table.

"You know these guys, Tyler?" Ruocco asked. "They say they belong to you."

Her eyes widened, but she didn't seem mad. "Um, yeah. Thanks, Ruocs." When the man left she said, "Hey, you two."

Cleary stood straight and lifted his chin, but Mike moved behind him. Cleary said, "Hi, Sophie."

"How'd you get out here?" she asked.

"Sinead drove us. He's eighteen."

"Your dad know you're here?"

"Nope."

She peeked around at Mike. "Hi, Mikey."

"Don't be mad."

"I'm not mad. Sit down."

Hannah stood. "Hi, guys. Bye, guys." She winked at Sophie and headed out.

They took chairs next to each other across the table from Sophie. Cleary spoke first. "We gotta talk to you."

"Go ahead."

"It's about Dad."

"Is something wrong?"

"He's sad, Sophie." Mike could see his father's face, always in a frown. "Like he got after Mom died."

"Oh, honey, I'm sorry." She grasped his hand and he felt okay being here. She went for Cleary's, too, but he drew back. "He'll get better, guys, like he did after your mom died."

"We couldn't do anything about that," Cleary said. His tone was mean.

"About your mom dying?"

"And dad being sad over it." Cleary faced reddened, and his eyes were bright. "But you can fix this, Sophie. You're not dead."

"Cleary, it's complicated."

"That's what adults say when they don't have any answers."

"I *don't* have any answers. Any good ones."

"We do." Mike thought about talking to his mom at the grave and to her picture. "My mom would want you to be with Dad."

Sophie shot a quick glance to Mike.

"It's okay, Cleary knows I talk to her. He said he did, too, sometimes."

"Dweeb, I told you not to tell anybody that."

Mike kept looking at Sophie. "Mom would want you and Dad together," he repeated.

"Guys, I appreciate your caring about us enough to come out here, but the stress of my job is too much for him. And for you."

"We can handle it." Again Cleary was . . . what had his dad called him . . . belligerent.

"You think that now."

"We love you, Sophie," Mike said.

"I love you, too. And your dad."

"Uncle Aidan says people in love take risks."

"This one's too big to take, Mike."

Cleary stood up fast and his chair fell backward with a bang. "Dad says you're a hero. But you're not. You're a coward." He started away. "Come on, Mike. She isn't listening."

But Mike stayed behind. He stood, circled the table, and threw his arms around Sophie's neck. "Please, Sophie, come back to us."

She held him tight, but he didn't look at her after he pulled away. He was afraid to, so he followed his brother straight out of the lunchroom.

LIAM REACHED UP to get a basket off the top of the refrigerator in his kitchen and a smaller one tumbled off. Tiny colored balls pinged on the floor and went rolling in all directions.

"Damn, Cleary. I told him not to leave those gobstoppers up there."

Great, now he was talking to himself. Well, he wasn't fit for company. Might as well take out his foul mood on himself. Swearing like a sailor, he crossed to the six-by-six-foot pantry and opened it. Kitty had wanted him to have a storage room, so in the course of expanding the kitchen, they had framed in this area. When the boys were little, they used to play in here. Groceries and toiletries were stocked on shelves that went to the ceiling and there was an area for cleaning supplies. He reached for the broom and when he bent to get the dustpan, the end of the long stick hit a shelf. He stood up just in time to dodge a can of shaving cream that came falling down.

What the hell? It hit the tile hard; foam spewed everywhere. Up several shelves. Onto his clothes. It spattered out over the floor, making a sudsy layer around him. Good Lord, who would have thought one can could hold so much foam?

"Fuck, what *is* this? The seven plagues of Egypt?"

Last week the basement had flooded in an unusually long

January thaw. He'd been ankle deep in water because of a failed sump pump. And the day before, a pipe had burst under the sink. Then the freakin' gobstoppers and now this sea of foam.

Suddenly, it was all too much. Leaning against the wall, he slid to the floor. The shaving cream seeped into his jeans, but he plopped right down into it and stared at the mess. No worse than his life, he thought bitterly.

Nothing was going right. He scrubbed his hands over his face and then swore again as he left traces of shaving cream on it. He couldn't stop thinking about Sophie and how they'd made love that last night. She'd come to him with no barriers, and because it was the last time, because they *knew* it was the last time, the intimacy had been acute. Even covered with shaving cream, his body responded to the memory. He'd left her asleep in bed that night, but kept her in his heart ever since.

The front door opened and closed and Liam checked his watch. Thumbing the cream off the crystal, he saw it was four in the afternoon. Mike was with Cleary and he expected them home any minute.

But the voices he heard were too deep for his kids. His three brothers appeared at the entrance to the pantry.

"This looks like fun," Dylan said, laughing at him.

"Hell, buddy, you could have just gone out and played in the snow." Patrick was snickering, too.

Aidan shook his head. "You're pathetic."

"Fuck you," Liam told them.

"Yeah?" Dylan took a bead on him. "I don't take kindly to insults." From the doorway, he bent down, scooped some foam from the floor and plastered it in Liam's hair. "There you go."

"Oh, that's mature."

Aidan muscled Dylan out of the way and got inside the pantry. Leaning over, too, he slipped and fell on his butt. Shaving cream splattered all over him.

"Good move, kid," Pat said.

Aidan scooped up cream and covered Pat's jeans from knee to toe.

"Hey, I gotta go to work."

Next thing Liam knew, Pat had snagged a fresh can of shaving cream from the shelf and squirted Aidan's face and hair.

"My eyes," Aidan yelled.

"Baby," Pat said.

Dylan grabbed a third can. Why had Liam stocked the pantry yesterday? This time the stream was aimed at Pat.

There ensued a forty-second shaving cream war, which no one escaped. And after which all four brothers were ass deep in the foam—by now it had spread out to the kitchen—and laughing their heads off.

"That's good to see." Dylan was cleaning off his eyebrows with a paper towel. "You've been Saint Liam of the Perpetual Grimace again."

At Liam's chuckle, Aidan scowled. "Hey, when I called him that last fall, he decked me."

Dylan scoffed. "He can't stand up, it's too slippery."

"Why are you assholes here?" Liam asked, snatching the towels from Dylan. "Other than to torture me?"

"We were gonna take you out and get you drunk," Dylan told him. "It's Monday, so the pub's closed."

"No, thanks."

Pat said, "We're worried about you, man."

"I'm not going to do anything, if that's what you mean."

"That's what we're afraid of." Dylan again, with a long sigh. "You're just gonna suffer again for three years."

"Sorry if my problems affect your lives."

"Shut up." Pat's tone had turned serious. "You know we care about you. And we don't give a flying fuck about our lives."

"That'd be a first."

"What does that mean?"

"You guys got a shitload of your own problems. Deal with those first."

"At least we're working on them." This from Aidan.

"I don't get it." Now Liam was even more pissed off. "You all told me to get out of this relationship if I could. So I did."

"Don't go back to her. Fine with us." Pat finished wiping his boots with paper towels, tossed them aside and took a bead on Liam. "But you're in a bad place. We aren't gonna stand by and just watch."

"How's the counselor working out?" Aidan asked.

"I stopped going."

"Why?"

"I made my decision. No need to hack it to death. End of story."

"Jesus, you got a hard head." Pat started to say more when they heard someone in the foyer.

"Dad, you here?"

In minutes, Cleary, Mike and Sinead appeared in the kitchen.

"Holy shit, Dad," Sinead said. "What are you doing?"

"Fighting a lost cause." Pat looked at the boys. "Where you been?"

"Just driving around." Sinead didn't look at his dad.

"We're cool," Cleary added.

"We went to see Sophie," Mike blurted out.

The other boys groaned.

"I thought she was at the academy." Pat's eyes narrowed on Sinead. "Tell me you didn't drive out to the Rock, son?"

Guilty looks all around.

Cleary shook his head at his father. "Don't worry, Dad. She was a lost cause, too."

TWENTY-FOUR

*"I'm coming, I'm coming." Fuck, I can't get any freakin'
sleep these days.*

*I need to take a piss. More banging. Hold your damn
horses. I'll stop at the bathroom, maybe they'll go away.
Christ, look at me. Bloodshot eyes. Sagging puffs under them.
Not good. Shit, I'm coming. Halfway to the door, knocking's
louder.*

*Wait! Don't go too close. Look out but be careful not to be
seen. Got a lot of practice at this. Fucking son of a bitch. It's
that cunt that's been nosing around. Okay, okay, don't panic.
Just open the door and see what they want. Just in case, get
your gun first.*

SOPHIE BROUGHT LUNCH to Joe Carusotti at his office. It
was his first day back at work, and she wanted to see how he
was doing. When the ceiling had fallen on him in that ill-fated
fire, he'd cracked three vertebrae in his back. After six weeks
of recovery, he was finally healed enough for desk duty. She'd
spent a lot of time with him during their simultaneous

convalescence, seeking comfort in the kind of family she had with him. Now that he was back at work, she didn't want to lose touch.

His office was huge and airy with plaques decorating the wall space. His desk, where he sat now, was backdropped by several accolades from 9/11 when Joe had worked tirelessly at the Pile. There was also a poster that read "Remember Our Brothers." When he sensed her presence and raised his head, his face looked pale in the white captain's shirt. "Hey, Sophie baby, what are you doing here?"

She held up a bag from a local deli. "Just brought you lunch."

"You done at the Rock?"

"The class isn't even halfway through. But I gotta meet with Mackenzie today about coming back to the line and so I decided to stop in and see you first."

"Give me what you got then."

They moved to the conference table and were working their way through meatball sandwiches slathered with mozzarella cheese when Joe's partner, Olivia Marsh, came to the door. Even dressed in the fire department uniform—but with a navy skirt not pants—her brunette good looks were evident. She smiled at them, but Sophie could tell something was wrong.

"Hi, there. I don't mean to interrupt."

Joe tensed. "What is it? You look like you lost your best friend."

"I have some very bad news." She glanced at Sophie.

"Want me to leave?" Sophie asked.

"No, I think it's best you stay. This concerns you, too." The woman came inside and took an empty chair at the conference table. She folded her hands and met her partner's gaze. "Joe, while you were out on medical leave, I started running the investigation of the arson cases in lower Manhattan."

"I know. You ran some things by me."

"Not everything. I had some suspicions that I didn't tell you about at the time the fires happened, or even after I took over. I followed up on them."

"What were they?"

"We caught the arsonist."

He dropped the remains of his sandwich onto the paper it had been wrapped in. "What? When?"

"This morning."

"I was here." Sophie felt his anger from where she sat next to him. "Why wasn't I in on this?"

"I'm sorry, Joe, but the arsonist is your brother Tommy."

Joe recoiled back as if he'd been slapped. "Fuck that. He couldn't be."

"I'm sorry. He is. I noticed he was at the scene of the fires too many times to be a coincidence. We investigated further and got a warrant. We found evidence in his garage."

"There must be some mistake." Joe shook his head wildly. "Somebody set him up."

Olivia looked pained. "He confessed, Joe. He was arrested an hour ago."

"No." He scrubbed a hand over his face. "No."

"Oh, Joey." Stunned, too, Sophie grasped his arm. "I'm so sorry." She looked at Olivia. "Why? Did he say?"

Olivia shot a worried glance at Joe. "He was tired of Joe being the hero of the family. Of taking second place. Your involvement, Sophie, was gravy."

"*My* involvement?"

"Toward the end, he targeted your group."

Sophie felt her stomach pitch. How could something like this happen? Tommy was her family, too. "I don't know what to say."

Reaching over the table, Olivia squeezed Joe's hand. "Your father has to be told. We're keeping it quiet until then."

Joe stared mutely at her shoulder.

"I'll drive you out to Brooklyn," Sophie offered.

Finally, Joe came around. "No, it'll be better for Dad if you're not there. He'd be protective of you, and he should be able to vent. My poor mother."

"Are you sure, Joey?"

"Yeah." He patted her arm. "You okay, honey?"

"I'm shocked, but I'll be all right. Don't worry about me. Take care of yourself and your parents."

"Keep your appointment with Mac." He stood, moving stiffly. "I just can't believe this."

Olivia rose, too. "I'll come with you, Joe. I'll drive. I'll stay in the car while you meet with your dad."

Joe nodded and they left together. When Sophie could move again, she followed them out in a daze. On the short walk to Company 14, she could barely think straight. Foul weather battered her face, but it was fitting for what was happening around her. God, everything was falling apart. Tommy. Joe. The O'Neil kids. Liam. She was so sick of it all. For the hundredth time, she questioned her choices, and what she'd given up for her job. She wondered if Joey was thinking about his choices, too.

She arrived at the station house conflicted. It didn't help that Yvette Trudeau was the first person she bumped into in the kitchen. Her face in its perpetual frown, she confronted Sophie right away. "If it isn't the golden girl. When the fuck are you coming back? You're behaving like a typical female, babying that arm. Toughen up, sister."

"I'm fine, thanks for asking."

Trudeau sniffed. "I can barely tolerate these morons."

"Feeling's mutual, sweetheart." Bilotti came out of the common area. He picked Sophie up and swirled her around. "Please, say you're comin' back."

She held up her arm. "Cast is off. Soon, maybe." Over Bilotti's shoulder, she caught a glimpse of Yvette watching them. For a second, the woman had this look of . . . longing in her eyes. Sophie knew her whole life was firefighting, yet the guys despised her.

Cooper and Jules and Murray greeted Sophie warmly, too. It felt good. But good enough?

"I gotta meet with Mac," she said after their greetings. "I'll see you all before I go."

Mackenzie was clicking off the phone when she walked in his office. "Hi, kiddo. I just heard about Carusotti."

"I can't believe it, Cap."

"Joe must be leveled."

"He is. I was with him when he got the news."

"You freaked, too?"

"Yeah. They're family."

"We all are, Soph."

"I came in to talk to you about coming back to the house."

"Music to my ears. Trudeau's driving us nuts."

She thought of family and of building one of your own. "But I want to talk about something else first."

"Okay, shoot."

Dropping into a chair, Sophie wondered if she was making the right decision to even talk to her officer about this. But what the hell? "I need you to tell me the truth about something, Cap."

"Always. What's on your mind?"

"A lot. Some things are just becoming clear."

DYLAN STOOD in the back of the church peering down the long, carpeted aisle. "Jeez, they said a small wedding."

"It *is* small for our family and C.J.'s." This from Patrick, who tugged at his tux collar. "I hate when I have to wear one of these things."

"Aren't her sisters lookers?" Dylan raised his eyebrows suggestively. "My jaw dropped when they came to the rehearsal last night."

"Aidan said they were beauty pageant material," Pat commented. "Even if they are blondes."

C.J.'s brother Luke, also in a tux, joined them. On his arm was another beauty who had soft brown hair, hazel eyes and a knockout face. "Hi, guys. I want you to meet somebody."

"Ah, you must be Kelsey." Dylan kissed her cheek. "No exaggeration on your beauty. And it must be a lie that you just had twins."

"This is Dylan, the ladies' man, though Bailey calls him the Taunter. Stay away from him. Pat, the Fighter by the way, this is my wife. Where's Liam?"

"Right here." Dylan watched Liam come into the back of the church and shake hands with C.J.'s brother. "How are you, Luke?"

"Liam, the Manipulator. This is my wife, Kelsey."

"Nice to meet you."

Kelsey smiled at them. "I'll have to watch my step with you guys."

Luke went to seat his wife, and Mitch Calloway and Clay entered the church through a side door. They were both wearing tuxes. Behind them, of course, was a team of Secret Service agents.

"All the groomsmen are here," Dylan said. "Where's the bride and her maids?"

Grinning like an idiot, Aidan strode out of the vestibule. "She's here putting on finishing touches. Not gonna stand me up, I guess."

Dylan watched Liam's face tighten. Today was hard for him. He had tried to get in a festive mood at the rehearsal party last night, and was putting up a good front today as everyone was seated: Brie and her kids; his Pa; Dylan and Liam's kids. And the mothers. Aidan had been right. *Matka*, C.J.'s mother, was the perfect Polish matriarch, matched only by their Irish ma, Mary Kate O'Neil, dressed in burgundy that set off her white hair. She asked Liam to take her down the aisle. Mama sensed his grief, too.

Dylan ducked over to the door off the side. He cracked it open and saw C.J. had indeed arrived, and the women were fluttering around her, including Bailey, who was also a bridesmaid. Three female Secret Service agents were standing guard; one gave him a warning look and closed the door.

From the corner of his eye, he caught sight of someone hovering in shadows. Sophie? But when he walked over, the figure receded. He grabbed for her.

It wasn't Sophie, it was Rachel Scott. "What are you doing here?"

Pulling back, she held up her arms, arrest style. "No cameras, Dylan, I promise. I just thought maybe I could do a small piece on the ceremony."

He stared at the lovely woman before him. She wore a simple black dress, but on her there was nothing simple about it. Gold jewelry completed the package. Watching her, Dylan felt something shift inside him. "I guess we owe you one."

"You do."

Scowling, he asked, "Is that why you did it? Called me from the fire?"

"No, of course not. I'm a decent person."

"Well, you're beautiful, I'll give you that. You promise no camera?"

"I do." Her delicate brows lifted and there was a hint of a come-to-me-baby smile on her lips. "You can search me if you want."

"Hmm, now there's a thought." Which lead to another. And another. What the hell? He grasped her around the waist, tugged her close and gave her a long, luscious kiss.

When she drew back, his heart was thumping in his chest.

She didn't seem offended, just confused. "What was that all about?"

"Damned if I know. Truce is off after today, darlin'. We're even."

She was sputtering when he left her. That made him chuckle.

LIAM WATCHED Aidan's face as he said his vows. His happiness for his brother was finally superseding the clawing ache he felt over Sophie not being here with him.

"I promise you, Caterina, that I'll do my best to be the husband you need. I'll protect and cherish you"—here he winked at his bride—"but not too much."

A rumble of laugher from those assembled in the pews who knew the couple's path to the altar had not been easy.

"I'll let you be your own person, and try to be reasonable. I'll give you my heart and we'll build our lives, one step at a time." He leaned in and kissed her. "I love you."

C.J., dressed in a floor-length, off-white strapless dress with lace and beads, and flowers in her hair, smiled back at him. "I promise to love you, too, Aidan. To cherish you always. To be unselfish and giving. And to do my best to stay safe and deal with your feelings on that." Did her eyes sparkle a bit with mischief, too? "I'll love you and care for our babies." Her hand went to her stomach. "Starting with this one."

Gasps went through the crowd. Had she just said what Liam thought she said? She kissed his cheek. "Happy wedding, Aidan. I hope you like your present."

Slack-jawed and silent, Aidan just held on to her.

Liam heard the clapping start and looked over to see Dylan

had begun it. Everyone else joined in. The priest chuckled, did
the ring and the do-you-take-this-woman thing, then ended with,
"I now pronounce you husband, wife and well, baby, I guess."

Aidan beamed.

C.J. glowed.

And Liam sighed. At that moment, he wanted what his
brother had so much, he thought he might be willing to do just
about anything to get it.

IN THE BACK of the church, Sophie wrapped the pink voile
shawl tighter around her shoulders and chest. The neckline of
the navy blue dress with a handkerchief hem she'd let Hannah
talk her into buying was low cut. The dress itself was form fitting. At the time, she thought she'd need all the ammunition
she could get. But now, here in church, she felt exposed.

She'd been shocked to hear C.J.'s news, given from the altar. But that was so *them*. Their relationship was and probably
always would be a roller coaster. And as they came down the
aisle arm in arm, they looked happier than any couple she'd
ever seen. Their courage to forge ahead shamed Sophie.

C.J. spotted her and grinned. Aidan gave a startled "oh."

Then the guys came with the bridesmaids. Patrick, Dylan,
Mitch Calloway, Clay and someone else she didn't recognize,
all with a Ludzecky sister on their arms. What a picture they
made, black tuxes with cummerbunds matching the wine-
colored dresses the girls wore. Last in line was Liam escorting
Bailey. He looked breathtakingly handsome in his snowy
white shirt and dark tux. Sophie couldn't take her eyes off
him. She thought her heart might leap out of her chest.

Just as he reached her pew, he looked over. And stopped in
his tracks. His gaze raked Sophie from head to toe. Bailey
stood on tiptoes and whispered something in his ear, then the
Secret Service closed in on her.

Liam couldn't believe she was here, but he sure as hell wasn't
going to let her go. Glancing from side to side and behind Sophie, he spotted what he was looking for, stepped into the pew
and grabbed her arm. Without saying a word, he led her through
the back of the church into a room labeled Baptismal Area. He

shut the heavy wooden door and leaned against it, folding his arms over his chest. "Take off the shawl."

"In church?"

"Yeah."

She let it slip to her hips.

He shook his head. "I've missed that beautiful body of yours, Sophie Tyler."

"I've missed yours, too. You look so handsome in that tux."

"I've been thinking."

"I've been thinking, too." She waited. "Come up with any answers?"

"Nope." He chuckled. "You?"

"Not a one." She moved in then, came flush with him so her breasts brushed his shirt. Her scent, so familiar, filled him, and made him remember what he really wanted in life.

She said, "All I can offer is a way to buy some time."

"Time? For what?"

"For us."

Reaching out, he traced the neckline of the dress. She looked so beautiful and vulnerable and, if he wasn't mistaken, willing to compromise. "And what would we do with the time you can buy?"

She glanced at his finger, which had made goose bumps on her skin. "That, too."

He laughed, then sobered, and slid his hand to her neck. "Time to figure out how to live together? To get married? To have a baby?"

"Uh-huh, time to figure out how to do all that. I've decided to stay at the academy until the end of the class, and give us the opportunity to work things out on both our sides."

"You have?"

"I talked to the cap. He's all for the respite. Besides, they're crying for instructors at the academy, especially women, so much so they'll save my spot with the group." A frown marred her forehead. "I don't want to mislead you, Liam. I intend to go back to line firefighting."

"What about the fear you experienced those few times?"

"I'll have to work on that, too."

"Well, darlin', I'm all for this plan. We'll take the time you bought us and find a way to be together." He kissed her lips gently. "I can't live without you."

"Me, either, without you. I want you and Mike and Cleary as my family, my real family."

"Thank God. They're mad at me and have been impossible to live with." He shrugged. "So have I."

"I'm sorry."

He pulled her close. Kissed her again, harder this time, with more passion.

She smiled when she drew back. "Does this mean I can have my job back at the pub?"

"That and more, *a ghrá*." He took her hand. "Let's go tell the boys."

"I don't want to steal C.J. and Aidan's spotlight today."

"That little stunt she pulled on the altar assures that we won't. Besides, it'll make everybody happy."

Holding hands, they opened the door and stopped short. All his brothers, Bailey, Clay, his parents and his two sons were waiting right outside the room. Briefly he was glad he'd controlled himself from any hanky-panky inside.

"So, is it good news, Dad?" Cleary asked, looking at their joined hands.

"Yep, son, good news."

Mike threw himself at Sophie and Cleary hugged Liam. Over the boys, he saw the acceptance on his brothers' faces. Even Aidan was there, smiling his approval, then left to find his bride. Finally they all traipsed out, except for his kids.

Liam was glad they stayed behind to celebrate the little miracle that happened in the Baptismal Area of their church. God, he guessed, had finally listened to his prayers. Liam felt a certainty and a sense of peace that Kitty was up there with Him, looking down on all of them, giving her blessing.

Mikey drew back and met his gaze, looked up to the heavens, too, then back at him. Liam nodded and Mikey smiled. He knew it, too.

Then the four of them left the church, hand in hand.